PRAI

THE KILLING FLOOR

a novel of THE INFECTION

AND THE WORKS OF CRAIG DILOUIE

"*The Killing Floor* is every kind of horror rendered down in one truly amazing apocalyptic novel."

—Peter Clines, author of *Ex-Heroes* and *14*

"Harrowing action so thrilling you can't help but get lost in DiLouie's nightmares."

—Joe McKinney, Bram Stoker Award-winning author of *Dead City* and *Flesh Eaters*

"Craig DiLouie takes readers on a wild ride into the darkest regions of zombie territory. Brilliant and terrifying!"

—Jonathan Maberry, New York Times bestselling author of *Dead of Night* and *Rot & Ruin*

"Not just another zombie story ... DiLouie takes everything you know and love about the world and turns it into something else entirely. Unflinching horror and surreal, almost dream-like imagery combine to make *The Infection* a disturbing, nightmarish read."

—David Moody, author of *Hater* and *Autumn*

"DiLouie carefully recreates our society and our military, populates it with people we want to know, then proceeds to bring the horror, devastation, and heroes we require."

—Fangoria.com

"[*The Infection*] is that rare novel ... that 'happens to you.' You are not merely a reader but a victim of the Hell it portrays. It leaves you numb from the assault. I highly recommend this book to anyone."

—HorrorReview.com

THE KILLING FLOOR

a novel of THE INFECTION

Craig DiLouie

Permuted Press
The formula has been changed...
Shifted... Altered... *Twisted.*
www.permutedpress.com

Acknowledgments

Special thanks to Renée Bennett, Jessica Brown and Elizabeth Stang for their editing support. I owe an additional thanks to former Chief Petty Officer James R. Jackson, who reviewed most military-themed content for accuracy.

Note

A significant amount of research went into this novel to make the setting and action as realistic as possible. That being said, all of its characters are completely fictional, and any resemblance to persons living or dead is entirely coincidence. Further, many places and organizations are either fictional or fictionalized. For example, liberties were taken in the geography, towns and roadways between southeastern Ohio and Washington, DC to enhance the story. Military units are also fictionalized, with the Fifth Stryker Cavalry Regiment being an invented unit borrowing elements of several existing units in the United States Army.

A PERMUTED PRESS book
published by arrangement with the author
ISBN-13: 978-1-61868-075-4
ISBN-10: 1-61868-075-7

For my beautiful family, my neverending worries for whom fuel these apocalyptic dreams.

OUTBREAK

On the second floor of the West Wing of the White House, the meeting adjourned for lunch early because the machine gun was too loud.

Dr. Travis Price, assistant director with the Office of Science and Technology Policy, stared out the window into the smoky haze that had settled onto the city.

Outside, the Marines were still shooting the Infected off the fence.

The conference room doors opened and servers entered in crisp blue suits, pushing carts across the carpet. They flinched at the machine gun's coughing bark.

"Oh my God," said Sanders, standing at another window.

"What?" someone said, his voice edged with panic.

"It's one of the gardeners."

Travis looked down at the green lawn, but saw nothing except for an infected woman climbing the fence. She flopped to the ground. The machine gun stopped firing.

"What happened to him?"

"Nothing. He's down there pruning the rosebushes."

A few people laughed.

"Now that's loyalty," someone said.

"Hope he's getting time and a half."

Amazing world we now live in, Travis thought, *where the mundane shocks us.*

The Continuity of Government Task Force had been thrown together on the epidemic's first day. The President wanted more authority to deal with the spread of the Wildfire Agent, the official name for the Infection. Congress had to approve everything. The room was packed with bureaucrats, policy wonks and congressional staffers; Travis had been attached to the task force as science adviser. They argued *posse comitatus*, the Insurrection Act of 1807, the lessons of Operation Noble

Eagle. Mostly, they fought over the boundaries of executive authority and ways to legitimize mass slaughter. Busts of George Washington and Benjamin Franklin, placed in niches on the far wall, observed the proceedings with mild disdain.

Travis wondered if all this debate over legal interpretations was some kind of institutional denial, the equivalent of Nero fiddling while Rome burned.

His stomach growled. He had eaten little over the past few days, and his body needed food.

He approached the lunch table, picked up a sandwich, and stared at it. Tuna fish, he observed, with the crusts expertly cut off. He marveled at the amount of care in its preparation. He took a bite, chewed, forced himself to swallow. Packs of Infected ran through the nation's cities on a series of TV screens recessed into the wall just above his head. Two of the stations, taken over by the Emergency Alert System, scrolled evacuation instructions.

So far, he had been asked to contribute little to the meeting—which was good, since he had no insights to offer. Everyone knew what he knew: Seven days ago, one in five people around the world fell down screaming. Four days ago, they awoke from a catatonic state and began attacking others and infecting them with some type of disease, plunging the world into hell. It was all right there on the TV screens.

The big question was why, and nobody had an answer to that.

CNN showed a mob tearing apart a squad of riot police in Chicago. Someone gasped. The violence was agonizing to watch. The Infected were like animals. The cops fought desperately, pushing them back and flailing with their batons.

"No, no, no," someone sobbed.

"Hey," Travis hissed to two men standing near him. Fielding and Roberts, clean-cut men with hard faces and astronaut builds. They worked for the office of the National Security Advisor. "Should we be allowing this on the air?" He felt sure the government should be trying to control the flow of information in a crisis like this. Censorship was wrong, of course, but could also be practical to prevent panic.

Fielding and Roberts exchanged a glance.

"Why try to cover up or deny something that's happening everywhere?" said Roberts.

"Stick with science, Doc," Fielding said.

Travis turned away, his face burning with embarrassment. He wondered why he'd bothered. Outside the realm of science in which he excelled, he was awkward around other people, always saying the wrong thing.

On the TV screen, three of the five fallen cops were getting back onto their feet. While it took three days for the screamers to awaken and attack their caregivers, once bitten, conversion took mere minutes. Heads jerking, the cops ran to join a pack of Infected.

"The biggest question is why they run so fast."

"What's that, Dr. Price?" Roberts asked him.

Travis blinked, unaware he had voiced the thought aloud. "Uh, the biggest question on the tip lines," he said. "Why the Infected can run."

The men stared at him blankly. Travis moved aside to allow other people closer to the sandwiches. The crowded room buzzed with gossip and debate.

He went on, "A lot of people think the Infected are zombies. Like zombies in old movies. Dead people who have come back to life. Zombies are slow, right? People don't understand."

"Probably a good thing too, Doc," Fielding said. "If people think their loved ones are already dead, fewer of them might hesitate. They'll kill them on sight, if they have a weapon."

"But we're not telling people to kill the Infected," said Travis.

"Of course we're not telling them that," said Fielding.

"I guess if they were zombies, they'd be dead and have no rights and then it would be okay to tell people to kill them," Travis said. "Too bad about that."

"Interesting," Fielding said flatly, his hard eyes betraying his contempt.

"Dr. Price, do you mind if I talk to you alone for a moment?" Roberts asked him.

"Certainly," Travis said with relief he hoped did not come across as too obvious.

The man gestured to the window and they moved away from the others. Travis winced at the man's breath, sour from endless tension.

"My wife fell down," he said.

"SEELS?" Travis asked. Sudden Encephalitic Lethargica Syndrome, or SEELS, was the formal, if somewhat broad, term scientists were using to describe the mystery disease that made more than a billion people collapse screaming, bringing the world to a crashing halt.

"Yeah," said the man, running his hand over his buzz cut. "I got her into a hospital. Now she's one of those maniacs out there."

"I'm sorry," Travis said mechanically.

"Listen, she's pregnant. Eight months."

"Oh."

"My kid—is he one of them or one of us?"

Travis opened his mouth and shook his head. Theories flooded his brain, fighting to be spoken, but he held them back. Roberts wanted some type of assurance, but Travis did not know the right words. He was as bad at platitudes as he was at small talk.

"The President," Fielding called to Roberts, pointing at the TV screens.

President Walker had spent most of the crisis underground in the Situation Room. Since the epidemic started, they had seen him only on television. Someone boosted the volume, filling the room with the President's address to the nation from his desk in the Oval Office.

"—functions of our government continue without interruption."

Roberts turned away to watch. Travis sighed with relief.

"Federal agencies in Washington are evacuating and will reopen at secure locations within the next few days. To ensure the safety of personnel critical to the continued functioning of our government, I am also ordering the immediate evacuation of the White House."

The room erupted with gasps and murmuring and people shushing each other.

"Quiet!" someone shouted.

"Excuse me," Travis said, stepping through the crowd. "I'm feeling sick."

They moved aside readily, staring at the screens. He did not even need the ruse. They were like sheep.

"—evil acts of terror perpetrated by people who were once our family, friends, neighbors."

He closed the door behind him.

A human train hustled past, shoving him aside. He caught a glimpse of the Attorney General flanked by stoic Secret Service agents and trailed by pale staffers clutching briefcases and stacks of files against their chests.

Travis fell in with them, glancing over his shoulder at the conference room doors. Fielding and Roberts and the others were still listening to the President's speech. He did not need to hear it. He had already gotten the message loud and clear: *Get out. We're leaving now.* Six thousand people worked for the White House. He had no idea how many were in the building right now, but it was a lot. He would take no chance at being left behind.

A large man wearing a business suit and ear piece appeared at the end of the corridor, waving them forward. "The stairs are clear," he barked. "Let's move it."

The group quickened its pace, suddenly interrupted by people pouring into the corridor from multiple doors. Everyone was getting the same message: *Evacuate.*

"Go," one of the agents said, pushing through the mob. "Make way for the Attorney General, people."

Travis tried to follow in their wake, but was blocked. He was now at the rear of a large crowd filling the corridor and trickling down the stairwell. Behind him, the thirty people from his working group caught up. A large portrait of Andrew Jackson frowned down at them from the wall.

The line ground to a halt. The staffers cracked open laptops and made calls on their cell phones. People sat on the steps and shared what they knew. Rumors rippled down the line.

Helicopters are taking us out. Marine One is in the air.

The President was already gone.

The line moved, and then stopped again. Travis chafed, feeling trapped. He had a bad feeling about the evacuation. He looked at the worried faces around him and wondered if they felt it too. He loosened his tie and tried to control his growing panic.

They finally reached the bottom and exited the building. Exhausted from working day and night to help steer the White House's lumbering decision-making process, officials and bureaucrats and secretaries blinked at the gray sky, looking for the sun. Ahead, more people streamed through the trees under the sentinel gaze of Marine guards with automatic weapons. A sniper on the roof fired his rifle with a sudden *bang*, making the crowd flinch in unison like startled deer. Travis hurried after them, coughing on hot, smoky air that smelled like burning chemicals. For days, he had watched the apocalypse on TV, and now here he was hurrying right into it. It was strange, but he thought he'd been in the safest building on the planet.

Emerging from the trees, Travis was greeted by the cathartic view of a massive Chinook helicopter standing on the broad South Lawn, the metallic chop of its rotors competing with the crackle of gunfire. The door was folding closed. Travis scanned the black haze drifting across the sky. Past the familiar sight of the Washington Monument, he saw the black dots of one helicopter receding, another approaching.

The helicopter on the ground lunged into the humid air, blasting the mob below with a strong hot wind that carried an oily smell. A briefcase spilled open and shed hundreds of sheets of paper that fluttered into the air. *This is not an evacuation,* Travis thought, feeling a rush of panic. *This is a meltdown.*

The Secret Service waved the crowd back, their mouths working, as the next helicopter landed hard and fast. Travis pressed ahead, ducking at the booming shots of the sniper rifles. He was so close now. If not this ride, he would make the next. Instead of assuring him, this idea inspired more panic. The people around him continued to shout into the roar of the blades, scream at the *crack* of Uzis, point at the Infected being shot down as they climbed the makeshift fence surrounding the landing zone.

"Come on!" he shouted into the noise.

People were moving again, climbing aboard the helicopter. Then the Secret Service closed ranks, blocking the way. The helicopter was full, the agents shouted. Wait for the next one.

So close, Travis thought. He looked at the sky past the Washington Monument and saw one helicopter disappearing, but none coming.

Someone screwed up. There's not enough transportation to get everyone out.

They're going to leave us behind to die.

Driven by his terror, he pushed forward until he stood face to face with one of the Secret Service agents. The crowd heaved and Travis found himself looking into the barrel of a large handgun, one short squeeze from oblivion. He dug his heels and pushed back at the bodies pressing against him, staring wild-eyed at the big gun in the agent's hand.

"Please don't shoot me," Travis said.

"Back," the agent told him.

"Listen to me," he said. "You have to get me on this helicopter."

The large man's expression remained inscrutable behind mirrored sunglasses.

"I'm a science adviser," Travis added. "The President needs me, do you understand? If you want this thing to end, the President is going to need me at his side. I'm a *scientist*."

The agent said nothing.

"You really think bullets are going to stop this?" Travis said in disgust, giving up.

The agent frowned and Travis winced, thinking he was going to be shot. Instead, the man turned and boarded the helicopter, grabbed the arm of a young woman sitting near the door, and pulled her from her seat. She burst into tears, obeying meekly until she stood in the opening looking dazedly at the crowd, mascara running down her face, her hair frayed around braids coiled into a bun. The roiling mob glared back at her in a state of fierce panic. The agent said something; she screamed and clawed at his face until he shoved her off. People surged around, trying to help. She continued to wail. The sound of it made Travis want to throw up.

Then he realized what was happening.

"Hey, wait," he said.

The agent slid his hand under Travis's armpit and squeezed, propelling him toward the open door of the helicopter.

"You can't do this," Travis pleaded. "You have to let that woman on too!"

The agent said close to his ear, "Don't try my patience."

If you want to live, live, he seemed to say. *If you want to die, die. Don't play games with me. I have to stay here. I'm a dead man doing his duty.*

His face burning with rage and shame, Travis climbed into the helicopter and took the woman's seat, avoiding the eyes of his fellow passengers. He sensed someone staring at him. He glanced up and locked eyes with John Fielding.

The helicopter lurched into the air.

He looked away, feeling Fielding's cold gray eyes boring into him as he fought back another urge to vomit. The machine banked in its long ascent, giving him a window view of the crowd surrounded by swirling debris. A sob ripped through him.

I just want to live.

The helicopter was still turning. Below, Travis saw a shiny black Lincoln Town Car, little flags fluttering on its hood, approach the South Lawn at high speed, pursued by a horde of running people. Some high-ranking official or diplomat seeking sanctuary. The vehicle accelerated as it neared the fence, then veered sharply as Secret Service agents opened fire on it. Moments later, the car crashed through and coasted to a smoking halt among the trees.

The Infected were streaming across the lawn into the guns of the Secret Service when the helicopter straightened out, cutting off his view.

THREE WEEKS LATER
PART I. TYPHOID JODY

RAY

The battle is over. The dying writhe in piles, softly hissing.

The man sits on the jagged edge of the broken six-lane bridge connecting West Virginia and Ohio, his feet swinging in empty space. His old work boots feel heavy and hot on his sore feet. A warm breeze moans across the gap, clearing the smoke from the air and drying the gore covering his body to a crust. Seventy feet below, the river is still clotted with corpses. Nobody will ever cross this bridge again. Less than an hour ago, he and his team blew a massive hole in it with several tons of TNT to stop the hordes, still pouring from the burning ruins of Pittsburgh, from continuing west toward the FEMA 41 refugee camp, otherwise known as Camp Defiance.

Just like the three hundred Spartans, he reflects with a harsh laugh, cupping his hands to light a cigarette with his steel lighter. *Camp Defiance is saved. They'll write legends about us. An incredible thing, but in the big scheme of things I'd rather not be dying.*

Ray inhales and coughs, his ears still ringing from the blast. Forty feet away, the Infected crowd the far side of the broken bridge, snarling and clawing at the air, still trying to get at him. They are people, once like him, now turned into monsters compelled by their viral programming to seek, attack, overpower, infect. An overweight man in a business suit loses his footing and falls shrieking into the river. Ray glances down and thinks, *There goes another CEO.* His gaze lingers on the sunlight sparkling on the brown currents and feels the urge to jump. Back on the bridge, a howling, hulking brute in bloodstained overalls takes the businessman's place.

Something blocks the sun; despite the heat of July, he feels a slight chill on his back. He takes a final drag on his cigarette and tosses it into the wind before turning to squint at the woman standing over him, the sun glaring around her head like a halo. Pain lances across his ribs, radiating from his wound.

"You must be Anne," he says, wincing. "You're Anne, aren't you?"

The woman nods. She is five-five and dressed in a black T-shirt tucked into dark blue jeans. Two large handguns are holstered snugly against her ribs. A black baseball cap rides low over eyes glinting like cold steel. Her face is disfigured with fresh scars running down her cheeks like scabbed tears. A cloth pad is sewn over the right shoulder of her T-shirt, put there to absorb the recoil of her sniper rifle. She carries herself like a soldier but he knows the truth, which is that less than three weeks ago, Anne Leary was a suburban housewife with three small children. She and her people showed up at the end of the fight, buying them enough time to finish the demolition.

If the PTA were a bandit army, Ray thinks, *she'd fit right in. As its general.* "Todd told me about you. How is the little pecker, anyway?"

"Todd will be all right," Anne says.

"Where is he?"

"On the bus. Sleeping. He doesn't know."

Ray nods, running his hand over his handlebar mustache and stubble. It's better Todd doesn't. "He's a—" He almost said Todd is a better man than him. He probably should have. The kid fought like a maniac during the battle. "He's just a dumb kid. Take good care of him."

Ann unholsters one of her guns and taps her thigh with the barrel. Ray frowns.

"So that's how it is," he says.

"It's just an offer."

"Of what, exactly?"

"Mercy."

He snorts with laughter; Anne does not strike him as the merciful type. The woman stares down at him as if he is a block of wood. She knows he is infected. To her, he is not a real person anymore. All she sees is the organism in his blood. For his part, all he sees is a cold-hearted bitch all too happy to put a bullet in his head.

On the other hand, it *would* be a mercy. He has a few hours at most to live and they promise to be insanely painful, culminating in the final horror of being eaten alive by the thing growing inside him.

Bone cancer would be a pleasant death compared to what I got ahead of me. But a few hours of pain is still life. And living is still better than dying.

"So that's what I get for what I done here today?"

It's not fair.

Anne shrugs. All of that does not matter. The only cure for the bug is death. The one choice you have, if you get one at all, is how you want to go.

"I don't want to die," he tells her.

"You're already dead."

Anger burns in his chest. She reminds him of the busybody neighbour who always gave his mom a hard time about her dog barking. The upright citizen type who called the cops on him when they found him sleeping one off on the bus stop bench. A lifetime of judging and now this, the final insult.

"Yeah? What about Ethan? Was he already dead too, when you shot him?"

The woman winces.

He feels a brief moment of triumph. *That's right: When it's your friend, it's not so easy to call them dead, Miss High and Mighty.* The moment passes, and he finds he no longer cares. He turns and regards the vast blue sky and remembers something Paul, the chain-smoking preacher, said to him: *The earth abides.* The thought makes him feel warmly detached.

"Do it, if that's what you want," he says. "I can't stop you. In fact, I'm honestly too tired to give a shit."

Do it now, he prays. *Do it before I change my goddamn mind.*

Ray tenses and waits for the gunshot to split his head open. The sky has never looked so blue. The muddy river flows deep under his feet. Birds chirp in distant trees. *The earth abides*: He tries to hold that thought and make it his last but his scalp starts to itch. He can almost taste the metal of the bullet coming out the front of his face, taking his teeth with it. The more he thinks about it, the more it fills him with mindless, screaming terror. In a moment, he will enter oblivion.

The dead don't even dream. They don't even know they're dead. They are a person and then they are nothing. Just meat.

"No," he moans, sobbing.

Behind him, boots splash among the dead. Anne is leaving without a word.

Ray exhales. He realizes he was not breathing. *Mercy, indeed.* He wonders why she did not go through with it, but it does not matter why. All that matters is he has a little more time. Time for what? He pulls another cigarette from his crushed pack and lights it with a cough. Time enough for one more smoke. Funny how he used to worry about lung cancer.

Gunshots echo across the bridge, sending his heart lunging into his throat. The others who'd gotten infected are taking Anne up on her offer of mercy. He hears the rest of the survivors piling their gear and casualties into the truck beds. They will not let the monsters take their dead. The bodies will be buried in a special place where nothing will be able to dig them up and eat them.

Soon, Ray will be alone with the hundreds of Infected still crowding the edge of the shattered bridge, growling and reaching for him with outstretched hands. Behind them, smoke blackens the horizon, where heat waves ripple into the sky as Pittsburgh continues to give up its ghost.

Everything is busy becoming something else.

For him, the change will happen soon.

♦

The convoy of heavy vehicles drives away. Ray wanted them to leave, but now feels tired and lonely. Around him, the dying have stopped moving, congealing into a single rigid mass. It is hard to distinguish individuals among the piles of torn and mangled bodies. He sees a hairy wrist with an expensive watch, and suppresses the urge to lift it. It has no value to him now other than to remind him he is running out of time.

The sun hangs low in the sky. Tonight, the real monsters will arrive, sniffing the air, and eat the dead. He wants to be somewhere else when they come. His instincts tell him to seek out a private place to curl up and die.

He works his way onto his hands and knees, gasping at the pain in his side. The puncture site has swollen to the size of a grapefruit, waiting patiently to be born. Behind him, the Infected on the other side of the torn bridge stop clawing and hissing and begin to moan. He reaches his feet through sheer willpower, hugging his throbbing ribs, and sees the Infected reach out to him as if pleading.

"What the hell?" he says. He finds this raw display as unnerving than their constant rage.

A distant monster bellows like a foghorn, reminding him that not all of the children of Infection wear human faces.

Get out of here, his instincts warn. Even now, he obeys the will to survive. If the juggernauts find him, they will grind him into paste and suck the blood from the remains.

Ray staggers among the bodies, trying to keep his footing. He finds a rifle lying on the ground, picks it up and peers through the scope, aiming at a woman wearing the shreds of a nightgown. He wonders if it still works.

One way to find out—

The rifle fires with a metallic *crack*. The back of the woman's head explodes, splashing the Infected behind her with smoking pieces of bone and brain. The shell casing rings on the asphalt. The woman crumples to the ground, rolls in a tangle of limbs, and tumbles into the river.

"That was for Ethan," he says, certain now he is holding what was the teacher's rifle. Ray hardly knew the man, but they fought together on the bridge, and Ethan became infected covering him and the others as they fell back to fire the charges and destroy the bridge.

He detaches the magazine and counts three bullets. He hopes it will be enough to get him to Steubenville and into a nice soft, clean bed to lie on and die. He sneezes on the puff of gun smoke and swears at the shock of pain arcing through his chest.

"Kill all you bastards," he mutters.

His mother's voice: *You do what you think is best, Ray.*

"Damn straight."

The Infected reach out to him, moaning and wailing, their eyes glimmering in the growing twilight. *Come back*, they seem to say. *Don't go just yet.* Ray coughs and spits a gob of black phlegm. It is easy to forget sometimes they were once average people. That they were loved.

The foghorn call booms across the dead landscape, closer now, sending a jolt of adrenaline through his system. *Time to go. Now.*

He starts walking. It is difficult to move; the right side of his ribcage feels like a giant fishhook is stuck in it and someone is trying to reel it in. The cancerous grapefruit throbs hotly, continuing its relentless growth.

He carries a special strain of the bug. He was not bitten; he was *stung.*

Some of the Infected do not look like people. The only way to describe them is to call them monsters. One particularly horrible species of these things, called a *hopper* by most people because of their oddly articulated legs allowing them to leap high into the air—but also going by the names *jumper, imp, goblin* and *humper*—stung him during the fight on the bridge. He imagines trying to explain it to Tyler Jones back at the Camp Defiance police station, where he worked as sergeant of Unit 12.

Well, Tyler, think of a whining hairless monkey the size of a German shepherd tearing you a new asshole and then fucking it with a syringe full of acid.

And that was just the beginning. The injected material immediately got busy converting his cells to start another hopper growing right out of his rib, like Adam making Eve.

Congratulations, Ray. You're going to be a daddy. And when it's born, it will eat what's left of you. At that point, you'll be so drained, all you will be strong enough to do is watch.

Is this really worth surviving for?

Breathing hard, he staggers off the bridge and stares blankly at the outskirts of Steubenville: several white buildings, houses, gas stations, distant smokestacks and church steeples under a dimming sky. From here, the town has no visible scars from the epidemic. No charred homes half burned to the ground, no abandoned wrecks of vehicles, no piles of corpses drawing flies in the heat. The only oddity is the eerie quiet, the lack of any living human. Nonetheless, he feels watched. The waning summer sun casts long shadows across the features of this ghost town. He hobbles along the street, passing under dead traffic lights, tears streaming down his face, driven by a need to survive he no longer understands.

Goodbye, sun.

The blue house calls to him. It reminds him of his mother's house back in Cashtown. *This house*, he decides, *will be a good place to die.*

◆

Ray tries the front door. Locked. The garage stands open, but its door is also locked. He limps to the side of the house, stumbling over a garden hose sitting in the tall grass like a patient snake, and finds an open window over an overgrown flowerbed. All he has to do is tear out the mesh and pull himself up and over—something he's done at least a few times during his long career as an asshole—but he wonders if he has the strength to do it now. As if sensing his ambition, the monster growing from his side pulls against his ribcage, warning him to stay put.

Don't rock the boat, mister, he can picture it saying, *or I'll suck one of your lungs through your ribs.*

"Shut the fuck up," he tells it.

Ray returns to the garage and drags out a short ladder, which he props against the window. Even with its aid, his progress is slow and agonizing. By the time he steps gingerly onto the floor of the house's kitchen, he is drenched in sweat and has given the growth in his side a full-fledged malevolent personality, something other than God to bargain with.

He needs water. The tap in the sink produces nothing but a single constipated groan. He eyes the refrigerator warily and decides not to open it. Its door is plastered with kids' drawings, a shopping list and a calendar filled with scribbled appointments and X's leading up to the day of the epidemic. The day all calendars stopped.

"Damn it," he says, rubbing his eyes. He left his rifle outside, propped against the wall, like the idiot in a horror movie that everyone yells at. There goes his suicide option. His face feels hot against his hand. Fever. His body trembles as his energy drains out of him and the simple act of standing becomes tiring.

"Ray?" a voice calls from behind the wall. "Is that you home?"

"Who's there?" he whispers.

"Ray?"

"Whoever you are, please don't mess with me."

The ghostly shape floats out of the gloom of the dining room, a giant woman in a white nightgown, her short hair mussed from sleep.

Ray blinks. "Mom? What are you doing here?"

"I'm so glad you're home, sweetie."

"Are you a ghost?"

His mother laughs. "Of course I ain't a ghost."

"Mom, you'll never guess what I did."

His mother checks out the kitchen, wearing a sad frown. "Does it smell musty in here? This place needs a good cleaning. So much dust."

"I'm a cop now. A real cop."

"So much work to do—did you say you're a police officer now?"

"That's right, Mom. At the refugee camp."

"Oh," she says with a worried expression. "Well, you do what you think is best."

His smile falters. "No, Ma, listen. We just blew up the Veterans Bridge. The Infected were coming out of Pittsburgh because of the fire, and we had to blow the bridge to stop them from crossing over and coming after the camp. I volunteered. I was one of the few who survived."

"Oh," his mother says again, touching her face. "Whatever you think is best, Ray."

"Stop saying that!" he roars. The creature inside him awakens and turns over, pulling at his internal organs. The shock strikes his body like lightning. He wakes up on the floor curled into a ball, still screaming. "Don't say that to me anymore!"

Several monstrous foghorns blast in unison outside, one of them close. The house trembles from the vibrations. The windows shiver in their frames. Glasses and plates rattle in the cupboards. A distant car alarm honks.

His shouting expended the last of his energy, but broke the sudden delirium. *Mom's not here. They put her in one of those mass graves outside of town.* Mrs. Leona Young died during the Screaming, drowning in the bathtub as

Ray slept one off downstairs in his basement apartment. So many people died during the Screaming that nobody could give his mother a proper burial. The public health department came to pick up her body for disposal in one of the mass graves the county dug outside of town. The health workers were unable to lift her three hundred pounds, and settled on dragging her from the house on a mattress. *We're going to need a bigger hole for this one, ha ha.* Even in death, Leona could not find dignity.

"Don't give up on me, Momma," he says, crawling out of the kitchen.

Whatever he thought was best was never any good, but she loved him anyway. All that mother's love, unconditional, abundant, wasted.

The couch in the living room looks deep and inviting. Gritting his teeth, Ray starts his journey across the dusty-smelling carpet, pausing often to rest. He tries to spit, but his mouth is dry. *Maybe I should just give it up. What does it matter where I die?* But he makes it. He may have lived like a dog, but he does not intend to die like one. He pulls his body up onto the couch and sits gasping, his face burning with fever as his immune system wars against the invader in his blood. Outside, the light is failing fast. Night is falling for the last time on Ray's world. *Time enough for one last smoke, and then good night and good luck.* He puts a wilted cigarette between his lips and lights it, staring out the big picture windows at the empty street outside.

Ray looks around, surprised to see no TV. He notices an unopened can of beer on the end table, hiding in plain sight, and blinks away a tear.

"Merry fucking Christmas," he says.

He opens the beer and smells it. Sips it. Pours some on the bulge in his shirt.

"You like that, you little bastard?"

The growth throbs in response.

The brew is warm and a little flat and not his brand but it is the best beer he ever drank in his life. Finding an unopened beer is almost enough to make him believe in a kind and merciful God. After savoring a few sips, he chugs half of it and belches.

The can falls from his hand to spill foaming onto the carpet.

"Get out of here," he whimpers, waving his good arm. "Go. Git."

The picture windows are filled with Infected. They stand motionless, peering in with dark eyes, their breath steaming the glass.

Why don't they attack?

"Leave me alone," he cries. "Just let me die in peace."

Are they real, or am I seeing things again?

Ray curls into a ball on the couch and closes his eyes, pressing a pillow against his face.

Lord, have mercy, he prays. *Don't let them eat me.*

As he loses consciousness, he begins to change.

Outside, the Infected scream in the dark, slapping their hands against the glass.

TODD

The convoy grinds west along U.S. Route 22 with the headlights off, navigating by moonlight. Near the front of the battered yellow school bus leading the convoy, the boy huddles against Anne's shoulder, her leather jacket draped over his body, lulled into a gentle doze by the droning engine. Three weeks ago, he was acing tests and dodging bullies in high school; now he is a veteran fighter in a war that is just getting started but has already changed him. Some of the other survivors weep in the dark. Outside, the Infected suffer their own pain. He can hear them wailing in the trees, mourning the lost world, until falling silent one by one as sleep overtakes them.

Pressed against the warmth of Anne's body, Todd feels safe.

"Where have you been?" he whispers.

She does not answer; he wonders if he spoke the words or only thought them.

"Going back and forth on the earth, and walking up and down it," Anne finally says.

"That sounds like a quote. Who said that?"

"Satan," Anne tells him. The angel of light who was cast out of heaven for hubris.

Todd used to coolly remark the apocalypse beat high school, but now realizes how stupid it was to say such a thing to people who lost everything. For most of his life, he had intelligence but little experience; he envied the natural gravitas of adults, whose sense of themselves ran deep with time. Now he understands. He senses the pain behind Anne's answer. She is no longer just a mother figure for him. She is a woman battling her own demons.

"Why did you leave us?"

Anne fought hard to get Todd and the others to the refugee camp, riding out of Pittsburgh in the back of a Bradley fighting vehicle, only to disappear just as they found it.

"My family died," she says. "They died because of me. I don't get to come back."

"But you did. You found us at the bridge."

"Blind luck," she tells him. "I was just passing through with some other survivors. I'm their guardian angel now. In any case, that's not what I meant."

"I know what you meant," he whispers.

Something large collides with the bus, with a metallic *boom* followed by a flurry of screams. Todd clutches at Anne, wide eyed and gasping, his arteries turned into wires carrying electric current instead of blood. The monster snorts like a giant pig, grotesquely loud, its hooves clashing on the asphalt. The driver roars, stomping on the gas. Todd feels the sudden pull of gravity as the bus lurches hard to the left. The hooves strike the side of the bus, making the entire vehicle shiver. The boy buries his face against Anne's shoulder, biting her jacket. Then the thing falls behind, its hooves clattering, shrieking in the dark.

"What about me?" he cries. "Do I get to come back?"

Anne shushes him and strokes his hair until he regains control of his breathing and his heart stops hammering in his chest. *It's all right*, the voices shout in the dark. *We're all right now. What about the others? They're still behind us, thank God.* Someone else says, *What was that thing? What was it?* Nobody answers. Nobody talks about the monsters. To talk about them is to give them your power. You start a conversation ready to fight to survive and end it ready to give up. Todd smells tobacco burning as survivors light cigarettes in the dark. As the others settle into an uneasy silence, Anne tells him, in a warm whisper close to his ear, a story about a woman who was a simple housewife—a loving mother, a devoted wife, a respected neighbor—who had everything until suddenly she didn't. When Infection arrived, she refused to accept what was happening. She sent her husband out into the storm of violence on a fool's errand. She left her kids with a neighbor to go search for her husband and realized, too late, she had left them to die. The woman wanted to die herself but could not overcome her instinctive need to survive. And so she made her survival a mission—a mission of vengeance.

Todd listened closely, his body slowly uncoiling as he relaxed, but now says nothing. He does not ask her if that is how she got the scars on her face. Her story makes sense to him. He spent two weeks with her in the back of the Bradley. She has the fury of Captain Ahab—if Moby Dick were a virus. Most people are just trying to get by these days, just trying to survive. Anne is at war. Her enemy is one of the tiniest forms of life on the planet.

"Is that why you hate them so much?" he says.

"Who?"

"The Infected, obviously."

"I don't hate them, Todd."

"Never mind," he says, frowning.

"Todd, those poor people deserve nothing but our sympathy."

"Then why do you like killing them so much?"

"Is that really what you think?"

"Well," he says.

"I enjoy nothing about it. But they're already dead. The second the bug takes them, they stop being people. Everything that makes them who they are dies. As far as I'm concerned, they're the walking dead. It's not the people I kill. It's the virus controlling them. That's my enemy."

He does not understand. *The Infected are evil, yes*, he reasons, *but they wear the faces of our loved ones. Perhaps there is something of those people left inside. Even if they only remember themselves when they dream, does this not still make them human?*

When he shot Sheena X in the face on the first night of the outbreak, he was not killing a virus, he was killing his friend. When Anne executed Ethan on the bridge at the end of the battle, how could she not see the man, but just the virus controlling him?

"Thank God," the driver shouts back at the survivors, switching on the headlights. "It's the camp! We made it!"

Todd tightens his hold on Anne. "Are you coming this time?"

"For a while," she tells him.

"Can I stay with you?"

"Todd, I'm going to get back on the road as soon as I can scrounge up a few things. You know what it's like out there. There is no life. It's no place for you."

I want to be safe, he wants to tell her, but does not know how to explain how he feels. He knows he will be safer in the camp. But he feels safer on the road, close to his fears.

Even after everything, he already feels its call to stay out here among the monsters.

Get on the road and keep moving, and they will never get you.

He remembers Sarge, the battle-hardened commander of the Bradley, falling apart during the orientation session at the camp. He stopped moving, and it nearly broke him.

Even the strongest sometimes are not strong enough to fight themselves.

Anne shakes her head. "All right, Todd. If you don't feel right tomorrow, come and find me and we'll talk."

Todd nods and sits up, sniffing and wiping his eyes with the palm of his hand.

"Camp Defiance," the driver says, pointing.

The sprawling camp looms ahead, the ragged outline of its makeshift walls and watchtowers silhouetted by the warm glow of searchlights and thousands of cooking fires. The warm breeze carries the sound of cheering crowds. Random snatches of machine gun fire. The smell of wood smoke. Overhead, helicopters roar through the night.

Home, Todd thinks. *I want to go home. Where is home?*

♦

The convoy grinds to a halt in front of the gates, churning dust that swirls like angry ghosts in the headlight beams. A machine gun rattles on the wall, tracer rounds spitting toward the distant trees. The sound of cheering grows in volume, responding to a voice squawking through a megaphone. The bass line of a pop song vibrates through the vehicle. Despite the notes of celebration, at night the camp has the atmosphere of a siege slowly being lost. Blinding white light floods the bus and then fades out. The gates open with a bang of gears.

"Show time," Anne says to Todd, nudging him with a wink.

Todd smiles at the inside joke. Sarge always said that before a scavenging mission.

"Welcome to FEMAville, Anne," he says.

This is the place he fought the horde to save. The place for which Paul and Ethan died.

The vehicle rolls into the compound and comes to a stop, the rest of the convoy stacking up behind it. The driver turns off the engine and opens the door, allowing the omnipresent camp smells of cooking food and open sewage to waft in. Bulbs on wires strung between wooden poles light the area, surrounded by moths. Music blares from a speaker mounted on one of the poles in a tangle of thick wires: Queen's "We Will Rock You." Todd peers out the window and blinks in surprise at the cheering faces. *Holy crap. They're cheering for us.*

A military officer climbs aboard the bus and speaks to the driver, who shakes his head, turns in his seat, and points at Anne. The officer approaches, introduces himself as Captain Mattis, and fires questions, his voice barely audible over the roar: *Lieutenant Patterson? Sergeant Hackett? Sergeant Wilson?*

Dead, dead and trapped on the other side of the river, Anne tells him.

"Too bad about Wilson."

"He'll make out all right," Anne says. She knows Mattis is noting the loss of the Bradley more than its commander.

"So who are you, then?"

"Just passing through with some other people. We heard the shooting and helped out." She tilts her head toward Todd. "He made it. Some engineers, some National Guard. That's it."

"The mission was a success, though," Mattis says.

Anne nods. "The Infected won't be crossing that bridge."

"Outstanding."

"Is that what all this is about?"

The Captain sighs. "Not exactly. The good citizens are celebrating because the military has arrived. Army units are dropping at refugee camps around the East Coast. A single company showed up and now everyone thinks it's going to be over in a few days and they can go home."

"It's about time the Army pulled its weight, in any case," Anne says.

Mattis smiles and shrugs. As a military man, he can say no more.

"People at the camp know what you did, though," he tells her. "Word's been going around all night about it. It's a day of wonders."

"It's the worst day of my life," Todd says.

"You saved all of us," Mattis goes on, holding out a box. "You're giving these people hope, son. That's an important thing. Make sure you get your ribbon."

Anne holds one up and laughs, startling Todd, who never heard her laugh even once in all their time together.

"It's a dog show ribbon," she says.

"Best of breed, to be exact," Mattis admits with a smile.

Todd stares at the purple and gold ribbon clutched in his hand. He can hardly speak; it's ludicrous. "What the heck is this?" he demands.

"We can't pay you. We don't have anything to pay you with. All we can do is try to honor you. Everyone at the camp knows about what you did and that you are wearing these ribbons. You're going to have a hundred and thirty thousand people treating you like a hero for the next few weeks. Extra food, extra showers, you name it."

Anne takes the ribbon from his hand and pins it to his T-shirt. Mattis stands back and salutes.

"Welcome home, son."

One by one, the survivors stagger off the bus and are welcomed by the cheering crowd. They huddle together, blinking tears. The more the people applaud, the more the survivors cry. Someone whistles and Todd flinches. He keeps seeing gray faces lunge out of the crowd. Faces of the Infected howling for his throat, spraying spittle rich with virus.

No, no, no. You're way too young to be this screwed up, Todd old man, he tells himself. Yet it takes every bit of mental energy he has not to yank out his pistol and start shooting.

"If you don't feel right in the head tomorrow, come and find me," Anne says. "I'll be here."

"Wait," Todd says, scanning the crowd. "Where's Ray Young?"

He turns back, but Anne is gone. And Ray is nowhere to be found among the sea of empty, grinning faces. Someone presses a warm can of beer into his hand and tells him to drink up.

"Ray!" he cries.

A girl walks out of the crowd. He catches a glimpse of her blue eyes and wild red hair before she cups his face in her hands and kisses him. The crowd applauds heartily and whistles, the sound blending with the roar of blood rushing through his ears.

"Erin," he gasps. "It's you."

"Come on. Let's get out of here."

She takes his hand and leads him through the clamoring mob. Hands clap him on the back and seek out his to shake. He gives someone the can of beer. As they reach the rear of the crowd, they disappear into the darkness, navigating by the dim light of cooking fires. Erin appears to know the maze by feel alone.

Todd can smell her on the breeze. His hand sweats against hers. She leans against him as they walk through the warm, humid night, and he becomes aware of her chest pressed against his arm. He remembers she does not wear a bra.

"Where are we going?"

"I'm taking you home, baby."

He wonders if he is hallucinating. He feels like he could sleep for days. Just a few hours ago, he was standing on the bridge in the sunlight, screaming for his friends, as it exploded in a blinding white flash. The monster charged, a giant thing covered in flailing trunks, each bellowing its deafening foghorn call. He and Ray stood their ground among the piles of dead, emptying their guns at the thing until it fell through the bottom of the world.

"What's wrong, baby?"

Then he is back at Camp Defiance, walking among the shanties with this beautiful creature he thought he'd never see again.

She asks him again if there is something wrong.

"I don't know," he says.

"You're not hurt, are you?"

"I don't think so."

"I had to ask. You may not know this, but you're, like, covered in blood."

"Oh," he says, touching his chest. His shirt feels stiff as cardboard. His entire body hurts, but he does not believe anything is broken. "I didn't know."

"You also smell like smoke and sour milk," she laughs. "Come on."

Erin leads him into the small shack and lights two candles, revealing a bucket of water and a stack of towels on a blanket.

"Take off your clothes," she says.

"I don't have anything," he tells her. "You took it all already."

"Do as I say, mister."

He obeys, peeling off his grimy shirt and tossing it into the corner. Then his boots and socks and pants. None of it is salvageable. He is going to have to burn all of it, and find more. Last, he tosses his gun belt and pistol on top of the pile.

"Now lie down."

He stretches out his long, gangly body on the blanket. Erin dips a sponge into the foamy bucket, wrings it out, and gently rubs him down. Pure bliss.

"Why did you come back?" he asks her. "You really hurt me."

Todd arrived at the camp with a bag full of DC-powered electronic gear, hoping to use it as capital to set up a trading business. Erin marked him, seduced him and robbed him. Reeling from the blow, he sought out Sarge and Wendy and signed up for the mission to destroy the bridge.

"I'm sorry for what I did to you," she says, blinking tears. "I didn't know. What you did, going to that bridge. . . You're an amazing boy. I really hoped you would make it back."

"My friends are dead," he says.

"Tell me about it." She pulls her shirt up and over her head. "Tell me everything."

♦

The Infected shriek down at him, kicking and clawing with faces twisted by rage. The shotgun roars and their bodies explode in a shower of blood and smoking entrails.

The deep voice booms: "Don't you touch that boy!"

He opens his eyes. Paul, the old reverend, stands over him, chambering another round and firing again. The Infected squeal and crumple in a wave in front of the blast.

"Don't you touch that boy, I said!"

BOOM. Reload. BOOM. Bodies splash in piles onto the bloody roadway.

The boy looks up at the Reverend through a blur of hot tears. The man's grizzled face looms large, frowning. He grips the boy's hand in his own, his eyes burning with worry and love.

"You're all right now, son. I'll get you out of here."

A rumbling sound fills the air, the monster purring deep in its throat. The boy can feel it deep in his chest. The Reverend gasps, his eyes wide with sudden knowledge.

"You all right, Rev?"

The Reverend smiles sadly.

"God bless you, Kid—"

Paul lurches thirty feet into the air and into the chomping mouth.

Todd screams.

"I've got you, baby," the girl says, hugging him from behind.

Todd sits naked on the floor of his shack, arms wrapped around his knees, screaming.

"It was just a dream," Erin tells him. "Just a dream. You're okay. See? Everything is fine."

He stops, panting for breath. Tears and snot stream down his face. His skin is slick with sweat and Erin's body feels like fire against his back. Sunlight streams through cracks in the walls, illuminating the dust. The small shack feels like an oven.

"What was your dream about?" she asks him.

"I was being saved," he says hoarsely, barely recognizing his voice as his own. He wipes his face with the back of his hand.

"That sounds like a good dream."

His face twitches. He notes the symptom.

"Not for the guy who saved me."

Todd tries to stand and sits back down with a grimace. Every muscle in his body is stiff and sore. His lungs seize from the smoke he inhaled during the fighting on the bridge, and he coughs loud and hard into his fist, just trying to breathe. His throat feels like it has been burned raw from smoke and screaming.

"I'm glad I'm not alone," he rasps, pulling on his glasses. The left lens is cracked.

"Oh baby, I'm right here," Erin tells him, squeezing hard.

He did not mean her, but says nothing.

"I have to go see Anne."

"Who's that?"

"One of my friends who made it."

Erin kisses the back of his neck. "Let's stay in bed all day."

"No, I have to go."

"Come on, baby."

"I'm sorry."

"Then I'll come with you."

"Erin, please."

She pushes away from him and pulls on her jeans. "Fuck it. I thought you liked me."

"I do like you," he says, watching her nudity disappear with longing.

If he had more energy, he would try to please her in some way, but he has none to spare. He stands, pulls on a clean pair of boxers, and buckles the gun belt around his waist.

"You're going out like that?"

He drapes the blanket over his shoulders. "My clothes are contaminated with Infected blood. They shouldn't even be in the camp. Put the ribbon on for me, okay?"

"I'll wait for you," she says, pinning it over his chest. "I'll get us some lunch, okay?"

Todd smiles. *God, she's beautiful.* "That sounds perfect, Erin."

He steps outside and enters the mundane chaos of FEMAville. The air is so humid it is difficult to breathe. The smell of wood smoke sets off another coughing jag. Water glistens on the ground, evaporating in the sunlight. Hard rain came last night; he fell asleep to the sound of it drumming on the roof. His bare feet sink into soft, warm mud.

First stop, latrine, then the showers.

Paul flew through the air into the gaping mouth of the monster.

Todd gasps, his heart racing. The dream, so vivid.

He cannot figure one thing out. Why was Paul smiling?

"Coffee?" says a voice.

Todd is aware of everything. Dogs bark and military vehicles groan on the other side of the camp. A few boys play horseshoes, wagering cigarettes on the outcome, while a woman shouts at her children to be careful running. Someone chops firewood while someone else practices the harmonica. Two grinning men carry a large painting that Todd recognizes from the Andy Warhol Museum.

"You want some coffee, buddy?"

Todd focuses on the bearded man sitting on a plastic cooler, brewing a pot of coffee on a Coleman stove. His wife kneels on a tarp, filling plastic bottles from a rain collector.

"Sure, thanks."

The man glances at his wife, who nods. "Want some sugar in it?"

"That'd be great."

Todd accepts the mug of coffee and blows on it, savoring its aroma.

"You look like you're going somewhere," the man tells him. "You can bring the mug back later, all right?"

"Thank you," he says again. The sweetened coffee is an incredible gift and this act of basic human kindness brings him close to tears.

The bearded man nods to Todd's ribbon. "No need to thank me."

"God bless you, boy," the man's wife says.

God bless you, Kid—

Todd takes a deep breath, gritting his teeth. His heart gallops in his chest. Is this what PTSD—post-traumatic stress disorder—is like? The older survivors of the epidemic always talked about its symptoms, but he was never able to relate.

Lying in the jaws of the beast, Paul stared into Todd's eyes and smiled sadly.

Even in death, he smiled. Why?

Clouds drift in front of the sun, turning the world gray.

♦

At the market, the traders give him new clothes and boots, rainproof poncho, handful of bullets, toothbrush, two packs of sugarless gum, three condoms and a plastic baggie filled with coffee.

So this is what it's like to be popular. Clean and clothed and eating cold spaghetti and meatballs from a can with a plastic fork, he starts to feel whole again. He always wanted to be popular. It's a strange feeling.

I wonder how fast it wears off.

He remembers something Erin told him last night: *We can make a life here.* The hero fights the monster and gets the girl and the treasure. Perfect story, right? He wonders if Prince Charming also screams in the dark during the happily ever after, dreaming about his fight with the Dragon.

His eyes wide with sudden knowledge—

Paul knew he was going to die. The monster's long, revolting tongue, studded with slimy suckers, had already gripped the Reverend's ankle.

And yet he smiled. In the air too. In the mouth of the beast.

Paul: the man who loved God but feared death. Who loved his enemies as he killed them. Who tried to reconcile the forgiving, loving God of the New Testament with the apparent return of the judgmental, violent God of the Old. Who could not live without his wife even though Sara would have wanted more than anything for him to go on living.

A fellow traveler of the thin line of survival, that limbo between living and dying. Torn between forces larger than himself, he gave himself to others, ultimately giving his life, and in doing so, welcomed death. With his wife now at last, either in heaven or oblivion; it did not matter which to him. Was this the peace the Reverend found? Could this be why he smiled? He had given up worrying whether he would ever see her again. All that mattered was they were together one way or the other. In the end, Paul welcomed his death.

Todd wonders if he will ever love anyone as strongly as that. He wonders if he could ever love Erin so much. Before the bridge, he would have said he already did. After the bridge, he does not know. He doesn't know much of anything. All he can think about is the road.

He limps past dozens of shacks, each leaning on the next for support in the endless shantytown. People sit on lawn chairs watching over their children, cook, tend gardens, stack wood, stoke fires, hang laundry, gossip, trade. They fall silent as he passes. Chickens cluck in a series of pens, filling the air with the acrid smell of shit. Several men swear over a tractor coupled to a water tanker, both of which are stuck in the mud. A teenager pushes a wheelbarrow filled with plastic jugs, surrounded by smaller children splashing through puddles acting out the fight at the bridge, holding back the Infected onslaught while the engineers lay their charges.

"On me!" one of the kids cries. "Come on, we'll make our stand here!"

Todd smiles at them, idly swatting a mosquito on his neck.

"Are you one of those people from the bridge?"

He turns and sees the teenager pushing the wheelbarrow, staring at him with something like awe. The kid is only younger than Todd by two years at most, filthy and dressed in rags. One of the many orphans of Infection.

"No," Todd says. "You are."

He unpins the ribbon, gives it to the surprised boy while the smaller children howl in disbelief, and walks into the compound adjacent to the gate, a hive of constant activity: salvage coming in, waste going out. A five-ton driven by men in bright yellow hazmat suits rolls through the gate, carrying corpses stacked in shiny black body bags. A squad of tired National Guard in olive green rainproof ponchos watches the truck leave, smoking and yawning and rubbing their eyes. Workers unload salvaged goods from a white pickup scarred with hundreds of tiny scratches made by fingernails and jewelry. Men fill out paperwork and hand over receipts. A large American flag hangs wetly from an overhead wire. This land is still the USA.

He finds the bus parked between a Brinks armored car and a pickup truck with a cobwebbed windshield. Dressed in greasy gray coveralls, Anne bends over the engine, talking to a mechanic. Another man paints camouflage colors over the bright yellow skin. A woman scrubs the V-shaped snowplow mounted on the grill, a retrofit enabling the bus to slam into human beings and toss them broken into the nearest ditch. Todd notes the metal plates welded over the windows, creating slits useful as firing ports.

Looks pretty ninja, he decides.

Anne senses his approach and turns to watch him limp stiffly, like a zombie, across the mud. The mechanic, a giant of a man with long blond hair, tightens the grip on his wrench, scowling at him. He takes a step forward but is halted by Anne clicking her tongue.

"Hello, Todd," Anne says, wiping her hands on a rag.

"Who are these guys?" he asks her, glancing nervously at the mechanic.

"I guess you could call them my crew. Marcus here I brought with me. Evan and Ramona heard about me and came here. They don't want to stay. They want to go back out."

"They call us Anne's Rangers," the mechanic tells him.

Todd likes the sound of that. "I thought you said there's nothing out there."

"I made a deal with Mattis," Anne explains. "The Camp will supply us with diesel, weapons, some other things. We'll find more survivors and bring them here. Run supplies and mail to the other camps. That sort of thing."

Todd nods. "That's a good job for you."

"What about you? You staying, then?"

"I want to go home."

Anne gives him a grim smile. "All right."

"Is that okay with you?"

"Marcus will get you some gear. Then rest. Tomorrow, we go back out. We can use you."

"Thank you, Anne."

The blond giant nods and extends his hand in welcome.

Todd smiles as he shakes it and thinks, *I always wanted to belong somewhere.*

MARCUS

He was a good mechanic and this got him steady work at auto repair shops. Mufflers, brakes and shock absorbers, mostly, plus body repair and painting. After his wife died, leaving him with two growing boys, he quit Sears Auto Center and got a job closer to home as a service technician at a Toyota dealership. He was welding when the Screaming swept through town.

After hours of starting and stopping, swearing and leaning on his horn, Marcus pulled into the high school parking lot and lunged sweating from his truck. Inside, he pushed through the roar of red-faced parents and teachers and into the gym, where the survivors had laid the bodies of the fallen, students and teachers alike, in rows on the floor. Both Jack and Michael lay on their backs, their bodies still jerking in tiny spasms. He swept them up, one boy over each shoulder, and carried them to his truck. A teacher approached to challenge him but dodged aside after seeing the terrible expression on his face and his hands clenched into fists.

On the way home, he listened to the radio. They were calling it a syndrome because nobody knew what the hell it was. There was a lot of talk about *exploding head syndrome, frontal lobe epilepsy, nanotech terrorism.* None of it made any sense. A doctor said some of the victims exhibited *echolalia,* the automatic repetition of sounds. His ears perked up at that. After arriving home and getting his boys into their beds, he told them he loved them, hoping to hear it said back to him.

His cousin Kirsten, who worked as a nurse at the hospital, dropped by first thing in the morning to set up bedpans and intravenous tubes. After she left, Marcus could not cope with the empty, funereal silence and went to the liquor store, where he stood for hours in a line that went out the door and around the corner. Returning home, he found his boys lying in the exact same position he'd left them. He changed their bedpans and IV bags, exercised their limbs a little, gave them a quick sponge bath. When he moved Michael's arm, he noticed his younger son had *waxy flexibility*, which he'd heard was another occasional symptom of the syndrome. Wherever he put the boy's limbs, they stayed frozen in whatever position they were last left.

This done, fighting tears, Marcus went back downstairs, poured a few fingers of Wild Turkey bourbon, topped it up with Coke and ice, and turned the TV on. A blowhard on the cable news was saying things like *brain drain* and *national inventory* and *precipice.*

None of it made any sense to him. The world began to blur.

Two days later, he heard shouting on the TV. The screamers were waking up, and they were attacking people. Nobody knew why. Apparently, if a screamer bit you, you caught the disease. Marcus watched Cleveland fall apart for an hour before realizing his kids had woken up as well. He could hear them stomping around upstairs.

Still reeling with hangover, Marcus staggered to the foot of the stairs. He considered calling Kirsten, or maybe the cops, and felt ashamed. Why was he afraid? What was there to be afraid of? The boys were his own flesh and blood.

He climbed the stairs slowly, one step at a time.

"Jack," he said when he reached the bedroom door. He felt out of breath; he could hardly speak. "Michael?"

He heard snarling on the other side, fingernails scratching at the wood.

"Are you guys okay?" Marcus whispered, suddenly scared of his own voice.

Something large thudded against the wall on his left, making a picture jump off its hook and clatter to the floor. Moments later, something crashed against the door, making it shiver on its hinges, followed by more growling and pacing.

Shit, Marcus thought, afraid to say anything. Terrified to even move. Even breathe. His body would not stop shaking. After a minute, he held up his trembling hand and stared at it as if it belonged to someone else.

I'm afraid of my own sons, he realized. *My sons. My own flesh and blood.*

It was like being afraid of yourself. They were a part of him.

Even worse, he was afraid he would open the door and they would have hate in their eyes. That they would look at him as if they didn't know him.

In the end, he had no choice. He opened the door.

"Boys? It's your dad. I'm coming in now. Take it easy, okay?"

Jack came at him first, hands splayed into claws. Marcus pushed him onto the nearest bed as Michael lunged at his legs. He kneed his younger son in the face, hard enough to make him yelp, and would have apologized if Jack weren't flying at him again. He shoved Jack to the floor, trying to buy time some to figure out what he was going to do. He was stronger than them, but he knew how much energy they had; they could keep this up for hours, while he was already breathing hard and sweating.

Retreating into the hallway, he slammed the door as the boys launched themselves against it, and moved a massive dresser from his own bedroom to block it. He listened to them howl and scrabble at the wood with their nails.

"You can bang on that door all you want," he said. "I'm not letting you out." The father in him felt the urge to add, "until," but until what?

Until never.

His body tingled with shock. His own children were trying to kill him. They had turned into the monsters he saw eating the dead on the cable news. He stumbled downstairs feeling fuzzy, as if he were floating. A part of him had been amputated, leaving nothing behind. The TV was still on, showing another talking head saying things like *we've lost contact with John* and *apocalypse*. Marcus poured another tall bourbon and Coke and wondered how long the door and dresser would hold his kids before they broke out and came for him.

The world blurred again. A tank rolled past the house on shrieking treads. People swarmed on top of it, clawing at the armor, trying to get in. Inside, dishes rattled in the cupboards. Pictures fell off the walls and crashed to the floor.

So this is the way the world ends, he thought.

The blowhard on the TV was saying, *God help us all*, when the power failed and plunged the world into darkness. Marcus sat on the couch sipping his bourbon in long stretches of silence periodically shattered by distant screams. The air smelled like smoke.

No son of mine is going to be a monster, he decided. His boys needed mercy only a loving father could give.

He drank until he had the courage to do what needed doing.

As dawn paled the sky, he lurched to his feet and searched until he found Michael's baseball bat. He hefted it, feeling the weight in his large hand.

Then he went upstairs to say goodbye to his sons.

COOL ROD

Back in Kandahar, the Fifth Dragoons played death metal battle anthems like "Bodies" and "Die Motherfucker Die" as they rode into battle in their Stryker vehicles, pumping up their courage and scaring the shit out of the Afghans. Now, roaring along the service road adjacent to Ronald Reagan National Airport near Washington, DC, the boys of Comanche Company are listening to the plaintive sound of "Paranoid Android" and still searching for the right note.

Sergeant Hector Rodriguez—Nimrod in elementary school, Hot Rod in high school, Cool Rod in the Army, and just plain Rod to his friends—doesn't mind. To him, this is a Radiohead war. Surreal music to go with the surreal scenery: a desolate, post-apocalyptic America. He feels like a sailor on a submarine, returning home after fighting a nuclear war, only to find his country destroyed.

In any case, at least it's not Enya. Some smartass cranked up "Only Time" as they stormed the airport a week ago, and nobody challenged it. It actually fit their mood.

The small VDT screen mounted next to the driver shows a digital map of the southeastern quadrant of Arlington, Virginia. Blue icons reveal friendly forces, so massively concentrated at the airport, now a forward operations base, that it is hard to pick out their column of LAV IIIs turning north onto Crystal Drive. There are no red icons. It is assumed the enemy is everywhere, dispersed in small formations.

In neat white letters on the back of his green helmet, the driver has stenciled, how's my driving? call M2-BOOM. The Stryker commander stands on a platform with the upper half of his body outside the vehicle so he can operate the fifty-caliber machine gun.

Rod scans the anxious faces of the eight beefy kids sitting with him in the hot interior of the vehicle. They look formidable enough. His squad of shooters is armed to the teeth, highly trained, part of a military that once projected American power almost everywhere on the planet. Modern legionnaires, lean and fit and hungry. He wonders if they will have what it takes to shoot and kill American civilians. Not just some, but hundreds, even thousands.

More specifically, they will be battling monsters. How do you train for that? Rod had been forced to sit through endless PowerPoint presentations discussing the type of monsters encountered and known capabilities and weaknesses. Few traditional tactics apply. The enemy knows no fear. Flanking accomplishes nothing. Ground cover is not important anymore, just concealment. Flamethrowers, which fell out of military use in 1978, are starting to be manufactured again in fortified factories. Shotguns and pistols are in high demand. The bayonet is making a comeback. Some soldiers are being trained as *mules*—lightly armed troops solely responsible for carrying spare ammunition.

Everything is changing. They must unlearn everything they know, then relearn it fast or die.

As the soldiers notice Rod's attention, they look away. The whine of the rig's Caterpillar diesel engine fills the dim passenger compartment.

It's going to take time to earn their trust. They can hate him for what they think he did. That is fine. But they must believe he is competent, and follow his orders, or he cannot lead.

Most of the boys in Fifth Stryker Cavalry Regiment's Company C are orphans from other outfits. Rod and Lieutenant Pierce, assigned to Comanche's Second Platoon, the Hellraisers, are the sole survivors of Battle Company's Third Platoon. Rod is new to the Hellraisers and some of these soldiers are new to each other, the result of higher command consolidating understrength units on the fly after the catastrophic losses the regiment took in Germany during the first days of the epidemic. The regiment had flown to Ramstein Air Base as a pit stop on their way home after a violent year in Afghanistan. Then the Screaming struck down one out of every five of them.

Three days later, the screamers rose from their beds.

Many soldiers could not fire on their comrades. They tried everything to subdue them without using lethal force. They wrestled and clubbed them and shot at their legs and gradually became infected themselves. Rod knows soldiers ultimately fight and die for the guy next to them. Why else would they do it? Death is final, and it is eternal. Looking death in the eye, country and apple pie and bringing democracy to the Middle East don't seem as important as they did at the enlistment office. So they do it for the other guys in their foxhole. It is a brotherhood bred not from the rigors of war, but from facing death together—a will to survive demanding mutual support and sacrifice.

The Infected left their beds and attacked their comrades.

Many of the soldiers could not shoot.

Rod's old squad had revered him back in Kandahar, calling him Cool Rod for his icy calm in a fight. But when his boys came running at him, he had not been able to shoot them. The entire platoon had been infected, along with a number of support personnel, and they ran at him and the Lieutenant in a wave. The young officer shot them down, killing thirty-one uniformed men and women, a heroic act in a battle where heroes eventually became despised. The Infected could not be subdued. They had to be killed. It was a horrible necessity, and anyone who pulled the trigger had blood on their hands. These boys see him as a monster.

Rod claimed the kills and Pierce did not contradict him. Pierce thought Rod was protecting him, but he was really protecting himself. If he admitted he froze, he could no longer lead men into battle. He would rather his new squad see him as a devil than a coward.

The boys glance at Rod with distrust, wondering if he would sacrifice them, if they got infected, as readily as he did his entire platoon.

Devil or coward. Soon he will be confirmed as one or the other. Because the Hellraisers are going to shoot American civilians today, and he will be asked to pull the trigger.

♦

Rod opens the hatch over his head and takes a look outside. The Stryker column snakes along the road at a reserved thirty miles an hour. They are in no hurry. Ten feet both high and wide and nearly twenty-five feet long, the squat metal titans look like ungainly boats on eight giant rubber wheels. Most are still clad in cages of slat armor to protect them against rocket-propelled grenades and piled with gear, making them look like something from *The Road Warrior.* The commander of the next vehicle in line grins at Rod under his Ray-Bans and spreads his arms as if to say, *Look at all this. Can you believe this shit?*

The combat engineers spent two days clearing a twelve-foot-wide path through what was a bumper-to-bumper traffic jam of abandoned cars and trucks choking Crystal Drive all the way to their objective. Judging from the scattered luggage, these folks were probably trying to get to the airport, which had already been shut down. The vehicles, stripped of gas and useful parts, are now piled along the sides of the road awaiting towing. It is like driving through a junkyard. Rod scans the wreckage for improvised explosives out of habit. Bodies are entombed in some of the cars. Loose trash floats and rustles on the breeze.

The plaintive notes of a religious song fall on his ears from one of the lead vehicles. It's "Ave Maria," Rod realizes with a frown. Christ, what a downer. And yet it fits.

Ave Maria, gratia plena.

Hail Mary, full of grace. Roger that.

The Strykers ahead disappear into a wall of black smoke billowing from a distant hill of burning corpses, and Rod follows, emerging coughing on the other side. The entire city is shrouded in haze, ashes of torched people floating on currents of hot air. An automatic cannon booms in the distance, drowning out the crackle of small arms fire that is so omnipresent it is only noticeable when it stops. Fighter jets roar through the distant murk, barely visible in this false twilight at nine hundred hours. One of the fighters breaks formation, veering toward the earth like a bird of prey to fire a missile at a target on the ground. Light flashes on the horizon. *BOOM.*

The battle for the capital is in full swing.

On his right, C130 cargo planes drop from the sky in a steady stream of screaming metal and disappear behind Terminal B of the airport, where they will land and disgorge even more troops and equipment. Rod's regiment has been bivouacked in Terminal A for the past few days, one of the first units to arrive, and it is already getting crowded. The troops swarmed Washington's key facilities and most defendable and sparsely populated patches of ground—Reagan Airport, East Potomac Park, Theodore Roosevelt Island. The engineers began the herculean task of clearing the major arteries. This beachhead secure, the invasion force now needs to expand to make room for more troops as well as civilian refugees starting to trickle in.

Something about the whole operation still smacks of a massive Army foul-up. Oops, we invaded ourselves by accident. Nice going, General Stupidity, you're relieved. General Chaos will take it from here.

He can't get used to it.

A foghorn booms in the west, answered by another in the south. Rod knows they are not real foghorns. They are giant monsters browsing their way through the city. He can't get used to that either. An MH60 Blackhawk gunship catches up to the column and paces it, the thumping of its rotors drowning out even the foghorns. It will provide top cover for the rest of the trip.

It's good to be back in the USA one way or the other. They all feel this way. They are back on sacred ground, that much closer to the people who matter most to them. They are home. When they captured the airport, a grizzled veteran dropped to his knees and kissed the tarmac. *Mecca's the other way, Sergeant*, one of the boys said, slurring the word as *Sarrunt* as so many of them did, but nobody laughed. Rod nearly kissed the ground as well. Leading his squad across the tarmac, he half expected to see the Washington Monument wrapped in monstrous tentacles or the Lincoln Memorial covered in vines or half buried in apocalyptic sands. Instead, he saw a typical airport with stately jumbo jets at rest among fuel trucks, water trucks, ramps, hoses and other white utility vehicles. Some scattered luggage offered the only clue something was wrong. That, and the total absence of people. Everything was abandoned. The city appeared to have been converted into a massive, derelict parking lot.

The column winds through an artificial canyon formed by rows of boxy office buildings, street-level retail stores and the ever-present piles of cars pushed to the side of the road. One of the buildings boasts in large letter signage that it is the corporate home of general dynamics. Rod grins. They're the company that makes the Stryker. The vehicles pass their maker. Minutes later, the column grinds to a halt in front of another large building and sits idling.

This is their objective. Seven floors. Three hundred and forty rooms.

The Crystal Palace Hotel.

◆

The plan is to unfuck America, starting with Washington, DC, their new area of operations. That is how Captain Mack, call sign Outlaw, put it during the mission briefing back in Germany. The Brass dubbed the invasion Operation Yellow Ribbon, but the grunts call it simply the Home Front. It is the largest and most complex military operation in America's history, involving units staging from around the world, and thrown together in less than a month.

Rod considers liberating Washington to be a symbolic gesture. There is nothing special about the city itself. No weapons manufacturing, food production, vital scientific facilities. The scuttlebutt is the Brass did not want to do it. The generals wanted to fight a campaign somewhere else with less risk to gain a secure foothold on the mainland and gain experience fighting this new enemy. The President, however, wanted something big and decisive to raise morale.

"We're going to take it back," Captain Mack told them.

Washington. Rod can feel the raw power in the air, even with the city fallen to the Wildfire Agent. Talk about symbols and myths. Washington was where taxes came from. Where the establishment ran the country. Where politicians clowned and fought in neverending political theater. It was a bag of dicks, in Army parlance, even before Wildfire. Some guys Rod served with over the years considered Washington a foreign power. For his part, he cannot help but feel massive anger and pride actually being here. Anger at seeing his capital in the hands of the enemy. Pride at being part of a massive invasion force that will take it back.

This is the first army in the history of the world, Rod muses, called to war to fight a virus. A war fought not over religion or resources or territory, but pure survival.

Mack said the Regiment would be fighting within miles of Arlington Cemetery, where thousands lie buried having died fighting for freedom. *Let's do America proud,* he told them. *Let's do the Army proud. Our families are back there. Our homeland is under siege. It's time to take it back.*

Standing at attention on the tarmac, the boys roared the regimental war cry.

AIEEYAH!

An hour later, they filed onto Russian-made AN-124 cargo planes for the long flight to Andrews Air Force Base in Maryland. After refueling, they hopped to Ronald Reagan National Airport ready to fight, crossing a Potomac swarming with Coast Guard cutters and supply ships, only to find the facility already secured by a unit of Marines and combat engineers, now banging away at Infected on the roads and clearing the traffic jams.

The Dragoons found themselves with nothing to do. Hurry up and wait, as usual. Welcome back to the Suck.

The EUCOM, CENTCOM, AFRICOM, PACOM and SOUTHCOM strategic commands were all heading home to be folded into NORTHCOM headquartered at Peterson Air Force Base in Colorado. From all over South America, Europe, Africa and the Middle East, troops poured into Andrews and were then flown to Reagan, while troops flying home from Pacific Command established a bridgehead on the other side of the country in Santa Barbara, California. Chinook helicopters filled the sky over Washington day and night, ferrying troops to bivouacs established on Theodore Roosevelt Island and East Potomac Park. The grand strategy was to expand these pockets to link up with Bolling Air Force Base, Fort Myer and the Pentagon, creating a secure zone supported by other installations in the region such as Quantico, Fort

Belvoir, Andrews, Dahlgren and Indian Head. From this expanded beachhead, the invasion force would cross the Potomac and drive east through the Mall to secure the White House and the Capitol.

Apache and Battle Companies were called away on missions. Then Comanche Company got its turn, a solid operation that would take it outside the wire: secure the Crystal Palace hotel. The invasion force was beginning its expansion phase and, besides that, needed the extra housing for troops and refugees.

This is what war looks like to grunts. The grand strategy is sweeping and covers the entire region, but is ultimately comprised of small units capturing small objectives. Being a veteran, Rod understands that these small steps win campaigns. For Company C, the next day of the war will be spent seizing a hotel, searching and destroying.

Rod's mission is much more personal than recovering Washington, DC, however. He needs to get home to his wife and children.

His marriage with Gabriela started off stormy. They tied the knot while the wars in Iraq and Afghanistan were in full swing, and he spent most of those years in the Sandbox. When he came home he was angry, restless, difficult to live with. They foolishly decided having kids would fix things. Oddly, it did. Children changed him. His kids became his center; their chaos gave him a sense of stillness he needed. He wanted a hundred and settled for three: Kristina, age four, Lilia, age three, and Victor, the youngest, still a baby.

Rod cannot imagine what happened to them. He has had no contact with his family for twenty-three days. They lived on base at Fort Benning, Georgia. The base was evacuated, and Rod still has not been able to find out where they went.

If he finds his children okay at the other end of this thing, he will hand in his rifle and become a priest. If not, he will curse God. He does not know what he would do if he lost them. He heard the Infected kill and eat children instead of convert them. He cannot even imagine someone eating his Victor. Just trying would destroy his sanity.

Captain Mack is right. They are going to have to take America back one house, one building, one city at a time. Rod will be there, fighting every step of the way, until he gets home.

♦

The column coils in front of the hotel, the vehicles grunting like giant metal bulls as they nudge into their final positions. Rod closes the hatch and touches his front cargo pocket, where he keeps his mission notes. The boys glance at him with wondering expressions, sweating in their armor and fatigues. It's still hot as hell today, especially inside this metal box on wheels.

Outside, a voice blaring through a megaphone addresses any locals in the area, competing with the final strains of "Ave Maria."

Attention! Attention! Military personnel are present in this area.

"All right, listen up," Rod says. "The hour is at hand. If anyone's got any last questions, now's the time."

The boys stare at him. Half of them are clean shaven. The other half are working on wispy combat mustaches.

Troops are preparing to advance. To avoid injury, please remain in a secure location and wait for further instructions.

Finally, PFC Tanner, a gangly kid from Wisconsin, raises his hand. "Do you think you could see the Washington Monument from the roof? Maybe even the White House?"

The other boys crack grins. They are afraid of Rod. They're not even sure of his humanity. But they cannot help themselves. Following an unspoken Army tradition, they have to test their sergeant.

Tanner explains, "This is my first time in DC."

"You're not a tourist, fuckchop," Rod says, fixing him with a hard stare. "You're a soldier. I want you watching your sector, Private, not seeing the sights."

"Is it true there ain't gonna be any light inside?" Lynch wants to know. "We'll be doing this by flashlight with the night vision goggles?"

"You afraid of the dark, Corporal?"

"No, Sergeant. Just what's in it. Those little jumpers are fast."

The boys wince. They hate the ugly, whining little hoppers more than anything. They see the stinging as sexual—violent rape by another species.

"We don't know what we're going to find in there," Rod says, acknowledging their feelings. The truth is the hoppers terrify him as well. "But this is what we do. You did this a million times over the past year in Afghanistan. You're good at this. The stakes may be higher here, but the job is the same."

The boys glance at each other and nod. The ramp drops, flooding the passenger compartment with gray light.

Do not run at military personnel. Repeat. Do not run at military personnel.

"All right, let's roll," Rod tells them.

The squad files out of the vehicle and fans into a circle around it, establishing security. The other squads are also dismounting. The soldiers from the new flamethrower units pull their tanks onto their backs and help each other fasten the belts; these units, along with the Stryker gunners eyeing the street, will provide outside security for the operation. The street is sprinkled with shell casings. It stinks of blood and death here. The Marines and combat engineers have been through this street clearing obstacles, and left them a present: A bulldozer stands next to a large pile of corpses surrounded by a cloud of flies at the bottom of the steps leading up to the hotel doors. Dozens of gray faces and arms and legs clad in the clothes of home: the soldiers crane their necks for a quick look. A few sneak pictures with their cell phones.

Lieutenant Pierce, trailed by Tom Ford, the platoon sergeant, walk away from their huddle with Captain Mack and the other platoon leaders.

Rod jogs forward to join his fellow sergeants gathering around the Lieutenant.

"The OpOrder is the same," Pierce says. "First Platoon is the designated entry team and will secure the lobby, first floor and maintenance facilities. Third and Fourth will take the second through the fifth. We Hellraisers are going all the way to the top. We'll be clearing the sixth and seventh floors as well as the roof. Got it?"

"Aieeyah, sir," says Sergeant Jake Morrow, grinning. Like the other non-commissioned officers, he is sick of the endless PowerPoint presentations, and is feeling gung ho being back outside the wire doing the Lord's work. Rod and the other men nod.

Pierce unfolds a map, actually a photocopy of an architectural blueprint. The non-coms huddle closer, whistling. It's a large building. Behind him and Ford, First Platoon rushes up the steps into the hotel, equipment rattling. Rod listens for gunfire but hears nothing.

"Tom and I will take Headquarters and Weapons Squad and establish our base in the elevator lobby here," the Lieutenant says, pointing to a section of the map. "Jake, you're going all the way across the floor. I want you to take this hallway and all connecting rooms, and establish security at the opposite stairwell. Rod, you'll push out from the elevator lobby and take the nearest stretch of hallway and adjoining rooms." He glances at Navarro. "Joe, you'll cover this area between them. We'll be in radio contact at all times. Watch the corners and don't get bunched up in any fatal funnels. I want good trigger discipline inside. I don't want any blue on blue. . ."

A wave of horror crosses the young lieutenant's face, transforming him into a man old and tired long before his time—a man with more ghosts than a haunted house. Only Rod knows the source of the man's pain. The Lieutenant glances at Rod, who turns away, his face burning.

The two men share the same shame, but for different reasons. One fired his weapon, the other didn't. In doing so, each failed his ideals.

"Remember the rules of engagement," Ford grates in his gravelly voice. "Yes, we're in someone's house here. Specifically, our house. There may be Americans in there. But the ROE is clear: Shoot on sight any individual who's got the bug. Shoot to *kill*. If somebody runs at you, assume he's got the bug. You take no chances. Worry about staying alive now and your conscience later."

"Roger that," the men respond.

Ford is good people, Rod knows. As the platoon sergeant, he will take good care of Pierce. The Lieutenant is in good hands. He'll be all right.

"Then get your men ready," Pierce tells them. "We step off in five."

♦

The sergeants tell the Hellraisers to form up in ranger file. The squads stack behind them, waiting for the order to advance. Captain Mack growls at First Sergeant Vinson to put the church music out of its misery, and Mozart's ethereal "Ave Verum Corpus" abruptly dies. In the ensuring vacuum, the distant gunfire presses in a little closer. The music lingers in Rod's mind, comforting and pure, and he finds himself humming it. One of the flamethrower units sprays a jet of fire onto the pile of burning corpses, setting them ablaze and filling the air with a nauseatingly sweet, rotten, beefy stench Rod can almost taste.

"Flashlights on, weapons hot," he tells his squad, giving them a quick once over to make sure they're ready to go. The boys stare back at him with wild eyes.

Pierce gives the order to step off and leads the platoon into the hotel. The anxious looks transform into professional frowns as the training takes over. Leading his squad, Rod raises his AA12 automatic shotgun with its attached SureFire flashlight and blinks in the gloom. The lobby is massive. After weeks of neglect, it smells like an old couch. Beams of white light play in the corners; that's First Platoon doing their jobs. Someone shouts that he found a body. The boys sneeze on dust in the air. They sweep their sectors with their weapons without breaking stride, boots stomping on clothes and hairdryers and books that spill like entrails from discarded luggage. Rod aims his flashlight over his head and watches the beam sparkle along a dead chandelier.

A rifle discharges in the manager's office with a loud bang.

"Lord, please don't let it be jumpers," Corporal Lynch hisses.

First Platoon's got this, Hellraisers, Pierce's voice buzzes in his headset. *Keep moving, out.*

The stairwell door opens ahead of them. Boots thunder on the metal steps. That would be Jake Morrow's squad, Rod knows. After them, Joe Navarro, then him, then Headquarters and Weapons.

Rod leads his shooters onto the stairs with weapons cocked and locked and night vision goggles on. The stairwell has no windows and is pitch black. Their flashlights flicker across cinderblocks and handrails coated in generations of paint now rendered in their grainy, monocular vision as shades of green. The boys cut off their muttered prayers and bitching as they enter the danger zone, breathing through their noses.

Above, a door bangs open. Rod's radio fills with chatter as Sergeant Morrow narrates what he sees and his progress toward achieving his objective.

Nobody here. Smells like sour milk, though. Stay frosty. Out, here.

Third Squad enters the elevator lobby and pauses in the hallway beyond. They made it to their objective without incident. Now all they have to do is sweep twenty-five rooms and a vending area, without getting mauled and bitten, to earn their pay for the day. Behind them, Headquarters and Weapons enter the elevator lobby and set up the machine guns.

"It's time to earn our money, *vatos*," Rod says. He orders Corporal Davis to take Fireteam A and clear the rooms on the other side of the hall, and then gathers Fireteam B in front of a nondescript hotel door reading 6101.

"U.S. Army!" he calls out. "If you are inside this room, get down on the floor now."

Silence.

"You're up, Sosa," he says.

The giant soldier grins and steps forward with the handheld battering ram. He takes pride in being the big kid, the bully. The fireteam makes way for him.

"Wilco, Sarge," he says.

He rears back and swings the ram into the door, which bangs open. The fireteam rushes past, weapons leveled and sweeping the room. Tanner breaks left and Arnold breaks right, circling back to Rod, who provides overwatch at the door. Lynch checks the bathroom.

"Clear," the boys sound off.

"Clear," says Lynch.

Rod scans the room again. An open suitcase lies on the unmade bed, half packed with wrinkled clothes. He joins Lynch, who shines his flashlight at the bathroom mirror. Someone wrote a message in red lipstick.

Sorry Sean I had to leave to find Liz

The sink is filled with bloody bandages.

The corporal shakes his head. "Like one big haunted house, Sergeant. I wonder what their story was."

Rod barely hears him. The lipstick reminds him of Gabriela.

The hopelessness of their mission feels like a sudden weight on his chest. The country is huge. How many miles, how many rooms, how many bullets until he reaches his family?

"Holy shit," one of the boys says back in the room.

Rod and Lynch rejoin the fireteam grouped around the window, and raise their night vision goggles. Someone pulled back the curtain, filling the room with bright gray light. From this high up looking northwest, Arlington sprawls before them behind a veil of smoke. Gunships buzz over the distant buildings, covering the combat engineers. Several circle a distant point, dropping Hellfire missiles before veering away. The boom reaches their ears and shakes the window for a fraction of a second just before a fireball blooms over the spot, dissipating in a mushroom cloud.

"It almost feels like we're winning," Arnold says over the grinding thunder.

"Winning?" Sosa snorts. "Shit, man, this is easy. The Infected don't shoot back, right?"

Jake Morrow reports to the Lieutenant that he has reached his objective. The constant chatter on the radio reminds Rod they have a job to do.

"All right. Enough sightseeing. Let's get back to work."

They have twenty-three more rooms to go.

Davis calls out from the hallway: "Contact!"

"Coming out!" Rod calls back, and rushes outside in time to see a man approaching them from the other end of the corridor. The flashlight beams converge on his face and chest.

"Sergeant, we got a civilian," Davis tells him.

"Stop where you are, sir," Lynch orders.

The man obeys, sniffing the air, his fists clenched against his chest.

"Some of these doors must be open," the corporal says. "He was in one of the rooms."

"Does he have the bug, Sergeant?" says Tanner.

Rod shrugs. He believes the man has the bug, but such speculation is pointless. The rules of engagement are clear. "If he makes a run at us, he does."

As if hearing an invitation, the man sprints at them, growling on the exhales, closing the distance. A wave of nauseating sour stench precedes him.

"Stop where you are, sir!" Davis shouts as the soldiers aim their weapons, waiting for the order to fire.

"Sergeant?"

The man rushes at them, his pale face shining in the glare of the flashlights, teeth gleaming, feet pounding the floor.

Rod doesn't want to shoot.

He also cannot order his boys to do something he wouldn't.

"What do we do, Sergeant?"

Rod raises his shotgun and growls back at the Infected.

"Fuck you, Jody," he says, and squeezes the trigger.

♦

The man's chest explodes with a burst of smoke as the high-velocity buckshot rips through his body, filling the air with a bloody mist. His legs give out, sending him careening into the wall, where he leaves a long smear of blood and bits of flesh.

Pierce's voice buzzes in his ear, urgent.

Hellraisers 3, this is Hellraisers 6. Sitrep, over?

Rod realizes he was not breathing. He takes a long, shuddering breath.

Repeat, Hellraisers 3. What's your sitrep? How copy?

Rod looks at the grinning corpse smoking on the carpeted floor at the end of a long trail of blood and guts and feels nothing but horror at himself.

The boys are laughing like crazy people.

"What the hell?" he says with disgust. "This man is dead."

"Sorry, Sergeant," says Tanner, coughing into his fist.

"Get your shit together," Rod snarls. He keys the push-to-talk button on his headset and reports in. "Hellraisers 6, Hellraisers 3. We engaged and eliminated one hostile, over."

"Not just any hostile," Sosa says, setting the boys off again.

Hellraisers 3, that's a solid copy. Stay in touch, out.

"Roger, sir," Rod says, glaring at his squad. "Out."

"Sergeant," Lynch explains, "you called him Jody just before you fired."

Rod grunts in surprise. "I did?"

In Army folklore, Jody is the sweet, sensitive civilian man who screws your girlfriend or wife while you're away fighting for your country. You spend months getting shot at in some bombed-out shithole where even the sand hates you, and then one day a Dear John letter comes from your old lady telling you how Jody was there for her while you were away. How his poetry speaks to her. How things sort of just happened. How she wants the uncomplicated life Jody offers.

Everyone in the Army, from the lowliest private to the Chief of Staff, hates Jody's guts. If Rod wanted to demonize the enemy and help his boys find humor in the horror, he couldn't do any better.

"Well, then I guess he had it coming," he says, sending the squad into hysterics.

Everyone is looking at the corpse. None see their sergeant wincing, blinking tears.

This isn't war. It's murder. Genocide. And Rod is no longer a soldier. He's an exterminator.

I'm sorry for what happened to you. I'm sorry I had to end your life, whoever you are. Please consider it a mercy and recommend me to God as a friend.

God, karma, whoever is out there, he prays, at the end of this I will answer for anything I've done. Do not punish my family for my actions, for they are innocent.

Amen.

"Ice cold, Sergeant," says Sosa, glancing at Rod with new respect.

Hellraisers 3, this is Hellraisers 6.

"Hellraisers 3. Go ahead, Hellraisers 6."

We got people in the elevator, over.

While the Lieutenant talks, Rod hears a metallic boom in the background. Someone is pounding his fists against the elevator doors, trying to get their attention, wanting out.

"Copy that, Hellraisers 6," Rod says. "Are they infected, over?"

No way to know until we get them out of the elevator, over.

"Hellraisers 6, do you need assistance, over?"

We could use you pulling security in the hallway, Hellraisers 3. Stay close, over.

"Roger, Hellraisers 6. Hellraisers 3, out."

More hurry up and wait. They'll have to finish clearing the rooms later.

Rod leads Third Squad back toward the elevator lobby. Turning the corner, he sees Weapons Squad prying open the elevator doors while the

Headquarters guys cover them with their rifles. He wonders how long those people have been trapped inside the elevator. Infected or not, they will be too weak to stand up.

Refugees are going to defeat the invasion, Rod believes. Thousands of people are still alive in Arlington alone, he is sure of it, barricaded in basements and other safe places. Hundreds have already reached the airport. They need food, water, shelter, medical care. Many of them are so psychologically damaged they present a danger to themselves and others.

The worst part is the military took their guns. Never did this country need a draft more than it does now, but the government has not yet done this. Many of the refugees are willing to fight alongside the Army, but they are not allowed, not even as mules, not even behind the lines. So they sit around and drain resources the military needs to win this war. It's a giant waste, and just thinking about it makes the old rage boil inside him.

A strange smell—a dry, antiseptic scent, like rubbing alcohol—strikes his nose, making him cough. He keys his headset in alarm. "Hellraisers 6, this is Hellraisers 3, how copy, over?"

Hellraisers 3, Hellraisers 6. We almost got it open. Wait, out—

The elevator lobby fills with the crash of gunfire and strobing muzzle flashes.

♦

The firing stops, replaced by screams.

"Move, move!" Rod roars, surging forward with his automatic shotgun up and leveled.

The lobby fills with chittering black creatures swarming over the bodies of the soldiers. They look like giant flies, their backs covered in greasy mesh wings, their limbs sharp edged and hairy, their eyes massive and pure white, their bodies ranging size from as small as a dog to as big as a cow. They smell like rubbing alcohol. One of them hunches over Sergeant Ford, its multiple limbs folding the man into a box shape, ripping flesh and bone like cardboard.

Ford screams in agony.

"Jesus Christ," Arnold says.

"Don't shoot!" Rod says. "That's our people in there."

"What do we do, Sergeant?"

"Follow me!"

They're going to have to kill these things at close quarters.

A voice calls from the elevator lobby: "Fire!"

"We're coming to get you, sir!" Rod says as he rushes forward.

"That's an order!" Pierce shrieks. "We're done!"

The squad hesitates in the corridor with gasps of revulsion and dread. Rod realizes he is alone.

Pierce is still screaming: "Fire! Fire! Fire!"

The words turn into a long keening wail. In front of Rod, the thing that folded Sergeant Ford into a neat box is now spinning him while shooting a stream of viscous webbing around the body. Another of the things picks up the shrieking radio operator, expertly lops the AN/PRC-119 radio off of his back, and then hacks off his limbs, chirping musically while it works. Its glistening wings tremble, making an oily, leathery flapping sound that gives Rod the skin-crawling sensation of cockroaches on his body.

He fires the AA12, which discharges with a deafening boom. The thing cocooning Ford explodes in a spectacular splash of carapace and white slime. He fires again, blasting another of the things into wet pieces.

Navarro's voice buzzes in his ear: *Hellraisers 6, this is Hellraisers 3.*

"Lieutenant!" he cries, ejecting the smoking twelve-gauge casing and chambering another round. The men in the elevator lobby have stopped screaming. The buglike things continue their grisly work on the bodies, ignoring Rod, their bulbous white eyes inscrutable and seemingly blind.

Rod turns and sees his squad flinching away from the sight.

"Fire your goddamn weapons!"

Hellraisers 6, how copy?

More of the things pour from the blackness of the elevator shaft and swarm across the ceiling and walls and floor in a single chittering mass, their wings trembling.

chk-chk-chk-chk-chk

"We've got to get out of here!" one of the soldiers shouts.

Rod flicks the selector switch on his thunder gun to auto and rains buckshot into the things, splattering them. He backpedals quickly, reloading, as the squad opens up, screaming their heads off. The monsters fly apart under the storm of shot.

For every creature they kill, another takes its place.

Any Hellraisers unit, this is Hellraisers 1. Identify source of gunfire, over?

Rod shouts into his headset, "All Hellraisers, all Hellraisers, this is Three. Six is down. We are engaged at the elevator lobby. Request assistance, over."

The voices of the other sergeants crash in his ear, talking over each other.

Copy that. On the way, Hellraisers 3, out.

Hang on, Rod. Wait one, out.

The wall next to them begins to crumble. Through the hole they hear the buzzing of wings.

"Fall back, fall back!"

The squad turns and sprints down the hallway, their boots slamming the carpet, surrounded by an omnipresent scratching sound.

The walls are dissolving.

Rod pauses to fire his shotgun. The gunstock hums against his shoulder. Shell casings fly into the air. The bloated black bodies explode under the fusillade.

The gun clicks empty.

chk-chk-chk-chk-chk

"Go, Sergeant!" Sosa roars, shouldering his SAW and opening fire. The tracers arc down the hall into the thickly massed creatures, splattering dozens of them.

Bits of dust and paint sparkle in the air around him, almost beautiful as seen through his night vision goggles.

Rod grabs the man's collar and pulls hard as the ceiling collapses under the weight of a pile of the things, landing on the floor with a thud. The bodies explode on impact, spilling guts and organs across the carpet.

Davis and Lynch wave the men through, shoot into the swarm and then run after the squad.

Rod sees lights flickering ahead and calls out, "Third Squad here!"

The squads almost collide at the corner. It's Navarro and his shooters, wide eyed and gasping.

"Where's Jake?"

"Don't know," Navarro tells him. "What the hell did you guys do? I'm being chased by giant flies, for Chrissakes."

"No time," Rod says. "They're right behind us too."

"If they are, we're trapped."

"Then we make our stand here. See to your men. We got your back."

Navarro nods, paling. "Good luck, Rod."

Rod hears muffled gunfire erupt on another floor of the hotel. Whatever Lieutenant Pierce unleashed is spreading through the building. With just seconds to act, he points and calls out names, positioning his two grenadiers against the walls and the SAW gunners next to them, where their overlapping cones of fire will cover the hallway with minimal shifting fire. Two riflemen kneel in the middle with Rod and his shotgun, while the other two stand behind them.

The swarm is nearly upon them when Rod gives the order to fire.

He shoulders his shotgun and squeezes the trigger, the gun booming in his hands. The grenadiers shoot their thumpers, sending multiple projectile rounds deep into the elevator lobby. The SAW gunners, lying on the floor, fire hundreds of rounds, tracers zipping downrange in blurred streams. The riflemen fire in an endless series of metallic bursts.

The corridor's volume fills with hot, flying pieces of metal. The creatures disintegrate under the withering fire. The grenades burst, sending a thick, rolling cloud of smoke and dust surging toward the soldiers. They cough on it, blinded, and continue to shoot.

"Loading!"

Light flashes in the smoke as another grenade bursts. The building trembles. The concussion blows a fresh wave of particulates into their faces. Dark shapes swarm toward them through the dust, like ghosts.

"Loading!"

Rod empties his shotgun and reloads until he has no more full drums in his pouch. Hundreds of warm shell casings flicker in his peripheral vision and roll across the carpet to gather in piles.

One by one, the rifles click empty.

"Last mag!"

"I'm out!"

Rod orders the boys to fix bayonets as the SAW gunners empty their belts.

The last gun sputters, falls silent, leaving a deafening ringing sound in their ears.

Rod draws his knife and offers a brief prayer for his family. Around him, the firing line, emptied of ammunition and bristling with bayonets, waits for the end.

The smoke and dust dissipate, revealing a jumbled carpet of black pieces of carapace and limbs crushed into a thick layer of white slime.

"Joe, what you got?" Rod calls out.

"I can't see shit," Navarro answers. "But I don't see any bugs either."

Several creatures squirm wetly through the sticky remains, their legs broken, making clicking sounds. At the end of the hallway, near the elevator lobby, the ceiling is on fire, the flames obscured by a growing haze of smoke. Another threat. They are going to have to move within the next few minutes.

"They ain't coming," Arnold says in disbelief, blinking. "We got them all."

"Kicked their ass," Sosa says, but without force.

"Aieeyah," Lynch answers mechanically, spitting into the dust.

Tanner slumps against the wall hugging his ribs, his body shaking. Davis lights a short length of foul-smelling cigar and sighs. Some of the other boys pass around a can of wintergreen dip.

"Hellraisers 1, this is Hellraisers 3," Rod says into his headset. "How copy, over?"

The platoon's private channel hisses with static.

"Do you copy, Hellraisers 1?" He glances at Navarro, who looks back at him with a grim expression. "Check the Comanche net, Joe. Outlaw needs our sitrep. Tell him the Lieutenant is down, the building is on fire and we're coming out." Then he tries to raise Jake Morrow again, fearing the worst.

"Rod," says Navarro, his eyes glassy as he listens to the chatter on the company net. "It's a shit storm. Captain Mack is wounded. We'd better get moving."

RAY

The children walked among the trees, feeling the energy of the crisp autumn air, their sneakers crunching dead leaves. Ray knows this place; it's Cashtown Elementary. And he is seven years old again, guiding a blindfolded and laughing Shawn McCrea.

His father, Ray Senior, got drunk and beat his wife and sucker punched his son until one day he died of a heart attack. Ray Junior adapted to a world where you were either a taker or a giver. Whatever goodness his mother had to offer was not enough. Ray had nature *and* nurture going against him.

People are not born greedy or violent or cruel; the world teaches them.

The children drifted among the trees, the sighted leading the blind under the watchful eyes of the teacher. The point of the game was trust. You trusted the person guiding you. It was an exciting game.

When Ray pushed Shawn face first into the oak tree, he thought he was winning.

♦

Infection rages in his blood. In his fevered dreams, the memories blur one into the next, settling on him sitting hunched over the counter at Pete's Tavern, slowly converting his last paycheck into shots of Wild Turkey and mugs of draft. Just three years out of high school, he had already been hired and fired from Walmart, the local Exxon station and the facilities department at a local hospital. As for next week, he had no idea what he'd be doing. A friend at a moving company had said he could use him, so maybe he'd do that for a while and see how it went. Anything but the Army. Ray liked to do what he wanted, when he wanted to do it.

He glowered at his image in the mirror behind the bar.

If I see that bitch Lola again, I'm going to slap her good.

(Whatever you think is best, Ray.)

And if I ever see her little jerk college boyfriend, I'll break his goddamn face.

(If you think that's best, Ray.)

Damn straight.

Lola Rivera was the one good thing that happened to Ray in high school. School had been like prison to him, a place to kill time smoking in the boys' room and terrorizing the weaker kids and thinking deep thoughts during detention. She was a good girl attracted to his unintentional bad boy charm, which smacked of honesty to her. For his part, her beauty and intelligence awed him, made him want to be a better man to give her what she deserved instead of what she was really getting.

Then Lola went to college, while Ray got a job wearing a blue vest. She called him a few times and they had awkward conversations about her exciting new life. Gradually, the calls stopped as they drifted apart, or rather, recognized how little they actually had in common. He hadn't thought of her in years until hearing she'd brought a guy home with her on Christmas break, some pansy ass named Bob. The happy couple had been spotted holding hands at the mall. Ray counted the years and realized she would be graduating soon. She would start a career, get married, buy a house and have kids, while he'd be stuck in Cashtown for the rest of his life, one of the losers he'd always ridiculed and sworn he'd never become.

Stewie and Brian entered the tavern, laughing and slapping snow from each other's shoulders, and joined Ray at the bar. Ray scowled at them.

"You'll never guess who's right behind us," Stewie said.

"Merry Christmas, Ray," Brian snickered.

The door opened with a jingle and a young couple stepped blinking into the warm neon gloom. Ray squinted and recognized Lola. His heart fluttered unexpectedly in his chest; she had flowered into a beautiful woman over the past several years. Bob struck him as your typical mild-mannered jock with his clean white oxford shirt and powder blue sweater, his blond hair neatly combed to the side. More Clark Kent than Superman, though; Ray believed he could push this college boy around pretty easily if he wanted. Lola called out to Pete to bring a pitcher. Bob pointed to a booth, and they took their seats and shucked their coats.

Lola laughed and socked Bob playfully in the shoulder while he grinned, apparently teasing her.

She used to do that to me, Ray thought, feeling sorry for himself. He realized he'd let something great slip through his fingers due to sheer laziness.

Stewie and Brian snickered while Ray glared at the couple. Eventually, Bob noticed and bristled. Lola saw Ray and whispered into Bob's ear.

Listen to your girl, Bobby, Ray thought, giving him an evil smile. *You'd better stay put or you're going to get hurt tonight.*

Bob gently shrugged off her hands and stood. Ray downed his shot and made a show of cracking his knuckles as Bob approached.

"You're Ray Young," Bob said uncertainly, glancing at Stewie and Brian and sizing them up before leveling his gaze at Ray.

"You found me," Ray said.

"All right," Bob said. "Well, here it is." He took a deep breath. "I heard you've been talking shit about me and Lola. Saying how you're going to kill us or something."

Before Ray could answer, Bob stepped forward and stared into his eyes from inches away. "Is that true, Ray?"

Ray's height and size and scowl intimidated most people, but not this kid. His fantasy of how this was supposed to roll dissolved in an instant. His alcoholic bravery abandoned him, leaving him feeling naked. He smiled, fighting to keep his cool.

"I don't know who told you that," he said.

He realized the bar was growing quiet. Everyone was watching.

"People told me," Bob said. "Worse, they told Lola."

"Well, they're liars. I never said anything like that. No, sir."

It might have worked if Jeff Vogler, standing at the other end of the bar, didn't laugh.

Bob's eyes narrowed. Ray couldn't believe this guy's self control. He felt what little courage he had left drain away.

"Let me put it this way," Bob breathed into his face. "Do we have a problem?"

Ray smiled again. "You've got a lot of heart coming in here, Bob. I'm willing to let it go." He raised his half-finished mug. "In fact, let me buy you a beer. You and Lola, for old times' sake. Peace offering."

The room relaxed a little. Ray had chosen an honorable withdrawal. Now it was up to the college kid to do the right thing, which everyone knew he would. Back at Bob's booth, Lola's eyes were wide and glassy. Pete started to fill a pitcher, which he would offer on the house.

Bob shrugged. "All right—"

Ray swung the mug into his face, spraying beer and blood and sending a chipped tooth skidding across the countertop. Then Ray was on top of him, straddling his chest, punching him with both fists.

When they pulled him off, he couldn't stop laughing because he had never felt such joy.

♦

Twelve years later, the Screaming changed everything. This is where his fever takes him next. That day, Ray woke up moaning in his basement apartment, his head pounding like a drum. He snoozed for another hour and decided it was time to get up. Rubbing his belly, he plodded into the bathroom and noisily emptied his bladder while he inspected his bleary eyes, bristling stubble and wild handlebar mustache in the mirror. *What a night.* By now, Ray accepted he was a loser, but took an odd pride in the fact he was somehow good at it.

He paused while brushing his teeth as he realized he had not heard his mother's characteristic plodding around upstairs. The floor was always creaking.

Pulling on a clean T-shirt, frayed jeans and his trademark STEELERS ballcap, Ray lit a cigarette, coughed up a ball of phlegm, and thought about hitting the old lady up for some breakfast.

He stepped outside and climbed the stairs to the main house. The air was filled with distant sirens. A haze of smoke hung in the sky. That figured. He'd joined the volunteer fire department to try to experience a little excitement that didn't come from a bottle or between a woman's legs. There was finally a big fire, and he'd missed it.

Ray opened the side door and walked into the house on bare feet. Too late, he remembered his mother's injunction against smoking and rushed to drop it into the kitchen sink.

"Mom?"

No answer.

"Ma, it's me, Ray."

He checked the couch and her bedroom, wondering if she was taking a nap, but there was no sign of her. He speculated that she'd gone out for a walk. *Miracles do happen*, he thought. For years, his mother had been a shut-in for the most part. He made a strong cup of coffee and sipped it, feeling a little better. Any minute now, she would squeeze herself through the front door and make him some bacon and eggs, all the while muttering some vague assurance that he was a good man, destined to do something special.

Ray noticed the bathroom door was closed. It was never closed unless his mother was actually using the toilet.

"Mom? You in there?" He knocked. "Can I come in, Mom?"

He opened the door and gasped. His mother lay sprawled in the bathtub, her massive belly rising above the gray water like the back of a whale, giant breasts swaying in the murk.

"Ma!" he roared, falling to his knees and trying to pull her slippery bulk out of the tub. He settled on raising her head. Water spilled from her mouth, open and stretched wide in a horrific, soundless scream.

Soaked with soapy water, he reached under her back and pulled the plug, letting the water drain out. He kissed her cold face, sobbing.

"No, no, no," he told her. "Don't die."

As a volunteer firefighter, he was trained in CPR. First, he had to get help on the way. Running to the kitchen, he grabbed the cordless phone and dialed 911 on the way back to the bathroom. The phone beeped in his ear, telling him all circuits were busy. Roaring a string of obscenities, he clasped his hands and pushed his mother's sternum, cracking it. The bathroom filled with the smell of shit. He breathed into her mouth, counting. Her body was freezing.

"Don't give up, Ma," he whispered.

The tears flowed. He could not stop crying. She was a giver and he was a taker but he had never looked down at her for that. Ray loved his mother more than himself. He loved her because she had given him whatever shred of goodness he had.

He finally got through to 911 after two hours, continuing to give CPR with his aching arms while shouting his address into the phone.

The ambulance never came.

Ever since that day, he had the nagging feeling her death was somehow all his fault.

♦

Three mornings later, Ray climbed into his battered pickup after a twelve-hour stint at his rent-a-cop job guarding a self-storage facility, and started his drive home. He was exhausted from the long night shift, his grief and battling with the mortuary people to take his mother's body and put her into the ground with some dignity. It was a fight he'd lost; several guys in bright yellow hazmat suits had loaded her corpse onto a truck the day before, and had handed him a receipt. Leona Young would be buried in a collective grave outside of town. Later on, when resources freed up, he could arrange to have her dug up and buried right. Meanwhile, the government had plenty of other problems to worry about. One in five people had fallen down. It had just been Leona's bad luck she'd caught SEEL Syndrome while taking a bath, which had led to her drowning. Most of the screamers were still alive, and needed around-the-clock care.

He was so preoccupied by these things he nearly missed the pajama-wearing lunatics running down the paper boy and ripping his body apart by the handful.

Ray slowed his truck, gaping, as they crammed his flesh into their mouths while the kid was still screaming.

"Hey," he hollered. "Hey!"

They reared their heads, still chewing, their chins stained black.

"Mike, what the hell are you doing to that kid?"

A woman stood, snarling, and sprinted toward his truck.

"Oh shit," Ray hissed, throwing the vehicle into drive and stomping on the gas pedal, pulling away on squealing tires.

He drove from the scene feeling shaken and unsure of what had happened. Did a group of people—one of them Mike Parsons, who got up early every morning to walk his dog—really run down the stupid redheaded kid who delivered the papers?

They were eating him, bro.

Naw, impossible.

All he knew was whatever they were doing to the kid, he didn't want anyone doing to him. He never claimed to be hero material. He would drive into town and call the cops; they could handle it.

Ray turned the wheel, feeling the truck bang over something. People ran across the street in front of him, chasing a screaming woman wearing a jogging outfit. She ran toward the truck, waving her arms.

He stepped on the gas and sped past, knocking down a mailbox. His truck glanced against one of her pursuers and sent him spinning through the air onto a parked car. The others tackled the woman, bearing her down onto the road.

"Shit, I'm sorry," Ray sobbed, and then flinched as a man stormed onto a porch in a bathrobe, firing his shotgun.

Sirens wailed in the distance. A dog bolted across the road, its head down. A car fishtailed and crumpled around a light pole. The driver looked at Ray in a daze as he passed.

"Sorry," Ray whispered, keeping his eyes on the road.

Something big was happening, something horrible, even worse than the Screaming. He turned on the radio, set to his favorite station. At this time of morning, Kaptain Kyle and Betty Boo did their morning zoo program. A muffled voice was shouting.

I swear to Jesus I saw this. The school bus was shaking. People were shoving at each other to get inside. Swarming. The bus was packed with people. They could barely move in there, there were so many. There was blood all over the windows. The windows were streaked with it. Those people were doing something awful to those kids—

Kaptain Kyle: And you're done. Another caller bites the dust. Look guys, it's a funny joke, but enough's enough already. I'm not falling for it. From now on, I'm cutting you off immediately. Even think the word "zombie" and you're gone, okay?

Betty Boo: It sounded real though, didn't it? Jeez, it gave me the willies. A school bus.

Kaptain Kyle: Some kind of War of the Worlds *thing going on today.*

Betty Boo: Is today the anniversary?

Kaptain Kyle: You'd think after the Screaming, people would show a little class. Should we take another caller? Dare we risk it?

Betty Boo: What's she doing?

Kaptain Kyle: Ladies and gentlemen, our producer, Sharon, is waving her arms at us. That is how cutting-edge modern producers tell their on-air talent to go to commercial, instead of using their microphone. They wave their hands in the air like they just don't care.

Betty Boo: Must be important. She's kind of freaking out. Is she crying?

Kaptain Kyle: Curioser and curioser. Ladies and gentlemen, we will return after the break.

Ray's truck rocketed down the street until coming to a skidding halt on the sidewalk in front of his house. He killed the engine, cutting off an ad for a better mattress, and jumped out. The air felt warm here and he smelled smoke. He had a rough plan sketched in his head. He knew a place where he could hole up for a while, but he needed supplies.

Inside the house, food, beer, liquor, cigarettes and dip, jugs of water, flashlight, packets of Kool-Aid, burritos and TV dinners all went into a plastic cooler until it was full. He had no idea how long it would last him, but it was all he had.

He ran back outside, the cooler perched on his shoulder, and nearly dropped it as someone fired a gun in the house next door. Old Wexler lived in that house with his poodles. The guy was pushing eighty. Ray wondered if he should go help him out.

In the distance, a woman screamed as if being tortured. The sound froze the blood in his veins. Wexler fired his gun again, BANG BANG. Ray saw the flashes of light in the living room window.

"Oh, God," he sobbed, heaving the cooler onto the back of the truck and jumping into the driver's seat. "Holy shit."

The radio was still playing commercials. He worked the dial until he found the local AM news station, which blasted the angry klaxon honk of the Emergency Alert System. He turned the radio off. He didn't need it. He had plenty of information. Everything he needed to know was happening right outside his windshield.

Squinting against the orange glare of the morning sun, he threw the rig into drive and turned onto Oakland, swerving to dodge cars and crazies. He drove blind through a billowing hot cloud of pitch black smoke, screaming *hail Mary*, and emerged in time to narrowly miss ramming a wailing ambulance in the process of swerving off the road. Another car, its windows streaked red, crashed through a phone booth and into a wall. Galveston looked clear and he floored it, pushing aside the worry a cop was going to pull him over. Figures ran in the distance. Bodies lay on the sidewalk. As he passed, they sat up and stared at him.

Minutes later, his truck idled in front of the self-storage facility's chain link fence while Ray panted as if he'd run, not driven, the entire trip. Sweat stung his eyes and he wiped it away with the back of the sleeve of his uniform. He had to talk himself into leaving the truck. Opening the door, he walked to the gate on trembling legs and unlocked it. He drove into the compound and parked in front of one of the storage cubicles.

As he jumped down from the vehicle, a deep thud reverberated through the ground, making him stumble. Car alarms shrieked across town. A massive fireball rose over distant houses. He paused, feeling curious. *What's over that way? Gas station?*

The gate rattled. Someone was trying to get in.

Breathing hard, Ray cut the lock on one of the storage cubicles with a pair of bolt cutters. He opened the door and squinted into the darkness, wondering. A strong musty smell poured out of the room. It was half filled with dusty boxes, some old furniture, a few floor lamps, an area rug rolled up and bound with masking tape. Good enough. He tossed in the cooler and a few blankets and clothes he'd scooped up back at the house and pulled the door shut. The darkness enveloped him. He felt safe in it.

Footsteps pounded outside, receding.

◆

For five days, he lived like a rat in a hole. At least, he thought it was five days; after a while, he lost track of time. At first, it was like a party. If this was the end of the world, he might as well drink up. His mother was dead, everyone had gone crazy outside, and he wanted to forget it all. Two days later, he woke up in the darkness to the smell of his own vomit, barely able to remember where he was and how he had gotten here.

Boredom set in. He spent hours rummaging through the boxes with his flashlight and found nothing useful. Just the detritus of some other loser's life: photo albums, knickknacks, children's toys, women's magazines, portable heater, computer mouse, mystery novels, videotapes, dishes and cutlery, blankets, dead cell phone, bras and clothes and a broken wristwatch. Nothing he could eat or drink or fight with. He used one of the boxes of clothes as his toilet. Filled with self pity, he had his first crying jag.

The batteries in his flashlight failed on what he thought was the third day. He started to panic. He pressed his ear against the big metal door but heard nothing outside, wondering what that meant. Maybe the entire town was on the other side of the door, waiting for him to come out so they could yell, *Surprise!* and laugh at him. Then he imagined Stewie and Brian standing on the other side of the door listening for *him*, drool leaking from grinning, chomping, red-stained mouths. The lockup had filled with stale cigarette smoke and the nauseating odors of his own vomit, shit and piss, but he didn't dare open the door even a crack to let in some fresh air. This made him wonder if the lockup had any ventilation at all. He imagined suffocating in his sleep, and spent the next hour taking deep breaths until his mind moved on to something else.

Between the fear and the isolation, he was starting to go crazy.

On the last day, still wearing his rumpled brown security guard uniform, he pulled open the cubicle door and emerged blinking into the light. The darkness had driven him out. His terrors lived in that darkness. His memories. More than food or water, Ray craved light.

In his fevered delirium, he recalls what happened next. Instead of a wasteland overrun by crazy people, which is what he half expected, he saw the watchtowers of a thriving refugee camp. He saw people unloading the storage lockers and staring back at him just as curiously. He figures on some level a bad guy like him was supposed to join a roving post-apocalyptic biker gang raping and pillaging and making things worse, just like in the movies. If he'd left the storage lockup and found such a gang, he supposes he would have signed up if he thought they could keep him alive. But he didn't find that. Instead, he found a struggling community making a stand, people working together to maintain something like normal. This was fine with him. He wanted nothing more than to help fight for that normalcy, even to the point of becoming a cop. The truth is the apocalypse scared the hell out of him. Sure, he was bad to the bone, as the song went, but he would rather be a bad guy among good, honest folk than a bad guy among homicidal maniacs. The apocalypse changed him—made him want to do better before it all fell apart. That's why when he met Wendy, the rookie cop from Pittsburgh, he pledged to watch over her. Even after every other cop was dead or run off and her city burned to the ground, this poor, innocent girl still fought the good fight, and it broke his heart. She deserved a guardian angel. He followed her to the bridge at Steubenville—perhaps the one selfless thing he ever did—and entered the nightmare of Infection.

In his delirium, however, he opens the door and does not see watchtowers or people looting the storage lockers. He does not hear dogs barking or men hammering boards or five-ton trucks churning up clouds of dust. This twilight world is barren, as quiet as the Moon. Infection is not showing him what has happened, but what might have been, or what might yet be.

He tries to start his truck, which clicks in response. The battery is dead. Outside the storage facility, he walks past an abandoned Laundromat, car dealership, appliance store, fast food restaurant, daycare. The pawn shop has been burned out. His boots crunch on broken glass. His footsteps are loud in his ears. The town looks like it has been bombed. The street is torn up and strewn with rubble. Trash rustles across the ground. Someone spray painted giant letters across the front of the police station: WE HAD IT COMING.

For hours, he explores his old town as little bits of ash flutter to the earth. His own house has been burned to the ground. None of the cars will start. The houses have no power. He sees no bodies, no animals. He finds a battery-powered radio but it hisses across the entire band.

It is a dead world.

Then he sees the distant walking figure.

Ray calls to him. The man turns and grins and waves as Ray grunts with recognition.

Tyler Jones, still wearing his CASHTOWN FIRE DEPARTMENT *cap and dark gray work shirt with a pack of Marlboros in the breast pocket, waits for Ray to catch up. Tyler is half friend, half mentor and, in semiretirement, something of a professional bum. Like so many people who lived in Cashtown, he did a little of this, a little of that, to make his beer money. Unlike other people, he wore his lack well. He always seemed completely comfortable with what he had, right down to his skin.*

Tyler squints at him, chewing on a toothpick. "Where you been, boy?"

"What happened here, Tyler?" Ray yells breathlessly as he jogs close. "What happened to the camp?"

This question appears to irritate the man. "Hell, there ain't no camp, Ray."

"The camp, Tyler. The camp! Camp Defiance."

"Check this out, bud. Look what I found. It's going to blow your mind."

Ray gasps in revulsion as Tyler steps aside, revealing two creatures bound to him with leather leashes. They're four legged, the size of deer, and covered in hairless green skin. The barrel-chested one on the left totters on tapering stalactite legs, its skull covered in long, straight horns. The other has bloated legs with wrinkled knees and a head covered in a briar patch of fleshy antlers throbbing like veins.

Ray glances down at the ground and sees a chunk of concrete on the rubble-strewn road. He picks it up, feeling its weight.

"What the hell are they?"

Tyler laughs wetly, wiping yellowish mucus from his mouth onto the back of his hand. "This," he announces proudly, "is Life."

Ray stares at them in horror. They are starving, weak, disgusting. They have no mouths, no teeth, no claws. They appear harmless, and yet he has never been so afraid of anything.

Tyler adds, "Come on over here, Ray, and meet the family. They ain't gonna bite."

He whistles and the creatures stir and totter forward. Ray is too terrified to move. Close up, they appear to be blind, without eyes, and yet he knows they can sense his presence—knows that they've been looking for him, that they're happy to finally have found him. They smell like pus.

As the creature with the antlers nears, its head shifts as if to nuzzle and its body shudders, releasing a cloud of musk. Ray cringes in disgust, fighting the urge to vomit. Make your pecker fall off, his mind blurts out irrationally. His instincts are howling with fear. He realizes he is not looking at another hideous spawn of Infection. He is looking at Infection itself.

Specifically, he is looking at his own infection. The sickness that right now is turning him into something else. It is like having cancer and being forced to say hello to your tumor.

The antlered thing scuttles toward him in a surprising burst of speed, straining at the leash and releasing another cloud of musk. Ray can feel its raging fever heat.

"Oh, we got a live one," says Tyler, laughing.

Ray reels from a massive wave of nausea. He looks at his hand and sobs in horror. It is bright red and swollen and covered in warts and blisters, one ruptured and leaking bloody fluid. His index finger has been bitten off. He is afraid that if he screams he'll start vomiting and won't be able to stop.

The thing shudders again, releasing another cloud of musk. This is how it eats.

Ray roars and crushes the creature's head with the chunk of concrete, the antlers stinging his hands as his skin brushes against them. The dark green skin splits easily, spurting pus and wriggling things that splash wetly onto the road. Its head destroyed and sagging like the ruins of a burst balloon, the creature continues to skitter back and forth on its leash, spilling squeaking parasites and fluids rich with alien bacteria and viruses.

Heaving the concrete over his head, Ray smashes the body into a puddle of green flesh.

Tyler laughs. "What do you think that's going to do? Shit, you can't kill Life, boy."

Ray says nothing. He no longer understands language. He no longer has a mouth. The heat is incredible—the heat of his own blood pumping through his body. Tiny monsters swim in the soup, spreading fresh diseases his body receives and catalogs with joy. He peers out from rubbery green skin with millions of microscopic eyes, sensing Tyler's presence. His hooves, chapped and raw and bleeding, clomp on the road.

He has become Infection.

Red mist veils his vision as he dreams the dreams of the Brood, the dreams of home. He floats over an endless plain under a copper sky filled with red dust and countless screaming winged things. As far as the eye can see, the land below swarms with monsters—naked things of all shapes and sizes constantly fighting and eating each other in teeming mountains of flesh. An entire ecology based on meat and waste in a circular food chain where everything eats everything else. Life filling every bit of space, eating and breeding and fighting for scarce nutrients and air and sunlight. This ecology is harsh and brutal but also rich, diverse, changing. Soaring through the humid, oily air, Ray watches as species rapidly evolve in endless competition. He wonders which of them is the Brood.

Then he understands. They are all the Brood.

As the myriad species fight and fuck and die, the Brood sighs content, flush with cheerful health. Oh, the joy of life. The wonder of endless creation. The brilliance of evolution. The Brood infected their world, and turned it into a laboratory for distilling perfection.

A dark shape veers shrieking from the left, and the dream ends.

Ray awakens and feels the constant hunger. He scuttles toward Tyler on his four legs and shudders, flushing powerful enzymes into the air.

"That's right," Tyler says, his eyes swelling shut, his face red and shiny with fever. "You eat. You grow up big and strong. It is time for you to become, Ray. Become perfection."

DR. PRICE

Travis sees the woman head into a side tunnel terminating at a three-story office building buried under the west portal, part of the underground world where he now lives.

Don't go, Travis wants to call after her. He mouths the words but cannot say them.

Every morning, she appears somewhere on the way to his job, but he has never had the courage to approach her. The truth is he is afraid of her, just like he is afraid of everything down here. His job may sound heroic—searching for a cure to the plague—but mostly he spends his time competing for scarce resources against the rest of the bureaucracy and staring at the ceiling in a state of mild, blank terror. Wondering if all those thousands of tons of earth, just over his head, will one day come crashing down.

Pale faces flash in the gloom of the crowded tunnel, people heading to their jobs or wandering around with nothing better to do. There are thousands more people than there are jobs. The stale air smells like minerals and concrete and sweat.

If the ceiling collapses he will be crushed like a bug, with as much awareness of his fate. The world will tremble violently; then darkness.

A man shoulders him, muttering an irritated apology. Travis catches a glimpse of blond hair in the crowd ahead and changes course, following her into another tunnel.

His stomach trembles with an odd falling sensation, reminding him of descriptions of love he has read. He wonders why he is doing this. He has no idea what he is going to say when he catches up to her.

Where are you going? he wants to ask her. *I don't even know your name. How did you survive?*

Nearly three weeks ago, Travis gazed down at Washington from a thundering Army transport. Riding high in the sky, the city looked normal, as long as you ignored the columns of smoke and the omnipresent distant boom of gunfire.

Heading west, the helicopter left the city and flew over green fields that gradually turned into the treed slopes of a mountain. At its base sprawled a complex of bland, utilitarian buildings and roads girdled by miles of fencing. Beyond, the Shenandoah Valley looked lush, green, untouched by the violence. The helicopter circled the facility and landed on a broad concrete pad occupied by several aircraft, their rotors still turning. Crowds of refugees were being herded by Marines toward the yawning mouth of a large building built from corrugated steel against the base of the mountain.

My God, Travis thought, pausing to look at the buildings. *This is the Mount Weather Emergency Operations Center. The Alamo of the U.S. government.*

A man in a business suit holding an M16 grabbed his arm and pushed him toward the tunnel. *Follow the others*, he said. *Obey all instructions.*

Travis glanced up at the sky and that was the last time he saw the sun.

Inside, the refugees streamed into what appeared to be a massive bank vault carved into the rock and waited their turn to plunge deep into the earth, emerging into the sunless world they were told was Area B.

The chase leads him to the mass transit station.

He hurries after, pushing through the crowd, trying not to lose sight of the young woman. She wears coveralls, common among the rank and file refugees who fled Washington with just the clothes on their backs. He grits his teeth and works to control his breathing, fighting his constant claustrophobia.

We're just rats in a cage, Travis thinks. The Mount Weather facility was designed to support two thousand people. He guesses at least three times that live here now. The top officials and the Congress and their rich friends have lots of space, he heard. They have their own private apartments and tennis courts and movie theaters. Everyone else lives and works in overcrowded dormitories, locker rooms, office buildings and cafeterias that are spartan, gray and washed out by fluorescent light that never seems bright enough.

He tries not to think about the overworked ventilation systems struggling to supply fresh air for this many people. Every time he has a headache, he believes it is carbon dioxide poisoning.

Stay focused. Follow the girl.

The walls here are painted with a red stripe, indicating he has reached a mass transit zone. Giant letters and numbers spell out his location in code. The air feels humid here and stinks like raw sewage. A crowd of people waits for the train, reading or working on electronic tablets. Behind them, a wall sweats, beads of water glistening on its surface. Travis guesses a wastewater pipe broke behind the wall. He hopes someone is repairing it.

What if the repairmen died on the surface and never made it down? What if the mains burst and the underground chambers fill with water and human waste?

We'll drown like rats in a toilet, that's what.

The terror of his claustrophobia takes so many forms, and it is neverending.

Every night, as he tries to sleep to the sound of a hundred other men snoring, he remembers the Infected charging across the White House lawn and envisions the same scene playing out three hundred feet over his head. In his mind, the Infected break down the fence and overrun the guards and pound their fists against the door to the complex, built thick enough to withstand a nuclear blast. Thousands of them mill around the buildings put there to communicate with the Situation Room, now empty and gathering dust back at the White House.

In chambers carved into rock deep inside the earth, Travis would never know he has been buried alive. The leadership would never tell him. He and the other refugees would go on doing their jobs, cut off from the surface, until one day the food runs out. Then the competition for resources would begin.

It won't matter if you're a Supreme Court Justice or the Secretary of State or the President of the United States. If we get cut off down here, we'll end up eating each other.

Travis believes it may be inevitable. One day, the Infected will migrate out of the cities. They will discover this complex. The electrified fence will not stop them. Human security systems provide deterrence based on an assumption of interest in self-preservation. The carriers of Wildfire do not understand that concept. Only the Wildfire Agent itself does, and it is all too happy—another homocentrism, as it does not *feel* anything—to sacrifice any of its hosts, like pawns, to win its never-ending game of dominance and survival.

The question is whether Wildfire has Mind. Is it intelligent, or just blind programming? Another thought that keeps him up at night.

The public address system bleats a muffled message about the cafeteria being open to second shift. The noise startles him, making him forget his fears and focus again on following the woman. A different cheerful automated voice announces the monorail is approaching the station.

The woman walks away from the crowd, stepping onto the track platform and turning so he can see her face. Just as he remembered, she is a stunning creature, tall and frail and beautiful.

Travis pauses, feeling breathless, wondering what he is going to say. How does one apologize for what happened to her? Perhaps that is all he should say: *Forgive me.*

She stares straight at him, mouthing words he cannot hear but his brain translates as, *Save me.* Travis watches in horror as the monorail approaches. She spreads her arms as the train's lights bathe her in white glare, swooning exactly as he remembered her standing in the door of the helicopter, just before the Secret Service agent shoved her into the crowd.

A scream catches in Travis's throat.

The train passes through the woman, who disappears as if she were a ghost.

♦

The bulletin board is plastered with orange public notices advising the denizens of the Special Facility on everything from dormitory schedules to daycare options to personal hygiene to general propaganda.

Travis scans the notices hungrily, searching for psychiatric help.

He has a choice. The Special Facility offers individual counseling for claustrophobia and depression as well as group grief counseling. He writes down the exchange number for both, hedging his bets. It doesn't matter whether claustrophobia or loneliness or survivor's guilt is driving him mad; he is seeing ghosts. He needs as much help as he can get.

This task done, he hurries off to work. He is not afraid of being late, as nobody cares about his hours. The fact is he spends far more time at work than he does in his overcrowded dormitory. Work takes his mind off things, steadies him.

His office building is set up like a Russian nesting doll, with various levels of workers authorized access to certain floors or zones. As an assistant director with the Office of Science and Technology Policy, Travis is Level Seven, enjoying broad access to both his office building and a special Biosafety Level 4 laboratory in another building buried farther west.

That's where the scientists keep the specimens and experiment on them in ways that would make the Nazis blush. Travis has to remind himself the Infected are not people anymore. In any case, it's the end of the world. If ever was a time when the ends justified the means, he reasons, this would be it. Recently, the scientists received a shipment of bodies of strange monsters for autopsy, sending rumors buzzing throughout Area B. Travis, of course, knows about these strange creatures that recently started to appear, as he now specializes in studying them. He has seen photos of the bodies, shaky video from the field. He has read countless reports, most of which sounded like folklore. He personally has not yet seen one of the creatures. Perhaps today he will take the time to enter the Lab and view the bodies up close. It is difficult to believe they are real. In the photos, they look like Photoshopped monsters from an Internet hoax. It feels like he is studying the Loch Ness Monster. Looking for a cure to Bigfoot.

In particular, he hopes one day they can catch the big monster commonly called the Screamer, King Monster, Rex, Godzilla, Demon. This rare and powerful beast shows up frequently in reports but has rarely been seen and as far as he knows has never been killed or captured. He believes the Demon has some sort of special role in the monsters' ecosystem, but he does not know what it is. Many of the monsters appear to be sickly and struggling to survive. They eat constantly but exhibit signs of starvation. Entire species born just days ago seem to be dying out already. The survivors are adapting, however. Growing stronger. The Demon is one of these survivors. Another fact that keeps Travis up at night.

He runs his ID card through another access control, glaring at the door as it pauses for the usual three seconds before opening with a loud beep, as if reminding him that it alone decides whether he is allowed to enter. He remembers when he used to consider this kind of thing exciting. Just a few weeks ago, he craved access. Now each entry feels like walking deeper into a prison.

The ID card reads, THE PERSON DESCRIBED ON THIS CARD HAS ESSENTIAL EMERGENCY DUTIES WITH THE FEDERAL GOVERNMENT.

The officials constituting what is left of the Office of Science and Technology Policy work in tiny offices ringing a room where a clerical pool works a reception desk around the clock. This is where Travis Price, PhD, an atomic scientist specializing in nonproliferation, came to study monsters. Scientific and policy journals and texts fill shelving against one of the walls. A soldier, helmetless in bulky black body armor, sits on the edge of the desk, flirting with the secretaries. Travis blinks at this uncommon sight, but has no energy for questions.

The soldier stares at him with cold gray eyes and says, "You don't remember me, do you, Doc?"

The woman fought the Secret Service agent, only to be tossed like a doll at the desperate crowd screaming into the powerful wash of the rotors. Sitting on the helicopter sobbing into his hands, Travis looked up and met Fielding's glare with his own.

That's right, I did it, he thought. And I'd do it again. I'm alive.

Fielding nodded slightly as Travis turned away to regard the city they were abandoning. Without its government, Washington seemed drained of its power, an empty shell.

There is no right or wrong anymore, he thought. There is only living and dead.

The flashback dissipates, leaving Travis feeling exhausted.

"Fielding," he says. "You're Fielding. So you're a soldier now?"

"Something like that."

"What does that mean?"

"Most of the Secret Service was lost during the evacuation. The President, the Cabinet, the Supreme Court, the Congress; everyone wants a security detail. I'm ex-military. I was recruited."

"So the government has a paramilitary organization now."

"We're more like the Praetorian Guard, Doc."

The secretaries pointedly ignore the exchange, sensing the tension between the men. Travis hears one of them typing randomly.

"*Quis custodiet ipsos custodes*?" he wonders aloud. Who will guard us from the guards?

Fielding laughs. "Who indeed?"

Travis is already tired of the sparring. A few weeks ago, he would have been terrified of a man like Fielding, and in fact was at their first meeting. Now Travis has real problems that make Fielding seem like small fish.

"So why are you here?"

"I'm here for you."

"Let's go into my office, then. Do you want some coffee?"

Fielding gets off the desk and stands erect, an imposing figure. "No time, Doc," he says. "Do you still have your suit? The one you wore the day you came here?"

The suit is neatly folded in Travis's locker. It still smells like fear.

"What's this about?"

"Doc," Fielding says, grinning, "you're going to meet the President of the United States."

♦

Travis remembers the first time he entered the White House. He tingled as he presented his credentials. A young, attractive aide led him to where he would be working. He glanced into private offices as he followed the woman down the hall and was surprised to see average people hunched over computers in tiny offices, hacking away at keyboards. Phones chirped discordantly, the sound muffled by the carpeted floor. File cabinets bulged with yellowing paper. If he didn't know where he was, he would have guessed he was in some kind of old, regal, shabby hotel converted into offices for law clerks paid to make deals. And yet that breathless 9/11 feeling permeated the building; the White House was a massive *zeitgeist* generator. Travis felt connected to mighty levers that turned the world. Even on days the President was traveling and not much was happening, each day felt like the cusp of history.

Travis never met the President, however. Not for two years. The closest he came was when the White House needed some warm bodies for a press photo.

Now, it seems, President Andrew Walker wants to meet *him*.

He remembers how strange it was. Often one meets a famous actor and later remarks at how much smaller he is in real life than he appears to be in his films. But the President seemed even larger to Travis. He is a giant of a man, making everyone around him appear insubstantial.

Fielding studies him with an expression of subtle amusement. The secretaries stare. One takes off her glasses and squints as if trying to see something in Travis she hadn't seen before, something she'd missed.

"I don't understand," Travis says.

Fielding acknowledges the women with a nod and gestures toward the door.

"Let's get a move on, Doc."

Outside in the corridor, Fielding walks a step behind Travis, his eyes never leaving him.

"Am I under arrest or something?"

"No," Fielding tells him. "You would know if you were."

"Then why do I feel like I'm under arrest?"

"I've seen you in action, Doc. You're a slippery one. I'm going to keep an eye on you."

"Slippery," Travis says, the word bitter on his tongue. *It's not my fault she got left behind*, he wants to scream. *There wasn't enough transport for everyone. The agent pushed her off. It wasn't me.* "If you're the good guy, what are you doing down here? Why aren't you out there saving the world?"

"That's what Roberts did—remember him? Stayed behind to look for his wife. Haven't seen him since. There's plenty of work around here for a guy like me, Doc."

"The fact is that the only person who's going to save the world is someone like me."

"God help us, then."

"I'm not joking. You know the military is in Washington. But do you know how many buildings there are in the city? How many people lived there who became infected? We're throwing what's left of our military into a meat grinder. There aren't enough bullets, Fielding. There aren't enough soldiers. We're going to lose."

Fielding says nothing, regarding Travis with narrowed eyes.

"Bullets can't fix this," Travis says. "Only science can. We just have to figure it out."

"All right, Doc," Fielding says, ending the conversation.

They enter the mass transit station, Travis glancing at the spot where the girl mouthed *Save me* before dissipating in the path of the train. Fielding sees him shudder but says nothing. They board an outgoing monorail, which drops them off near the dormitories. Travis's dorm is a large open space packed with cots on which men sleep in the dull glow of a few red light bulbs and exit signs hanging from the ceiling. So few cots are available that people use them in shifts. In four hours, according to the clock set to military time, Travis will be able to use his cot again for sleep, first brushing the other man's dandruff off the pillow they share.

In the locker room, Travis changes into his suit, shirt and tie, still wrinkled and smelling a bit gamey. It will have to do. One does not visit the President of the United States wearing an orange coverall like a penitentiary inmate.

"Very presentable, Doc," Fielding says, inspecting his nails.

Travis unravels his tie and tries again, eyeing his reflection in a small mirror. Women often told him he was good looking, even though his social awkwardness and general lack of interest otherwise kept them at bay. Now he appears downright frightening. His stubbled face is pale and his eyes look dead.

"Can you at least tell me what this is about?" he asks.

Fielding shrugs. "Don't know, actually. Policy is your field. But I would suspect it's not a social call. Whatever you're working on regarding Wildfire, the Boss thinks it's important."

Travis experiences a sudden flash of panic. *Does the President expect me to make a presentation on my research now? Why didn't the Director tell me about this?*

Outside the dormitory, the two men walk east along the crowded sidewalks framing a main road leading into the heart of Area B. People come here to stroll because of the high ceiling and extra lighting. Travis wonders if he should take the President's interest as a good sign. His theories are controversial and have not been accepted by what passes for the scientific establishment down here. Maybe they're ready to hear him out and give him some real resources.

Earth is being colonized. Not just colonized, but terraformed. The Earth is, to put it plainly, infected. And humans, other life forms? Fertile soil.

The prevailing theory is humans did this to themselves. People tinkering with nanotechnology. Bioweapons designers creating a beast they could not control. The beast escaped its cage, replicated using resources in the natural environment, and covered the planet within days. Once the nano reached a critical mass, one out of five people fell down screaming within hours of each other. The Wildfire contagion descended from this original nano. End of theory.

The problem is they can't find it. For that matter, they can't find evidence of whether Wildfire is a molecular engine or virus or a bacterium. They keep testing and cutting open bodies looking for it, without result. The theory also does not explain the monsters.

Travis has been championing an alien colonization theory. Earth has been seeded with biological software that responds differently to various genetic markers. Spores, in other words. A bit of seemingly harmless organic matter clinging to a falling meteor that thrived and spread and entered the global food chain and, eventually, its resident species. Some people fell down screaming while others did not. Some life forms were transformed into monsters, others not.

This is not to say evil humanoids with big gray heads are flying around in spaceships, manipulating these tragic events. Travis suspects Wildfire is not intelligent in the way most people would define it. He believes it may simply be an adaptive, self-designing but otherwise mindless extraterrestrial life form. Not quite colonization, not an invasion as it would typically be defined, but instead a viral entity, one that infects planets. In people and animals, it disguises itself as a normal virus or bacteria and is only triggered by certain genetic markers.

What this means, of course, is that everyone is infected in one form or another.

It also means the only way to unmask the Wildfire Agent is to examine a huge number of cells. This would take many months even if Travis had the resources he wanted.

What he really needs is a pure sample of Wildfire. If they could get that, they would have a solid chance to win this fight.

An electric jeep whirs up to the curb, driven by a soldier dressed similarly to Fielding, and parks.

"Good afternoon, Captain," the soldier says, addressing Fielding.

Fielding gestures to the backseat. "Hop in, Doc. Mustn't keep POTUS waiting."

♦

Wearing his old suit and riding in a car makes him feel normal again after weeks of living like an inmate in a dystopian prison. The breeze on his face raises his spirits.

The jeep halts in front of a wide, bright passage leading to a gleaming vault door guarded by more soldiers in black body armor. One of them, a tall, athletic woman wearing a black beret and a large handgun on her hip, approaches the vehicle.

"End of the line, Doc," Fielding says.

"What's this place?" Travis says, trying to control his sudden panic.

"This," Fielding says with a grand gesture, "is the Executive Branch."

"Dr. Price," the woman says. "I am Lieutenant Lateesha Sanchez."

She extends her gloved hand and helps him from the jeep.

"Good luck with that saving the world thing," Fielding tells him.

Looking at Sanchez's phony smile, Travis is a little sorry to see Fielding go. They may hate each other, but at least everything between them is out in the open.

Before he can say a word, the jeep lurches back onto the street.

"Come with me, please," Sanchez says, motioning toward the massive door, which the soldiers are pulling open, their machine guns slung over their shoulders.

They enter a long white corridor, dim but regularly cleaned; the floor glistens from a recent waxing. The air is fresher here, with no random pockets of hot or cold air, no sudden blasts from a filthy ventilation duct. Portraits of past presidents, liberated from the White House, adorn the otherwise blank walls, like placeholders for ghosts.

"What's behind these doors?" he asks, his voice loud in his ears. He pictures large control centers like the bridge of a starship or the set of the old TV show *24*, with lots of people hunched over various stations.

"That's not your concern, sir," Sanchez says.

Travis glances at a sign reading, EAS STUDIO. The Emergency Alert System. The President can talk to the entire country from here by radio or TV. He can also override or turn off any local broadcasting he does not like.

President Walker's emergency powers give him the power of a dictator.

"Everything is so clean here," Travis says. "Even the air. Do you get to live here?"

"I am not authorized to discuss anything with you, sir," Sanchez tells him.

More corridors, more doors, until Travis becomes convinced they are walking in circles. A door slams and a group of people in suits scuttle from one room to another. Black-armored soldiers scrutinize his ID at checkpoints and wave him through.

She finally stops at a door; the nameplate reads FRANKLIN ROOM.

"This is Lieutenant Sanchez," she says into her headset. "Package Papa Three is delivered." With a final smile, she adds, "This is your stop, Dr. Price."

Travis taps on the door and opens it, peering inside at what appears to be some sort of waiting area filled with men in suits clutching briefcases.

"I was told to come here," he says.

The men take in his stubbled face and wrinkled suit with contempt. Two large men stand in front of a second set of doors on the other side of the room, giving him a quick once-over. Travis surmises these are Secret Service agents, the last of the old Praetorians.

These doors open and an older, balding man peers at him over the rims of his glasses. Travis recognizes him as Terry Goodall, the Director of the Office of Science and Technology Policy. His boss.

"Ah, Travis," Goodall says. "Come on in. We're ready for you."

Travis walks across the waiting room, trying to ignore the baleful stares of the other men. "What's all this about, Terry?"

Goodall reaches and grips his arm. "You are about to meet the President of the United States, who at this moment is under a lot of pressure and has more power than Caligula," he hisses close to Travis's ear. "We all understand you do not have prepared remarks. Just play off the slides provided and answer the questions as best you can. It's all in your field of expertise. Okay?"

"I guess it will have to be," Travis mutters.

Goodall eyes him. "Don't screw this up, Travis."

"Of course not, sir."

"You look like shit. The least you could have done was gotten yourself cleaned up."

Travis shakes his head. "No time."

Goodall grunts and ushers him into a bright room. At first all Travis can do is stand at the threshold, half blinded by the sudden change in light, blinking tears.

"Dr. Price, is it?"

Travis blinks again and sees twenty stern-faced people seated around a conference table, observing him with open distaste. Some wear military dress uniforms with chests crusted with medals, what men like Fielding would call a fruit salad.

The man sitting at the center is President Walker. He is older, grayer, more tired than Travis remembers. But still formidable.

"Yes," Travis says with a weak voice, then clears his throat. "Yes, Mr. President."

"You realize everything you see and hear in this room is classified."

"Yes, Mr. President."

"Based on your area of expertise, you already enjoy a number of special clearances. Today, you're going to be privy to information classified as Top Secret. Understood?"

"Absolutely, Mr. President."

"Good. You've kept us waiting long enough. You may begin."

Travis approaches the screen at the front of the room, his stomach doing flips. *This is it*, he realizes. He is meeting the President of the United States. The world is ending, and his nation needs him. Nobody listened to his theory, but now he gets this one chance to make his case. The President will be grudgingly persuaded before committing to decisive action.

Dr. Travis Price saves the world.

On the screen, he sees a map of downtown Miami overlaid with a bull's eye pattern rendered in shades of red.

What does this have to do with the monsters?

"I don't understand," Travis says, staring at it.

The President grunts with irritation, folding his large hands.

Goodall places his elbows on the table and says, "Dr. Price, your area of expertise is the weaponization of nuclear fission, is this correct?"

"Nuclear nonproliferation," Travis mutters.

The Director reads highlights from his resume, focusing on his support of exercises by the Office of Nuclear Counterterrorism and the Nuclear Emergency Support Team, as well as development for the

Radiological Assistance and Consequence Management at the Los Alamos Lab.

"You are one of the nation's leading experts on the effects of nuclear device combustion on populations in urban centers," Goodall says.

"That is accurate."

"Good. Then explain the graphic on the screen, if you please."

The realization makes him gasp. Even with the world coming to a violent end, the terrorists could not give up their grudge against the Great Satan.

They finally did it. They blew up an American city.

"Who did it?" he says, his face reddening. "What kind of madman would do this?"

Even in collapse, America could, and would, retaliate. He heard America still maintains twenty-four-hour flights of strategic bombers able to drop nuclear warheads virtually anywhere in the world.

Goodall smiles. "This is purely a hypothetical, Dr. Price."

"Hypothetical, sir?"

"Options," the President grunts. "All options are on the table."

"I see," Travis says, feeling sick.

Terrorists did not bomb Miami. The President wants to bomb Miami. Miami, and perhaps other cities as well.

Pure madness. Things must be worse on the surface than he thought. The cities are filled with Infected and have become breeding grounds for the monsters.

Drop the bomb, and they all go away.

But so do the cities themselves, and millions of survivors still living in them.

During the Cold War, a U.S. Minuteman missile crewman once asked the chain of command how he could verify whether a launch order was coming from a sane President. The generals removed him from his post.

If I voice any dissent, I wonder what they'll do to me?

"This graph shows the effects of detonation of a one hundred fifty kiloton device at ground level in North Miami," Travis murmurs. "That's the average size of a single warhead in the U.S. nuclear arsenal."

"Speak up, Dr. Price," Goodall says.

"It's about ten to fifteen times the size of the bombs dropped on Hiroshima and Nagasaki. Everything in the center ring would be exposed to explosive force equaling fifteen pounds of pressure per square inch of overpressure. Everything would be destroyed. People, buildings, everything."

The bomb explodes in an intensely hot fireball, creating a giant crater hundreds of feet deep and sucking tons of earth into a massive mushroom cloud. Within the blast, buildings and people, normal and Infected alike, vaporize in a flash, becoming part of the cloud. Structures and bodies fly apart in the earthquake and sudden change in pressure. Debris rockets through the air with the force of bullets. Shattered windows turn into flying knives of glass. Miles away, thousands of fires burn, merging into raging firestorms. Flesh melts in the fierce heat; internal organs cook; brains boil. The smog blots out the sun. Dirt and ash rain down as radioactive particulates for miles in every direction, even farther on the winds.

"At a little over a mile from the blast, buildings would suffer heavy damage, and intense heat from the blast would start numerous fires. At a little over two and a half miles, covering El Portal in the south, Pinewood, Golden Glades, most houses—would be—crushed flat—"

His stomach leaps into his throat. He stumbles toward a metal garbage can and vomits. Behind him, he hears a woman mutter, *Christ.*

"Excuse me, I'm not well," Travis says, wiping his mouth.

"You may continue when you're able," says the President, and turns to ask another man at the table a question about his afternoon schedule.

Travis does not hear the answer. His stomach lurches again, producing a trickle of bile. He spits several times before standing and facing the room with watery eyes, his face burning with embarrassment.

"I apologize, Mr. President. I may have a touch of flu."

"Tell us about the fallout," the President says.

"Fallout," Travis says mechanically, as if he has never heard the word before. "Yes. For a surface burst, outside of ground zero, the area impacted by the blast and the initial nuclear radiation will be less severe than, say, an air burst of similar yield. Local fallout can be dangerous over a large downwind area, however—"

A single gunshot cracks, startling them. The President's advisers gasp, some already half standing. The President glares at the door.

People are shouting outside in the waiting room.

"John," the President says to one of his people. "Go take a look."

"I don't think we should open the door, Mr. President. You would be exposed."

"It's all right, John. I think our people have things under control now."

The door opens from the outside, giving Travis a clear view. The waiting room is filled with men and women in black body armor. One of the Secret Service agents kneels with his hands on his head, while the other lies grimacing on the floor with a soldier hunched over him, applying a tourniquet to his leg. The other men in suits cower in their chairs.

The President watches them, his face turning from red to purple.

"WHAT THE HELL IS GOING ON HERE?"

The soldiers glance at him. The wounded agent cries out in pain. Two men in desert combat uniforms enter the conference room, pistols holstered on their hips.

"Mr. President," the first man says, taking off his cap.

"General," the President says. "Glad you're here. What's the meaning of all this?"

General Donald McGregor, the chairman of the joint chiefs, is a wiry stringbean of a man compared to the President, but just as intimidating. Travis once met him during nuclear terrorism exercises. He is a ruthless son of a bitch, much like Fielding, and with incredible power at his command.

The General pauses in the doorway, taking in the red rings radiating from downtown Miami on the screen. Travis steps away from it, trying to disappear. McGregor frowns. His eyes flicker to meet the President's.

"That, sir," he says, pointing at the screen, "is not going to happen."

The man behind the General whistles. Soldiers in black body armor file into the room, carrying automatic weapons.

RAY

Unsure of whether he is struggling toward air or plunging deeper into abyss, the man swims against warm tidal currents. Light sparkles in the thick, murky depths. He lets go and drifts weightless toward consciousness.

Ray awakes gasping for air, sucking it greedily into his lungs.

The light, so bright it is blinding.

He does not know anything; it is like being born.

Mysterious dark shapes coalesce into normal things. A television set. A bookshelf packed with books, knickknacks and a bowling trophy. A table lamp. A large picture window covered in smeared handprints, making the world outside appear shrouded in gray fog.

He closes his eyes and tries to return to those warm currents, but his curiosity betrays him, forcing him up into a sitting position. Throbbing pain at the base of his skull makes him groan. He looks at his dirty hands and remembers how he got here.

I'm supposed to be dead. How long have I been on this couch?

The light outside—Christ, it's the sun.

He survived the night. The Infected are gone. He touches the monster in his side, now just a raw, achy swelling covered in flaky skin. His touch ignites a horrible itch inside the growth, which scratching just makes worse.

Fine. Itch all you want, you little bastard. I beat you. I won. I'm alive.

His body rejected the growth, or perhaps the growth rejected him. Too much smoking or drinking, who knows. He never heard of someone becoming infected by a hopper and surviving it. Then again, after Infection, Ray's world got a whole lot smaller. Maybe people survive it all the time in Colorado. Maybe California has no epidemic at all. He wouldn't know.

The floor is covered with empty bottles and jars of food and multiple sets of muddy footprints. People brought him food and water while he slept. His mouth tastes like raw sewage and his teeth feel mossy. His pants are crusted with his own waste. The ammonia smell of his piss makes his eyes water. *Something is not right here. How long have I been out?*

Feeling frail and shaky, he peels off his clothes, hardened to the consistency of cardboard, and retches at the sight of his waste caked in his pants and clinging to his ass and thighs. It feels good to be naked, however; the house is hot and his body is covered in a slick sheen of sweat.

After gaining his feet, he plods into the kitchen, half expecting to see his ghostly mother doing dishes in the sink, and pulls a squat, ugly looking steak knife from a drawer. *Safety first.* The window is still open and the outside air smells fresh and clean. He finds a bathroom and spends several minutes examining himself in the mirror with blunt surprise. A gaunt lunatic stares back at him. His acne-scarred cheeks are sunken. His handlebar mustache is now part of a beard. His shaggy hair has grown even longer, greasy and lank, a full-on Jesus mane.

Has he been here for days, weeks? Who was feeding him this whole time?

I'm alive, says the leering lunatic in the mirror.

Dude, you are seriously fucked up.

His caregivers left him two buckets of water. He's not sure if these are any good for drinking but they look all right for washing. Squatting in the tub, Ray soaks a toilet scrubber with tepid water and liquid soap and scrubs his body until the water turns black and he feels somewhat clean. He scrapes his mossy teeth with his fingernails, gargles and spits the mess into the sink.

Upstairs, he finds a T-shirt and jeans that fit, and puts them on. His STEELERS hat is riddled with charred holes and stinks like old grease, but he puts it on anyway. He checks out the neighborhood through a window. A car is parked at an angle across both lanes of the street below, all of its doors open. The asphalt glistens; it rained recently. The lawns and bushes on the other side of the road look overgrown. Beyond, the bridge invites him back to its scenes of horror. The eastern horizon is no longer blackened by the fires of Pittsburgh, but still shimmers with a polluted brown haze. A flicker of movement down in the street grabs his attention.

A large woman dressed in a filthy halter top and sweatpants limps past the car with her hands clenched into fists against her breasts, one of which sags out of her shirt, scratched and bloodstained. Ray watches her, wondering who she was before the bug turned her into a violent maniac. He feels like he understands Anne a little better now; this woman is no longer human, but a malicious, mindless organism wearing the face of a human, like a mask.

The woman pauses, doing the odd jittery neck roll favored by the Infected. Her head, jerking, turns to the window to look right at him, and tilts to the side, like a dog's.

He leaps aside, his heart hammering in his chest. He expects to hear feet slapping against the asphalt, the rasping bark, the door crashing open, the pounding on the stairs. His eyes take in details of the bedroom, searching for a hiding spot or a weapon.

Nothing happens. Fighting to control his breathing, Ray glances back at the road. The woman is gone. He snorts.

Maybe I look so bad she thought I was one of them.

He trudges downstairs and puts his boots on, still heavy with dried blood, and walks onto the porch. The abandoned houses stand in silence, bugs buzzing in their overgrown lawns. A deer browses in a garden until bolting across a driveway into someone's backyard. A light breeze dries the sweat on Ray's face. He closes his eyes and savors being alive.

There is just this. Nothing else. And that makes this good.

He finds his rifle on the side of the house, wet and spotted with rust, and inspects it. He considers finding some oil and a toothbrush and trying to clean the weapon, but decides to leave it in the grass. Cleaning it would take a long time, and besides, it only has a few bullets. With just a few hours of daylight remaining, Ray feels an overwhelming urge to get moving. He was lucky here, but he has the strong feeling his luck has run out. The open road beckons. His steak knife will have to do until he can find better. The road will provide.

Ray checks out the few cars and trucks abandoned on the streets and writes them off as well. He can fix just about anything with wheels, but none of the vehicles he inspects have keys in their ignitions, and, despite his checkered past, he has no idea how to hotwire a car. The idea exhausts him; the only thing that inspires any energy is getting the hell out of this ghost town as soon as possible.

Guess you're walking, bro. This is going to take a while. You can hit some houses along the way for some supplies. But it's time to get moving.

Sticking to backyards, he emerges from town to the north and decides to circle through the woods along Route 22, heading west. Back to Camp Defiance.

He pauses as a foghorn booms close, a vibrating sound he can feel deep in his chest. The sound ignites a flock of birds from a tree, black shapes darting through the air. A distant foghorn answers, then another and another, for miles around it seems.

Ray closes his eyes and listens as if they are communicating something he might understand. For the next few minutes, the air becomes filled with the melodic song of the monsters, a symphony of sounds like tubas and didgeridoos, plaintive and hopeful. Ray smiles, tingling from the vibrations. Their song speaks to him.

We are not alone, it appears to be saying. *We are afraid and we may die, but we are not alone.*

◆

Shucking his Army surplus backpack heavy with cans and bottles, Ray tramps through a garden eating raw peas and any tomatoes spared by the insects. Unable to eat more, he stuffs his cheek full of Copenhagen dip and lets out a satisfied sigh. He has twenty miles to walk, which will take him two, maybe three days in his condition and carrying the weight of the pack on his shoulders. Climbing over a barbed wire fence, he angles west and starts marching through the trees, knowing Route 22 is about a hundred yards on his left. At the base of an old sawtooth oak, he picks up a good walking stick, a long wizardly staff that helps him find a steady hiking rhythm.

As the sun falls toward the horizon, his eyes roam the landscape, searching for shelter. Wind rustles through the branches and the atmosphere feels moist against his skin. The sun drops behind western rain clouds, dimming air already darkened by the forest canopy, and Ray quickens his pace as a few random drops splat on the rim of his STEELERS hat. He emerges from the trees onto a grassy field covered with a riot of dandelions. At the other end of the field, a farmhouse stands quiet, its windows boarded up, three rotting bodies drawing flies on the porch steps. A tire swing sways from the stoutest branch of a massive oak tree.

He pauses here, listening to the buzz of insects in the tall grass. The world is so lush and beautiful it is sometimes hard to believe it is coming to an end. Then he remembers the world is not ending, just its dominant species.

The sky continues to blacken. Moist wind strikes Ray in the face, carrying a few drops of rain, and he opens his arms to it. The air feels electric. The clouds rumble with distant thunder, a melancholy sound. He takes a deep breath and decides to try the barn to ride out both the night and the rain. The house appears occupied and dangerous. Get too close to that place, he might get a lungful of buckshot, looking the way he does right now. He studies his hands—workman's hands, hairy and powerful—and realizes his survival and recovery from Infection is not a get-out-of-jail-free card. He might have to fight again, and kill again, if he wants to make it home alive. Ray has a lot for which he wants to live. Nothing ambitious, just a deep, abiding appreciation for breathing in and out. When he thinks about his fever over the past few days—weeks?—it terrifies him because he remembers little of it. He dreamed; many of the dreams were horrible. But mostly, just darkness. Trying to remember those long days of nothing is like trying to remember the time before he was born.

Rain pelts the roof as he enters the barn. Rats flee squealing from his advance, melting into the dark spaces. The building has a rich smell of farm animals and hay and old dung, but the smell is stale, a memory; the animals are long gone, the hay is rotting. Ray sniffs the air again just to be sure, but detects no sour milk stench, the calling card of the Infected. Something crunches and scatters under his boots, and he looks down, only to wish he hadn't; the floor is strewn with little piles of bones and children's clothes. Bloodstains have turned the dirt floor the color of rust. The barn was a nest, then; a pack of the Infected killed here, ate here, slept here, but they moved on long ago. Ray waves away a small cloud of buzzing flies and thinks about burying the bones, but he is tired and it is getting late.

"Sorry," he grumbles, spitting a stream of tobacco juice into the dust. Ray feels like an empty husk. Something in him died when the bug took him. Or maybe he was reborn, and is still finding out who he is. Either way, he has no fight in him anymore.

He climbs a ladder leading to the hayloft, pulls it up after him, and spreads out his old rolled-up blanket on a bed of moldy hay. He pulls off his boots and then his socks and sighs with relief despite the stink, wiggling his toes. Fishing in his pocket, he finds a couple of Band-Aids and applies them over the blisters on his heels. Minutes later, he falls into a deep, blissful sleep to the soothing sound of rain pattering on the roof. Mosquitoes feast on his blood during the night.

The next morning, Ray pisses hard into the hay, smokes a stale cigarette, and cuts open a can of cold SpaghettiO's pasta, which he eats with a plastic spoon. The air is warm and humid; his body is already slick with sweat. His legs are sore and a part of him wants to sleep the day away again. He stares into space scratching at his bug bites until boredom drives him back down the ladder and into the farmer's yard. Beyond, winter wheat stands hunched and wet under a dim, heavy mist that shrouds the distant fields and woodlands.

He decides he likes the mist. The mist could be his friend. As long as it lasts, he can hide in it. The house still stands quiet, but Ray is certain he is being watched. He feels a sudden urge to wave, or better yet flip them the bird, but doesn't have the energy for it.

Shouldering his pack and gripping his walking staff, he disappears into the treeline.

♦

Minutes later, the mist surrounds him like a living thing. It feels cool and wet in his lungs. He cannot see more than a few feet in front of him but has the skin-crawling sensation he is still being watched. He is in danger here. Coming into the mist was a mistake, but it is too late to go back. He already no longer has a sense of where he started.

He closes his eyes and pictures sitting at a big desk in the station's holding pen, where Unit 12, his old police unit at Camp Defiance, made its home. He and Tyler and his kid Jonesy and all the other guys in the unit, Cook and Salazar and the rest, laugh at some joke as they pass around a can of warm beer they scrounged up.

Ray just wants to go home. He does not have the stamina to live under constant threat like Anne and Todd. He needs people. He wants to be in a nice, safe place among friends.

Over time, his inability to see amplifies his hearing. Things tramp through the forest all around him. His own footfalls sound loud to his ears, as if he is walking on garbage bags filled with crumpled paper. But standing still is worse than making noise. Standing still is worst of all.

He remembers a dream he had while fighting his infection. A dream of something that happened to him when he was a kid. The dream so real, the actual memory so long ago, he wonders if it actually happened, or if he just dreamed it. In the dream, he shoved Shawn McCrea's face into a tree while playing a trust game. That's how he feels now, being led through the forest blinded by mist. At any moment, he is going to get sucker punched.

His father's voice: *Hey Ray, come here a minute.*

Ray breaks into a run, hands splayed to ward off low-hanging branches. In his mind's eye, his father is about to hit him. The fog is so blank it is easy to write one's memories and worst fears onto it. He wants to outrun the old man, but, as in a dream, he cannot move. In his memory, he loves his father too much to leave, so he obeys; he walks meekly to his dad. And gets slapped. It feels good to get it over with. The worst part is the waiting. The cat and mouse game.

Leona, stay out of this or you're next. Kid's got to learn. He's got to toughen up.

The sad thing is, Ray believed him. He believed his father was trying to help him when he got drunk and slapped him around for not being strong enough.

A black shape forms in the mist, coalescing into a gaunt, looming monster. Ray gasps and falls to his knees, his heart galloping in his chest.

This is it. I'm going to die.

It almost feels good to get it over with. As always, the worst part is the waiting.

It registers in his panicked brain that the monster is a tree. Ray curls up at its base, shaking with terror. It is like being back in the storage locker, trapped with his own memories and thoughts. It was his past that drove him back out into the light of day.

Ghostly voices call in the mist. The sound rakes across his already tattered nerves. A motor engine revs before cutting out. Then silence.

He feels light on his face and blinks into the fleeting glare of sunlight winking through the forest canopy above. The fog is dissipating, retreating into shreds and wisps.

The voices shout again, clearer this time.

Ray peers out from behind the tree. A Winnebago sits parked on the shoulder of the highway, a battered state police cruiser next to it. A man with a hunting bow stands guard near two men hunched over the RV's engine, while a woman sits behind the wheel of the police car. They look as terrified as he feels.

"Hurry up, the fog's lifting," the man with the bow says. He wears a tank top and fluorescent blue jogging shorts, exposing hairy, thickly muscled arms and legs.

Shaking, Ray stands, hugging the tree, and considers how to approach them. Should he call out? The alternative is to walk out there nice and calm, hands in the air. Either way, he might get one of those arrows in his ribs. They might think he's infected. They might not be friendly to strangers.

No choice, then. He will have to call out and see if they'll welcome him. He is starving for human company, driven by a need to be in the middle of the herd. He made it this far, but he knows any luck he's had is running out.

Something thrashes in the foliage. Ray drops his pack and draws the steak knife. A pair of Infected, a man and a teenage girl, burst from the bushes snorting, leaves and twigs falling from their hair. Ray crouches, willing himself not to be seen, his body electrified by a shock of adrenaline. The Infected run past his tree, heads wagging, their faces and arms a ghastly patchwork of livid red scratches. The girl snarls, revealing braces black with decaying meat.

An arrow thuds into the man, who falls thrashing in the tall grass just outside the treeline, shrieking like an animal. The bowman notches another arrow and shoots the girl through the hip. She falls, gets up, then falls again, writhing and bleeding on the grass.

More Infected emerge from the woods, drawn to the sound of the cough of the Winnebago's engine as it tries to start. The woman in the police cruiser screams when she sees them, covering her ears. The man with the bow crosses himself and gets back to work.

Another arrow whistles though the air, flying through a young woman's throat before piercing a man behind her in the face. The man howls and runs in circles, batting at the arrow flopping around his head; the woman continues to run, coughing blood with each stride, until pitching forward into the grass.

"Right on," Ray hisses. He feels a strange kinship with the archer wearing the ridiculous shorts. He wants to get into the fight and help. He pictures leaping from behind the tree, joining the pack of Infected running past and cutting their throats one by one with his carving knife.

Welcome, stranger, they'll say. He and the archer will clasp hands warmly, recognizing in the other a warrior of the apocalypse. Because he helped them, they will trust him. Then they'll get the Winnebago running and drive it to Cashtown in comfort. It's a good plan.

The fantasy over, he does not move. He clings to the tree, feeling rooted to the spot, watching the Infected close in on the group. *It's not my fight*, he decides. *Not my problem. Sorry, sorry, sorry. I'm too tired. All I have is a knife some family used for carving rib roasts.*

But the truth, again, is there is no fight left in him.

More Infected run across the field behind the survivors. The man with the bow sees them and fires another arrow, which misses. He shakes his head and says something to the men working on the Winnebago, who ignore him. The archer roars at them to move. The man hunched over the engine raises his head, blinking at the Infected rushing at him, and bolts for the police cruiser with the other man at his heels. The group slams the doors just as a man punches the windshield, cobwebbing it. A woman climbs onto the rear of the car, scratching at the back window with her nails as the vehicle growls its way to life.

Go, Ray wants to scream. *You're surrounded. Get out of there.*

The car lurches and bangs into the man, knocking him down with a sickening crunch. The woman tumbles off the back and the car roars down the road, trailing a massive cloud of exhaust and a score of screaming Infected.

Ray waits several minutes, picks up his pack and approaches the Winnebago. He spots the problem with the engine, but lacks the tools to fix it. Inside, he finds food and water, a bucket for a sponge bath, shaving kit, and personal knickknacks. The vehicle smells like people, a comforting smell.

He decides to stay the night here. Eat, sleep, shit and maybe try to get cleaned up a little so the Camp Defiance guards don't shoot him on sight thinking he's one of the crazies. Ray tries the stove, and permits a brief smile. He is going to eat hot food tonight, and bathe and shave with hot water. By tomorrow, with hope, he will feel human again.

He spots a photo album and opens it. Weddings. Family vacations. Births. He smiles at these highlights of a normal life, but after a while the images become difficult to look at. A proud fisherman with a prize catch. Children building a sandcastle at some beach. An attractive woman smiling flirtatiously at the camera. The photos portray memories too painful to remember, even for a stranger. And yet whoever owned these pictures is going to regret leaving them behind.

The past haunts everyone, even the good stuff. Especially the good stuff.

♦

Ray gets an early start the next morning, setting a brisk pace with his walking stick. He stays on the highway, hoping to find other survivors, but the road is deserted.

He passes an abandoned van resting on flat tires, and peers in through a gaping hole in the windshield. Animals rustle and hiss in a pile of torn luggage and seat stuffing in the back, probably a family of racoons. The interior smells like dung. *It doesn't take long for things to fall apart*, Ray realizes. *By the time we're all dead, most of what we've built will crumble into dust.*

He returns to the road, scanning the trees on both sides for ambush, but he's not used to living so close to fight or flight, and zones out, thinking about everything and nothing. For some reason, his thoughts turn to Lola Rivera. He dreamed about her while he fought Infection, he remembers. He dreamed his entire life, it seems. It would be nice to believe some kindly force made this happen to teach him something about his life so he would make the most of this second chance, but the memories had a forced quality about them, as if they were being taken from him. Ray woke up feeling exhausted, docile, violated. All of the fight was sucked out of him. *I don't want anything*, he understands, and experiences the shock of this, being a man of constant need and habit, a creature of deep drives and dark urges.

Now all he wants to do is continue living. Nothing else but live. Breathe in, breathe out.

Whatever the source of the dreams, without his rage, he can only look back on his life with remorse. He regrets what he did to Lola, how he treated her. After he sucker punched Bob at the bar and made bail, he went to the hospital and told Lola he did it because he still loved her. Every day, he went, and said he'd do it all over again, just to have her back. Eventually, something in her snapped and she gave herself to him. That night, while lying beneath him on his bed, she opened her eyes and, seeing only spite written on his face, realized he did not love her. She wept until he threw her out in a fit of anger. Rage came so easily to him, the urge to lash out instead of do the right thing. It was his automatic defense against both love and shame.

You do have a second chance here, bro. Maybe when you get back to camp, you can try to make things right with a few people, if they're still alive.

He finds the idea surprisingly appealing.

As the sun dips low in the sky, he finds the exit for Cashtown and walks off the highway, pausing to flinch at the bang of a high-powered rifle. Ray grimaces with relief. He is not far from Camp Defiance now. The rifle shot was one of the snipers in the watchtowers doing his monotonous, grisly duty.

As he gets closer to the camp, the air fills with white noise, the sound of thousands of people and vehicles punctuated by the distant pop of gunfire. The breeze delivers the faint but familiar odors of wood smoke and human waste. He breathes deep, enjoying a sudden rush of memories. Tyler in his ridiculous red suspenders, chuckling over a book, his reading glasses perched on the end of his nose. Doug Foley loading shells into his shotgun between nips of Jägermeister, getting ready for patrol. Jonesy licking his hands and slicking back his hair in front of the mirror, announcing he has a hot date. *Boy, are they going to be surprised to see me*, Ray thinks, feeling good for the first time since he woke up.

Topping the next hill, the camp spills across the horizon, a mass of densely packed buildings and tents and vehicles all shrouded in a haze from thousands of cook fires. Mountainous walls of heaped sandbags, tractor trailers and barbed wire, buttressed by watchtowers, surround the bulging mess like an old belt, keeping it from vomiting onto the neighboring smoking fields, keeping Infection out one day at a time. Ray gazes at it for several minutes, wiping away a tear. Never did this sprawling dung heap look so good to him, not even when he crawled out of the storage locker, fleeing his fears lived over days in darkness.

He spots a series of windmills churning over the southern side, near the big circus tent, the start of a power grid. When he left to blow up the Veterans Memorial Bridge at Steubenville, the windmills were just a plan championed by the do-gooders. The people must be starting to accept they're going to be here for a while. Ray wonders again how long he has been gone, decides he doesn't care. The camp is still here; that's all that matters.

He gasps, unable to breathe, wondering how fast he can run back into the trees. A man stands rock still fifty yards down the road, dressed in a ridiculous Santa costume, one arm frozen in a wave. It takes him several moments to realize it's a store mannequin, one of many dotting the no man's land surrounding the camp as bait for the snipers. The Infected make a beeline for the color red. *Ho, ho, ho, welcome to FEMAville. BANG. Splat.*

In the distance, he sees a figure running toward the wall. A woman doing the hundred yard dash, hoping to get in and spread her disease. The effort strikes him as both heroic and suicidal. The echoing roar of a single rifle shot rolls across the fields. The figure spins and falls. Ray watches as the woman continues to drag her broken body along the ground, still fighting for her cause even while she bleeds into the mud. Behind the wall, life in the camp goes on as if nothing happened.

The cracked road plunges down the hill and leads straight to the gates. All he has to do is walk down there and he's home. But he is unsure how to get there without getting shot. It's too dangerous to move now.

Best to wait until dark, he decides. *The hour just before dawn.*

◆

Ray wakes during the night to the sound of machine gun fire. It stops abruptly, leaving him wondering if he dreamed it. He wipes drool from his mouth and sits up, slapping a mosquito on his cheek. A flare traces a burning arc over the distant fields, washing the ground in a bright, eerie glow. Shadows gradually infect the light, lengthening as the flare continues its long descent. Ray sees figures moving in a mad rush. The machine gun starts up again, sounding tinny and ghostly across the fields, like someone clapping chalkboard erasers together. Tracers burst in the dark. The figures now lie on the ground, melting into the darkness as the flare falls to the earth.

For several minutes, Ray sits in the dark waiting, but nothing happens. It strikes him his plan to wait until the hour before sunrise would work better if he actually knew what time it was. He gazes at the night sky but there is no Moon, no stars. Massive clouds still blanket the atmosphere, the tail end of the storm passing over this part of the world on its way to the Atlantic. The lights of the camp are his only beacon.

Something tramps through the woods behind him. Whatever it is, it's tall enough to rustle through the branches of the trees, snapping twigs that rain onto the forest floor. Ray hears a deep, nauseating gurgling, like what he would imagine a motorcycle idling underwater to sound like. The gurgling ends in a throaty chuckle. Ray knows the sound; it is one of the tottering monsters that ate the Reverend on the bridge. The rustling becomes violent thrashing. The thing smacks its wet lips. Leaves flutter to the ground around Ray, tickling his face.

Time to move. Now.

Ray lopes from the woods at a brisk pace, trying to stay as low to the ground as he can, grunting under the weight of the backpack. He pauses to shrug it onto the ground behind him and keeps moving, breathing hard.

The machine gun fires again. He throws his body into the mud face first, but the tracers flicker into the woods to his right. He grunts, gets back onto his feet and keeps going, running blindly now, the camp lights swimming in his gaze. He hears feet splashing to his left and hurls himself down again as a flare bursts high overhead, turning night into day. Face pressed into the mud, he hears the crash of rifle fire and bodies falling. A body thrashes nearby in the muddy water. The machine gun joins in, sending bullets plopping into the earth around him.

Hail Mary, full of grace, hail Mary, full of grace, hail Mary, Jesus and God—

The firing stops. The gates are just fifty or so yards ahead.

Screw this.

"Don't shoot! I ain't Infected! Don't shoot me!"

No answer. That's not good.

On the other hand, nobody's shooting at me either.

Ray gets onto his feet, shaking violently, and raises his hands. Standing in the flare's light, he feels like he is on stage, in full view of an audience he cannot see.

"I'm coming in now," he announces, marching forward. "Open the gates for me."

"We can't," someone shouts from the wall, using a megaphone.

Ray staggers to a halt. "What do you mean?"

"The gates stay closed until sunup. That's the law. It won't be long. Just hang tight."

"Come on! I'm Ray Young! I'm a cop. I almost died to save this goddamn place." He is babbling like a madman, but cannot help himself. "I blew up that goddam bridge in Steubenville—"

Muzzle flashes pop along the wall like paparazzi. Ray flinches, but realizes they are not shooting at him.

"Hurry up," the voice shouts through the megaphone. "Come on."

He turns and sees a small group of Infected racing into the dying light of the flare, their eyes black and their yellow faces twisted in hate. Two of them disintegrate into smoking body parts, flopping to the ground.

Another flare bursts high overhead, revealing a hundred more running behind them.

"What the f—"

His words turn into an incoherent screaming flood of obscenities as he throws his exhausted body into a full sprint toward the wall, reaching it in less than a minute and falling to the ground gasping for air. One of the gates grinds opens inch by inch as gunfire crashes overhead.

The horde pauses twenty yards from him in a wide semicircle, ignoring the guns cutting them down.

"Move it!" a man says, standing next to him.

Ray rolls aside as several fighters rush through the partially opened gate in single file, holding what appear to be fire hoses attached to tanks on their backs.

The Infected reach out to him with an odd pleading gesture as blinding jets of fire pour across their ranks, turning them into a massive bonfire of dancing, shrieking figures. The heat blasts Ray's face, making him wince.

One of the men kneels next to him and takes his hand.

"It's a goddamn miracle," the soldier says. "Are you injured?"

"No," Ray croaks, unable to look away from the Infected flailing in the wall of fire like a vision of hell. "I don't think so."

"Were you bitten?" The man has to shout to compete with the screaming.

"No," Ray says. "I ain't bit."

The man grins and squeezes Ray's hand. "Welcome home, Ray."

"Let's go," another voice roars.

"I hope he's worth it," another voice says. "The Captain is going to have our heads for this."

"Don't matter," the first man answers. "Look, it's already sunup."

"He never would have authorized us going out there with that many Infected outside."

"Thank you," Ray tells them. "Oh Jesus, thank you."

"You're home now, Ray. You're safe—"

Several men lift him roughly and carry him through the gap and into the safety of Camp Defiance.

♦

They set him down on a plastic tarp as the gate grinds shut. Ray gapes at the bearded faces and thanks them repeatedly, babbling. The men crowd around, pressing in for a look, most of them soldiers, some disposal workers in yellow hazmat suits, some salvage operators from outside the camp. They tell him he's going to be okay and ask him questions about where he's been, how he survived. They don't know whether they are looking at a living legend or a ghost. A plastic bottle is shoved into his hand and he gulps the warm water. Someone yells to *break it up, let the guy have some air*, and the crowd loosens, giving Ray a view of the sky, already paling with the sunrise and dotted with a flock of birds in flight.

The man who yelled—a stocky, clean-shaven soldier with friendly blue eyes set far apart on his large head—kneels next to him and introduces himself as Sergeant John Riley, U.S. Army. Ray stares at him, finding it hard to understand what is being said to him.

"I'm Ray Young," he says.

"You're a lucky bastard, is what you are," Sergeant Riley grins. "So what do you need, Ray? We don't have much here in the compound, but we got hot coffee, water, food, a medic—"

"Unit 12 station."

"Settle down," the sergeant yells at the crowd, quieting them. "What's that, Ray?"

"I want to go to Unit 12 station," Ray repeats. "That's my police unit."

The man nods, considering the request. Behind him, the other men frown with disappointment. They obviously hoped they could do more for him.

"And a smoke," Ray adds.

One of the men leans in to offer a cigarette jutting from an open pack. Ray takes it with two shaking hands and accepts a light.

"I'll drive you wherever you want to go," Sergeant Riley tells him.

"He'd better report to Captain Mattis," another soldier says.

"He can do that later," Riley growls. "Let Mattis sleep. This man's just been to hell and back. He wants to be with his people. They'll take care of him."

The sergeant extends his gloved hand and pulls Ray onto his feet.

When Sergeant Wilson told him and the others about the lunatic plan to blow the Veterans Memorial Bridge at Steubenville, he thought they would drive out there and probably die and nobody here would care. Life would go on as if they were just another band of Infected dying outside the wall. Road kill of the apocalypse.

He had never been so wrong. Sergeant Riley and his men had risked everything to save him. If Ray was anyone else, they would have left him out there to die.

His luck is still holding, just as it was the moment the horde was upon him, when they hesitated instead of tearing him to shreds.

Why didn't they attack? Maybe they were just trying to scare me to death. He snorts. *They came damn close to succeeding.*

Minutes later, Ray is bouncing along through the camp in Sergeant Riley's Humvee. Sagging in his seat, he looks out the window at the bustle of the early risers starting their day. They pass what used to be Meade Park, now a dense sprawl of motor homes and campers looking like a traffic jam that went on for so long the drivers decided to live there. A man anchors a tarp into the ground, observed by his young son, while a woman hangs faded laundry from a clothesline strung between two RVs. Another man brews coffee using a contraption consisting of two soup cans, while a woman connects a car battery to a power drill. A pair of tired-looking, scantily clad blondes walk arm in arm—prostitutes going home after a long night's shift by the porta-johns. A work crew pulls planks of lumber from the back of a pickup truck, laying them in the mud end to end to form pedestrian pathways. The world may be ending, but people still need to brush their teeth and cut their toenails and patch holes in the knees of their jeans. Life abides.

Ray looks at these people living hand to mouth at the edge of survival and thinks, *I nearly died for this?*

"It's going to be another beautiful day," Sergeant Riley says, whistling.

It's the first time the soldier has spoken to him during the ride. Ray nods and Riley says nothing more. Ray is grateful not to have to talk. He glances at the man's earnest profile and feels a little ashamed. The soldier just led a squad of flamethrowers outside the wall to torch dozens of Infected bearing down on him, with the fate of the entire camp in his hands, and has survived fights that were most likely far worse in the past few weeks. What Ray went through is probably nothing in comparison. The old Ray would have converted his shame into anger—gotten mouthy and ruined the man's generosity—but again, it isn't in him anymore.

He's one of the centurions, Ray tells himself instead. *Our one chance at ending the epidemic. If these guys can't do it, God help us.*

"This is you," the sergeant tells him, turning the wheel and bringing the Humvee to a halt at the curb.

Ray sees the worn police station building and feels a strange sensation in his stomach. Butterflies. He never thought he'd miss this shithole as much as he had. It's like a homecoming. He watches two burly cops exit the front doors, grim-faced and toting shotguns, dogs yelping around their legs. People on the sidewalk jump aside to let them pass.

"Thanks for the lift," he says. "Thanks for, uh, everything."

"Don't mention it," the man says. "Listen, I got a bottle of old scotch under my bunk I've been saving. If you ever want to share a drink and some stories, look me up. I'll bet you've got one hell of a story to tell."

"I'll do that, Sergeant," Ray tells him, and steps out of the vehicle.

As the Humvee pulls away honking, Ray stands on the sidewalk. The few people out at this hour stare at him as they pass. He guesses he looks pretty screwed up even by camp standards. A speaker mounted at the top of a telephone pole, surrounded by a dangling spaghetti of wires, whines with feedback just before a tinny voice wishes Camp Defiance a good morning and launches into a public service announcement.

Taking a deep breath, Ray enters the police station, ignoring the confused stares of the cops behind the big desk, and slips into the hallway leading to the holding pens.

Tyler Jones sits behind the desk in the empty Unit 12 barracks, an open space with jail cells once used to hold prisoners but now used as bunks. Just as he remembered him, reading glasses perched at the end of his nose and ridiculous red suspenders and all. Instead of reading a cheap paperback as his usual habit, Tyler is poring over some paperwork on his desk, his lips moving while he reads, cursing someone named Benny under his breath. A large poster mounted on the wall to his left shows a photo of a smiling little girl under the words: WHY WE FIGHT.

Ray grins. "Tyler Jones, you old shit."

"Get out of my ass, Ray," Tyler says, then blinks, his mouth hanging open. His eyes flicker and take in Ray leaning against the doorframe. "*Jesus*, Mary and Joseph."

Ray shrugs, enjoying the sight of Tyler staring at him with his paling face. "I'm back."

"I can't believe it."

Tyler half stands, still bug eyed, and Ray waves him back into his chair. "I'll come to you."

"Well, sit down then! You want some coffee?"

Ray takes a seat opposite Tyler with a painful grunt. Every muscle in his body aches, the result of burning massive amounts of adrenaline over the past few days. He feels like he could sleep for a year. "And a smoke, if you got one."

Tyler shuffles to the pot, pours a metal cup full of hot, black coffee, and returns, slamming it on the desk in front of Ray. He snaps his fingers, as if forgetting something, then pulls two cigars from the breast pocket of his gray work shirt.

"Wow, look at you," Tyler says as he lights Ray's cigar.

They say together, "You look like shit."

Tyler laughs. "This is the best day of my life, Ray. I mean it."

"I can't believe I'm here."

"What the hell happened to you?"

"Never mind that right now, Tyler." He reaches for the coffee and sips it, humming with pleasure. "How long was I gone? I kind of lost track of time out there."

"You left two weeks and three days ago, champ."

Ray shakes his head. He was asleep for roughly two weeks. *I'm a regular Rip Van Winkle.* "What's been going on around here?"

"Progress, Ray," the old man tells him, puffing on his cigar. "The government is digging wells and building windmills. We even got a radio station now, telling happy stories about loved ones reunited and teaching everyone how to make a vegetable garden. People here started getting a little more hopeful when the Army invaded Washington, DC. They've got a big piece of it cleared out already. A whole company of them showed up here, too."

Ray thinks of Sergeant Riley, how he was regular Army. "The Army's here? When did that happen?"

"As a matter of fact, they showed up the day you left."

Just a couple of hours, and Ray would not have had to go to the bridge. The Army would have taken care of it. The Reverend Paul Melvin would still be alive, and so would Ethan Bell, the teacher, and thirty-three National Guardsmen. And Ray would not have been stung and infected.

He sobs, unable to tough it out. He sniffs and wipes tears from his eyes.

Tyler shakes his head. "Jesus, Ray, look at you. Your nerves are shot. Let me get something stronger." He holds up a small key and uses it to access a file drawer in his desk, from which he produces a bottle of Wild Turkey and two glasses. "I know it's a little early, but let's have a snort."

"Why not?" Ray forces a smile. "I just can't believe I'm actually here."

"Shit, boy, I can't believe you're here either!" Tyler laughs. "We had a funeral for you and everything. We even said nice things about you. Anyway, drink up while you still can. The good stuff won't last forever. We'll all be swilling dandelion wine and mead pretty soon."

Ray grins at Tyler and remembers his dream. His friend holding two green monstrosities that strained against their leashes, trying to get near him. *Whoa, we got a live one here.*

He feels a sudden hot flash followed by the urge to vomit.

The thing shivers, releasing a cloud of musk. This is how it eats.

Tyler is staring at him with obvious concern. Ray reaches for his glass and slams his drink back, gasping with pleasure.

"So how's your dumb kid?" he says.

Just before he left for the bridge, Jonesy and Wendy had been attacked by camp riffraff while on patrol.

"Jonesy is great, thanks for asking. He got over that knock on his head in about two days. All the guys should be done with their shift in about a half hour. You can say hello. They're going to shit themselves when they see you." Tyler taps the end of his cigar against the edge of the ashtray. "Listen, Ray, they made me sergeant. But you're still in charge here as far as I'm concerned. I'm happier doing dispatch. You rest up and take command whenever you're ready."

Ray frowns. He had not thought about it, but right now does not welcome the idea of being a cop again. Does he have any responsibility to other people anymore? He remembers standing next to Todd Paulsen on the bridge, emptying his pistols into the greasy pale hide of the tentacled giant, screaming his head off as it bore down on them. Last time he stuck his neck out to save the world, he got infected. He beat the bug, but far from feeling invincible, he dreads everything now. *Let the Sergeant Rileys fix this mess and leave me out of it,* he decides. *I deserve a break. I've got a second chance, and I have to figure out what to do with it so I don't waste it. And for that, I need a little time. No worries except breathing in, breathing out.*

"Any word from Saslove?" he asks.

Tyler nods. "I heard our dear Wendy's shacked up with that big Black fella, Toby Wilson, and they're traveling around with an outfit called the New Liberty Army."

"Good. Sarge will take good care of that girl."

"She was the real thing." Tyler snaps his fingers. "Hey, I almost forgot. Get a load of this." He goes into one of the holding cells, rummages around in a box, and returns with a mint-condition black STEELERS cap. "Try this on for size."

"I can't believe it," Ray says, blinking another round of tears.

Tyler laughs. "Boy, that old hat of yours has seen better days."

Ray takes off his old STEELERS cap and puts on the new one.

"How does it look on me?"

"Like lipstick on a pig." Tyler laughs so hard he starts coughing. "Lipstick," he repeats, his face turning red. "On a pig."

Ray watches with mounting alarm as the veins in Tyler's throat stand out hard and dark like wires. The man is choking. He grimaces and wheezes: "*Pig.*"

Then he slams both hands on the desktop, stands and sprays a geyser of vomit from his open mouth. Ray lurches back in his chair as the old man's breakfast splashes across the desk and onto the floor.

"Tyler!" he roars, standing.

The man collapses to the floor, convulsing.

Ray kneels next to him, pressing down on his shoulders, trying to hold him still. "Aw, shit," he says. He has no idea what to do. "Help! Help me!"

Run, Tyler hisses just before his eyes roll back into his head.

Ray jumps to his feet and races down the hallway to find most of the cops on the floor. The men still on their feet stare at them helplessly, their eyes wild, shouting at each other to do something.

Outside the building, he stops in awe. Everywhere, bodies are flopping in the mud like fish while the survivors stand over them, crying for help. A man hobbles away on crutches, raising the alarm.

"Infection! Infection!"

A cop wrenches a pistol from his shoulder harness and fires into the face of a woman lying on the ground. People shrink away in revulsion from the roar of the gun. Even from two feet away, he misses two shots before the woman's head explodes across the sidewalk.

"They've got the bug!" a woman says, drawing her own gun and emptying half a magazine into another convulsing victim.

Another woman screams at her: "We don't know they've got it!"

"Are you blind?"

A man roars: "That's my mother! Put that gun down!"

The shooters raise their guns. Ray flinches at another round of gunshots. The cop and a bystander collapse to the ground. People are running, trying to get away.

"Stop it!" a woman shrieks, hugging a wailing toddler against her chest. "Stop it!"

The people on the ground stop twitching. They sit up, looking around in a daze. Slowly, they get back onto their feet.

Ray's vision shrinks to the size of a small circle.

"Aw, shit," he says.

Screams rise up from all over the east side of the camp, an exciting wall of sound, like being in a football stadium during a dramatic play. The dogs go berserk, yelping and howling. The first gunshots follow within seconds, a random pattern that rolls into an avalanche.

This is everywhere.

The Infected stand with their arms at their sides, hands clenching and unclenching rhythmically, heads darting to follow the progress of the fleeing survivors. The voice droning over the speaker on the telephone pole stops and a deafening air raid siren begins to wail.

The Infected are running.

Two women drag a man down, one pulling his hair out in fistfuls while the other scrabbles at his clothes with her nails, looking for a place to bite. A fleeing woman runs into a plate glass window and bounces off it, stunned; a teenager in a hoodie lands on her back, gnawing at her scalp. A man's pistol clicks empty just before a pack surges over him. A tow truck roars down the street, Infected swarming over it, running down anything in its path. A dozen people wrestle in a pile at the curb. A dog with bloody jaws hovers at the edge of the melee, snarling and barking, lunging in to bite and tear the flesh of the Infected.

Ray pulls out his carving knife and turns in place, waving it vaguely at these threats.

A man staggers past, blood trickling down his forehead, wearing the dazed, panicked expression of someone who has just been bitten. The man stops, turns and frowns at Ray, his face twitching. He begins to chew his lips.

Move, bro, a voice screams in Ray's head.

He runs back to the police station but pauses at the steps leading up to the main doors. Dark shapes struggle inside. A shotgun blasts twice, and then goes silent. The shape of a man fills the doorway, hunched and snarling, blood splashed down the front of his shirt.

"No," Ray says, horrified. "God damn it, no!"

Tyler Jones jogs down the steps and stops in front of Ray, his face bright with fever. Ray glances at the knife in his hand, but cannot make himself cut the old man.

"Look at me," he pleads. "I'm Ray Young. I'm your friend."

Something like recognition flashes in Tyler's eyes.

"That's right," he goes on. "It's me."

Tyler's head jerks as if trying to see something more interesting behind Ray, and lunges snarling after a screaming woman. Ray watches him go in amazement and realizes the street is filling with Infected.

A military helicopter hovers low over the rooftops, its thundering rotors sending bits of garbage swirling through the air. Ray holds up his hand to shield his face against the wash, watching the Blackhawk turn in place until the machine gunner, crouched behind his M60, comes into view. Another soldier, crouched next to him, makes a chopping motion with his hand.

A burst of smoke appears in front of the roaring gun. The air buzzes with flying metal. People collapse where they stand, large parts of them missing.

A storefront explodes with a burst of light, raining the street with glass, as Ray throws himself onto the ground and covers his head with his hands.

The Blackhawk stops firing and moves on, searching for fresh targets.

Ray refuses to move. Lying on the road with his face pressed against the warm asphalt, he is going to stay right there and hide in plain sight for as long as it takes.

Feet stomp the ground as people run past him with howls of rage.

This is the last moment of your life, he keeps repeating in his mind, while praying it isn't.

ANNE

From a nearby hilltop, Anne studies the death throes of Camp Defiance through binoculars. A drifting pall of smoke hangs over it. Helicopters circle low, pulling the smoke into fantastic swirls, dropping missiles that burst on the ground in sudden flashes. Gunfire crackles along its length. Two Chinook transports rise above the airfield in a hard ascent, one of them wobbling unsteadily in the air, people cartwheeling out of the back in a swift return to the earth. The muffled screams never stop, rubbing her nerves so raw she has to fight the urge to join in.

This has been going on for hours. FEMA 41, Camp Defiance, is devouring itself.

Her Rangers stand in a line behind her, hands over their mouths, gasping as an explosion rips apart a patch of ground on the north side, hurling bodies and debris into the air. Jean, whom they picked up in Hopedale two days ago, cries hysterically in Gary's arms, dressed in her wrinkled Chanel suit. Ramona and Evan lean against each other until standing cheek to cheek, watching. Marcus, the toughest of them all, wipes tears from his eyes. Anne spares a glance at Todd, standing ramrod straight and pale with his hands over his ears, watching the open gates with rigid hope as vehicles emerge singly and in groups, going south. One of the vehicles veers off the road, crawling over the muddy field, tiny figures struggling in the cab.

The Chinooks pound overhead, heading east. The hum of their powerful rotors drowns out the screaming for a few minutes. Anne gasps with relief.

Hundreds of camps have been set up across the country, she knows, possibly thousands. She tries to tell herself the human race can survive the loss of even this massive battle. That they can still win the war. But this corner of southeastern Ohio has just gone dark. It belongs to

Infection now. And Anne and her team are in no man's land, at ground zero. She knows they should already be back in their bus and moving. She returns the binoculars to her eyes and stays.

"What are we going to do?" Marcus says.

"It isn't over," she says.

"Can't we do anything to help them?" Todd asks her.

Anne shakes her head, watching a squad of soldiers emerge at the top of the wall and begin climbing down the other side to safety. *Even the Army is bugging out.*

"Erin," he says, and sobs, covering his face, giving in to the feelings he has been holding at bay all day. "What's happening to her?"

"It isn't over," she repeats, but it is.

She tries not to think of the children. Everyone knows the Infected do not convert them. They eat them. Thousands of children are in the camp. Her hand flickers to her scars, where she scratched her face in grief when she discovered the dead bodies of her own children six weeks ago.

As the endless day grinds on, the others drift away to process what has happened and mourn lost friends. When the sky dims toward twilight, only Todd remains with Anne, watching, hoping for his miracle.

Camp Defiance is dead. A convoy of military vehicles shot their way out an hour ago, and then the entire camp fell silent.

Anne rubs her stiff and tired arms. A lone figure emerges from the camp gates and moves south. She raises the binoculars to her eyes and swears under her breath.

In her magnified view, the man runs splashing through the mud, looking over his shoulder with blank terror. She would recognize that mean face anywhere, even without the ballcap.

"Do you know him?" Todd says. "Who is it?"

"It's Ray Young."

"But you said he got stung. The hoppers got him. Nobody can survive that."

"It's flat out impossible, Todd, but there he goes."

She chews her bottom lip, wondering how he survived both the hopper sting and the sudden fall of the camp.

"Look," Todd says. "More people are coming out."

She turns slightly, giving her a view of what he is pointing at. Infected are pouring from the mouth of the camp. Scores of them, walking hesitantly, hands pressed against their chests, heads cocked to study Ray's retreat.

One by one, they trickle after him.

"Are they survivors, Anne?"

She understands. It is a miracle, true, but not all miracles are good. Some miracles are evil. Some miracles, like Infection itself, can end the world.

"Do you see Erin?"

She lowers the binoculars and spits.

"Anne?"

"I should have killed that motherfucker when I had the chance."

PART II. ENDGAME

RAY

They are gaining on him.

Ray stumbles through the cornfield crying and laughing and screaming. He flails blindly against the cornstalks with sticky, stinging hands, driven by memories: *The Infected raced into gunfire time and time again, some of them taking a dozen bullets to put down, overrunning scores of last stands. Military helicopters screamed low to the ground in high-speed strafing runs, heavy fire striking down both the normal and the diseased. People clawed screaming at the base of walls that once protected them. Officials evacuated the burning school that housed the government, trying to push their way out as the Infected forced their way in, the air filled with burning posters reading,* ASK ME ABOUT RESETTLEMENT.

Choking on smoke, Ray fled across the camp, searching for sanctuary until the last strongpoint fell. Realizing the camp was finished, he ran headlong through the slaughter, ignoring screams for help and mercy alike, until he reached the eastern wall. Hours after he entered the camp, he ran back through the gates and disappeared into the woods from which he came.

A massive human pile writhed like worms in the bloody mud. A woman engulfed in flames walked past without a sound until collapsing in a burning heap.

Now he runs through this endless cornfield, his exhausted body driven solely by blind terror, as insects shriek in his ears and the thrash of pursuit grows steadily closer. The sun dips toward evening, bathing the corn the color of blood as the dark closes in.

A running mother, bleeding from multiple bite wounds, suddenly turned against her child, eating him while he cried and struggled in her arms.

Ray bursts gasping from the field and staggers into a large yard. He pauses to catch his breath, his heart thumping at an alarming speed against his ribs, and scans the area for weapons, a place to hide, anything that can help him. They are close behind.

A farmhouse stands with its back door open and inviting. An aboveground pool stinks like rotting plants near a clothesline. An old swing set rusts among the dandelions between a vegetable garden and a barn. A solitary wooden baseball bat leans against an apple tree. Ray lopes to the tree, scoops up the bat and turns to face his pursuers.

The backyard is empty. Insects rip the air like distant chainsaws.

Still gasping, he slaps corn dust and tiny bugs from his T-shirt, wondering what happened.

People were chasing me. Where did they go?

A flock of birds flutters into the air, swirling around the sky before falling into formation and heading east. In the twilight, the wall of corn is dark and impenetrable. As his eyes adjust to the light, he realizes the stalks are trembling.

People are moving across the cornfield.

Ray stands his ground, sure he is being watched. Slowly, his muscles uncoil. He lowers the bat. *If they were Infected, they would have attacked by now.*

"Hey," he says. "Who's there? Come on out of there. It's all right."

The movement stops. The ring of cicadas crescendos and ebbs. *Please*, he thinks, pleading. *Don't go.* He needs people right now. He doesn't want to be alone again.

"I ain't dangerous or anything. It'll be safer if we stick together."

A man appears, bugs and bits of cornstalk clinging to his hair and clothes, followed by two women.

"It's all right," Ray tells them. "My name's Ray. I was at the camp too."

The people pant, watching him. Dozens more appear. Then a hundred. Behind them, hundreds more stream into the yard. The cornfield ripples with the movement of a horde.

Ray laughs with relief. He can't believe how many. He takes several steps forward and then stops, his lungs constricting.

Can't be.

He turns toward the house. The open door now seems impossibly far away.

Can't be.

The people continue to gather, staring at Ray. Some of them reach out to him, moaning.

Can't be, can't be, can't be.

They're Infected. All of them.

TODD

The bus rumbles along the road toward Trimble Airport, a tiny commuter airfield outside of what used to be a small town called Appleton. Anne's Rangers converted one of the hangars there into a safe house. Harsh red light flickers through the metal-slatted firing ports, fitted where the windows used to be, as the sun bleeds into the horizon. Todd is too preoccupied to worry about being caught in the open at night. They'll reach the safe house soon enough. He does not care what happens in the meantime.

The Rangers sit scattered around the bus, each taking a seat as far as they can from everyone else to be alone with their thoughts. Hugging his assault rifle, Todd tries to process the horror of what he saw today. Jean cries in the back while Gary tries to console her. The Rangers rescued the pair from an art gallery in Hopedale two days ago. She is taking it the worst. Her wailing scatters Todd's thoughts until he begins to hate her.

We have all suffered, lady. We've all lost people.

Todd knows he will never see Erin again. The best he can hope for is somehow she survived and is on her way to a safe place. He shuts his eyes and pleads with God to let her live.

Spare her and I'll do anything. Just name the price.

He wonders if this is how the Reverend felt when he prayed. Bargaining with a God who does not answer. Who may not even be listening. And yet it feels good to bargain.

I should have tried to save her. I did nothing. I just watched.

If you tried to save her, you'd be dead by now. Dead or infected.

I could have tried.

Around and around his mind goes.

The Rangers lived on the road, searching for survivors and bringing them to the camp. Defiance was their port—a place to rest, retool and resupply. Without it, they are adrift, anchorless, in a sea filled with monsters.

Erin was Todd's port.

Everything he'd enjoyed doing as a troubled, geeky teenager before the epidemic was gradually forgotten along with the millions of other things people liked doing, such as going to the movies, ordering takeout from a Chinese menu, buying flowers for a date, catching up on reruns of a favorite series. Even the things Todd found exciting about the epidemic—the boyish thrill of living without school or parents, shooting guns, living life dangerously, the freedom of the apocalypse—had all turned sour with repeated use. Todd was growing up in a world filled with risk and death. A world he looked at with the resentment of a boy cheated of his inheritance. Erin was the only thing in that world offering him any real happiness, and now Infection has taken her from him, just as it took his parents, Sheena X, Paul, Ethan and so many others.

The vehicle shudders as it drives over rubble and shards of timber. Unknown to the people of Camp Defiance, the storm that lashed the camp several days ago was the northern front of a small tornado ripping through southern Ohio. Most of the buildings here took damage; some of the weaker structures were crushed flat. The road is blanketed with leaves and branches, wires, furniture, soggy books, broken plates, shattered electronics, the bloated bodies of people and cattle.

The bus drives over it all with a crunch.

♦

The Rangers would visit Camp Defiance for a day or two and then return to the road for as long as a week. The more Todd stayed away, the more Erin wanted him. Each time he left, she cried and screamed and called it quits. After sex, he studied her body, feeling helpless. His happiness with her felt as fleeting as life itself, and just as doomed. He believed someday she would leave him not because of his separate life on the road, but because he was not who she thought he was. Todd believed she was too good for him, and would one day realize it.

His life among the monsters appeared to be a constant source of attraction to her. Erin called him the coolest guy she knew. She said how all the other guys she'd ever liked had the trappings of being a bad-ass. Todd had none of the trappings, and yet he was the biggest bad-ass she knew.

He would just laugh. *If only you really knew*, he would say. *If only you saw what was out there. You wouldn't think I was bad-ass. You'd think I was certifiably bonkers.*

She told him she loved him. *Isn't that enough?* she said. *What more proof do you want? Stop trying to think and feel and choose for me. I know how to think and feel and choose. And I choose you. I am giving myself to you completely. Just accept it.*

Like a fool, he did not allow himself to believe her. He survived the end of the world, but still suffered from the low self-esteem that had plagued him in high school. Now Erin was dead or infected in the camp with its massive walls and watchtowers, and he was alive out on the road, the most dangerous place in the world.

He remembers scavenging around Pittsburgh with Anne and several other people in a Bradley fighting vehicle during the first weeks of the epidemic. After settling into a building they hoped to make their home, Todd asked the Reverend what he missed most from the time before Infection. Todd started listing off a lot of things—Buffalo wings, wargaming, computers, ice cream.

What about you, Reverend? he asked. *What do you miss the most?*

Paul grimaced, excused himself, and left the room. At the time, Todd put his brooding down to the dark, odd behavior of people whose age placed them closer to their death than their birth. His own dad had him when he was forty; for most of Todd's childhood, his dad seemed paranoid the world was going to end, that his family would be attacked or robbed, that the government was going to take everything away from him and give it to lazy poor people.

Then, one day, his dad stopped caring about these things. His dad realized his own parents were dead, some of his friends were dying, his brother was fighting cancer. His attitude went from, *Fight for what's yours* to: *We're next.* He no longer seemed paranoid. He seemed resigned. That's what Paul was like when Todd asked him what he missed. Resigned to his fate.

It wasn't until later Todd realized the one thing Paul truly missed was his wife, Sara, who had become infected.

Now, above all things, above even his parents, Todd misses Erin.

Now he finally understands loss.

◆

Marcus parks the bus in front of the hangar and lets it sit idling. The survivors stir, gathering weapons and equipment, but nobody gets off. He kills the engine and they sit and listen to the pulse of insects for a while. After several minutes, Anne says, "All right, let's move."

Todd exits the bus and jogs to his designated position, sweeping the area with his carbine. Regardless of his despair, he has a job to do, and people's lives depend on him staying alert. He scans his sector looking for threats. The airport is a disaster, covered in a jumble of leaves and branches and scattered equipment. The orange windsock and antennae jutting from the dark control tower have been swept away. He notices a small metal sign, bent double but still standing: LEARN TO FLY HERE!

He sees no Infected. *Maybe I won't have to shoot anyone today.*

Marcus opens the hangar doors with a grind of metal. Todd lowers his weapon and jogs back to help unload their gear. The survivors fall into the routines of survival, filling buckets with water from the rain barrels they installed under the building's rainspouts, collecting and cutting firewood, servicing the bus's engine. The safe house is just as they'd left it. Nobody says a word unless it is necessary. Night is falling, and they have to get inside.

One by one, however, they stop moving. The Rangers gather on the tarmac, gazing at the eastern horizon. The cloud cover glows like burning coals, reflecting the light of vast fires on the ground. The story of the battle of Washington, written on the sky.

"Let's get a move on," Anne tells them.

Todd shoulders his rifle and helps Evan bring a cooler into the building. Inside, their footsteps echo across the massive, empty space.

The Rangers settle in for the night, eating a hasty supper around their small fire, listening to monotone voices on the radio mourn the fallen and encourage all Americans to continue to fight Infection. Nobody says a word. Any conversation taking place is the internal kind. The silence suits Todd just fine. The fall of the camp calls for a night of silence just to process it.

Then he realizes Anne is staring at him. He looks away, feeling like he failed some sort of test. Like the others, he is a little afraid of her.

And yet he understands her a little better now.

He is learning how to hate.

WENDY

The juggernaut gallops on its four thick legs through the half-empty parking lot of the Lebanon Costco, scattering garbage and vehicles and making the ground tremble. It stops, its lungs swelling against its ribcage. Dozens of tentacles sag from the body, swaying tentatively, as if groping. They straighten and shiver, flailing, blasting like foghorns.

The sound fades, replaced by the growl of advancing machinery. A Technical—a pickup truck with a heavy machine gun bolted onto its bed—races through the empty adjacent dirt lot, sending a rooster tail of mud flying behind it. The driver wrestles with the wheel while the gunner holds on for dear life. On the other side of the parking lot, another Technical, a Toyota with bumper bars welded onto its face, slams through a snarl of shopping carts under a dead light pole, sending them flying with a crash of metal.

The gunners open up at the same time, sending rounds arcing across the parking lot to fall into the flank of the monster, punching holes through hide and muscle.

The drivers whoop at the sight of the elephant-sized thing limping away on legs thick as tree trunks. They step on the gas and lean on their horns while men in the passenger seats shout reports into radios. They are pushing the thing into the rest of their combat team, which even now is circling the other side of the Costco.

The monster lows in pain, so white now it is almost translucent, leaving a trail of blood that fills the air with a copper scent. One of the trucks splashes through it moments later.

The man in the passenger seat sees a gray blur and screams a warning.

Five tons of flesh and bone slam into the vehicle and shove it into a crashing roll that sends the gunner flying and leaves the truck lying on its back, parts of it scattered all over the parking lot. The second juggernaut embraces and lifts the wreck with its swarming tentacles. Two of the tentacles punch through the cobwebbed windshield, latch onto the dying driver, and start sucking, throbbing scarlet as they drain the man's blood.

The other truck veers away, its gunner hanging on, as the Bradley fighting vehicle crashes through a chain link fence and hurtles onto the parking lot on screaming treads. A wreath of wildflowers trembles on its metal chest like a necklace. A faded American flag waves from one of its antennae. The crew of the Technical raise their fists and whoop as the armored vehicle rushes past, its turret rotating to align the cannon for its first shot at the monster.

The men glimpse the words BOOM STICK stenciled on the side of the turret, partly erased by deep grooves in the armor, as the cannon fills the air with manmade thunder.

♦

Gum cracking, Wendy sits at the gunner's station in the Bradley and feels the surging power of five hundred horsepower flow through the rig's twenty-five tons. She applies gentle pressure to the joystick with her gloved hand, keeping the giant monster centered in her integrated sight unit as the cannon continues to boom.

"Target," she says, announcing they are making solid hits. "Target."

The tracers surge into the monster, which sags, collapses. The tracers begin to flow over it. Instead of correcting, Wendy ceases fire.

She finishes: "Target destroyed."

"Rapid scan," Toby says.

"Hotel Bravo identified," Wendy answers, referring to the monster type known among their militia as *horn blowers*, then adds, "One." *One hundred meters.*

Another of the monsters has entered the parking lot, bellowing in rage. Wendy confirms range on the RANGE-SELECT knob and that the AP LO annunciator light is illuminated on the weapons box. They're going to fire armor-piercing rounds from the cannon at a rate of about a hundred per minute.

"Line it up," Toby tells her, watching the thing on his optical relay.

"Wilco," Wendy says. She pushes the joystick a little, making the turret rotate until the reticle falls center mass on the new monster on her screen.

She was once a cop and now she's a tanker, a monster slayer. It used to be exciting. Now it's just slaughter. *Every day*, she thinks, *some of us get killed, some of them. It never ends.*

Toby puts his ear against the instrument panel, listening to the Bradley's beating heart. Wendy breaks from her mental routine and watches him. Armored vehicles are impervious to most children of Infection, but not malfunction.

He shakes his head. "It ain't nothing."

She catches the reticle drifting and feathers the joystick to stabilize it. Then she realizes the thing is moving. Galloping straight at them. She blinks sweat from her eyes, ignoring the sweltering heat inside the tank.

"One thing at a time," Toby tells her. "Fire."

"On the way," Wendy responds.

She presses the trigger switch, feeling the stresses of the cannon's recoil spread through the rig's frame. Like Toby, she knows every inch of the rig by feel as well as sight and touch. She can tell if one of the guns is malfunctioning before the annunciator lights confirm it.

She knows when to use the coax MG and when to use the twenty-five-millimeter cannon. She knows which creatures require a high rate of fire to bring them down. She knows when to use the heavy explosive ordnance and when to use the armor piercing.

"Target," she says with cold familiarity to the task. She remembers when firing the tank's cannon filled her with a primitive joy, enough to make her whoop as it sent its devastating ordnance flying down range. Now Wendy and the gun are an old married couple. "Target. Target destroyed."

"What's wrong?" Toby asks her, sensing her mood.

"I don't know," she says, shrugging. "Everything?"

The radio crackles.

Sarge, this is Joe. Sherman Tully and his boys didn't make it.

Toby glances at Wendy, who winces, but says nothing. The New Liberty Army is made up of people who do not expect to live long. Death is so commonplace, when one of them dies in the fighting, it is expected, not mourned. And yet every death weighs on her.

"Roger that," Toby says into the comm. "What about the equipment?"

The truck's a total write off. The gun too from what I can tell. We're salvaging the ammo and some gas and whatever else we can.

"We'll provide overwatch from here until you're done," Toby tells him.

Much appreciated.

"Then we'll camp inside that Costco tonight."

This is Russell, Sarge. My boys missed out on all the fun. We'll get to work clearing the Costco.

"Fine with me," says Toby. "Any word from Ackley? Moses Ackley, how copy?"

Moses, here.

"What's your sitrep?"

We found a litter of their young, Tobias. You should see the yard where they built their nest. It's covered in bones and hair. Small animals—I'm guessing dogs, mostly. Some human kids in there too from the looks of it. We killed the adults. We're gonna torch the little brats next.

Wendy winces again. She hates the idea of killing children, even the children of monsters. But it has to be done.

"Roger that," Toby says, and takes a deep breath. "Lebanon has been liberated."

The men cheer over the radio. A few pop off rounds into the sky. Tonight, they will break out the whiskey and drink until oblivion.

Toby turns to study her. "Tell me what's wrong, Wendy."

"How's she doing?" Wendy says, extending her arm to touch the instrument panel. She feels its pulse flow through her hand and into her arm.

"We're going to need some real maintenance soon," Toby says, frowning at her evasion.

"Sergeant," Lieutenant Chase says from the back. His young face appears past Wendy's shoulder, frowning at them. "Why are we stopping here for the night?"

"We're stopping here because we're done," Toby tells him.

"You said we'd sweep through and continue on to Washington. That's our mission."

"Don't worry, LT," Toby tells him, pronouncing the word as *el tee*, an abbreviation for lieutenant. "The war will still be there by the time we show up."

"From now on, I expect us to do what we agree to do," the young officer says.

Toby's voice becomes low and menacing. "Lieutenant, you should know by now that the NLA ain't the regular Army, and that it follows its own impulses."

Wendy stifles laughter. To claim the New Liberty Army follows its own impulses is an understatement, to say the least. The outfit was created by men who cannot live in the refugee camps, who have the stomach for constant slaughter, and who do not fear death. They've been mopping up towns all over eastern Ohio and western Pennsylvania for the past three weeks. They are good at what they do. They are damaged people; they can never go back to the way things used to be. After the war, they will have to be put down like wild dogs.

Wendy does not worry about that too much. She doesn't think the war will ever end. And if it does, she doubts any of them will live long enough to see it.

"It may not be the regular—"

"Besides," Toby adds, "we are providing overwatch for the salvage operation. We are still in combat. Now's not the time."

"I just wanted to point—"

Wendy wrenches her eyes from her display and says, "Sit the fuck down, sir."

Lieutenant Chase blinks and glares at Toby, who shrugs. "You heard the lady, sir."

As the young officer returns to the passenger compartment to retake his seat with the squad, Toby sighs and says, "So are you going to tell me what's eating you today?"

"Nope," Wendy tells him.

♦

The fighters shoot out the skylights in the Costco to create smoke vents, chop up some of the empty shelves, and settle into lawn chairs around their cook fires. The beards, sunglasses, bandanas and leather make them look more like a biker convention than a military force. The women look even fiercer than the men, some of them wearing bits of armor and body paint and necklaces of ivory monster teeth. At any one time, roughly six hundred men and women to serve in the New Liberty Army. Outside, the sentries stand guard on the beds of the trucks arranged in a line in front of the store. Inside, a boom box blares an old Jimi Hendrix song, rebellious and nostalgic. The fighters swap war stories and pass around chewing tobacco and mason jars filled with grain alcohol. Franks and beans and Ramen noodles bubble in pots set over the fires, filling the store with the rich smell of camp food. The fighters play cards for hundreds of dollars looted from the cash registers. They trade toilet paper for cigarettes, chocolate bars for antacids, silver dollars for porno mags and Percocet. A man tries to sell a handful of gold wedding bands, but gets no takers. Everyone knows carrying such things around is bad luck.

Each night they are alive is cause for as big a party as they can put together with whatever they have on hand. Tonight, the fighters are happy to be camping inside, away from the rain and the mud and the mosquitoes. The New Liberty Army is a nomad army, always on the move, living off the land and leaving a vast swathe of death and destruction in its wake. They are an unforgiving army; wounded fighters are left behind with a gun and a little grub to die or get well. Their sole mission is to purge Infection from the region, scavenge what they can, and then move on. They are hard men and women, civilians who fight like professionals. An army of psychopaths, a legion of the insane, a homegrown militia of monster slayers. These people are here because they can do nothing else. They are damned. They don't mind killing; some of them enjoy it. Some hotwire mannequins with dynamite, and laugh when the flash and boom turn the Infected into jelly and pieces of bone. Some mutilate the dead. What some of them do to infected women, Wendy doesn't want to know. Most have lost everything and hold a grudge.

Anne would fit right in here, Wendy muses.

And yet it is a tranquil army, one where many of the old divisions do not exist, or at least have been put aside. She remembers Paul telling her about the demonstrations at Camp Defiance and the old hates pulled into the new world they lived in, some of them even amplified. Some believe God hates the Infected, while others believe the Infected are specially chosen instruments of divine wrath. Some argue abortion can no longer be justified during a time when more people are dying than being born, while others argue the option of abortion makes even more sense in this harsh, dying world. On and on. None of that stuff matters in the New Liberty Army. Nobody cares Toby and Wendy are a mixed-race couple, for example, or that Billy Weaver's crew is openly gay, or that the Ackleys are Jehovah's Witnesses. They are united in their single purpose to stamp out the plague, without mercy, with fire and shot.

She walks away from the others, picking through the shelves looking for something useful. With hope, she'll find some gum. Looters have already been through the store, however, and taken almost everything. The candy aisle has been stripped clean. It's not over, however; you just have to know where to look. Getting down onto all fours, she feels under the bottom shelf, her hand sweeping through the dust, until settling on something. Bingo.

She pulls it out and holds it up in the dim light. It's a Tootsie Pop. Not gum, but it will do.

"Wendy Saslove?" says a man's voice.

Wendy stands, feeling a little silly and also foolish for having made herself so vulnerable. The last time she dropped her guard, she was on patrol with Jonesy back at Camp Defiance, working as a police officer for Sergeant Ray Young in Unit 12. She was violently attacked by three scumbags, two of whom she beat senseless, the third she fought off after he attempted to rape her. She hadn't felt safe since that night unless in Toby's arms or in the gunner's station of the Bradley.

She faces the large, bearded man, feeling the reassuring weight of her Glock on her hip, her hand near her pepper spray and side-handle police baton. She is a beautiful woman; she has been told this enough times to be sure. Most of the men are afraid of Toby, who is something of a living legend in the outfit, but a few made a move on her anyway when his back was turned. They didn't know Wendy was a cop before she became a volunteer gunner. Too bad for them: She stomped them so hard, many of the boys grew even more afraid of her than Toby.

"I'm Dennis. Dennis Warren."

"Nice to meet you, Dennis," she says.

"I joined the outfit about a week ago."

"I've seen you around," she says. "How's everything?"

"I don't mean to bother you or anything, but I heard you were a cop. Over in Pittsburgh."

Wendy relaxes a little. "That's right."

"I just wanted to say thank you."

She knows what he wants to do, so she asks the question. "For what?"

He wants to tell her his story. That's always what they want when they mention they find out she was a police officer.

There were four of them trapped in a supply closet in an office building, two women and two men, one of them a cop suffering a severe concussion, floating in and out of consciousness. Outside, an Infected man scratched at the door like an animal, grunting, while the survivors gaped at the noise, sweating and paralyzed and feeling nauseous. One of the two women worked in Finance; Dennis didn't know her name, even now, but he had seen her around the building for years and always thought she was pretty. She was trying to help the cop. She said there were dozens of Infected out there, maybe even a hundred. She insisted on this until Dennis believed her. He was out of his mind with fear. The Infected heard their voices and pounded at the door, screaming loud enough to send fresh waves of adrenaline through Dennis's body. His brain went numb with fear. *One little bite*, he knew, *and I'm as good as dead.* The Infected outside wanted to bite *him*. The door trembled on its hinges.

The center splintered. The woman took the cop's gun from its holster and aimed it at the door, her arm shaking, taking deep breaths. *Leave us alone*, she screamed. *Stop it!* The Infected outside howled in a blind rage and crashed against the door. She said it was no use. She said the Infected would get in and tear them into pieces. *Best to end it now. Janet, I'm so sorry.* The gunshot blasted in Dennis's ears, making him flinch. When he opened his eyes, Janet sat on the floor gaping at nothing, her brains splashed up the shelving behind her and coating the neatly stacked Post-Its and legal pads and pencil sharpeners. *I'm sorry*, the woman with the gun said, turning back toward Dennis with eyes glazed with shock. *I never got your name.* Dennis lunged and wrestled her to the floor. *Don't hurt her*, he told himself. He felt like he knew her after sharing elevators with her for two years. He'd always had something of a crush on her. She fought like an animal, pulling on his tie until pain lanced through his neck, trying to free her wrist so she could shoot him or herself in the head. *Kill me*, she begged. *Quick, before they get in. I don't want to turn into one of them.* Dennis slapped her hard. He just wanted to make her be quiet, but she kept screaming and clawing at him. *Everyone just settle down now so I can think*, he said, hitting her again. His hoarse whisper sounded like someone else speaking. He wrapped his hand around her throat and squeezed for a while to stop her screaming. *Just be cool for a minute.* He couldn't think straight. She stopped struggling. *Oh shit. Oh shit, I didn't want that.* Crying now, he untangled her fingers from the grip of the cop's gun and pointed it at his own head as the door splintered further and the Infected face appeared snarling in the hole. Dennis blinked in surprise; it was Paul Dorgan, VP of Product Development. *Wait*, a voice said. Dennis turned and saw the cop pushing himself up trembling onto one elbow. *Give the gun to me. I'll do it.* The cop accepted the Glock, raised it calmly and fired through the hole. The body fell heavily to the floor.

"If the cop hadn't been there," Dennis says, "I would have died in that closet. Simple as that. The fear made us crazy. I was out of my mind. I owe that man my life."

"What happened to him?"

"He didn't make it. He died that night in his sleep. His name was Matt Prince. He was a Pittsburgh cop. Did you know him?"

"Sorry, no," Wendy tells him. "I didn't know any Matt Prince working Northside."

"Well," Dennis says. "I was just wondering."

"What did you do, Dennis? Before?"

"I worked in the IT department."

Wendy smiles. His appearance fooled her; she thought he was just another lost redneck like many of the others. "You're a long way from that world."

"I wish I were," Dennis says. "That would mean it was still there."

She hears boots stomping down the aisle behind her, and knows it's Toby. She turns and sees him approaching.

"God bless you, Wendy," Dennis adds, and turns away to return to the camp.

Toby folds his arms around her shoulders and chest. It is like being hugged by a bear. The familiar odors of his body push away the irritating smells of wood smoke and dust. Wrapped in his large arms, Wendy feels like she is back in the Bradley, completely safe.

"He heard you're a cop," Toby guesses, kissing the back of her head.

"The police did amazing things," she says, as if she were describing heroes of ancient legend. "The ones who stuck it out and didn't run. They really helped people."

He hugs her tighter. "Some of them still do."

"No. The police are all dead now. There are no police. Not real police, anyway."

He kisses her again. "You're a real cop."

"I'm not police anymore, Toby. I'm an exterminator. A gas chamber operator."

Toby sighs and releases her. "It's almost suppertime. You coming?"

"Where else would I go?"

He frowns. "I keep pissing you off. Tell me what's wrong, Wendy."

"It's not you," she tells him, placing her hand against his muscular chest, over his heart.

"Maybe this will make you feel a little happier." He reaches into his pocket and pulls out a handful of moist toilettes in their wrappers. "I got these off one of Ackley's boys. I know how you like to stay as clean as you can."

Wendy's eyes flood with tears. "I don't want this."

Toby stands with his hands at his sides. "You don't?"

His tone of rejection only makes her cry even harder. "This, Toby. *This*. I don't want *this*."

"It's all there is," Toby says as gently as possible.

He tries to pull her back into his arms, but she shoves him away and dashes into the dark aisles. *That can't be true. There must be something else. There has to be.*

It's been less than two months since the screamers woke up and the epidemic began. How can I do this for another two months? A year? A lifetime?

◆

They turn off the music so Tom Ackley can play his violin. Nothing white trash; pure Stravinsky. The stark notes fill the empty spaces and make the fighters feel melancholy. It gets so quiet they can hear a distant radio droning advice to *stay indoors* and *wear dark clothing* and *isolate and abandon loved ones who have been bitten.* The fighters chew slowly; the music makes them remember. A woman pauses while cutting her toenails and trembles, sobbing, as she relives some past event. Tom breaks into the warm rhythm of a waltz, making them glance at each other and smile. Laughing, the boy switches to bluegrass, sawing the strings like a fiddle and tapping his feet. The fighters clap as the music makes them forget.

"Here you go, Wendy," Will Barnes says, handing her a paper plate loaded with franks and beans, Ramen noodles tossed with grilled vegetables, and canned pears.

"Thanks," she says, taking a seat far from the others, her eyes on Toby, who sits at another fire with Steve, the driver, telling the story about being attacked by the Demon. The militia never gets tired of hearing that one. The Demon is a legend. They heard one screaming in the hills once and ran across its tracks, but never saw one themselves.

Which is why you're still alive, Wendy muses. *If you saw one, it would have eaten you and shit you out already. The one thing that saved me and Toby and Steve was the Bradley's armor. Even then, it was a close thing.*

The men's eyes gleam in the firelight, hanging on every word. Wendy notices Toby's hair is going gray. He is going to look like the Reverend Paul Melvin in no time. Thinking this, her heart goes out to him. *He is my man.*

"Mind if I sit with you?"

Wendy glances up, her mouth full of beans, and motions for Lieutenant Chase to join her.

"Thanks," he says, sitting with his own steaming plate of food. He takes a sip at the clear liquid in his mason jar and gasps, then laughs. "Wow, that's strong stuff. Like drinking a bayonet."

"Sorry I yelled at you earlier today in the Bradley, Lieutenant."

"That's all—"

"But lives were depending on me paying attention to the ISU display. I couldn't have you yelling in my ear about military strategy."

The officer nods. "Fair enough."

Lieutenant Peter Chase showed up several days ago and latched onto Toby as the only non-com in the outfit who is regular Army. What he doesn't understand is Toby isn't in his Army anymore. And the New

Liberty Army doesn't have a general. Each of the Technicals has its own commander, and all of them decide as a group where to go next. They all want the same thing, and none of them mind doing their part. Often, they debate little over what to do, and a formal vote is not required. At least, that is, until the young lieutenant—yanked from West Point, put through a special counter-Infection training program, and thrown into the field—showed up. *The Army is invading Washington*, he told them. *We need you in the fight, each man to his duty.*

Wendy likes the young officer, who isn't even old enough to legally drink in most states, and has a penchant for the melodramatic. *Who will follow me to Washington?* he actually said once. Another time, Wendy could have sworn he said, *We will drive east, toward the sound of the guns.*

The New Liberty Army is not a field army, however; it is a militia made up of people from the region who see no reason to fight outside of it. Moses Ackley said America is dead and they need to take care of business here. He pointed out that if they go, they may leave the entire region vulnerable to Infection. This ground here is not America; it is their home. They know the area intimately, making them successful in battle, and they are highly motivated to defend it. To men like Moses, America has become an abstraction, without meaning. Without the NLA, the refugee camps like Camp Defiance might be threatened. Most of the commanders are not ready to write off the United States, however. They still believe in America, if only in the ideal.

Lieutenant Chase offered them a deal. He said, *If you follow me to Washington, we will supply you. Fuel, parts, weapons, ammunition, medicine, food and water, and payment in gold.* Moses Ackley called it a trick, and besides, he said, the NLA is not for hire. Other commanders wondered what choice they had. The NLA is mechanized and without resupply, they will end up on foot. They're always running out of things and what they have is steadily deteriorating.

"I was wondering," says Chase, "if you would put in a word with Sergeant Wilson for me."

"He's right over there," Wendy tells him. "Go tell him what you want. He's reasonable."

"Wendy, the mission is in Washington. We need to be moving at a faster pace."

"And you think Toby can make that happen?"

Chase blinks, considering how it could be any other way. "Of course."

She laughs. "Lieutenant, everyone here looks up to Toby. But nobody reports to him. Even I don't report to him. Not even Steve, who used to report to him. This outfit is not military, LT. It's a gang. I'm amazed it's lasted as long as it has. One little thing could tear it apart."

"And you think I'm that one little thing?"

"Yup," Wendy says, scooping noodles and corn into her mouth.

Chase stares at the fire. "About two hundred miles from here, the Army is fighting for its life. Everything is riding on this one big battle. Higher Command wants me to get this militia into it as fast as possible. If I don't make progress, they won't deliver the supplies I promised."

Wendy nods. "You're in a bad spot. If you don't deliver any supplies soon, you're going to lose these people. It's on you, LT. Not Toby. You're going to have to find a way."

"Shit," he says, and then blushes. "Excuse my language."

"No, you're right," she says. "It's shit."

"Shit, shit, shit."

As if on cue, she watches Moses Ackley stand, dust off his pants and approach Toby, no doubt to make his case to strike west instead of east, and screw the Feds. His Biblical beard spills down his chest, giving him a stern, fearsome appearance. Behind him, some of the boys finish a shopping cart race that ends with a metallic crash and laughter.

Wendy remembers driving to Camp Immunity near Harrisburg. It's the biggest camp in Pennsylvania, even bigger than Defiance, and better organized. They hid the Bradley outside, walked in and found Ethan's family. Wendy recognized them from the photo Ethan carried around; she felt like she already knew them after living with Ethan for weeks. Carol Bell sat in terrified silence, hugging her little Mary tightly on her lap, while they told her everything. The weeks scavenging in Pittsburgh. Following a theory into one of the hospitals. The flight from the fire that consumed the city. The refugee camp, the bridge. Ethan's infection and death.

Ethan was brave, they told her. *At the end, he died fighting. He saved our lives time after time with his intelligence and intuition. He never stopped searching for you. You were his sole purpose for going on. He never gave up hope. At the end, he believed he had found you. He died knowing you are alive. His last thought was of you.*

Carol could not stop crying. She wanted them to tell Ethan she was sorry she left the city during the evacuation. Surely, he would understand she was only looking out for Mary. She refused to acknowledge he was dead. When hope is all you have, it's hard to give it up.

Hours later, they left her and had a look around the camp. *This is a good place*, Wendy said. *They have their shit together.*

We can't stay, Toby told her. *You know we can't stay. None of these places are good for us.*

Toby had barely been able to stand Camp Defiance. None of his group of survivors had been able to really stomach it. They fought so hard to survive long enough to reach sanctuary, just to find out they would rather live on the road.

Now she thinks about that camp and wants to disappear into the crowd. Forget the NLA and the epidemic and the neverending slaughter. Just her and Toby. They could build something like a home there. Wendy is tired of the war. She could handle the fighting if she could believe there might one day be an end to it. She would even lay down her life if it meant victory. But the slaughter never ends. It just goes on and on.

She remembers asking Toby if they have any responsibility to other people. She's a cop in a lawless land. He's a soldier without an army. Do they owe people anything? Even if she does, she signed up to be police and help people, not butcher them. Steve sometimes calls the Infected "crunchies," after the sound they make when the Bradley runs over them. Wendy doesn't like it; the Infected never quite feel like the enemy to her.

She longs for home.

We've done our part. God knows we have. It's someone else's turn to fight the war. It's our turn to live in peace.

But she knows it could never be. The refugee camps are noisy and crowded, filled with people who cannot be trusted, and neither she nor Toby believe they could truly live in one of them again. She just wishes there was a way.

Lieutenant Chase nudges her. "I think something's happening."

Tom Ackley has stopped playing. Toby and Moses jog toward a group of fighters gathering around the radio. People are shouting, their voices edged with panic.

"Oh God," Chase groans.

"What is it?" Wendy asks him, fighting the urge to run to the Bradley.

Instead of answering, he throws his plate into the fire, swears loudly, and buries his face in his hands.

Wendy stands, her hand on the grip of her police baton, and approaches the huddle. "What's going on?" She shoves one of the men. "Hey! What's happening?"

The man turns, his eyes wet and feverish. It's Rick Combs, one of Russell's guys.

"We just heard it on the radio," he tells her.

"Heard *what?*" she grates, her patience exhausted.

"Camp Defiance has fallen. It was overrun. It's fucking *gone*."

♦

Many of the fighters had friends and family living in Camp Defiance. They sit alone or in huddles around the dying fires, wailing into their hands. Aside from the crying, everyone talks and moves as quietly as possible in the funereal atmosphere. Wendy's brain tingles with shock. She thinks about Todd, Anne and Unit 12, the police unit at the camp where she served with Ray Young, and wonders if any of them made it out. So many people died in Steubenville to save that place: Paul Melvin, Ethan Bell, Ray Young and the rest. All for nothing. To hear the entire camp has collapsed is too much to take in at once, forcing her into a state of denial. *An entire camp. More than a hundred thousand people. Wiped out. Just like that. All of them infected or dead.*

The commanders of the Technicals crowd around Toby, arguing in hushed whispers, the hissing turning into shouting that startles even those doing it. Chase stands next to Toby, visibly wilting. Some of the commanders blame him for distracting the New Liberty Army. Their shame fuels their fury. If they blame the Army, they don't have to blame themselves. Wendy pushes through the mob until she reaches Toby and Steve and the Lieutenant, her hand on her baton. She stares back at the angry and terrified faces, angling her body into a fighting stance and planning where she is going to hit them. Her despair craves its own outlet. A part of her is hoping they will give her an excuse to stomp some ass.

"This is why we need to stay in our territory," Moses says in his deep baritone. "Washington is an empty gesture. The fight is here. If we leave, there will be nothing to stop the bug."

"We *are* in our territory," Russell tells him, scratching at his beard. "And we didn't do nothing to stop shit. The camp was wiped out on our watch."

"There's still the smaller camp at Mason," Joe Hanley chimes in. "Camp Nightingale. They need protection, too."

"Cashtown couldn't hold out," Martha Grimes says in her raspy voice. "How can Mason hold out, shit for brains?"

"They're next," Russell mutters. "You can bet your ass they're next."

"We don't know that. There are forty thousand there. They need us."

"Your country needs you," Chase says, but it falls flat. Some of the men openly laugh at him.

"My country is Ohio, boy," Moses growls. "And we need to take it back before it's too late. As for America, it can take care of itself. I don't see it looking out for me and mine."

"America expects each man to do his duty," the young officer grates. "I would expect all of you, being military men, to understand that."

"Dumb shit thinks this is the real Army," someone snickers.

"Who said that?" Toby roars, shutting them up. "We are, in fact, nominally an Army operation, which means we will give the LT real respect as an Army officer. Whoever disrespects him again will get my boot so far up his ass, he'll be flossing with my shoelaces."

The men grumble, sizing him up. Wendy tenses, putting on her game face. There are dozens of commanders here, and just four soldiers. But nobody challenges them.

"So what do you think, Sarge?" someone calls from the back.

"This is not a local problem," Toby answers. "If we don't take all of America back, we'll never be truly safe anywhere. We got to start someplace, and that place might as well be Washington. That's where the Army is, and we should help if we can. Plus the LT says he's going to get us supplies that we need. It's a good deal. We should honor our end of it."

"Sarge, with all respect, I am sick of this man's empty promises," Russell says. "The Federal government promised help on the first day of epidemic, and it never came. They promised to protect us in the shelters, and those shelters didn't last a goddamn week."

The fighters growl, remembering. The shelters became deathtraps.

"They promised us a vaccine, and there was no vaccine, and no cure," he continues. "They promised to send troops, and then sent them all to Washington."

The fighters glare at the officer with open resentment.

"I'll tell you what, sir," Russell tells the Lieutenant. "If those supplies don't show up by tomorrow morning, I'm taking my crew and going west." He glances at Moses. "All right, Ackley?"

"That's fine," Moses tells him.

"What about Camp Defiance?" says Joe. "There could be survivors."

"We could split the NLA in two," Fred White chimes in. "Half head west to Defiance, and half east to Washington to join the fight."

"And be too weak to do either one right," Martha says.

"Put it to a vote," Fred says.

"Vote for suicide?"

"We'll go," Wendy says. "Me and Toby and Steve, with our shooters and the Bradley. We'll backtrack to Morgantown and then go north to check out the camp. We'll catch up with you in Washington."

The men glance at Toby, who shrugs. "You heard the lady," he says. "All right, Fred?"

"That'll work, I guess," Fred says. The other commanders nod at this, but reluctantly; they'd all rather have the Bradley riding along with them.

"It's on you, then," Russell tells Chase. "All this talk is pointless if our resupply don't show up here tomorrow. If it don't, then, well, we're all going west."

The mob breaks up. Toby and Moses exchange a nod of understanding. Wendy blows air out her cheeks and tries to relax; she feels like she could run a mile.

"Wow, I thought they were going to crucify the LT," Steve says, grinning.

"By the way, Sergeant Wilson, thank you for supporting me," Chase says.

Toby shakes his head. "Next time you see a fire, LT, try throwing water on it instead of gas."

"So if you go west and the rest of the NLA goes east, who am I going to ride with?"

Wendy says, "Try to find the crew that hates you the least, sir. In the meantime, I'd lie low if I were you. A lot of people here still blame the Army for what happened to Defiance."

"But why?" Chase asks in a childlike voice.

How to explain human nature? She shrugs. "Got to blame someone."

"So it's going to happen?" Toby says. "You're going to be able to deliver?"

"I don't know. Look, can I be honest with you guys?"

"Please," Steve tells him.

"The policy is only the militias that make it to Washington get the supplies. Otherwise, there's too much risk they'll take the resources and do nothing, or get killed on the way to Washington and waste them. It's supposed to be an incentive."

"Well, LT," Toby says, "I'd say you have a pretty strong incentive to get on the horn with your people and convince them to cough up the gear, or they'll get no help from the NLA and you'll be hitchhiking to Washington."

"Assuming I can even convince them, will your people honor your side of the deal?"

The tank commander shrugs and says, "Probably."

Wendy takes Toby's hand.

"Enough of this," she says. "Come on."

Once they are out of earshot of the Lieutenant, Toby asks, "Why do you want us to go west?"

"You know why. These idiots wanted to split the army."

Toby shakes his head; he doesn't believe her, but it doesn't matter. "Are you going to tell me why you're pissed at me?"

"I'm not pissed at you."

"Are you going to tell me why you're pissed at the world?"

They stop in front of their tent.

"No," she says, ducking inside.

"Tell me," he says in the dark.

She whisks her T-shirt up and over her head, steps forward and kisses him. Minutes later, they make love on top of their bedroll. She clings to him fiercely, squeezing him so hard it makes him gasp. *Come on*, she says. *Harder.* She wants to forget everything. She wants to fall inside of him. *That's it.* They grind against each other in a growing frenzy. *Oh, fuck, yes.*

He climaxes just after she does and they fall asleep sweaty and panting.

The next morning, she straddles him.

"Sergeant *Wil*son, it's reveille. I want you at attention, bud."

Toby awakes and grins, studying her face, the spill of her blond hair covering her left shoulder and breast. "Christ, you're beautiful."

Wendy places her hands against his chest, covering his tattoo of a bear claw, the symbol of his dead regiment.

"Shut up," she says, maneuvering her hips, and then gasps as he enters her.

She wants him to know that despite whatever she may feel about her life, he is her man. That every time he touches her, she feels safe.

Outside the tent, the fighters cheer as a dull metallic roar fills the store.

Toby and Wendy throw on their clothes and emerge from the tent to see the fighters streaming out of the camp, leaving their frying pans and coffee pots untended, and toward the parking lot, where a massive Chinook aircraft lands in the light of the morning sun.

ANNE

As the sun pales the eastern sky, Anne steps outside the hangar doors and inhales the stench of wet decay. Trimble Airport features a forty-five-hundred-foot runway, now blanketed with fallen leaves and branches, as well as landing facilities and fueling, maintenance and other services for a variety of aircraft. Private operators here once ran aerial tours, commuter flights to the big cities in the region like Cleveland and Pittsburgh, and weekend jaunts to private cabins around Tappan and Piedmont Lakes. Now the planes and helicopters are gone, the fueling station drained and idle, the facilities falling into rust and ruin, the ground covered in garbage and debris swept here by the storm. *The world is starting to look more apocalyptic every day*, she muses. *Everything is falling apart.* She finds it sad nobody will clean up the mess. Anne has always been a bit of a neat freak.

The others huddle around the fire, staring at the flames in a daze. Todd tosses in one branch at a time and watches the sparks flutter into the air. Marcus gets the coffee boiling and calls to Anne, telling her it's time to talk about what they are going to do next.

She accepts the coffee and sips it, savoring its rich taste and trying to commit it to memory. She knows it is the last of their supply and that it will be hard to get more. Soon, she believes, people will eat only what they can grow locally, behind walls topped with barbed wire. She has gotten used to living out of an old backpack and does not really care what she eats, as long as it gives her the calories and energy she needs to survive another day. But she will miss coffee.

Its loss reminds her of the loss of so many people at Camp Defiance, which reminds her of the loss of her husband and children. *My good Peter. My big, grownup boy, so brave, just like his daddy*. She closes her eyes and sees a bloody baby tooth resting on the mantle of a fireplace in a dark suburban living room while a bright TV blasts the Emergency Alert System signal.

Her hand flickers around the scars on her cheek, feeling the damaged skin.

Anne suppresses her feelings until they boil back up as rage. Rage, she can use.

♦

She sets out a cloth, makes sure her pistols are unloaded, and field strips them for cleaning: frame, rod and spring assembly, barrel, slide. Her Springfield nine-millimeters don't have the stopping power of her sniper rifle, an old military-issue M21 with telescopic sight. They are light and have little recoil, however, and with nineteen bullets in the magazine and one in the firing chamber, she can punch holes in any Infected that get too close with a fair degree of accuracy.

"We need to figure things out," Marcus says, gazing at the fire as he feeds it another branch. "Unless someone has a better idea, I think we have two choices. We can either go to Camp Nightingale, or stay here until things cool down, and then backtrack to Defiance."

"Why Defiance?" says Gary, his arm around Jean. "They're all dead or Infected."

"There's a huge amount of food and equipment just sitting there now."

"Sounds dangerous," Evan says. He is a small, wiry man who has survived for so long because, like Ethan Bell, he is able to think several moves ahead; that is why Anne chose him for the team. In the time before, he was an electrical engineer.

"The Infected will migrate," Marcus points out. "They'll leave a giant stockpile of gear we can use. We could pick up enough supplies to keep us going for months. If we grab another decent vehicle, even longer."

"That's right," Evan counters. "There are possibly a hundred thousand Infected, and they'll be migrating everywhere. And all those dead bodies are going to attract monsters looking for an easy meal."

Marcus glances at Anne to gauge her reaction, but she ignores him, dipping her bore brush into her bottle of solvent and running it through the barrel with the cleaning rod.

Normally, she and Marcus act as a team. After leaving Sarge's band of survivors, she found Marcus alone, bloodied and wild and liable to be mistaken for Infected himself, wandering the wasteland killing with bat and axe. The willpower involved in killing another human being, face to face and with a blunt weapon—not to mention the strength and stamina required to survive long bouts of hand to hand combat—amazed her.

He recognized in Anne a kindred spirit, and decided to follow her. But while they share a vision of wiping the Infected from the earth, they are doing it for different reasons. Motivated by hate, Anne kills for revenge against the organism that destroyed her life. Marcus kills to release lost souls enslaved by the virus; he kills for compassion. For him, it is about mercy.

While they have never touched, they are something like lovers. More feelings to suppress. Anne knows Marcus would follow her off a cliff if that is what she wanted.

Today is different, however. Today, Marcus must make up his own mind. Anne is planning her own mission, and it is not up for debate.

"Some of us have people back at Defiance," Todd says. "I want to go."

"You know what the odds are," Evan says. "I'm sorry to say it like that, but we're making decisions that will affect our survival. Even if she survived, by the time we go back, she will probably be long gone."

"I have to see," Todd says.

"And you're willing to put our lives on the line for that."

"Yes," the boy says, glaring back at him.

Anne smiles, pushing a cotton swab through the barrel.

"He doesn't have to justify his vote," Marcus says.

"We should be logical about this," Evan tells them. "The smart move is to go to Nightingale. They're picky about who gets permanent citizenship, but we know people there who will vouch for us. Once we get in, we could organize a scavenging expedition to Defiance."

"If they let us in, we'd have no say in what we would do," Ramona says. Slim and athletic like Anne, she sits cross-legged near the fire, eating Spam from a can. Overweight people are rare these days, at least outside the camps; they either dropped the pounds due to exercise and change in diet, or died out. "They run a tight ship at Nightingale. They have people at the top making all the decisions. They might break up our unit and make us scrub toilets. That's how it is."

"We formed this unit so we didn't have to be citizens of anything," says Marcus. "We've always worked on the outside. I think it's best if we keep it that way. We're better off on our own."

"We might have to rethink some things," Evan answers. "The fall of the camp changes everything. We need to be flexible. I'd rather scrub toilets than throw my life away."

Anne pauses in her work to squint at Evan. *If you value your life so much, what are you doing here at all?*

"What about us?" Gary says, staring at Jean, who gapes wide eyed at the fire, shivering. "Don't we get a vote?"

"Fine," Marcus sighs. "That all right with everyone?"

The others murmur their assent. Gary and Jean are refugees, not part of Anne's Rangers, but the situation is unique, with extreme stakes.

"We need to get to the other camp," Jean says, struggling with the words, her face and voice straining with effort. Anne studies her briefly, noting the symptoms. "Can't you see that? Are you blind? We're out in the open here. We're all going to die if we don't get somewhere safe."

At one time Jean was a beautiful woman, Anne believes, and this is the person Gary sees when he looks at her. Now her hair is disheveled, her eyes puffy and glazed, her mouth twisted into a grimace. They locked themselves inside the Wild Arts Gallery in Hopedale during the first days of the epidemic, and survived there for weeks. People will do whatever it takes to survive. The only problem is they have to live with what they've done afterwards.

They do not know Anne found the trash can in the back office, next to the gas grill, filled with human bones.

"So that's three for Defiance, three for Nightingale," Marcus says quickly, obviously regretting agreeing to give the refugees a vote. He turns to Anne, who rubs a drop of gun oil across the slide of one of her reassembled Springfields. "Anne, it seems you're the tie breaker."

Anne loads the pistol and holsters it.

"Anne?"

"I'm going south."

The survivors glance at each other. Marcus clears his throat and asks why.

"I'm going to kill Ray Young."

The Rangers watch her in stunned silence.

"This is the guy you think is some kind of Typhoid Mary," says Evan.

"He murdered a hundred thirty thousand people," Anne says. Most of them are not dead, are in fact Infected, but it is all the same to her. "He's a walking neutron bomb. He needs to die."

"Even if he did what you believe," Evan ventures, "what's the point of revenge?"

"If he goes to Washington, he will infect the soldiers fighting there," she tells them. "The military is our last hope. If they can't retake the city, it will be over for us. The war will be over."

"How would we even find him?" Todd wants to know. "He could be anywhere."

"He's heading southeast," she says. "That was his heading when he left the camp. He knows the Army is in Washington, and might go there thinking someone can help him."

For the next hundred miles, a single east-west road cuts through the Cherokee Valley, linking up with the highway system just east of Morgantown. They will need to move fast, and hunt and catch him on this stretch of road.

The survivors grow quiet, considering this.

"We don't know that for sure," Evan says.

Anne stands, wiping the gun oil on her hands onto her camo pants.

"I'm leaving," she adds. "You can do whatever you want."

The survivors shift uncomfortably at this news.

"Anne, we need to talk about this," Marcus growls.

"No, we don't," she answers. "If you're coming with me, we're leaving on the bus in fifteen minutes. If none of you are, I'll leave now and track him on foot on my own."

Marcus appears hurt, but she cannot help that. "We still need to vote on it."

"There is no vote. You are either with me, or on your own."

"But how would we find him?" Evan asks.

"I'm going to follow the Infected. They're following him."

Jean groans, burying her face into Gary's shoulder.

Marcus stares at her, raising his eyebrows. *Are you sure?*

She returns his stare. *This has to be done.*

"All right, let's get ready to move," Marcus announces, standing. Anne stifles a sigh of relief. She was partly bluffing; she is not sure she could stand to part with him.

"You could at least drop us off at Nightingale," Gary tells her.

"No," she answers.

"It's the moral thing to do."

"No." Anne barks a short laugh at this. "It isn't."

"You're crazy," Jean says.

"The sane thing to do is to save as many lives as possible. More lives than just yours and Gary's. Wouldn't you agree? That means killing Ray Young."

"But we were safe in that art gallery. It was hard and we suffered but we were safe. Now you want to drag us along on some quest. We never would have left if we had known."

Anne shrugs. Things have changed. She can do nothing about it.

"You don't understand," Jean says, her tone pleading. "I've lost everything. I can't do this anymore. You have no idea what I've been through."

The Rangers bristle at this. Shaking their heads in disgust, they move away to collect their gear to load back onto the bus.

"That's a good point," Anne tells Jean. "I have no idea what you've been through. So tell me about it. What did you do to survive back there in Hopedale?"

"Wait," Gary says, startled.

"Leave her," Jean hisses in a sudden ugly rage, glaring at Anne with open hatred. "If she wants to die so bad, let her. Let her go to her Infected. They'll rip her apart and stuff the pieces in her mouth to shut up her lies."

The Rangers ignore her, focusing on their tasks. Anne pats one of her holstered pistols pointedly, and then hurries to catch up with Todd.

"I'm glad you're with me," she says close to his ear.

He blinks, lost in his thoughts, as if surprised to see her there.

"If I lost you and Marcus," she adds. It is too painful to finish the thought.

"Anne, I'm not with you," Todd tells her.

"I thought you were coming," she says, surprised at how hurt she feels.

"I am. If what you're saying is true and the Infected are following Ray, then going with you is my best chance of finding Erin if she was infected. But don't make the mistake of thinking I'm *with* you. I won't kill Ray Young. I won't do it. I won't even help you do it."

Anne grunts in surprise. "What is he to you? He caused Erin's death, you know. I'm sorry to be blunt about it, but it's the truth."

"Every couple nights, I have a dream," the boy says. "I see Paul pulled up into the mouth of one of those tall monsters—the ones that look like giant heads on skinny legs. I see Ethan pushed to the ground and infected. Sarge and Wendy drive the Bradley into the smoke to fight the Demon, and don't come back. In the end of the dream I'm alone and the juggernaut is coming straight at me. Then all of a sudden I'm not alone. Ray is there and we're screaming our heads off and shooting at the thing together. My last thought before the monster falls through the broken bridge is I'm happy I won't die alone."

She hears the unspoken accusation clearly. *You abandoned me. Ray didn't.*

"Infection killed her, not him," Todd adds. "I don't hold him responsible."

"Fair enough," Anne nods, once again suppressing her feelings. "Just stay out of my way when the time comes."

JEAN

She was starving. Someone was going to have to go out for food, but they were too weak to do it. And Prendergast would not shut the hell up.

They'd been stuck in the art gallery for six days. Instead of sanctuary, it had become a tomb. They were dying by inches, surrounded by Prendergast's massive, horrible paintings.

The artist himself lay spread eagled at the foot of one these paintings, sweating profusely, his wrinkled black shirt riding up to expose his round white belly.

"My work connects the real and the imaginary," he said.

"Your work idealizes ideology through literary exposure, and yet real ideology is a hidden force, a political prime mover, not something you can frame and point to," Jean whispered, laboring to speak clearly. "The paintings juxtapose the real and the imaginary in conflict, not connection."

"The connection is within the conflict of these opposites," Prendergast insisted. "My work is fascism expressed as a brand. You can buy it, you can use it, you can throw it away."

Jean closed her eyes. She did not have the energy to say anything else.

At the other end of the gallery, Gary sat huddled against the wall, hugging his knees and rocking, watching them with narrowed eyes that appeared sunken into his skull.

Getting Ricky Prendergast and Jean Byrd together at the gallery had been his idea. He owned the gallery and considered Prendergast the local boy who made good. The artist's paintings and their declaration of a stark totalitarianism repulsed and attracted at the same time. Their size enveloped the viewer, threatening his or her individuality, and yet were strangely seductive, promising an existence without thought, whispering, *you kind of want this.*

Jean was an East Coast art critic who wrote for several important art magazines. Her pen had made a few careers, and broken more than she could count. She and Gary had fallen into bed together after Grady Tallman's opening (which she later skewered) in New York three years ago. Hearing she was going to be in Akron, he'd convinced her to visit his gallery in Hopedale and review Prendergast's exhibition at Wild Arts. After the Screaming screwed everything up from air travel to basic utilities, he'd doubted she would show, but she did.

"You'll love it," Gary had told her when she'd appeared at his door first thing in the morning. "His paintings are like propaganda for a fantasy regime built on absolutes. They make you want to punch a Nazi in the face. Wow, Jean, I'm so happy you're here!"

He'd kissed her, laughing, and handed her a mimosa in a champagne flute. He told her how good she looked in her black and white Chanel suit. She sipped her drink, smiling back at him. Gary was strictly small town, but he was extremely cute, and she had always had a soft spot for him.

Jean had toured the gallery, aware of Gary's eyes on her, and concluded Prendergast's work stank. His paintings were childish in their assumptions, their one saving grace, in her opinion, being their rich colors and sheer size made them audacious—suggested maybe they weren't childish after all, but profound, perhaps even threatening.

Gary had sensed her vibe, mistook it for ambivalence, and told her she would really come around once she met the local genius himself.

Prendergast, a giant of a man dressed in a black suit—his height and size squandered on fat, however, making him appear as if he were made of spheres—arrived late, complaining of the ungodly hour. His big, bright grin, framed by dimples and surrounded by a beard, forced you to like him, if only for a moment. He extended his large, sweaty hand, and Jean shook it. They agreed to have breakfast at the cafe around the corner, and discuss her impressions of his work.

As they'd left the building, a policeman shot a woman sprinting, dropping her to the asphalt. The gunshot electrified them. The cop screamed, waving them back inside, as more howling figures appeared. Before Jean knew what was happening, she was back inside the gallery and Gary was pulling down the metal gates to cover the windows.

The police officer's pistol had cracked several more times as Gary darted back inside and locked the door, his eyes bulging and his chest heaving, babbling about crazy people in the street. Whatever he'd seen outside, it had terrified him.

Gary did not have a radio or television in the gallery, but they'd had their cell phones, and both Prendergast and Jean had iPad computers. They spent the day surfing and sharing information. They finished the orange juice and champagne, getting drunk and treating the whole thing as an adventure. In a few days, the government would resolve the crisis, they believed, and then they would have a great story to tell when it was over.

Jean had slept on the floor curled into a ball, using her purse as a pillow, and woke up starving in the middle of the night. She hadn't eaten all day, and she felt weak and nauseous. After an hour of pressing her fist against her stomach to try to quell the growls and pangs of hunger, she fell back asleep.

The next day, the street belonged to the crazies, cutting them off from the outside world. Things appeared to be getting worse by the hour. They felt lightheaded and jittery. Their blood sugar levels were crashing. The room stank of bad breath. They drank as much water as they could, and spent hours checking the Internet and talking through their options, each of which led back to staying put inside the gallery doing nothing. As the day wore on, Jean became unable to focus on what she was reading. All she could think about was food. Every time they opened the door, screaming maniacs charged them. They were trapped. For hours, they sat in a fearful silence.

"Maybe we could talk about your impressions of my work," Prendergast had offered.

Jean had actually appreciated the request. Anything to pass the time.

"I don't like your paintings," she'd said. In fact, she was terrified she was going to die surrounded by them, and Prendergast's *Iron Eagle*, an art deco portrait of an angry stylized war bird surrounded by light beams, would be the last thing she saw. "Sorry, Ricky, but I don't."

That was five days ago, before the power went out, before they began to die.

"My work is a complete rejection of post modernism, offering one truth," Prendergast said.

They had argued for most of that time, but now Jean just moaned. Her body had burned through what little fat remained on her rail thin body, and had begun eating itself to recover proteins it needed to keep her heart and brain and nervous system functioning.

She could not believe how empty she felt. She'd once thought art could change the world. Now thoughts of food occupied every horizon of thought, left room for nothing else. Everything important in her life before the epidemic now struck her as pointless next to food.

"One truth," Prendergast repeated, "but one that is painful to look at."

Jean opened her mouth. Her tongue felt like it was covered in moss. Her breath smelled sour.

"Okay," she whispered. "I like them. I like your paintings. I will write a good review."

Prendergast lay silent, and then said, "Thank you."

For what, the capitulation or the argument that took his mind off his contracting stomach, she wasn't sure. In the ensuring silence, she fell into darkness.

When she awoke, Gary and Prendergast were gone and the gallery smelled like burning meat, overwhelming the open sewer shit smell emanating from the bathroom with its dead plumbing. Her salivary glands squirted, flooding her mouth, and she wondered if this were a mirage—a bitter manifestation of her starvation.

"Gary," she hissed. If this was a sign of the end, she didn't want to go alone. She gathered her strength and screamed, "Gary, please!"

He emerged from his office smiling and knelt on the floor next to her. She had a hard time seeing him; her vision had gone blurry.

He unclenched his fist and showed her a sliver of steak cupped in his palm.

"Eat," he said.

Jean swiped the warm meat from his hand and jammed it into her mouth, swallowing it almost whole. It was amazing. Nothing she'd ever eaten, in fact, had ever tasted so good. It had tasted like God. She licked her fingers and cried.

"I have more food, but you have to go slow," Gary told her. "I know how hungry you are, but you have to take it slow, okay?"

"Thank you," she said. "Thank you."

"I chose you," he said enigmatically. He smelled like smoke.

"How did you get it?"

"After you fell asleep, I went outside to check things out. The crazy people were gone. So Prendergast and I scavenged around the neighborhood and found a butcher shop with some meat in a cooler that was still good for eating. I dug the hibachi grill out of storage; we used to cook shrimp out back for parties. I got it set up in my office. I'm trying to vent the smoke out the window."

Jean felt alarmed Prendergast was eating it all. "Where is he?"

Gary's smile turned into a hard line. "Ricky didn't make it, Jean. We weren't alone out there. Some of those people were around."

"I'm sorry," she told him. "I know he was your friend." Faced with the prospect of survival, she now regretted compromising her artistic principles by conceding the argument and saying she liked his work.

"Yes, he was. Thanks for that. Listen, the steaks are going to burn. I'll be back in a bit. You stay here, okay? Don't move. I'll bring you more food in just a minute."

Jean lay on the floor for some time breathing in the odors of roasting meat and moaning with need. Wisps of barbecue smoke drifted in the air like spirits. Burned, medium rare, raw—she didn't care, as long as she got to eat it. Now she started to panic Gary was going to eat it all, leaving her with nothing. He didn't understand; she *had* to eat. She had to eat *now.*

She raised herself to her knees, gasping for breath and feeling dizzy, and gained her feet. The floor looked very far away. Then she started walking toward the office, her mouth filling with saliva again.

Jean opened the door, squinting to see better, and gasped.

Gary stood at the barbecue shrouded in cooking smoke, his mouth open in surprise. The room was dim and smoky, but she could see, plain as day, a plate of steaming brown steaks lying on a silver serving tray, the one he used to serve champagne to guests for small showings to important buyers. Two champagne flutes stood filled with water.

He had scavenged a feast for her. This food would bring her back to life.

For a moment, she thought she'd seen something else, something evil and impossible, a trick of the gloomy daylight filtering through the smoke. She thought she'd seen a chopped up carcass hanging from hooks used to mount large and heavy artworks. It'd looked like the body of a naked obese man hung upside down with his head, feet and hands cut off, gutted and bled out, the blood and organs dumped into a large plastic garbage can beneath the body.

Then she blinked, and it was gone.

"You weren't supposed to see this," Gary shouted, his voice edged with panic.

"It's beautiful," she said, leaning against the doorframe. She couldn't take her eyes off the steaks. "It's so beautiful."

That night, Gary crawled to where she lay, hiked up her Chanel skirt and entered her. Jean put her arms around him, smacking her lips and thinking about her next meal. He had little energy; it was over fast. Afterwards, while they slept huddled on the floor, the carcass invaded her dreams. The pale carcass of a man, chopped and gutted, mounted on the wall like slaughtered cattle. Like an obscene piece of art, provocative and visceral.

Prendergast would have loved it.

DR. PRICE

Travis paces his small cell and pushes at the walls in claustrophobic despair, convinced they are closing in a fraction of a millimeter at a time. He wonders if the cell is properly ventilated until he finds himself on all fours, sucking on air and dust trickling in from under the door. Picturing the room imploding and entombing him in solid rock is actually the least upsetting thing on his mind right now. He believes any minute, someone is going to come and make him disappear down the garbage shaft. In his mind's eye it is Fielding who comes, grinning and wielding a big shiny knife. *Sorry, Doc, orders are orders.*

Travis has a bucket for his waste and a mattress mounted on the wall, but otherwise the room is blank. He has no idea how long he has been stuck here; assuming they are feeding him three meals per day, then he has been in this cell for four days. It is something of a miracle he survived this long.

Not long ago, he witnessed an actual coup d'état. Soldiers handcuffed the President of the United States and dragged him shouting from the room. The Chairman of the Joint Chiefs calmly eyed the Cabinet and asked if anyone knew where the Vice President was. It was the VP's lucky day; he was going to be President. Then someone noticed Travis cowering in the corner.

The funny thing is Travis happens to agree with General McGregor. Detonating nuclear weapons in American cities is a desperate measure that would accomplish little. In fact, it'd be like stabbing yourself in the brain with a knitting needle to get rid of a bad headache. In Travis's opinion, Donald McGregor is even a hero of sorts; he stopped a madman. But whether Travis agrees or not with the men who staged the coup does not matter. What happened *did not happen*, and that means anyone who knows the truth is a bizarre anomaly that must be corrected, most likely with a bullet in the head.

Sadly, Travis even agrees with the rationale behind his own murder. Outside Special Facility, Wildfire is rapidly paring the Federal government down to the military. Only the military has the command structure and resources to continue functioning on a large scale. The American people do not want the military to run the country, however. They will only follow the President, based on illusions of tradition, leadership, unity. Even most of the military would not obey McGregor's junta if it openly declared itself in charge. So the President has a "heart attack" and is lionized as a martyr, the Vice President is sworn in, the bombing plan is axed, and everyone tells the same story for the good of the nation.

Through simple bad timing, Travis was given a peek behind the curtain and saw the man working the controls. What he knows could shatter the illusion of civilian control of the military, and with it, unity and loyalty to the government. And for that, he must be eliminated.

The irony of his situation almost makes him laugh. Despite his claustrophobic terrors, deep down he believed he was in the safest place in the country. Then again, he also thought the White House was safe, until it wasn't.

Boots clomp in the corridor, growing in volume. Instead of a tray of food being thrust through the slot, the lock rattles. Someone is coming in.

Travis realizes how little he will be missed after he is gone. He has no wife or children, no other family, no real friends, not even a hobby. A quiet academic at the University of Chicago, he wrote a paper about Iran's potential nuclear ambitions that found favor with hawks in the Walker Administration. After Walker won his second term, his people tapped Travis to join the Office of Science and Technology Policy. Travis had always hoped his study of nonproliferation would earn him some type of notoriety, but he never expected it would lead to a chain of events culminating in his execution by a junta now controlling what's left of the government.

All the knowledge he gained, leading to nothing. What has he done? Faced with the prospect of his death, he feels like he never lived. Is his life worth so much more than the woman the Secret Serviceman threw out of the helicopter?

His one regret, watching her be left behind to die, will go to the grave with him. It was the one time in his life he ever felt real empathy for another human being.

The door groans open, letting in a draft of air. Travis blinks at the figure dressed in black.

"Time to pay the bill, Doc."

Just as he feared, it is Fielding.

◆

Travis submits to handcuffs, his face burning with shame. Fielding grins; the son of a bitch is enjoying this. Travis braces for a lecture about karma, but it never comes. Instead, Fielding orders him to walk down the corridor. As he walks, Travis fantasizes about turning and knocking his captor unconscious, and then escaping to the surface, or making a brilliant case for keeping him alive, after which Fielding puts his own life on the line to help him escape the General's justice.

Any resistance would be a futile gesture with a man like Fielding, however, who would likely respond by beating him senseless and frogmarching him to his execution. Head bowed, Travis keeps moving, fuming at his lack of options.

"Stop here, Doc."

Fielding slides his gloved hand under Travis's armpit and pulls him toward a metal door, which he opens with a mocking gesture of welcome.

Under the glare of fluorescent lights, three broad-shouldered military officers in camouflage fatigues sit behind a desk, their backs ramrod straight. Their gray-flecked crew cuts, stern white faces and astronaut builds make them all look the same.

Fielding lifts Travis's shoulder again, forcing him to walk on his toes to a simple steel chair facing the desk. Travis notices the black stains on the concrete floor under the chair and stifles a yelp of panic. Fielding shoves him into it and remains standing somewhere behind him.

The officer in the center places his elbows on the desktop and rubs his leathery hands together before clapping once to call the meeting to order.

"Dr. Price, I am Colonel Slater. This is Major McMahon, and this is Major Buckner. We have asked you to come here today because the General thinks you're a person of interest. So they tell me you're a scientist. I'm curious. Tell me, Dr. Price: What do you think of our current situation?"

Travis blinks. "You mean—?"

"I mean in the country."

Travis studies the man's face briefly, searching for clues about what he wants to hear for an answer, but gives up. The soldier's rigid expression tells him nothing.

"I think we have less than a year before the winter finishes us or them."

Slater regards each of the men next to him in turn before returning his hard gaze to Travis. "See? I told you he was smart. Please elaborate, Dr. Price."

"We're putting everything into winning Washington, but it's a morale boost at best, not something we need to fight a war," Travis mutters, trying to muster the energy to speak. "We should retrench in regions that produce things we need, such as the grain belt. We should draft people to fight instead of herding them into refugee camps. We should put those who cannot fight to work rebuilding industries we shipped overseas years ago. We need to be able to make everything ourselves now, weapons and ammunition in particular, and we need to do it fast. All fiat currency is worth nothing. Goods are becoming scarce. The government is going to have to start paying in room and board and some type of new money based on a gold standard, and it might have to employ almost everyone in the country for a few years. But even if we did all of this, and did it now, we cannot sustain even what little we have saved. When the winter comes, we will suffer another mass die off. Our one hope is it will be harsher for the Infected so we have a fighting chance in the spring. We're so occupied with getting things normal again we fail to realize that no matter what happens, Infection has already permanently changed the world."

He stops talking, hoping at least something he said was pleasing to this man who holds his life in his fist. The officers chew on his speech.

"So you think our current strategy pretty much sucks," Slater says.

"I did not use that word," Travis says. "And I may not have all of the facts."

The officer laughs. "It's even worse than you know. There were actually people in the government who did not want the military to be recalled. They were worried about our bases overseas. It's easier to leave, they said, than to ever return."

Travis realizes he is expected to say something. "I don't think the military strategy ultimately matters."

Slater's leans forward. "Why do you say that?"

"Ultimately, bullets cannot win this fight, only science can."

"Ah, right. The elusive cure, the Holy Grail."

"Or a vaccine, or perhaps even a weapon."

Slater smiles grimly at that. "Dr. Price, I'd like to show you something."

The door opens; a soldier pushes a projector into the room on a wheeled cart. Crouching, the man taps a few keys on a laptop, which produces a grainy video image on the wall showing a compound filled with soldiers and workers in hazmat suits. Men load body bags onto a truck while others unload salvaged panes of glass from another truck. Another figure in a hazmat suit feeds clothes from a garbage bag into a fire burning in a metal drum. Travis does not know who these people are or where they are other than they are somewhere on the surface.

The video has no sound. The room is quiet except for one of the officers clearing his throat. Travis can hear Fielding, still standing behind him, breathe through his nose.

Sensing this is some type of test, Travis studies the image intently. He blinks in surprise; a man has collapsed and other figures race across the compound to see what's wrong. Half of them never make it, falling as they run. All around the compound, people topple to the ground and lie twitching. Travis recoils, making his chair squeak loudly; it is like the Screaming. The survivors gesture at each other. One of the soldiers is shooting the victims in the head. Others gather around, waving at him to stop, unaware the rest of the fallen are returning to their feet.

"This is FEMA 41," Slater says, startling him. "A refugee camp in southern Ohio, yesterday morning, at about oh-six-twenty."

The video switches to a view of people scrambling around a lot filled with campers and trailers. People have been living here for some time; the space in front of each camper is cluttered with tarps and coolers and other junk laid out like a never-ending yard sale. Two of the figures tackle a third and fall into a fire pit.

"They never had a chance," Slater adds.

"So it would appear," Travis mutters. The violence is shocking; he swallows hard to keep from throwing up.

The video changes again, showing a mob of Infected surging over a retreating knot of police firing at them with shotguns. The bottom of a helicopter comes into view. Dozens of figures fly apart, filling the air with body parts. The image shakes. Smoke obscures the camera's eye just before the picture cracks and turns to electronic snow.

This is not satellite imagery, Travis realizes. *They had cameras at the camp.*

"I think Dr. Price gets the idea. Corporal, skip to the next part."

"Sir," the soldier says, tapping keys.

The video changes to a view of an empty field cut by an old road. A vehicle lies on its side in the distance. A man enters the image, staggering across the mud while glancing over his shoulder repeatedly. Seconds later, he exits the image on the right.

"This is right outside the eastern gate," Slater tells him. "Now wait for it."

Travis watches a trickle of people wander onto the scene in the same direction as the running man. The trickle becomes a flood. From their jerky movements and the way they stumble into each other, Travis can tell they are infected. The image fills with a massive crowd following the running man. Hundreds, then thousands.

"In every major camp in the country where we sent troops, we set up a sophisticated video surveillance system feeding data to local commanders and analysis teams here at Special Facility," Slater explains. "Our commanders use this data for rapid detection and response to outbreaks and riots. The cameras on the wall teach us how to improve camp defenses. In this case, it gave us a blueprint for how we lost more than a hundred thousand people to Wildfire."

"That man in the compound, the first who fell," Travis says. "Was he the index case?"

"You mean was he the first person in the camp who showed symptoms of Wildfire?"

"Yes," Travis says. "The primary case. Victim zero."

"He's the first one who showed symptoms, that's right," Slater tells him. "But not the first who caught the bug."

"Are you suggesting an Infected entered the camp who was asymptomatic?"

"Like a Typhoid Mary, you mean?"

"Yes. A carrier."

"The analysis team narrowed it down to a single uniform mike—an unidentified male. This man entered the camp a short time before Wildfire appeared. And he was the last to leave. That was him we just saw."

Travis stands, unable to contain his excitement. "But how? How did he spread it to so many people so fast?" Other questions race through his mind: *Why didn't the Infected attack him? Why are they following him?*

He feels Fielding's hand on his shoulder, pushing him back into his chair.

Slater shrugs. "We don't know. The important thing right now is to evaluate him for response. We know he is a threat. What we want to gauge is his potential value as an asset."

"If that man is a carrier," Travis says, "he may carry a pure strain of the Wildfire Agent, which offers amazing research opportunities."

"You see, Dr. Price, that's just the thing we're curious about," Slater tells him. "From where we sit, we can't tell if he represents a cure, or whether he's a superweapon created by the virus."

The corporal brings up another image. Glowing blotches of red sprawl across a black landscape, like diseased cells under a microscope. Travis realizes he is looking at a thermal image of a large area of ground, taken from the air. The blotches are large crowds.

"As you can see," the Colonel continues, "the uniform mike has built an army for himself. They were all moving southeast as of an hour ago, when they stopped and surrounded the farmhouse you see at the center."

"Does he know what he is?" Travis asks.

"We don't know anything about his range of free will. He might be a mindless agent of Wildfire, some poor guy who can't understand why everyone he meets falls down and turns into a monster, or something in between."

"We need to study him. This man's blood. . ."

Slater points at the thermal image and whistles, imitating a falling artillery round."Boom," he says.

". . . can end Wildfire," Travis finishes awkwardly, confused.

"The Chiefs want to drop some bombs and put an immediate end to the threat. That's the smart move, don't you think?"

"You—you can't be serious!"

"I'm dead serious. He's a little over two hundred miles from Washington, Dr. Price. If we do nothing and he shows up with a hundred thousand Infected tagging along, we'll lose everything. Even if he shows up without them, he could infect our troops."

"You don't know where he's going to go."

"Doesn't matter. The region is filled with refugee camps. The man's a threat to us wherever he goes."

"I know it's easy to see this man as a threat—"

"A threat?" Slater laughs. "He's a walking, talking biological superweapon, Dr. Price. Less than a day's drive from our front lines."

"Colonel. Sir. You have to listen to me. As far as we know, this man is a unique mutation of Wildfire. He's the chance we've been waiting for."

"What kind of chance are we talking about?"

"To beat Wildfire, we need to characterize it," Travis explains. "To characterize it, we need to identify it. We haven't been able to do that yet. This man's blood might be the key to a vaccine or even a cure."

"What about a weapon? A virus to kill the virus and anyone or anything that's got it?"

Travis considers this, and nods. "Yes. That's possible as well. A weapon, or maybe a repellent."

"You're sure, then, he's got such a thing in his blood? You're one hundred percent positive he could produce material we need to win?"

"Of course not," Travis says.

"Well, see, that means all you've got is a theory."

"A hypothesis, yes. If he does carry a pure sample, though, it could end all this."

"We're not even sure we *can* get him," Slater tells him. "Since we don't know how he spreads Wildfire, will a standard MOPP suit be enough to keep someone from catching the bug from him? Not to mention how we would separate him from a hundred thousand crazies."

"It's worth the risk," Travis says.

"For who?"

"You could send a—what do you call it, a search and destroy. . ."

"Snatch and grab?"

"Right," Travis nods. "A snatch and grab team. Special Forces. Navy SEALS."

Slater says, "Dr. Price, I hope you're listening to me carefully. There's no way I would risk our best men on your shit theory."

"Well," Travis says, stunned.

"Do you play poker, Dr. Price?"

"No, I don't." He enjoys cards, but not the social aspect of most card games.

"The General plays. Damn good, too. He's a man who likes to hedge his bets. That means if there's an even tiny chance you're right, he will want to give it a shot. If he does, we'll pull a squad or two off the line and drop them between Typhoid Jody and Washington. It will be their job to find this guy, grab him and bring him to an isolation facility."

"Perfect," Travis says, happy to see any effort made. "Since you've identified the carrier, do you have any records on him? Anything would help."

"We have no idea who he is."

"But you called him Jody."

Slater laughs, and even the stony-faced officers flanking him crack smiles. "Jody does not actually exist, Dr. Price. It's a nickname for the Infected going around. More military speak." He chuckles again. "Let's talk about why you're here. If the General decides to send some of our people, you will go with them as mission science adviser."

"Me? I'm not a soldier. I don't know how to fight the Infected."

"Who does? But millions are somehow managing. Now it's your turn to step up."

"But you'll need me here to run the tests after we pick him up," Travis pleads. "You're not being very logical about this."

"I heard you lost your lunch in front of the President of the United States when he asked you what was going to happen after he nuked one of our own cities," Slater says. "I almost admire you for that. It might have been the only sane thing to do. But it tells me something about you. It tells me you're a weak sister. You want to see the epidemic put to an end but only if you don't have to get hurt doing it. So let me put my offer to you another way, Dr. Price: Now would be a very good time to make yourself indispensable to the war effort. Do or die, so to speak."

Travis nods dully. He'd forgotten his knowledge of the coup makes him a liability to the new regime. "I understand."

"You'll have forty-eight hours to find the carrier," Slater informs him. "Captain Fielding will go with you. Bring him alive, bring him dead, bring his left foot—I don't care what, as long as you get what you need. If at any point it appears to the Captain you will fail, we will drop every bomb we've got on Typhoid Jody and his friends, and the Captain will tie up any final loose ends in the field. Do I need to explain what that means?"

"No," Travis mutters.

"Don't look so sad about it, Dr. Price. On the bright side, if you succeed, you will get more resources than you dreamed possible. If your theory is right—shit, Congress will probably award you the Medal of Honor. People will name their babies after you. You'll never pay taxes again as long as you live. I'll give you a big, fat kiss myself."

The officers smile again, like sharks.

"How does that sound to you, Dr. Price?" the Colonel asks. "Does its logic appeal?"

"It's a great opportunity," Travis says, feeling sick. "Thank you."

"See? I told you. Smart guy."

Travis shudders as he realizes he is about to be released from his imaginary terrors down here in this underground prison and face the very real terrors ravaging the surface. He feels Fielding's hand slip under his armpit, lifting him from his chair and propelling him toward the door.

I'm still alive. They're not going to shoot me, at least not right away. I have a chance to win this. I have a chance to survive.

"We'll let you know what the General decides," Slater calls after him.

WENDY

The Bradley hums along the road, its crew sweating at their stations and its squad of four shooters raggedly singing a rap song popular when the world ended. Wendy looks at the optical display, scanning repeatedly for targets, chewing on a piece of nicotine gum and blinking at the head rush. She is addicted to the gum, not the nicotine. Her eyes sweep the indicator lights, confirming the vehicle's big guns are ready to party. Then she glances at the man sitting next to her and smiles like a school girl.

I love you.

She says out loud: "It's like an oven in here today and I have to pee."

Toby grunts. "I'll turn up the air conditioning."

She laughs. "Now there's an idea. We spent over a million bucks on each of these things, and nobody thought it might be a good idea to put in some air conditioning? Come on, guy."

They are in high spirits after the supply drop. They now have a tuned-up engine, full tank of diesel with a good amount of spare fuel, functioning weapons systems and enough ammunition to obliterate anything in their path.

Toby produces a protective mask provided for crew use in the event of a nuclear, biological or chemical attack. A plastic hose dangles from its filter.

"Observe," he tells her. "This hose connects the mask to an air purifier that has a fan."

"I'm not peeing into that tube."

Toby grins. "I have a better idea."

He removes the hose from the mask and tucks a length of it down the front of her shirt.

"Oh my," she says.

"Now check this out."

The commander flips a switch, forcing air across her chest, drying the sweat pooled between her breasts.

"Now we're talking," she says. "Welcome to civilization."

Steve chimes in over the radio: *Did you show her the hillbilly AC, Sarge?*

Toby laughs. "You're in the Army now, Wendy. In the Army, we make do, right Steve?"

"That's all well and good, you guys," she says, "but I still have to pee."

♦

An hour later, the amored vehicle idles in front of a red brick school building. The clerestory windows installed along the roofline of the gym, dirty and glinting in the sun, are spray painted with giant, bleeding red capitals: PLEASE HELP US. Toby studies it on his optical relay, rubbing his stubbled chin and scowling. Wendy knows he does not like the risk, but this is the mission; they separated from the convoy this morning to strike northwest, back toward Camp Defiance, and search for survivors. She closes her eyes and listens to the beating heart of the engine, which sends tiny vibrations tingling along the surface of her skin.

"I guess we'd better check it out," Toby says.

"I'll go too," Wendy tells him, pulling off her headset.

"I guess we're all going, then."

They agreed they would stay together no matter what. It is an incredible thing to realize another human cannot live without you. She never felt that way before. Understanding it as she does now, Wendy wonders how so many people survived the first days of the epidemic. *The disease took the ones you loved, and then put on their face, demanding you kill them or die yourself. You have seconds to make this decision. How would you choose?*

The threat of this choice is neverending. It can be forced on you at any time. It is the plague's greatest weapon.

They follow the squad out the back of the Bradley and fan out. After a few minutes of squatting in the heat, Wendy realizes they are looking at her.

"It's your show," she tells them, shaking her head. "I'm just tagging along."

She remembers driving in the back of the Bradley during the first days of the epidemic with Paul, Ethan, Todd and Anne, warring with Anne for leadership of the gang. She was a police officer, and felt it was her responsibility to take care of the others.

Later, marching down a desolate highway in a blizzard of ash falling from the fires of Pittsburgh, she realized she was not a cop anymore. Her precinct was gone, and so was her city with its courts and jails and laws. She had no responsibility to anyone except a detective named Dave Carver, the man who saved her life when the Infected overran her precinct, and that responsibility did not require her to help others, only survive.

Charlie Noel nods and whistles at his shooters, who stand as one and follow, rifles leveled. They look and act like professional warriors, but just a few months ago, Charlie was a traffic cop, Stu Guthrie a bartender, Sharon Yang a paramedic and Ana Cruz an architect. Infection has gone on for so long it is the past that now seems like a dream, not the nightmarish present.

They briefly inspect a pile of bodies rotting away in the hot sun in front of one of the gym doors, partly open and covered in scratch marks and blood splatter. The stench is powerful. They raise handkerchiefs, soaked with cologne, to cover the bottoms of their faces.

"Where are you going?" Toby asks her.

Wendy squats by some nearby shrubs and urinates.

"Told you I had to go," she grins.

On the road, privacy is a dangerous luxury. If you want to be alone, you will eventually die alone.

Stepping over the bodies, Noel shoves at the door. "There's something blocking it." He shoves again and a pile of furniture, stacked behind the door to block it, comes crashing down.

Steve sighs and blows air from his cheeks.

"Let's do this quick," Wendy says, gnawing her gum.

"More bodies here," Noel says, disappearing inside. "Watch your step."

Wendy follows the others into the gym, ignoring the corpses' splayed hands brushing against her legs, and gasps at the assault of heat and smell. Their boots send empty shell casings clattering across the floor.

The flashlights converge on the bodies of four men and women, three dressed in casual clothes and one in a police uniform. All shot in the head and partially eaten. Wendy stoops and collects the cop's badge, pocketing it. Her eleventh, counting her own.

Noel signals his shooters to fan out and clear the room. They call from the dark corners: *All clear. No Infected here.*

Wendy approaches the other side of the gym, followed by Toby and Steve. The play of their flashlights reveals more giant red bleeding capitals painted on the wall:

GOD FORGIVE US WE TRIED TO SAVE THEM

At the base of the wall, twenty small children lie in a row, all dead from gunshot wounds.

♦

From what Wendy can see, the children were lined up facing the wall and executed. Sickened by the sight, they turn off their flashlights and stand in the dark.

"Jesus," Noel says, catching up. "Who would do such a thing to them?"

"They did it to themselves," Toby answers.

"You mean the cop? But why?"

"They were under siege," Wendy murmurs. "During the first day of the epidemic. Some of the schools had just reopened after the Screaming, remember? They barricaded themselves in with these kids."

"The Infected found out they were in here and started to force their way through the outside door," Steve chimes in. "There must have been a lot of them. Too many to keep out. Too many to fight. The Infected must have been in the school too. These people were trapped."

"The cop held them off until it seemed hopeless, then he shot the kids so they wouldn't be eaten, while the teachers held the doors closed," Toby says. "It was a mercy killing."

"Probably made a game of it," Wendy adds. "Turn around and close your eyes and don't open them no matter how loud the pistol shot next to you."

"And then he killed the teachers and himself," Toby finishes. "Right at the door so the Infected would eat them and spare the children from even that."

"It's horrible," Wendy says.

"I don't want the others to see this," Noel says, his voice cracking.

"Everyone out," Toby calls across the gym. "Back to the rig. Come on, let's go."

Guthrie, Yang and Cruz take the hint and file out blinking into the harsh sunlight. They are not curious to see what the others saw. They have already seen their share of bad things.

"My kids," Noel says. He does not finish the sentence. He sobs once, wipes his eyes roughly, and turns to follow the others.

"There's nothing we can do here," Toby says. "Might as well get back on the road."

"Hey, one's alive!" Noel says.

Wendy puts her hand against his chest. "None of them are alive, Charlie. They're all dead."

"I saw one moving!" He aims his flashlight, but she steps in front of him, blocking his view.

"You saw a trick of the light. That's it."

"Just let me check. I need to be sure."

"No. Go back to the rig. You don't want to see a dead girl."

"But you might be wrong," Noel says, his eyes wild. He turns to Steve, his voice pleading. "I saw her move. I need to make sure she's not still alive."

"I'll check," Steve says. He turns on his flashlight, and just as quickly turns it off. "Wendy's right, Charlie. The girl is dead. I'm sorry, man. Come on, I'll go with you."

Wendy listens to their footsteps echoing across the empty spaces. She turns to the body of the girl in the pink dress and watches her little face wink and nod in the dark. She knows the face is not moving.

The maggots are. Wendy can hear them rustling.

When she is sure Steve and Noel are gone, she covers her face with her hands and weeps.

◆

Toby wraps his arms around her, but it is not enough this time.

There is nothing here for them except death. They should get back to the Bradley, but Wendy lingers, staring at the blackened bodies of the children and wondering who they were before they were killed and left to rot here in this oversized tomb.

"Are you okay?" Toby whispers, but she does not respond.

Wiping her eyes, she wonders what kind of lives they might have had if they hadn't died. If the school hadn't reopened. If they hadn't come to school that day. If they'd gone to a different school. If Infection had never happened.

So much life needlessly destroyed, like ants crushed by a giant's foot.

Will I ever have children? she wonders. *If I did, would they survive longer than these kids?*

Would I one day be forced to tell them to face a wall with a gun in my hand?

"We should go," Toby says.

I'm done with this fucking war. I mean it this time. I want out.

Shrugging out of his embrace, Wendy points to the corpses.

"Toby, look at this."

"It's nothing we haven't seen before."

"I want you to look at it," she says. "Really look."

"Wendy, please."

"Look."

"I don't want to!" he snaps, then sighs. "Come on, Wendy, what's the point? Do you want me to say the world is shit? Yes, it's shit. I used to see things like this in Afghanistan even before Infection. It doesn't matter. This is the world now. It's filled with fucking dead kids."

Wendy shakes her head. "I don't want to live in it anymore."

His eyes widen. "Don't talk like that. Don't you ever talk like that."

"You're worried about me killing myself? If we stay in this world, we'll die soon anyway. It'll catch up to us. Look at what happened to Camp Defiance. Staying here is suicide."

"It's the only world we've got." His tone is pleading now. "I don't understand. What else is there? We're alive today. What else could we hope for?"

"If we stay in the NLA, one day the Bradley will break down or we won't be able to find gas, and we'll end up in one of those Technicals. Those guys die like flies. Who knows how long we'd last?"

"They aren't as good as us. We've made it this far, haven't we?"

"Training and skill don't mean anything on a long enough timeline. Eventually we would get unlucky, and then we would die or become infected. It's not a forgiving game."

"All right," he agrees. "You want to leave the NLA. And go where?"

"The fall of Camp Defiance tells us the refugee camps aren't safe anymore."

"Been there, done that in any case," Toby snorts. "Both of us have. No, thank you."

"Well, if that's the world, then we make a new world," Wendy tells him. "I've been thinking about it. We could round up some survivors with skills we need, drive down south where it's warm all year around, and find a nice island for ourselves."

Toby sighs as he finally understands what she wants. "You know I'd like nothing more than to do just that, babe," he says. They are whispering now, as if afraid to wake the sleeping dead. "But the fight is here. We're taking it back. We're winning, making real progress. Don't you feel it? So many towns have been cleared."

"Come on, Toby. We're barely scratching the surface. The fight never ends. It will never be over. Look what happened to Paul and Ethan. They died on that bridge to save the camp, and the whole camp fell a few weeks later. None of it means anything. Eventually, the bug is going to win."

"You're asking me to abandon my duty to my country. To the children who are still alive."

"Just as I abandoned my oath to the public," she tells him. "To protect and to serve. I'm not police anymore. The last real police died in this room. And you're not in the Army."

"But I thought we had a responsibility to other people. I thought we believed that together."

Wendy no longer cares about the survival of the species. *How can I explain this to him? It is a hard thing to think, much less say to another human being.* All she cares about is seeing Toby and the others in her group survive. That's all the responsibility she can handle anymore.

"If there was something decisive we could do, I would say let's do it," she says. "I would give up my life. But there is nothing like that. There is only death, and more death, until the end. Just like Paul and Ethan. What is the point? The one responsibility we have is to each other and the rest of our group. We have to find happiness while we can. I don't believe we are dead already, Toby. I am alive and I want to stay alive. And I want to be happy while I can. It's why I chose you."

Toby stands in the dark, saying nothing for a while. Finally, he takes a deep breath. "Is your mind made up about this?"

"It is, Toby. I'm sorry."

She didn't want it to sound like an ultimatum, but that's what it is. She hopes he does not call her bluff, because she knows she could never leave him.

But it must happen. We have to go. We've gotten away from the NLA, with supplies and a full tank of gas. It's meant to be.

"As long as we stay together," he says. "That's all I want."

She smiles, her eyes stinging with tears. "Hell, Toby, we're practically married at this point."

"All right then," he says, letting out another long sigh. Wendy can sense something breaking in him, releasing, letting go. "So, have you picked out an island yet?"

"Thank God for you, Toby Wilson."

"I love you, Wendy."

She grins, plants her hands on his chest, and kisses him on the mouth.

RAY

Ray creeps out of the farmhouse breathing hard and feeling his heart pound in his chest. Hundreds of Infected mill aimlessly in the morning light, filling the air with their random, anguished cries. They stagger along without purpose, bumping into each other and growling. Some trample the garden while others lie in the tall grass. A few hold their heads with both hands and scream as if suddenly remembering who they are and what happened to them. Each moment brings more tramping out of the cornfield, grunting and wailing.

Last night, they reached out to Ray as if pleading. Their eyes followed him as he retreated into the house, shaking with the disbelieving laughter of a maniac. They moaned softly, a sound like humming, as he entered a coat closet and curled into a fetal ball in the dark and the dust.

The tiny space was hot but at least it was quiet. He started awake repeatedly until exhaustion overcame him. He dreamed of standing with Todd on the bridge, screaming his head off; he woke with a sore jaw from hours of grinding his teeth, and the hopper sting in his side, shrunk to the size of an egg, throbbing gently as if keeping time with a favorite song.

Now Ray inches away from the farmhouse, at the mercy of thousands of Infected. He glances over his shoulder to confirm the open back door is directly behind him, in easy reach, in case he needs to make a run for it. Last night, a miracle: The Infected did not take him. Today, they appear to be ignoring him. But this does not make them predictable. At any moment, they might turn on him, snarling, and decide to have Ray on a stick for breakfast.

He gags, slammed by a solid wall of stink. Oblivious to discomfort, the Infected eliminate their waste in the clothes they were wearing the day they were converted. Their bodies emit a sour stench that makes him think of rotting food and warm, old milk turned into thick cottage cheese chunks by runaway bacteria. One of the Infected passes close by, studying him vaguely before continuing on her way, taking little excited bites at the air.

He can hear them breathe. The wheeze of air entering thousands of lungs. Some of them cry out with the sadness of slaves. Others shriek before lapsing into silence. The spaces in between are eerily quiet. Just the insects and the birds.

Feeling bolder, he walks along the edge of the crowd for over an hour, studying their faces one at a time. The Infected continue to ignore him. Some stare at their feet; others blink at the sun. *They don't look very scary. They look like sick people. Like very sad, very sick people.* Like him, they came from Camp Defiance; he recognizes a man who sold mead in one of the trading booths. He wonders how they ended up here.

What is so special about this house? And what is so special about me that the Infected don't want me for one of their own?

♦

Survival trumps any interest Ray has in solving the mystery. He made it this far, and he's not about to quit as long as his luck is holding up. He retreats back into the house to do some exploring. As soon as it gets dark, he hopes to sneak through the crowd and strike a path toward Mason, where he knows Camp Nightingale was established. He feels an overwhelming urge to be around normal people who will protect him. Before he goes, he needs to gather up supplies.

The house smells dusty and Ray experiences a vague sense of alarm entering the kitchen. It is abandoned, but it is still not his house. He feels like an invader here. A clock ticks on the wall. Through the sheer white curtain covering the kitchen window, he can see the tightly packed Infected roaming about on their mindless errands. The refrigerator is plastered with holiday cards and photos of smiling people he doesn't know.

First, he needs food and water. He takes a plastic bottle from a cardboard box that had been used as a recycling bin, and puts it under the tap. The faucet spits and shoots enough water to fill most of the bottle before the pipes groan and run dry. He takes a sip and decides to down all of it.

Skipping the refrigerator, he opens one of the cupboards, hoping to find some food.

"Shit!" he screams.

A large, greasy rat tumbles from the cupboard and scurries under the sink.

"Give me a heart attack," he says, and laughs.

The boxes of food have been torn open, their contents half eaten. The cupboard smells like rat turds. He can hear the little bastards writhing and sneaking inside the other cupboards, and decides not to open them. He's not hungry enough yet to fight rats for cans.

"No grub for Ray," he sighs.

He spends the next few hours wandering around the house, picking up items and then putting them back where they belong. Surprisingly little salvage turns up. The only useful item he finds is a replacement for his T-shirt in an upstairs dresser drawer, and a new backpack.

A door bangs open downstairs. He peers over the banister, listening for footsteps. Nothing. He walks down a few steps and listens again, then a few more.

At the bottom, he sees the Infected filling the living room, looking at him.

The moment he appears, they raise their hands in supplication, groaning.

Ray runs through the kitchen door, leaps down the back steps and lands hard on his feet, gasping for air. He does not remember running. He didn't even think about it. He just moved.

The Infected are not oblivious to him. At least some are interested in him. He wants to know why. Steeling himself, he waves at the nearest Infected tottering past, stumbling over a garden hose.

"Hello?" Ray says.

Several of the Infected stop and stare at him, baring their teeth. He extends his knife with one hand while wrapping the other around his head, covering his eyes. He peers out and realizes they have gone back to ignoring him. For all he knows, snarling is how the crazies express polite interest. He wonders if he should try again.

"I'm Ray Young," he says. He points to his chest and adds, "My name is Ray."

Some of the Infected stop and stare at him.

"Ray," he says. "Young. My name."

He cringes under their gaze, feeling ridiculous. The Infected study him, their heads bobbing, as if looking for the ideal spot to sink their teeth. Just as quickly, they lose interest and resume their wandering, leaving him feeling even more puzzled. He decides to try an experiment.

He picks the scrawniest man within view and stands in front of him. The man makes a half hearted growl and licks his chops, prompting Ray to take a cautious step backward, his heart skipping a beat. Staring over Ray's shoulder, the man tries to go around, but Ray holds him in place by his shoulders. The Infected yelps, but does nothing.

"It's like I ain't even here," Ray says, feeling bolder.

The man stares over his shoulder with glazed eyes.

"You're not so bad now, are you?" Ray says, giving the man a little shove, angry he'd been terrified for nothing. The Infected blinks, disoriented by the sudden attack. Ray laughs harshly and pushes him again. "You're not scary at all. All bark and no bite!"

The Infected lurches backward, holding its hands up to defend its face. *He's afraid of me*, Ray realizes. The thought makes him feel stronger.

"You screwed things up, you know that?" He leans in, pushing the man again. "Totally screwed it up!" Again. "Screwed it up real good, you son of a bitch!"

Why? Why did this happen? Why did you do this?

Driven by sudden rage, Ray believes this man made the world end. Every death, every lost friend, every ounce of misery and fear, was all this man's doing. Blood pounding in his ears, he shoves the Infected to the ground, kicks him once, and spits on him.

He draws the knife from his belt, but the rage fades, leaving him feeling drained.

"I hate you," he says, his vision blurring with tears.

All around, the Infected howl and rush at him with hands splayed into claws.

Ray is jostled roughly as the hot, sweaty bodies press in all around, eyes gleaming with hate. His arms forced against his sides, he cannot use the knife to defend himself. An elbow slams into his chest. He can hardly breathe. The Infected snarl through their noses like wild animals. Ray pushes back at them, struggling to stay on his feet.

Someone screams shrilly, ending in a choking gurgle. The man he pushed is being stomped to a pulp by a ring of snarling Infected. One of them hunches over the man's neck, slurping at an arterial fountain of blood. The others stop kicking at his body and reach down to tear off pieces of clothing and flesh and shove them into their mouths.

Roaring a string of obscenities, Ray doubles his efforts to get away from the crowd now swarming toward the fallen body and groaning with pleasure as they tear it to shreds. They chew on pieces of muscle, cartilage, cotton, denim. A woman holds a hairy strip of scalp over her head like a trophy, screaming a long stream of gibberish before consuming it.

Ray lunges from the crowd, falls to his knees and pukes long and hard into the grass.

Oh God, it's me, he realizes. *It's me. It's my fault. I didn't want that to happen, but it did.*

He remembers the Infected on the bridge, reaching out to him as if pleading. The Infected at the wall, trying to tell him something, oblivious to the arc of the flamethrowers. The Infected slapping their hands against the window of the house where he fought Infection.

He did not beat the bug. The bug won, and has been using him all along.

I infected all of these people, he understands.

And now they belong to me.

COOL ROD

The Hellraisers sit on the sidewalk with their backs against the wall of a burned-out bookstore, sweating in M50 gas masks with their rifles held on their laps, taking five. Ash flutters to the ground like snow in Hell; their uniforms are grimy with the stuff. Waves of heat radiate down the street, making them feel like they are being cooked in a microwave. A battalion of heavy tanks got lost and tore through Georgetown two nights ago, shooting everything they saw with Biblical flashes of light, and set fire to the entire district. The fires fizzled out, but not before filling the air with a solid, eastward-moving wall of smoke, heat and ash to greet the Dragoons' advance, hence the M50s. Saving this city, it seems, requires the Army to destroy it one block at a time.

An M88 Hercules recovery vehicle fills the street with its massive bulk, its thousand-horsepower engine growling as its seventy tons maneuver into position to tow a disabled Stryker. His back against a brick wall, Rod studies his squad and realizes they are spent. He can see it in their worried, bloodshot eyes, barely visible through the dirty lenses covering the top half of their black Darth Vader facemasks. They have fought hard and accomplished incredible things.

But you can win only so many times before it feels like you're losing.

Rod closes his eyes and feels his mind drift in the dark, searching for a happy thought.

The monsters boil up from the shaft, their wings buzzing—

The surge of adrenaline jerks him from his doze. He sits panting, his body electrified, until he notices the skinny soldier standing over him.

"You all right, Sergeant?" the kid drawls.

Rod wags his head, trying to get rid of the overwhelming feeling of dread left behind by the dream. "What do you want, troop?"

"LT says he wants to see you. I'm to show you the way."

The squad watches him stand, collect his weapon and follow the kid into the maze of giant vehicles idling in the heat, like cattle watching one of their own being led away to the killing floor of the slaughterhouse.

Georgetown still smolders in the northwest. Charred bits of garbage and clothing flutter to the earth, some of it burning as it falls, touching the ground as cinders. Rod walks through air filled with smoke and vehicle exhaust that drifts but never leaves. He feels dried out, tired and grimy to the bone.

A helicopter drifts overhead, its rotors stirring the ash thick as a sandstorm.

Thank God for these masks. Just need the new air filters.

"Over here, Sergeant."

The kid leads Rod through one of the blasted-out windows of a shattered diner. Rod's boots crunch on broken plate glass. The restaurant was designed with a retro flavor, with lots of chrome and vinyl. Neon signage sits dark and unused along with a jukebox. It is a disorienting sight; parts of the diner look the same as the day the epidemic started. A chalkboard announces specials and dollar-ninety-nine giant milkshakes. The stools in front of the counter are empty and inviting. On the walls, framed posters of Marilyn Monroe and James Dean have been defaced with obscene graffiti by another unit passing through. Lieutenant Willie Sims sits at one of the red booths with Jared Kelley, the new platoon sergeant, who raises his hand in greeting.

"How are your men doing, Rod?" says Sims, his voice muffled by his mask.

"We're still here, sir," Rod answers, taking a seat opposite the officer. In the past, he usually reported his boys were itching for a good fight, in the hopes of getting something solid to do in the field. But not today. Today, he is hoping to avoid asking his squad to do anything even remotely dangerous.

The new platoon leader is a straw-haired, overgrown Iowan the Hellraisers call Techno Viking, a second lieutenant from the Third Armored Cav who recently earned his silver bar. Rod likes the gentle giant who is his new platoon leader. The man listens to the non-commissioned officers, cares about his troops, and has no crazy personal ambitions other than to keep as many of them alive for as long as possible.

Sims's standing order is to kill anything that moves, and let God sort it out. This is not crazy bloodlust, but simple survival. The fact is they are fighting a war of extermination.

It's called total war. In military speak, a war with an unlimited spectrum. In civilian terms, it means we fight without pause or quarter until the enemy is all dead or we are.

Rod taps his gas mask and adds, "Any word on the new filters, sir?"

"Negative," Sims tells him.

"We can't do our jobs if we can't breathe."

"I hear you, Rod. We'll just have to make do until we get back to base." Lines form around his eyes and Rod guesses he is smiling. "Not that I could tell the difference. I feel like I can't breathe in this mask at any time."

"You get used to it, sir," Rod tells him.

"That's what my platoon sergeant keeps saying," Sims says, glancing at Kelley.

"You should have been around when we were using the M40s," says Kelley, an old-timer like Rod. "Made you look like a giant insect. You could barely suck enough air to breathe. We had to run five K in one as part of the training. Half the guys puked into theirs."

Rod laughs, a muffled barking sound coming through the mask. Kelley has tons of stories like this; he's been in the Army since Jesus was a corporal.

Sims leans forward, planting his elbows on the table. It's time to get down to business.

"Sergeant," he says, "I've got a job for you and your men."

Rod closes his eyes for several seconds. "Sir, I am hoping there is another way to do what needs doing. My boys have zero fight left. They need a good rest."

"I know I've been leaning hard on you," Sims says. "And you've done an amazing job getting your squad this far without even a scratch. But you are the best I got and I need your men to give a little more today."

Orders are orders. Rod is a professional.

"What do you need?" he growls.

♦

It's a recon mission. The heavy smoke cover is preventing their birds from seeing what's happening on the ground. Captain Rhodes wants eyes all the way up to the Rock Creek and Potomac Parkway, the projected edge of the advance by the end of the week.

The engineers cleared the road as far as the first few blocks. Third Squad advances along the empty street in a wedge formation with the flamethrower on point and Rod and the RTO, the radio/telephone operator, not far behind.

Rod watches them with paternal fondness and high expectations that they survive and become everything he thinks they can be. He wants them to kick ass; he wants them to live. He has led a dozen like Specialist Sosa, the overconfident big kid; even more like PFC Arnold and PFC Tanner, naive eager beavers; a few overthinkers like Corporal Lynch, always concerned with *why* certain orders are being issued; and too few like Corporal Davis—quiet, reliable men who know how to get things done under extreme stress. They are just like every other squad of big, dumb kids he has led during his career as a professional soldier. But they are his.

He knows the boys are calling him Cool Rod behind his back. After the fight at the hotel when they lost Pierce and so many others, they eyed him with a level of respect bordering on reverence. It was perhaps the one good thing to come out of that day—conquering the reputation he earned in Germany. Since then, they have fought every day, and between Rod's leadership and a hell of a lot of plain luck, Third Squad has taken no casualties. Now they think he's a god.

Rod does not care what they think, as long as they follow his orders and cover their sectors.

Visibility remains poor because of the smoke. On the left, a construction site reveals itself, giant cranes soaring into the murk, scattered orange traffic cones, a sign that says WAYNE CONSTRUCTION. Someone spray painted SCHOOL IS OUT FOREVER on the side of a trailer. Sosa chuckles, shaking his head. Rod remembers they are in Foggy Bottom, somewhere on the George Washington University campus.

As they near the next intersection, a wall of vehicles emerges from the gloom. This is as far as the engineers cleared the road; from here on out they will be in the shit. Cars and vans and trucks sit parked, many of them at angles, some seemingly fused together. Their drivers fought for every inch before abandoning them in this endless apocalyptic parking lot.

Rod splits the squad. Fireteam A advances first and pauses at a defensible location, and then provides overwatch for Fireteam B's advance. Their gear clatters as they wade into the mass of vehicles.

On the left and right, high-rise apartments flank the street. Rod tilts his head back, but cannot see the tops of the buildings. The sun is just a yellowish splotch smeared on the sky like an infected wound. Frantic pounding draws his attention to one of the windows. A pale young woman stares down at him from a second floor window, slamming her fists against the glass.

Lynch follows his gaze and turns to glance at him. *Refugee, Sergeant?*

Rod shakes his head. *Nope, Infected.* He considers calling it in, and decides against it. The woman is no threat. In Kandahar, they reported continual random snatches of gunfire from the areas they patrolled each night. Sometimes a mortar burst or a machine gun. In DC, they call in foghorns, screams, distant roars, stray monsters, roving swarms of maniacs.

Sosa snickers and hisses at Arnold, "I think she likes you."

Huffing under the weight of his flamethrower, Arnold shakes his head and says nothing, too tired to respond.

Ahead, a car door slams: Tanner, on point, clearing a path for them. The column threads its ragged course between the vehicles. They step over abandoned luggage. Sosa spots a pack of cigarettes on the ground and pockets it. The woman continues to pound on the window over their heads. The sound multiplies.

Rod glances back and sees more people at other windows, banging on the glass with their fists. As they clear the van, he sees even more in the building on his left as well.

Lynch glances at him again and Rod gestures forward. *Keep moving. We'll be fine as soon as we pass these buildings.*

People stand at most of the windows now, fists pounding like war drums. The sound becomes a roar. Over the drumming, Rod hears the tinkle of broken glass on the sidewalk.

"Pick up the pace, Tanner," he calls out.

Glass shatters overhead.

"Heads up!" Davis shouts.

A dark shape flutters through the smoke and lands heavily on one of the vehicles to their left, which groans and sags under the impact. Arnold cries out in terror, the grimy lens on his facemask dotted with sprayed blood.

Another body flies through the air in a rain of broken glass.

Tanner shoots at it, misses. The rest of the squad opens fire.

"Cease fire!" Rod roars, furious at the lack of fire discipline.

The boys obey the order, panting in their masks.

The gunfire shattered many of the windows. Bodies fall like human missiles, limbs flailing. Glass rattles across the cars. The crash of the impacts multiplies until it is continuous. A car alarm wails its grating alarm. Others join in.

The boys begin firing again, but this is not combat. The onslaught is nothing they can fight.

It's an avalanche. We can either weather it or get out of the way.

"Off the street," Rod roars, pushing at Sosa's shoulder until the man obeys.

He pulls his fireteam to the right side of the street while Davis pulls his to the left. Rod peers through the grimy glass windows into the building's lobby. No threats there.

"What the fuck is this?" Tanner screams, gaping at the bodies falling onto the cars, shattering windshields and splattering across the crumpled metal. "WHAT THE FUCK IS THIS?"

Sosa grips the back of his neck and forces him to look away while Arnold and Lynch bend close, telling him he's okay, everything is going to be okay.

"It's not okay," Tanner sobs. "Nothing about this is fucking okay."

"Stay frosty, *vatos*," Rod tells them. "All that noise is going to attract attention."

He feels vibrations in the soles of his feet. The sensation migrates up his legs to his knees. Ash dances on the asphalt. He turns and pulls on the building's front doors. They're unlocked. He holds one open and waves the fireteam inside.

"Get in there! Move!"

The soldiers enter the lobby, half dragging the dazed Tanner, and deploy into firing positions. Rod turns and sees Davis directing his men into the burned-out building across the street. The downpour of bodies has stopped. An incredible roar reaches his ears, the crash and pop of crumpling metal and shattering glass. The traffic jam trembles, cars shifting by inches.

Inside, his fireteam tenses, ready to open fire at whatever is coming.

"Get down," he says.

They look at him.

"Eat dirt!" he roars.

The air fills with a long blast of foghorns.

The thunder grows in volume until they are certain the world is ending. The first juggernaut bounds across the roofs of the vehicles, crumpling their frames under the impact of seven tons of flying muscle and bone. The rest of the herd follows, tentacles flailing around their brontosaurus bodies, crashing over the cars and flattening the traffic jam into crushed metal.

As the last monster leaps across the wreckage, Rod lunges to his feet and rushes to the RTO, yanking the handle from the field radio and shouting, "Hellraisers, Hellraisers, this is Hellraisers 3. How copy?"

Jared Kelley's voice responds: *Hellraisers 3, this is Hellraisers 5, go ahead, over.*

"Large herd of Bravo Mikes inbound on your position from M Street. Estimated size forty, fifty adults, moving at gallop speed, over."

Rod waits during the long pause as Kelley processes the fact a stampede of about three hundred tons of monster is bearing down on his position at twenty-five miles an hour.

"Bravo Mike" is the current Army slang for "big motherfucker."

Solid copy, out.

"They'll be all right, won't they, Sergeant?" Sosa asks him.

"I don't know," Rod answers, feeling shaken and humbled. He has not heard of Bravo Mikes attacking the line en masse. As far as he knows, this is the first time it has ever happened.

If the bug has a lot more monsters to throw at us, the U.S. military may have just lost the initiative in this fight. We will stop being attackers, and start being defenders.

Gunfire erupts to the southeast. Fifty-cal machine guns pound in the distance, followed by the WHAM WHAM WHAM of bursting grenades. The sounds roll down the street, filling the air with white noise.

It's over quickly; the firing stops.

Rod counts his ducklings and, satisfied they're all present and in one piece, orders them back onto their feet. They pause at the doors, waving at Davis and the other fireteam across the street, all of them shifting their gaze to the giant metal pancake blanketing the road. Getting across the wreckage is going to be like walking across a field of knives.

Treading with painstaking slowness over the jagged edges, slicing their uniforms and legs, they work their way back to the part of the road that is cleared, and jog toward their lines.

Minutes later, the outline of a Bravo Mike emerges from the gloom, lying on its side and defecating in its death throes. The soldiers give it a wide berth and find themselves confronted by a looming hill of dying monsters, their tentacles still thrashing. They hear men screaming.

"Over here," Davis calls from the flank.

He shows them a way around. Further down the street, they find more of the monsters lying dead or dying among trampled human remains. Several sprawl broken across the front of the Hercules. Beyond, even more lie among Stryker vehicles flipped onto their sides or jammed against each other. One vehicle has been shoved half inside the front of a Thai restaurant.

Men scream for medics. Soldiers run everywhere. A military ambulance lurches to a halt and discharges stretcher bearers moving at a sprint.

"Make a hole! Make it wide!" several soldiers shout at them as they race past, carrying a screaming man with a shattered leg. Rod jumps aside and catches a glimpse of bone jutting from torn fatigues.

Rod watches them go and feels an unnatural rage take hold of him. *What a waste of the world's finest combat infantry.*

"What are your orders, Sergeant?" Davis asks him.

"Sergeant Rodman!" Lieutenant Sims calls. He and Kelley stand in front of the diner where they gave Rod his orders less than an hour ago.

Rod jogs over to the Lieutenant with his squad in tow.

"Good to see you and your men back in one piece, Sergeant," Kelley says.

"You too," Rod responds. He tells the boys to get inside the diner and wait for orders, then turns to Sims. "How bad is it, sir?"

"As bad as it looks. We're still sorting it out. We made out okay, but First Platoon lost some good men."

"The big bastards slammed into the Hercules," Kelley says. "It was like watching tomatoes thrown against a wall. The guys were cheering. Then the rest of the Bravo Mikes just ran right over it. Plowed straight into Comanche."

"The Captain appreciates your heads up on the radio," Sims says. "That was good work."

"Thank you, sir," Rod says impatiently. "What can we do to help here?"

"Nothing," Sims tells him. "They're taking us off the line."

"To hell with that," Rod snaps, feeling the rage surge inside him again. "We can help the docs get the wounded into their vehicles for evac."

"Rod, our people are in good hands," Kelley says. "We're getting a lot of help. We've got to let the docs do their job. We'd just be in the way."

Rod sets his jaw. "Then we'll go back out and finish our recon."

"We're done here, Rod," Sims says. "We've done everything we can. Now get your men ready to move. Got it?"

"Aieeyah, sir," Rod mutters.

He turns and gazes across the chaotic scene still playing out around them: the dead smeared across the asphalt like road kill, the wounded being loaded onto stretchers, the soldiers wandering around dazed and crying until their comrades come to comfort them.

What a waste.

"Fuck this," he hisses under his breath.

Every time we win back some of this city, we get a little closer to losing all of it.

♦

The men ran at him in their torn and bloodstained uniforms, faces flushed, eyes gleaming with fever. Rod and Lieutenant Pierce watched them come, rooted where they stood. They were talking about redeploying stateside when the base alert siren started to wail; the Lieutenant's friendly question still hung in the air: *What's the first thing you're going to do when you get home?* Gunfire popped across the base. Soldiers fought with each other everywhere in view; a few of them were shooting. At first, Rod thought a couple of soldiers had gone nuts—not uncommon after the trauma of the Screaming three days earlier—and were shooting up the base, while the unarmed soldiers were trying to stop them. Then he realized something was wrong; the unarmed mobs were attacking everyone. They were coming for *him*. Rod raised his shotgun and roared at the snarling pack to stop or he would fire on them. The crowd resolved into the faces of the men he led for a year in Afghanistan, glaring at him with open hatred. His shotgun sagged in his hands, still a part of him, but now forgotten. Seeing the men he kept alive on Baghdad's mean streets for a year, howling at him in a blind rage, shocked him to the bone. *These are my guys and they want to kill me*, he thought. *They're coming to kill me and I don't know what I did to deserve it.* Pierce was screaming, *What do we do? What do we do, Sergeant?* Rod stared back into the eyes of his men and thought, *I'm sorry for whatever I did.* Pierce's rifle fired with a metallic *crack* and puff of smoke, dropping one of the sprinting figures. *Shit*, he said. *I just shot somebody. They won't stop. They just keep coming. Rod? Rod?* As the pack closed the final yards, the man blew air out his cheeks, shouldered his weapon, and shot them down with cold efficiency.

Pierce is screaming at him, What did you do, Rod? What did you do? Rod looks down in horror at the smoking barrel of his weapon and says, Christ, it was me. I did it. I killed them all. It was me.

Rod lurches out of sleep, sitting up and snatching his shotgun. The soldier who was kicking the sole of his boot jumps back with a panicked yelp. Rod glares at him.

"Why'd you kick me?" he says, furiously rubbing sleep from his eyes.

"I wanted to wake you without getting my head torn off," the soldier tells him.

He nods and stands, gritting his teeth at a dozen minor aches. The soldier takes a second step back, still unsure of Rod's intentions. Just another kid, clean shaven and dressed in an ironed uniform with two chevrons on the shoulder, signifying his rank as corporal. Obviously a "person other than a grunt," or POG for short. He's so small he appears to be fifteen. *Hell, maybe he is.*

Rod can't get past the horror of the dream. The boys of his old outfit looked just as he remembered them in life. He finds it strange that this time, he was the one who shot down his platoon instead of Pierce. Strange, but not too troubling; his survivor's guilt often makes him feel like he is responsible for their deaths in some way. The real horror is he remembers the faces of the dead so well, while the mental image he has of his wife and children continues to fade over time. Sometimes he cannot remember his son's face.

He hawks a black gob of phlegm onto the ground. "Why'd you wake me up at all, Corporal?"

"Captain Rhodes wants to see you, Sergeant. I'm supposed to take you to her."

Christ, he thinks. *We just got here. Why are they sending us back out so soon?*

"All right," he says. He spits again and takes a swallow from his canteen. He can't get the burned charcoal taste of ash out of his mouth.

"Here, Sergeant. Try this."

The kid offers a packet of flavored powder, which Rod accepts with a nod. He pours a little into his canteen and swirls it around. Instant fruit drink. He take another swallow. *Better.*

"Outstanding," Rod says, spitting again. "Thanks for that."

"Close of business is in an hour, so you have time to get cleaned up, Sergeant," the kid says quietly, adding the hint: "Captain Rhodes is in Major Duncan's office."

Rod sighs loudly, suppressing another surge of rage. You'd think the rear echelon motherfuckers like Major Duncan would change their tune and try to be useful during the end of the world, but some things never change, even during the apocalypse. The infantry often looks down on all the POGs—everyone in the service believes they are part of an elite unit and winners of the big dick contest—but they don't hate them. Rod does not hate the kid standing in front of him, nor does he hate the mechanics who keep his Stryker operational, the guys who cut his hair, the cooks who load his plate in the chow line. What Rod does hate is officers who bust men returning from combat for dirty uniforms and stubble and flaring sideburns. Officers like Major Duncan, the chairborne ranger the boys call Major Dookie.

The minute Fifth Dragoons returned to the forward operating base, many of them headed for the mess hall. They hadn't eaten since the previous day, and they were starving. Major Duncan pulled them out of the chow line and told them to get cleaned up. Outside the banquet hall being used as a dining facility, Rod told his squad to hit the showers and put on some clean uniforms, and then go get something to eat if there was still time. This done, he walked into a nearby park, stretched out on the ground at the base of a tree, and fell fast asleep. *Screw it*, he thought just before he went under.

"You work for Major Duncan, Corporal?"

"That's right, Sergeant."

"Did he order you to tell me to get cleaned up before reporting to Captain Rhodes?"

The kid swallows hard. "No, Sergeant."

"Then mind your own business. Nobody likes a busybody, even if your intentions are good. Understand?"

"Yes, Sergeant," the kid answers, paling. "My bad, Sergeant."

Rod sighs, letting go of his anger. "What's your name, Corporal?"

"Sam Carlson, Sergeant. Corporal Sam Carlson."

"Well, then, drive on." Translation: *Carry on with your mission, soldier.*

The kid smiles at this and leads him through the park toward the massive building across the street—the old Harry S. Truman Building, former home of the Department of State—that now houses the headquarters staffs of Rod's regiment and several other large units operating in the area. Along the way, he sees the familiar base personalities hard at work and play: chairborne rangers and the cheesers who suck up to them sunning themselves in the park, sick call ninjas smoking outside the infirmary, gung-ho-mo-fo lieutenants drilling their platoons mercilessly toward perfection, treads terrorizing the enlisted just for the fun of it, tough Jane Waynes out jogging and the shit patrol cleaning latrines, almost everyone sandbagging to stretch out the long, hot day. Observing the dicked-up routine he's known for years, Rod feels something like fondness for it. It feels normal; it feels a little like home. If nothing else, he knows he is safe here, safe enough to sleep.

Some of the boys from Third Squad call to him as he passes. They're cleaned up and heading back to the mess hall to get their supper.

"What's on the menu at the DFAC tonight, *vatos*?" he says.

"I heard cigarette soup, Sergeant," Tanner tells him with a laugh, referring to onion soup.

"Sergeant, we got mail," Davis says. "I think there's some for you."

Rod waves the boys on and turns to Corporal Carlson.

"We got about an hour, right?"

"That's right, Sergeant."

"Then take me to wherever you've put my company clerk."

♦

Dear Rod,

We're all okay.

Rod smiles. Gabriela always starts her letters this way when he is deployed, and they have an immediate healing effect on him. This last letter is dated a week ago. While he'd rather it be dated today, he feels assured his wife and children are alive and safe.

He leafs through the handwritten pages hungrily, as if getting acquainted with a brand new book by his favorite author. He has a lot of reading to do. Pages and pages of life.

Back to the beginning. He picks a spot at random in the first letter, and reads:

We're too close to Columbus, and can't handle all the refugees and Infected coming south. Shooting kept the kids up all night. I doubt anyone on base slept at all. I sure didn't. Today we were told that we're evacuating to Fort Hood in Texas. The trip is going to take a while since we're going to avoid the major highways, so we're being told to bring as much food and water as we can carry, while we can only bring a few personal effects. I didn't know it would be so hard to walk away from our home with almost nothing, Rod. I was allowed to bring a photo album and some toys and books for the kids to keep them occupied during the trip. Sitting on the bus as I write this, everyone is quiet, scared. We're all diving off a really high diving board and we have no idea of what's down there, you know?

Rod stops there, sniffing and wiping his eyes. He feels restless, but fights it. He wants to read the entire stack of letters in a single glance, but wants to savor every word. As a compromise, he skips ahead to the middle of another letter.

Fort Hood is serving as a refugee camp for military families, and it's huge. I heard there are something like thirty thousand of us here, pulled together from bases all over the country, and still growing. It's even hotter than Georgia, if you can believe that. Hot and dry. We've been here six days and we're still not used to it. I spend half my time chasing the kids around, making them drink plenty of water. The barracks are all full, so we sleep on cots in a big tent they put up for us. You can imagine what that's like: babies crying all night long, and the cot murder on my back. There's a lot of resentment between the families that were already here, who have houses and call this place home, and the newcomers like me who showed up scared and with nothing. I'm not getting caught up in any of that nonsense; the Army is taking good care of us. We've got everything we need. Things could have turned out a heck of a lot worse. We're all being given work—help with the daycare, tend the garden, type up memos, empty the latrines, collect firewood, wipe the dust that gets into everything, and laundry, laundry and more laundry —all sorts of jobs. The list of chores is endless. I feel like we're in the Army too. We eat, sleep, shower, work together. Almost everything we have is government issue and we share everything. I miss our house and old life but in a way it's kind of fun, like being on a camping trip. We tell stories about our men and it really helps to know so many of these people are feeling the exact same things as I am every day. Last night, some of the wives put on a play that had us all laughing for the first time since the Screaming. The kids are also making the most of it, and my only regret is I did not bring more clothes for them; they are wearing out what little I could bring as fast as they can. Oh, by the way, some drill sergeants are teaching us to shoot. I have a 9-mm and fired it a few times at a target and the drill sergeant told me to tell you that I'm good enough to earn the Bolo Badge, whatever that is, so there! You'd better watch your ass, Cool Rod! Mustang Sally is packing heat.

Rod laughs. The Bolo Badge is slang for the marksmanship badge they give to soldiers who score at the lowest possible grade, and yet still pass, on the shooting range. In other words, Gabriela can't shoot for shit. He's proud of her. He always tried, and failed, to get her to learn how to use a handgun for home defense while he was away on deployments, but she always refused; she hates guns. *Times have certainly changed*, Rod thinks. *I pity the dumb Jody who comes sniffing around our kids. My wife the pacifist will turn the bastard into Swiss cheese.*

He skips ahead again.

So we've got a plague of bedbugs now. The kids all have rashes, and there's not enough cream to go around, so we're washing our bedding every day to try to get rid of the pesties. What else? Victor is walking now, and if you can believe it, he's learned some sign language. Another family taught me a few basic signs for milk, eat, drink and sleep, and I tried them on Victor over the past few weeks. Just when I was about to give up, he asked for milk! Which I give him from the boob, as with everything that's going on, I decided to keep nursing. I wasn't even sure what he was doing at first, but sure enough, he kept squeezing his little fist together, which is the sign for milk! He cries so much less because he can tell me what he wants even though he can't talk yet. Lilia isn't doing so great right now, though. She asks about you all the time, cries a ton, and has nightmares that make her wet the bed. She's back in diapers, and sleeps with me now at night. Kristina's going the other way, thriving like a weed. She's doing well in the camp school. The one thing that worries me is she's starting to hoard food a little—she eats as fast as she can, and then squirrels away little bits—raisins, Cheerios, whatever she can get—under her cot.

Rod's vision blurs with hot tears. His heart aches; he can barely stand it. He can't believe how much he misses them. Can't accept how much of them he is missing. They are growing up fast, without a father, in a refugee camp, while he fights this crazy war.

You're so far away, Rod. I hope you're safe and that these letters are finding their way to you somehow and giving you some comfort that I know you sorely need right now. I want you to know I'm proud of you, and so are our kids, and we will wait as long as it takes for you to come home. Do not worry about us, Rod. I will look after our little ones. You can keep us all safe by getting rid of these monsters plaguing our country. Fight hard for us, and win, so that you can come back to us by Christmas.

He buries his face in his hands and bawls while Corporal Carlson looks away, trying to give him some dignity. Rod is like every father in that he wants his children to have a better life than him. That is the reason he is here fighting. But he has a feeling that even if they win, his children will face a life of misery. The feeling haunts him.

And yet they are alive. His family is alive. This simple fact gives him all the hope he needs.

Rod is crying because he is happy.

"Corporal," he says, carefully folding the letters and pocketing them.

"Yes, Sergeant?"

"I think I will get cleaned up before seeing the Captain."

♦

Showered, shaved and wearing a clean uniform, Rod enters the big building through a cordon of military police armed with billy clubs and flamethrowers. The building has electricity, although it is rationed; only the security lights are on in the gloomy corridors, and its eight floors are accessible using the stairs only. The air is hot, humid and smells like dust and mold.

The corporal sneezes several times, and then they hit the stairs. Refreshed from the catnap, a quick shower and Gabriela's letters, Rod follows alertly, feeling almost human again, rifle slung over his shoulder and his helmet held in the crook of his arm.

The fourth floor is busy with officers and aides and civilians clacking away on typewriters. Rod grunts with appreciation at seeing civilians contributing to the war effort. Mostly, the Army has been keeping the refugees penned like sheep—under martial law, no less—a complete waste of resources, in his opinion. No wonder they end up rioting. These people are not weak. They survived this long, didn't they? They just don't have the training, organization and security of the military. Someone needs to get them organized and into the fight, like those militias he's been hearing so much about. The Maryland Regulars. The Philadelphia Free Militia. The New Liberty Army. The Virginia Field Army. The Allegany County Partisans.

Natural born killers, from what he heard. And most of them streaming toward Washington to join the final push to liberate the city from Wildfire.

The hot, crowded little office smells like flop sweat and burnt coffee. The window is open and the light is off. Major Duncan sits at his desk, sunlight gleaming on his bald head and glinting on his round wireframe glasses. Captain Rhodes, a gung ho Jane Wayne that Comanche picked up from Army Intelligence, stands behind him with Lieutenant Sims.

Rod knocks.

"Come in, Sergeant," Duncan says.

He halts two paces in front of the officers and presents a tired salute. "Sergeant Hector Rodriguez, reporting to the commanding officer as directed."

The officers return the salute, giving Rod a moment to notice the other two people in the room sitting against the wall in office chairs, one of them a hard case in SWAT armor, possibly National Security Agency but probably a mercenary, and the other a pale, blinking specimen in a wrinkled business suit who looks like he hasn't seen daylight in weeks.

A spook? Rod wonders, but decides against it. The second man is definitely not NSA or CIA. He looks scared. Like he'd rather be anywhere but here. Like a prisoner.

"At ease, Sergeant," Duncan tells him.

"Thank you, sir," he answers, assuming the at-ease drill stance.

"Sergeant, of course you know Lieutenant Sims and Captain Rhodes. This here is Dr. Travis Price, a scientist posted at Mount Weather Special Facility, and Captain Fielding."

"Captain?" Rod says, giving the man a onceover. "First Maniple? Flying Column Corp?"

Few of the private military contractors escaped the Sandbox in the first days of the epidemic. Their dissolving companies pulled some of them out and were forced to abandon the rest. The locals chewed them up until the Army absorbed the survivors on the way back to the States.

Like many soldiers, Rod does not like mercenaries.

"I'm not a merc," Fielding says. He does not elaborate.

"Captain Fielding is paramilitary," Duncan tries to explain.

Rod lifts his eyebrows at this, but says nothing. Something big is being planned; the excitement in the room is as palpable as the scientist's anxiety. They'll get around to explaining things to him if he stays quiet.

"Rod, we have a special job for you and your squad," Duncan says. "This one comes straight from the top, and it could end the war."

Rhodes and Sims grin at this.

"Yes, sir," Rod says, his heart pounding.

Duncan turns to Rhodes. "Go ahead, Captain."

"About twenty-four hours ago, we spotted a uniform mike who carries the Wildfire Agent, but is not showing symptoms," she explains. "About two hundred miles northwest of where we're standing. As far as we know, the man is unique. First, he spreads Wildfire through the air, and second, the Infected appear to be aware of and submissive to him. How and to what extent, we don't know. Dr. Price here feels if this man can be captured, the scientists may be able to isolate a pure sample of the Wildfire Agent. If they can do that, they might be able to make a vaccine, a weapon, even a cure. Is that about right, Dr. Price?"

"Yes," Dr. Price says, clearing his throat. "That's right."

Rod nods, considering what he's heard. *About* two hundred miles, Rhodes said. *As far as we know*, the man is unique. The Infected *appear* to be aware of and submissive to him. How and to what extent, *we don't know*. Dr. Price *feels* they *may* be able to isolate a pure sample of the Wildfire Agent. *If* they can do that, they *might* be able to make a vaccine.

With so many qualifiers, he thinks, *my situational awareness has not gained a single inch.*

"The mission," Rhodes adds, "is to locate, contact and recover this individual for the purpose of obtaining a biological sample. Preferably alive."

And then we save the world and everyone gets a pony. Shit, even the Big Green Machine doesn't believe in this saving Private Ryan bullshit. Otherwise, they'd put Special Forces on it. They'd throw everything they had at it. Not yank a single tired-out squad off the line and dump them in the middle of no man's land to find some guy who infects anyone who comes near him, and is now surrounded by, and appears to control, an untold number of Jodies.

After dealing with all that, we just have to convince the unidentified male to surrender to a bunch of soldiers so that scientists can experiment on him in a government lab.

I'm sure this guy, alone and scared shitless, will be just fine with that!

The idea is so crazy he has to resist the urge to laugh openly at it. The Army seems to have found a very creative way to get him killed.

Dr. Price glances at him, his eyes filled with anxiety.

Rod chides himself. *What did you expect—that it would be black and white? It's a chance, and nothing more. In this war of extermination, a chance is everything.*

Major Duncan appears to sense his hesitation. He clears his throat and says, "Sergeant, I know you and your men have been through a lot in this war, and that this mission offers a great deal of risk for uncertain gain. I want you to consider something. Do you know the biggest threat to our forces right now? The leading source of casualties among our fighting men?"

Rod realizes the question is not rhetorical, and scrambles to think up an honest answer. "The monsters," he says. "The hoppers in particular, sir."

"The correct answer is suicide, Sergeant. Our people are killing themselves in record numbers." The Major takes off his glasses and cleans them with a handkerchief. "Let me ask you another question. Do you know why we still pay our personnel in dollars, and accept those dollars at the PX for goods available at normalized prices?"

"The dollar's the national currency, sir."

The man puts his glasses back on and regards Rod with a grim smile. "Gold is the closest thing this country has to a national currency right now, Sergeant. Gold and things you can touch—food, water, toilet paper. Hell, bullets are so valuable these days *they* should be the currency. So why bother with paper money, when so many people in the country have given up on it? I'll tell you the answer this time, Sergeant. One word: Morale. The illusion everything is normal. We pay dollars to soldiers to clear ground and scavenge goods, which we then sell to these soldiers in return for their dollars. We do a lot of things like that to maintain the idea that things are still normal, right down to busting balls about dress and appearance. But we all know they're not normal. This war is taking a massive toll and it's only just started. The fact is, Sergeant Rodriguez, we are falling apart a little bit every day. Even as we continue to gain ground, we are losing the war for the hearts and minds of our own people."

Rod nods in understanding. He underestimated this officer. For a rear echelon type, Major Duncan appears to know what he is doing.

"Do you catch my meaning, Sergeant?" says the Major.

"I understand if there's any chance to win this fight, we have to take it, and my boys are up to whatever it takes to get the job done," Rod tells him. "You can count on it, sir."

"Aieeyah, Sergeant," Duncan says, while Rhodes and Sims nod.

Rod meant every word he said. *It's a long shot, but any shot at all is enough to make me a believer at this point. After all, there are no atheists in foxholes.*

ANNE

The bus trembles and bangs over potholes marring the sun-dappled road. Anne studies the forest and open fields through the windows with her detached telescopic sight. A white-tailed deer bounds through the distant growth, fleeing the metal monster with its grinding hum.

"They could be anywhere," Todd says, studying the same ground with the binoculars.

Anne wants to tell him to stay focused on the mission, which is to find and kill Ray Young before he can infect more innocent people. But she knows what Todd is going through.

"They can't be far from here," she says. "We've got to keep searching."

"Of course. It just feels a little hopeless with so much ground to cover."

"Stop the bus," she says. "I think I've got them."

"You're kidding," Todd says, leaning forward, trying to see what she sees. The forest on the right drops off in a steep slope, revealing a valley divided into farms covering the land like faded patches on an old quilt. "I don't see anything."

"There," she points as Marcus pulls onto the shoulder of the road.

"That smoke? That could be anything."

"Not smoke. Dust. You were saying?"

"Wow," Todd says with a grin.

She resists the urge to tousle his hair.

A dust cloud could mean a lot of things. It could mean cattle, but she knows the cattle herds are gone from the area, eaten by survivors and the Infected. It could mean a refugee camp, but if there were one there, she would have heard about it. It could mean a convoy of vehicles, but the dust is too concentrated and localized.

By process of elimination, it is most likely a massive crowd of people.

These are the Infected of Camp Defiance, migrating east. Assuming they are following Ray, then he should be there as well, like Moses leading his people to the Promised Land.

"If I see Erin, I'll let you know."

"Promise me you'll look," Todd says.

"Promise."

Marcus cranks the handle, opening the door. Anne touches his shoulder and hops down onto the road, rifle slung over her shoulder and her boots crunching stones.

"You need me to watch your back?" he asks her.

"No thanks, I'm good," she says. "I'll be back in a couple of hours."

"You be careful," he says, and she feels his desire.

"I will," she says, holding his gaze.

"We'll be here," Jean calls from back of the bus. "Like sitting ducks."

Marcus grins, shaking his head. Anne rolls her eyes at him before turning and marching into the woods. *The sooner I dump you in someone else's lap, Jean Byrd, the better. Maybe they'll understand how bad you had it during the epidemic.*

For now, I've got bigger fish to fry.

She disappears into the trees, still tingling from the way Marcus looked at her, excited and afraid at the idea of his feelings coming out into the open. *Stay focused.* The gloomy forest envelops her, thrusting her into a darker, far more dangerous world.

Shrugging her rifle into her hands, she jogs through the foliage. The air smells like moist earth and greenery. The air is cooler here under the shade of the forest canopy, but more humid, covering her in a slick sheen of sweat. Her cap feels wet against her forehead. After fifty yards, she crouches, sweeping the foliage with the barrel of her rifle.

She hears a nasal grunt. Something else responds with a series of glottal clicks. Anne knows of just one thing that uses this form of speech. *Hoppers.*

She finds the little band hunched in a circle around the carcass of a dead deer, tearing off pieces of meat and chewing, their little cheeks bulged with meat. The monsters look like the product of a bizarre genetic experiment—hairless, barrel chested, albino baboons with legs shaped like a cricket's. They wobble when they walk, as if struggling, little arms outstretched for balance. When they sight their prey, they are capable of multiple jumps high into the air. Their wide mouths are lined with rows of jagged teeth.

Once they land on their victim, they bite and wrap their legs to prevent him from tossing them away. They then stab him with the erect stinger between their legs. This stinger injects a parasite that grows to become another hopper.

Anne hates the hoppers nearly as much as she does the Demon, the fiercest monster of all. She hates these particular creatures because they are parasites. Bottom feeders. Cockroaches.

As much as she would love to gun them down, she cannot afford to draw any attention to herself. If she shoots, more might show up, not to mention a hundred thousand Infected she believes are marching across the valley just past the next rise.

She goes around the hoppers, staying as close to the ground as she can.

Anne has bigger fish to fry today.

♦

Ahead, sunlight glares through the trees. Soaked with sweat after her journey, Anne slows as she approaches the edge of the forest, pausing every few paces to study her surroundings. The last thing she needs is to leave the woods and run into a pack of Infected.

She emerges at the top of a treed hill overlooking a farmhouse and surrounding cornfields swarming with Infected moaning in the sunlight. The horde seems endless, trampling the fields into ruin, large enough to raise a dust cloud seen from miles away.

So this is where you went.

The sight is breathtaking. So many people. So many lives destroyed just so that a mindless organism could survive a little longer. Sarge would have described the scene as a *target rich environment*, but she is not here to kill Infected.

Anne is looking for Ray Young, the man who caused all this.

She takes a drink of water from her canteen, breathes deeply, and gets to work. Peering into the eyepiece of the telescopic scope mounted on her rifle, she studies the crowd.

This might take a very long time. Might as well conserve energy.

She detaches the scope from her rifle and puts her back against a large tree, scanning the shifting crowds while she eats a granola bar.

Erin?

The girl drifts among the Infected with her arms at her sides, wearing a lost expression.

At least Todd will get some closure.

A flicker of movement far behind her catches Anne's eye. A group of Infected swarm over each other, covered in blood, eating one of their own.

Something is moving on their left. She shifts her scope.

Ray Young jogs away from the Infected, looking terrified.

A smile flickers across Anne's lips.

Got you, you son of a bitch.

She pockets her unfinished snack and reattaches the telescopic sight. Ray stops at the farmhouse and sits on the steps.

He believes he is still human. The tragedy is he is another product of Infection, perhaps the worst of all—a lie, a creature of deception, a Trojan Horse.

An abomination that must be killed.

Time for the killing.

The first step: find a good firing position.

Anne studies the ground, looking for a prone firing position offering support as well as concealment. Making herself as still as possible is necessary for an accurate shot, but is also exhausting. As muscles tire, they move, producing wobble in the crosshairs.

She cannot find a prone firing position on the hill with a decent line of sight. Not even a kneeling position. Anne will have to take her shot at Ray while standing.

Placing her palm against the rough bark of a tree, she extends her thumb to form a V and rests the butt of the rifle there, placing the stock against the pocket of her right shoulder.

Stay right there, Ray.

She flicks the safety to the FIRE position, pulls the bolt back to release the catch, and chambers the first round from the magazine. Locked and loaced.

Ray stands and paces, then stops. Anne rests her cheek against the worn surface of the walnut rifle stock and aligns her eye with the scope. The blurry image comes into sharp focus as she adjusts the magnification. As the reticle clears, she centers the crosshairs on Ray's chest, making an adjustment to the ballistic cam to compensate for her higher elevation.

This done, she closes her eyes and relaxes. When she opens them, the crosshairs have dropped to her natural point of aim, a little left and below the target. If she were to correct and shoot now, her muscles would tense, which could throw off her aim. Anne adjusts her firing stance and repeats the exercise. When she opens her eyes, Ray is still in the crosshairs. Now she can shoot without any tension. The man looks as scared and confused as he did earlier. Rather than evoking any sympathy, this makes her hate him even more.

In a minute, all of your worries will be over, and you can go to sleep, you prick.

She inhales, exhales.

As she breathes out, she delays her next inhale, knowing she has about ten seconds of perfect stillness to shoot. Her finger touches the trigger.

Just a little more pressure, and BOOM.

Ray grins just before a man steps in front of her shot.

Anne pauses, blinking, and lowers the rifle.

Something strange is happening.

A large number of the Infected are streaming through the crowd, converging on her target.

RAY

Ray sits on the porch steps and watches the Infected bring him gifts. He thought about how hungry and thirsty he was, spoke the words aloud, and now here they come like robot servants, dumping pieces of jerky, cans of pasta in sauce, bottles of water, warm sodas, lint-covered Life Savers, sticks of gum, trail mix and a bag of multigrain tortilla chips crushed to the consistency of sand. He wishes for cigarettes, and soon has his choice of brands. He wishes for a stiff drink, and is given a metal flask with a bullet hole punched through the top and a little vodka in the bottom.

Saying the words is not even necessary. Picturing it in his mind, and willing it to happen, is enough to get what he wants.

Ray laughs. *I'm king of the motherfucking zombies.*

He takes a long snort from the flask and gasps, raising it in a toast.

"I drink to your health."

He is starting to process what is happening to him.

The bug turned me into a superweapon. It allowed me to live for this, and this only.

The Infected stand around, staring at him with their glazed, needy eyes. He pulls his STEELERS cap lower over his face and wolfs down his meal of junk food and water. Ray doesn't want them to see him crying.

He feels defiled. Diseased.

"Sorry," he mutters. "Sorry, sorry, sorry."

"Sorry" doesn't begin to cover it, bro.

He looks up at the Infected crowding around and feels something else, too. A fierce pride. They belong to him now. They are, in a sense, his children.

Is that me feeling this, or the bug?

A dark defiant thought seeps into his mind and replaces his guilt. *The whole world can go fuck itself and become infected, as long as I live.*

That was not the bug thinking. That was him. He lights a Winston and leans back on his elbows. *I'm alive, and there is only this, and that makes this good. Whatever it is.*

Breathe in, breathe out.

You do what you think is best, Ray.

"You got it."

He smokes in silence, listening to the Infected growl, and tries to reason things out.

I'm a carrier for the bug. I can't be around normal people. That's the bad news. The good news is I can control the crazies. Maybe even the monsters.

In any case, it's nice to finally feel safe. Like a sheep in wolf's clothing.

On the other hand, the idea of living among the mindless Infected for the rest of his life is enough to make him doubt his sanity. He may be a bit of a misanthrope, but he is a sociable misanthrope. He may have a history of abusing people, but he needs people to be happy.

Ray smiles at the gray faces. If he can control the Infected, he can make them all walk off the nearest cliff, or turn on each other. He could be a major weapon *against* Infection.

He might, in fact, be capable of saving the world using this power. What would that idea be worth to the right people?

Maybe nothing. Maybe they'll kill me on sight. Just in case. Just to make sure I can't ever hurt them. It's the safest move for them.

Maybe we could do a deal, though. I make all of the Infected climb the nearest mountain and jump off and die, and they find a way to cure me. It's the least they could do for the man who saved the world.

He chooses to believe in this possibility. It is, after all, his one hope. Like he already learned, anything can happen.

Ray stands and stretches. *That's it, then. I'll try to contact the government. But where is it?*

The Army is in Washington. That's where he must go.

The lump in his side buzzes with appreciation.

"I'm glad the idea pleases you."

The solution is simple enough: All he needs is a vehicle with a full tank of gas. Maybe a pickup. He'll take a bodyguard of Infected with him, and ditch the rest here.

I know just who I want for the job.

"Unit 12," he calls. "Get your lazy asses over here."

His old police unit streams through the crowd. He can hear the clatter of their gear and their glottal grunts. They stop in front of him in their black T-shirts and load-bearing vests bristling with shotgun shells, grinning wolfishly, their heads cocked and their fists clenched at their sides. Two of them still wear pistols on their hips. Ray laughs and whoops.

"Holy shit. Look what the cat dragged in."

Tyler Jones shoves through the milling horde, ridiculous red suspenders and all, the front of his gray work shirt black with dried blood.

"Good to see you alive, buddy," Ray says. "Even with the bug."

He holds out his hand, but Tyler ignores it.

"I guess Jonesy didn't make it. Sorry about that, bud. May he rest in peace."

Tyler grimaces, but says nothing.

"You boys," Ray tells them, "will be my Praetorians. I'll bet you dumb shits don't even know what a Praetorian is. Maybe you, Tyler, but that's about it."

It feels good to talk, and oddly, it doesn't bother him to have a one-sided conversation with a bunch of crazies. It's not quite like talking to himself; it's more like talking to a pet dog.

"Now let's see how good you people really are."

He pictures a pickup truck and a set of keys.

Now fetch. Howl if you find it.

His mental image of the truck expands to include several big-chested blondes giving it a soapy wash. He laughs.

If you see any hot models hanging around the truck, bring them to me as well.

He is amazed by how powerful he feels. Before he made it to the camp, all of the fight had been sucked out of him. Now he feels like a king, with a nation to do his bidding.

Not to rain on your parade bro, but again, is that you or the bug feeling so good?

He finds the thought depressing. How does one know if he has free will? How much free will can you have if you have a parasite craving to be spread?

Does it matter in the end?

The women drift out of the mob, their faces twisted into frightening imitations of smiles. Brunettes and blondes and redheads. Beautiful, all of them, even with their unkempt hair and gray skin and feverish eyes.

His heart races. He has not been with a woman since before the Screaming.

What is this? Is Infection manipulating me again?

Nope, you imagined this. The bug merely delivered.

It wants you to be happy.

Several Infected howl from the front yard. The owner of the house left a truck behind. The women continue to approach, softly hissing, their heads jerking.

Stop, Ray projects.

The woman hesitate, confused at his mixed signals. One of them lifts her T-shirt and squeezes her scratched breasts together, licking her chops while the others inch their way forward, their eyes gleaming like knives.

Oh God—

He knows of some guys who worked over Infected women. They raped the prettier ones before killing them. They justified it by saying the women didn't even know they were being raped.

Ray remembers saying he would never sink so low.

But if I'm doomed to have the crazies as company forever. . .

Get away from me!

The Unit 12 cops turn and roar at the other Infected, shoving at them. The women shriek and melt back into the crowd.

Ray takes off his cap and wipes sweat from his forehead.

Shit, that was close.

As if I'd ever do something like that.

A little angel and a little devil perched on his shoulders, arguing over his soul.

But they wanted it.

Bro, they just wanted it because you wanted them to want it.

I'M LONELY.

His discontent passes through the Infected like a wind, agitating them. The crowd parts like massive curtains made of people. A single figure approaches. It is a woman, walking slowly like a bride coming down the aisle to join her husband at the altar.

The Infected howl again in the distance.

"In a minute," Ray says absently, waiting.

Her hips sway as she walks. Like the other women, her hair is wild, but while this makes the others look like broken dolls, it just makes this woman more attractive. She is older now than he remembered; he hasn't seen her in years—not since that night she looked into his face and saw only spite. He heard she married a pharmacist and returned to Cashtown to buy a house and raise a family. If anything, the years have been kind to her. She has put on a few pounds, but in the right places. Her face has aged, but she is still beautiful. Her legs, even covered in tiny scratches and insect bites, are still shapely and muscular. When she smiles, she appears human.

She was the only woman he ever loved.

"Lola."

He takes a step forward just as the top of Tyler's head disappears in a spray of blood.

A second later, he hears the rolling rifle shot.

ANNE

You screwed that up, Anne tells herself.

Ray took a step to her right, forcing a last-second correction. Then one of the Infected stepped to the left to get out of Ray's way, putting his head squarely in her shot as the rifle boomed in her hands.

The bullet left the muzzle at a velocity of more than half a mile per second, shattering the Infected's skull as if it were a melon.

She relaxes for her next shot, searching for Ray through the objective lens of her scope. The M21 is a semiautomatic rifle with a twenty-round box magazine, giving her nineteen more shots at him before she has to reload.

The Infected scream and wave their arms over their heads. *Shoot me*, they seem to be saying. *Shoot me instead of him.*

Ray is still there, staring up at the hills in terror. The likelihood of him seeing her is virtually nil. She is too far away to detect with the naked eye where she is standing against the treeline, and her rifle is fitted with a suppressor that reduces visible muzzle flash.

Inhale, hold the exhale, shoot.

She fires again, and another Infected falls. They crowd around him now, swarming on top of each other. Her body shudders with disgust.

This is getting weird.

She fires again and again, dropping bodies until Ray's pale face comes into view. He gapes at the hill where she is positioned, his mouth open in a large *O*.

Got you, you little shit.

More Infected lunge in front of him, absorbing her bullet and falling into a pile of writhing bodies at his feet.

Shit, shit, shit.

The rifle bangs, recoiling against her shoulder. Her view shakes. She inhales, holds the exhale and fires again. The roar of the rifle shot rolls across the valley. Her left arm trembles with the effort of keeping the weapon still.

I let you go once.

Another body drops, revealing a glimpse of Ray screaming with fear.

Not again.

The rifle dry fires with an empty *click*.

"Mother," Anne hisses, releasing the empty magazine and slamming a fresh one into the magazine well. She resumes her firing stance, but lowers the rifle, blinking in disbelief.

The Infected have stopped shrieking and waving their arms. Working in eerie silence, they are building a living wall in front of the farmhouse. Thousands of people scramble with unnatural speed and precision on top of each other, creating a series of swaying human pyramids.

Anne fires at the Infected at the bottom of one of the pyramids and it collapses, spilling bodies into a massive, squirming pile.

"God damn it," she says between gritted teeth.

She fires into the mass, draining the second magazine. When the rifle dry fires again, she flings it onto the grass with a long, bloodcurdling howl of rage.

RAY

"I never hurt anyone," Ray shouts at Lola as the truck rockets down the country road. "Sure, I beat on a few guys back in the day, but I never shot at nobody. I never killed a man."

Lola sits next to him in the front seat like a blow up doll, staring straight ahead with her hands in her lap, wind ruffling her hair. Behind him, in the truck bed, his cops hang on as the vehicle roars around a bend, tires squealing.

"But someone sure as shit is trying to kill me!"

Ray swerves hard to narrowly miss slamming into an abandoned utility truck blocking the right lane. The road is filled with wrecks. *I'm going to end up wrapped around a telephone pole if I keep this up.* A glance in his rearview reveals nothing but his own dust.

Slow down. Think. Think it through, Ray.

No way that was a random thing. No single shooter shows up to take on a freaking Mongol horde of zombies. It was an assassination attempt, plain and simple.

Whoever it was, he was trying to kill me.

He finds this a truly terrifying idea.

Someone wants to kill me.

Nobody else in the whole world. Just me.

The question is why but the answer is not too hard to puzzle out.

Someone knows what you did to Camp Defiance. It's called karma, bro.

"I ain't a bad guy," Ray growls, and spits out the open window. "It wasn't my fault."

Slowing the truck a little more, Ray lights a Winston with his steel lighter and blows a stream of smoke against the dirty windshield.

Was his attacker military? He kind of doubts it. He has a hard time believing the military decided to chopper in a single sniper to kill him.

If they really wanted me that bad, they would drop a cruise missile on my head.

No, he decides. Not military. The sniper was probably some vigilante. Whoever it was, however, he is still good. Not Ray's idea of Tom Clancy good, but good nonetheless. And there is a good chance the shooter is still hunting him.

Then he laughs out loud. Next to him, Lola blinks rapidly.

"Maybe I'm not the one who should be scared."

Ray remembers he has thousands, maybe tens of thousands, of people who would give their lives to save his without a second thought.

It was the most amazing thing he'd ever seen. As he ran from the farmhouse to the truck hidden under the tarp in the front yard, thousands of the crazies were clambering on top of each other like some kind of massive *Guinness World Records* stunt. Tallest human pyramid. Great Wall of China, made from human beings.

All to put themselves between him and the sniper's next bullet. It was kind of humbling.

They pass a state police cruiser abandoned on the shoulder of the road. It gives him an idea.

"Whoever it is, if he keeps screwing with me, he's going to get a bad guy. Am I right or am I right?"

Lola nods almost imperceptibly.

He slows the truck to a halt and shouts through the open window, "Leon, Foley, get out."

Two of the cops vault over the side of the truck, landing hard on their boots. They approach the driver's side window and regard Ray with open mouths, breathing like hyenas.

After he gives them their orders, he pulls back onto the road with a laugh.

Whoever you are, you made a serious mistake to fuck with me.

A roadside sign tells him he is approaching Sugar Creek. He slows the truck to a crawl, navigating a six-car pileup splashed across the road. Then he is on the main drag, driving past an ice cream shop and convenience store.

A man stares at him as he passes, too far away for Ray to tell if he is infected. More people are on his left. One of them waves. Ray waves back.

"Stay cool back there, guys. We're going to bluff this out."

He tries not to think of the spores floating out the window to be sucked into the truck's back draft, maybe infecting these people.

Ahead, more people leave their homes and businesses to watch him approach, some of them waving. Again, he waves back.

"These people are a little nuts," he tells Lola, who surprises him by laughing out loud.

Something is definitely wrong with these folks.

Then it hits him. They're infected.

Infected teachers and waiters and cashiers and housewives pour onto the sidewalks, all waving at him like he is some kind of celebrity. Ray knows it's fake. Either the bug is manipulating him or he is subconsciously controlling the crazies, but ultimately it doesn't matter.

I like it.

Ray drives along at a snail's pace, waving back.

"Look, honey. They're waving at you."

Lola raises her hand and waves feebly, her face a blank, more robot than human.

He stops the truck in front of a tangled pile of vehicles blocking both lanes of the road. Concentrating, he summons work crews to push the wrecks out of the way. Dozens of people swarm across the knot of vehicles. Ray lights another Winston and watches them work.

"Nobody ever treated me special like this before, Lola. Hell, I don't want you to think I'm getting a big head or anything, but I could get used to it. I honestly could."

The last wreck is moved aside. Ray throws the transmission back into gear and nudges the gas.

"Thanks for the help, you guys."

The waves turn into Nazi salutes. A forest of hands pledging absolute obedience.

"That's right," he chuckles. He sees a man wearing a pistol in a shoulder holster and broadcasts, *Bring guns to my boys here. And bullets. Whatever you can dig up.*

Within minutes, several Infected run out of the mob, chasing after the truck to hand rifles and pistols to the boys of Unit 12.

"Thank you, my subjects. I shall never forget you."

Now we'll see if anyone wants to screw around with me.

He laughs and stomps on the gas, roaring out of town on squealing wheels. Lola smiles at the sound of his laughter. Ray notices an ant crawling across her face and brushes it off.

"That's right, honey. It's you and me against the world."

What now? Stick to the plan. Go to Washington. Contact the Army. Make a deal.

Ray glances at the fuel gauge. The rig still has half a tank of gas in it. It feels a bit underpowered when he steps on the gas, but it runs true. It will get him to the city, or at least close enough to walk.

He pats Lola's knee and smiles at her while he drives. He was hoping his return would offer him a second chance, and here she is in the flesh.

"We're going to fix you, honey. We're going to make things right as rain again."

If they want me to cooperate, they're going to have to cure you, too. That's the deal.

COOL ROD

The lumbering Chinook heaves into the air with thundering rotors as the Stryker rolls out of the sunny field and onto the road, picking up speed as it heads toward its objective. Twenty minutes later, the Stryker's gunner, standing behind the heavy machine gun, crouches inside the passenger compartment and says to Rod, "You should check out the birds."

Rod opens the hatch and peers outside. The old, cracked country road, flanked by trees and telephone poles and marked by centerlines faded to mere suggestion, is empty. The wind in his face smells like green, living things. The sky is deep blue here, free of the smoky haze hanging over Washington like a permanent shroud. It feels free. It feels like home.

A cloud of black birds swirls over the distant town visible miles down the road. They are crows, scavenging, fighting over an unprecedented feast.

Crows will eat just about anything, including dead meat if it is soft from rot.

Rod's smile fades.

"What's it mean, Sergeant?" says the gunner.

"It means stay frosty on the fifty," Rod tells him, closing the hatch over his head.

Soon they will enter Morgantown nice and quiet, the way they did in Afghanistan during their nighttime patrols. His team will wait for their guy, grab him, and bug out.

He blinks in the heat and the gloom of the Stryker and regards his team. The vehicle holds a squad of nine, but today they are carrying the scientist and the spook and reserving an empty seat for Typhoid Jody. He brought Fireteam B and loaded them up with heavy weaponry and ammunition: Sosa with a flamethrower, Arnold with a machine gun, Tanner with a rifle, and Lynch with a SAW. He also brought Davis with a rifle and field radio. Between the Stryker's machine gun and the squad, they have enough firepower to make short work of anything in their way.

The young faces look back at him expectantly, but he just nods, and they return the gesture with some relief. No news is good news. Sosa gives him a cocky grin that looks like lipstick on a pig. Rod's shooters have faith in him, but they think the mission is screwed up. The scientist is dripping with sweat that smells like fear. Next to him, Fielding sits looking sour, probably resenting being taken out of the safest place on the continent and thrown into the shit.

Don't worry, Captain, we'll get you back to your cushy desk job. We're all going to get through this in one piece.

Major Duncan and Captain Rhodes made a big deal out of the mission. They made it sound like the squad was being sent to save the world. It's a chance, yes, but a long shot to be sure. Saving the world apparently is not even important enough for the Army to give him some air support and keep eyes on the package. Someone *is* watching, possibly by satellite, but they're not being very giving with their information, and what they do share, by the time it filters to Rod's level, is old. In short, this is going to be like finding a needle in a haystack.

A haystack that is on fire and trying to kill you and eat your flesh. The mission is important, but I'm not going to allow it to become a slippery slope where good men end up taking big risks and dying for nothing. We're going to do this like we do everything—as professionals.

The Stryker gunner swears loudly.

The nauseating smell has already seeped into the rig, making the boys wince. They know it well from DC. The sweet, beefy, putrid stench of dead bodies left rotting in the sun. They will never get used to it. It's just a hint now, but getting stronger by the second.

Lynch produces a bottle of menthol vapor rub from one of his front cargo pockets and wipes some under his nose with a cotton swab, sniffing. He passes it on.

"Two minutes," the commander announces.

Rod opens the hatch as the Stryker rolls into the outskirts of Morgantown on its eight wheels. Behind him, the commander sweeps the fifty across the length of an old red brick apartment building, its windows filled with cheap air conditioners.

Past that, a shopping center, and beyond, main street.

The Stryker passes five bloated, grinning corpses hanging from a traffic light, three by their necks with their hands tied behind their backs, two by their ankles. The calling card of the militia groups. Signs on their chests bear the inscription: INFECTED.

The militia, it seems, are every bit as ruthless as he heard through the grapevine. Some of them wear necklaces made from monster teeth. Others cut off the Jodies' heads and mount them on spikes to mark human territory. Rod has seen what men can do in war and believes these people are insane. He's just glad they're on his side.

A seething carpet of crows bursts shrieking into the air at the Stryker's approach, revealing piles of blackened, half-eaten bodies covering the street. As the birds take to the air and settle in the hundreds on the rooftops, thick clouds of flies materialize over the dead.

Armageddon visited this place. The storefronts lining the town's main drag are shattered and burned out, the walls peppered with bullet holes, the sidewalks glittering with broken glass and empty shell casings. The asphalt is coated with a paste of hardening blood. Rod covers his mouth and waves away the hungry flies buzzing around his face. The stench is incredible and he resists the urge to vomit, reminding himself that decorated combat infantrymen do not hurl on over three million dollars' worth of taxpayer-funded military equipment. He thinks about Gabriela's letters, about baby Victor squeezing his fist, signing for milk, and smiles a little.

The commercial district turns into a residential area, its homes waiting patiently for their owners to return and take care of them. Thankfully, the flies disappear and the stench of death loses its bite the further they get from downtown. Beyond, they drive through another commercial district made of up a car dealership, strip mall, small office building and Walmart store.

Rod slaps his gloved hand against the metal skin of the Stryker. The driver rolls the rig to a stop in the Walmart parking lot about halfway between the junction of the nearby east-west roads and the big box store's front doors. He closes the hatch and tells the squad to dismount.

"It's time to earn our money, *vatos*," he says.

♦

Morgantown dominates the entrance to a long, lush, green valley flanked by tall, thickly treed hills. From the west, two roads lead into town from the valley. On the other side, three offer multiple routes to Washington. If Typhoid Jody is in a vehicle and heading to Washington from Camp Defiance, Rod is fairly certain he will come through this town. If the man is on foot, it is at least probable he will come through the area rather than hoof it over the hills, with their steep approaches that would challenge even the physically fit.

All assuming, of course, the man is going to Washington at all. The last information they received indicated Typhoid Jody was on the move and heading east, based on the assumption that the large crowd of Jodies is following him. They have nothing else to go on. They do not know whether the man is leading his little army on foot, or whether he's gotten a ride.

They are not completely without sight, however. Higher Command gave them two James Bond-grade systems normally issued to recon units. The first is a tripod-mounted surveillance sensor offering radar capability. The second is a package consisting of a long-range TV camera, laser range-finder and thermal imager. Using the first sensor, they can detect any moving object within twenty kilometers. Using the second, they can see what's coming, learn how far away it is, and identify thermal signature—that is, see if what is coming at them is human or not.

The boys fan out around the Stryker, establishing security. Deciding there are no threats in the area, Rod whistles, calling them together.

"Aieeyah," he says.

"Aieeyah, Sergeant," they grin.

Rod eyes them with pride, noting their high morale. "Everyone clear on what they're supposed to do?"

The soldiers nod.

"Then get to it, *vatos*," he tells them.

Sosa and Lynch help each other unload motorcycles tied to the sides of the rig, and perform a last-minute spot inspection. Satisfied, they throw satchels over their necks, kick start the bikes, and roar out of the parking lot, leaving behind the acrid smell of exhaust.

Their job is simple: drive five miles down the road and spray paint messages on billboards, the sides of buildings and on the road itself along their return telling Typhoid Jody that they are waiting for him in Morgantown.

Rod does not want a panicked civilian trying to evade his people. He does not have the resources for an extended car chase. Typhoid Jody is going to have to want to come to them. Rod believes he will, as long as they do not make him feel threatened.

Arnold and Tanner, meanwhile, have unloaded the tripods and are jogging with them toward the Walmart. Their job is also simple. They will scale the wall, deploy the gear on the roof facing west, and return, running the fiber-optic cable back to the Stryker. Arnold will stay on the roof to operate the sensors and provide overwatch with his machine gun.

His shooters know where to go and what to do. Now they wait. Rod pats the bulge in one of his front cargo pockets, where he keeps Gabriela's letters. He has read all of them except the last one, and they have gotten darker over time. His wife is depressed, and there is nothing he can do about it except do his duty and win so that maybe he can get a little R&R with them at Fort Hood.

Tonight, he will read the last letter, aware it may have to last him for a while.

"What do you want me to do?" the scientist asks him, breaking his reverie. "Can I help?"

Fielding stands with his back against a light pole and stares at the scientist with an amused expression, as if the entire mission is an experiment to test the other man's response to stress. Rod senses he is not here to help, but as a minder. The good doctor is something like a prisoner.

During the airlift and subsequent drive in the Stryker, Rod found himself warming to the scientist. Dr. Price does not fit the egghead stereotype. The man appears to be socially detached and unable to connect with other people, but he is not haughty or arrogant. Instead, he beamed with obvious excitement at the chance to elaborate on his theories, half of which involved molecular biology that went straight over Rod's head. Otherwise, the man's entire being appears to be focused on coping with his terror and trying to stay alive.

Fielding is another matter. The man is unreadable. He appears to have no value to the mission other than to keep an eye on Price. Rod wonders what orders the man has, and who gave them to him. He will have to treat Fielding as a wildcard—a potential threat to mission integrity.

"We're going to set up our roadblock right over there by the entrance to the parking lot," Rod tells Price. "Just you, me and Captain Fielding."

He gazes down the road past the Walmart and takes in the bowling alley, gas station and seedy shopping center with a bar. On the other side of the street, the small office building stands dark and derelict. He imagines Typhoid Jody's approach and tries to visualize the outcome. If the man is on foot, they may be here for a while. Typhoid Jody will see the signs and have miles to ditch his entourage if he agrees to give up. If he doesn't, the Hellraisers will have ample warning to jump in the Stryker and get the hell out of here.

If the man arrives in a vehicle, he will be alone. They'll detect his approach from miles away and have plenty of time to get ready even if he's driving fast. When he sees the roadblock, he will either stop to negotiate, or keep driving. If he agrees to surrender, they will slap a bio suit on him and put him in the Stryker. If he does not, or if he tries to run the roadblock, they are authorized to use deadly force. Because if he does not surrender, he is a threat and must be terminated.

Is that why Fielding is here? To make sure Typhoid Jody dies?

"How much time will we have?" Price asks him. "When the time comes, Fielding and I will have to get into our Racal suits."

"Anywhere from ten minutes, if he's driving fast, to hours, if he's on foot."

"We should be able to make that work. You should know that our suits are yellow, and the subject's suit is orange, so you will be able to tell us apart at a glance."

"Dr. Price, you might as well ring a dinner bell."

The scientist gapes at him. "What do you mean?"

"The Jodies make a beeline for bright colors like yellow. Red, orange, anything like that."

"Well," Price says.

"Not to worry. We should have enough spray paint for you and the Captain to use."

"Thank you."

Rod nods. "So why don't you tell me how much danger we're in here?"

"Danger?"

"From Typhoid Jody. What kind of a threat is he, exactly?"

"You want facts or speculation?"

"Facts, please."

"The man you call Typhoid Jody is an asymptomatic carrier of an airborne variant of the Wildfire Agent. But we know about as much about how he does it as we do about Wildfire itself—that is to say, not a whole hell of a lot."

Rod laughs at the man's candor. *As usual, facts appear to be in short supply.* "So we don't even know if our MOPP suits will offer any real protection."

"I wouldn't bank on it."

"Great," he says dryly. "What do we know for sure about how he controls the Infected?"

"Again, very little," Price tells him. "All we know is the human Infected are drawn to him. Thousands are following him. But we don't know otherwise what level of control he has. With hope, he won't have any Infected with him."

"That's what we're hoping," Rod agrees, and then adds, "Do you really think he could end the war?"

"I definitely think it's very possible."

Another ironclad, definite, absolute, solid maybe, Rod thinks, and sighs.

And yet the world has gotten so bad even *maybe* sounds like something worth fighting for. He thinks about Gabriela, and his kids, and wants to believe.

It's a slippery slope for sure, but Rod cannot help but begin to feel hope.

ANNE

Anne whistles, letting Marcus know she is approaching and to stand to arms. The large man stiffens and snatches up his rifle.

She emerges from the woods, sniper rifle slung across her back, the brim of her cap pulled down low, casting her face in shadow.

She is finding it difficult to process what she has just seen; she wonders how she is going to communicate it to the others. Visions of the Infected swarming over each other like termites to build human pyramids continue to haunt her, making her feel nauseous and frazzled.

Evan and Ramona sit cross-legged on the ground, eating cold ravioli from cans with chopsticks. Evan nods to her, stands and throws his can into the woods.

"Thank God," Jean says, her Chanel suit now wrinkled to the point of looking like a wrung out washcloth. She and Gary sit huddled on the ground, their backs against the side of the bus. She looks furious. "Now we can go to Camp Nightingale, right?"

Anne ignores her, scowling.

"Was he there?" Marcus asks her.

"He was there."

The Rangers gather around, waiting for her to explain.

"What's with her now?" Anne says, tilting her heard toward Jean.

"She said you were dead and we should leave," Ramona tells her with a sigh. "The minute you left, she started in on us."

"Sorry to disappoint her," Anne says. "Where's Todd?"

The others glance at each other.

"He split," Marcus tells her. "Headed the same way as you, in fact."

"And you didn't think to stop him?"

His face reddens. "I'm not the boss of him."

Anne cannot argue. It is her own logic come back to haunt her. *We are here by consent*, she always told them. *When we are fighting, you will do your job or face judgment from the rest of us. But when the fighting stops, nobody owns you. If you want to leave, then leave.*

She herself was willing to abandon them all to pursue Ray Young out of a sense of a higher purpose that trumped her loyalty to the team she created. Todd must feel he has a greater loyalty to obey, and Anne can guess what it is.

The dumb kid is going to get himself killed over an infected girl.

"He said to tell you he'll catch up with us east," Ramona says. "And that he's sorry. He said he had to go see for himself."

Anne points toward the trees and says, "On the other side of that hill, there are tens of thousands of the Infected. That's where Todd is going."

"All right," Marcus said. "You want us to track him?"

"When are we leaving?" Jean says. "That was the deal, right? We help you kill this guy, and then you'll take us to Nightingale."

"I didn't get him," Anne says.

"We came all the way out here for *nothing?*"

Gary shushes Jean, starting them hissing and spitting at each other like cats.

Marcus frowns in puzzlement. "What happened? Didn't have a clear shot?"

"The Infected were protecting him," Anne tells him, again struggling to find the words. In her mind, she fires at the human pyramid, which collapses into a massive pile of squirming arms and legs. "He can control them. Once I started shooting, they blocked my shot."

"Control" hardly covers it. Ray has his own personal army.

His relationship with the Infected appears to be symbiotic, but what are the Infected getting out of it? Maybe nothing. Maybe only Infection itself is. If that's true, who is controlling whom?

The answer does not matter to her. Either way, Ray must pay for what he did to more than a hundred thousand people at Camp Defiance. Either way, he must be stopped before he reaches Washington.

"I'll need your help next time," Anne tells her team.

"Come on," says Jean. "You need to stop rolling the dice with our lives."

"What about the risk of exposure?" Evan wonders. "I thought the idea was we would provide security for you, and you would kill him with the sniper rifle."

"I need you to shoot at any Infected between me and him. Just get close enough for suppressing fire. Then throw everything you've got. Think you can do that?"

The others nod. Of course they can. And if that does not work, they can always wear the gas masks they keep stowed in their kit, and pray it is enough to keep from becoming infected.

"Come on," Anne tells them. "We've got to get back on the road."

"Do you know where he's going?"

"East," Anne says. "He took off in a white truck. We're on the only road through this part of the valley. If he hasn't passed by here, then he's still going east."

"What about Todd?" Ramona says. "You said he was in danger."

Anne groans. Her shooting stirred up the hornet's nest, and Todd is walking right into it. The whole thing infuriates her. *What does he think he is going to accomplish?*

She feels a wave of grief wash over her mind, leaving behind despair so deep it sucks the air from her lungs. She worked hard to master her emotions, rejecting love and attachment and embracing the strength of perpetual hatred.

The truth, however, is she loves Todd as if he were her own son.

"Are you all right?" Ramona asks her.

"I don't know yet," she says in a small voice.

"God, she's falling apart now," Jean says. She stands near them now, shrugging out of Gary's grip. "Look at her. This is who you're taking orders from."

Marcus turns and glares at her. "Shut the hell up, lady."

"Or what?" Jean laughs. "What else can you do to me? I'm practically a hostage."

"Nobody's holding you here," he tells her. "You can go anytime you want."

"I'd be happy to, Marcus, if I had food, weapons, a car and some directions, but I don't. Anything I had, I left behind in Hopedale. So I guess that makes me your hostage."

Marcus grunts. He doesn't care; he's not listening to her.

"Todd," Anne whispers.

She has a vision of cracks appearing in a dam.

Beyond, infinite darkness, seeping in.

"Jean, come back to the bus with me," Gary says.

"You should be supporting me," Jean hisses at him. "We need to go to Camp Nightingale now. We're out in the open. We're all going to die out here if we don't get somewhere safe."

"Anne knows what she's doing," Evan says. "We've survived out here for weeks together."

"Look at her," Jean shrieks. "Can't you see? She's lost it!"

"Anne?" Marcus says, looking at her worriedly.

Evan shrugs. "Hey, I have no problem going to Nightingale."

"Maybe she just needs a rest," Ramona suggests.

"Someone else needs to take charge and make a plan," Jean says. "I nominate Evan."

Anne blinks and the vision of the dam fades. "We need to get back on the road."

"I don't know, Anne," Evan says. "Maybe we should talk about it."

"Just drop us off at the other camp," Jean pleads. "Then you can go do whatever you want."

"Anne, do you have a plan?" Marcus says, frowning.

"There is no plan, you fucking moron," Jean screams, pointing at Anne. "This woman is crazy and she's going to get all of us killed if you don't listen to me!"

"That's enough," Anne says quietly, her eyes narrowing.

"Don't look at me like that," Jean tells her. "You don't get to look down on me like I haven't suffered as much as you. I'm sick of your act. You're not half as badass as you think you are with your guns and scars. You have no idea what we went through in that art gallery. What we had to do to survive. But even then we were better off than we are here. We had everything we needed, and we could make our own decisions without someone telling us what to do."

"Jean, please," Gary pleads.

"I'm not *finished*. We had everything we needed. Then you found us. You told us we would be safe at Defiance. You made a promise to us, and we believed you. Now you're off chasing some guy on a bizarre hunch and we have to get dragged along, regardless of the fact that every hour we spend out in the open we are in incredible danger. And you refuse to take us to the one place within fifty miles that's safe. You lied to us! You don't get to make decisions for us anymore!"

Anne unholsters one of her guns and taps it against her thigh.

It's time for you to shut up.

"And you don't fucking scare me either," Jean tells her. "What are you going to do now? Kill me in front of all these witnesses?"

Anne raises her pistol and fires, the gun discharging with a deafening report, the recoil vibrating down her arm.

The empty shell casing flickers in her peripheral vision. The slug punched a hole through Jean's throat. The woman stumbles away as if seeking a private place to bleed.

The others watch in horror as she bends over, hands on her knees, struggling to breathe as blood pours from the smoking wound onto the road.

She looks at Anne with wide, disbelieving eyes before falling first to her knees, then onto her side, where she curls into a ball, air bubbles gurgling from her torn throat, her face turning blue. Her body shivers briefly before stiffening.

"Jesus, Anne," Evan says, backing away.

She shifts her aim to Gary. "This is the new reality," she tells him. "Do you understand what the new reality is?"

Gary stares at Jean's body, wearing a pained expression. "Better than anyone," he says quietly.

"Are you on the bus, or off the bus?"

He takes his time answering. The rest of the team stares at the body in shock.

"I'd like to come with you," he whispers.

"Let's go," Anne tells her team, holstering the gun. "Todd will have to take care of himself, like a man. As for us, we're leaving right now."

TODD

Todd kneels in the tall grass on a hill overlooking the farmhouse and the thousands of Infected swarming the fields surrounding it. Hundreds trickle east but most mill around aimlessly, their heads bobbing in search of prey. The humid air fills with their neverending chorus of barks and moans, competing with the loud buzzing of insects and the laughter of birds in the trees.

Todd scans the Infected with the binoculars, feeling queasy. He has never seen so many of them before in one place. Rage and despair is written on their faces. The magnification makes them feel too close for comfort, and he wonders how Anne does it every day, looking at them through her rifle's telescopic sight. He glances over his shoulder as warning shivers slither down his spine, and it is just as unsettling to see nothing there than something. For months, he has survived because good people watched his back. Only the best can travel alone out here among the Infected. Only the best and the lucky. And sooner or later, everyone's luck runs out.

The sun beats mercilessly against his head; his old SWAT hat is soaked through with sweat. He can feel the back of his neck slowly frying in the light. Lowering the binoculars, he plunges his arm into his rucksack until his hand grips the familiar shape of his bottle of suntan lotion. He slathers it onto his neck and arms, then takes a sip from his water bottle.

Hours have passed, and still he has not found her. He will search for as long as it takes, one gray snarling face at a time. It does not matter to him that he has no idea what he will do if he does find her. For now, only the search itself matters.

He takes a break to stretch and rub his tired arms, and then returns to his task. Several Infected have broken into the chicken coop and are chasing the chickens, which flee into the swarm to be torn apart and eaten raw.

For the next hour, that is about as exciting as it gets.

His mind wanders while he works. He remembers the fight on the bridge, him and Ray running to one of the buses parked across the road to form barricades, the men inside screaming and shooting and dying, the hordes of Pittsburgh rushing at them in a massive, snarling flood. The bridge exploded in a blinding flash of light, flinging Todd through the air like a doll to land tumbling across the cratered asphalt. The juggernaut galloped straight at him, its rigid tentacles trumpeting its war song. Ray tried to pull him away and, seeing Todd refuse, stood with him, emptying his pistols into the thing before it crashed through the bridge and fell roaring into the torrents below.

I don't care what he is. I forgive him for what he's done. I'm not going to help Anne kill him. I have to get away from her. If I don't I'll end up just like her, filled with hate.

Todd gazes at the pathetic horde in the valley below and realizes he does not even hate them anymore either. When Anne sees the Infected, she sees only the monster controlling them like meat puppets. When Todd sees them, he sees people enslaved to a monster. It's hard to hate slaves.

He remembers coming home from the bridge in the dark, his face nuzzled in Anne's lap. How safe that felt even as the hoofed thing rammed the vehicle. They stepped off the bus, ringed by leering faces and clapping hands. Erin came and cupped his face in her hands and kissed him. She called him an amazing boy. She stuck with him even though he always returned to the road, maybe never to return. She said she loved him.

Remembering these things, Todd's heart feels like it is sinking. He was stupid to run away and live on the road with the Rangers. Erin offered him everything he wanted. She did love him; now that she is gone, he believes that.

We only realize what we have after it's gone, he understands now. It is a grownup thought, something Paul might have said.

He should have stayed with Erin and built a life together with her, no matter how brief it might have lasted. Happiness is a rare thing these days, and he'd squandered it.

That is what Paul's smile was trying to teach me, he realizes. *That home, as they say, is where the heart is.* He can picture the Reverend saying, *I used up all my chances, boy. You got your whole life ahead of you. This, too, is a gift.*

Todd lowers the binoculars, aware of a vaguely ominous sound. It is the crisp, aerosol roar of a distant jet, growing in volume until it becomes thunder. When he cannot hear anything else, putting him at risk from Infected coming up behind him, he snatches his rifle and glares at the woods, the blank blue sky. The sound crawls along his nerves until he starts to panic.

A formation of four planes appears, roaring high overhead.

The noise fades as the planes stream into the distance. Todd watches them go with pride—after all that's happened, the Air Force is still holding it together—then resumes his search.

Minutes later, the roar builds again, cascading over the hills.

You guys lost or something?

The planes scream into the valley, flying low like gray birds of prey. Todd flinches with alarm as their searing roar crescendos.

One by one, the planes release bombs that plummet toward the ground, whistling as they fall.

WOOOOOOOOO

Just above the ground, the payloads burst in flashes of light, replaced by clouds of black objects hurtling toward the earth.

Holy shit—

The ground sparkles.

Cluster bomb, he realizes as the air pressure around him changes.

Thousands of explosions ripple across the valley floor with an ear-splitting crackling, devouring it in seconds. The bodies of the Infected fly apart, trees explode into splinters, the farmhouse and outlying buildings dissolve in bursts of flaming matchsticks. The puffs of smoke congeal, roiling into seething waves of smoke and dust.

The planes split up, veering left and right, and circle the valley.

Todd looks down at the scene of devastation in disbelief. The ground is still trembling. Body parts begin to rain around him.

Holy shit. He dives under the nearest tree for cover.

The ground stops shaking but arms and legs, hands and feet, grinning faces and bits of bone continue to plummet onto the hill, shredded and smoking, along with flaming bits of wood and chunks of hot chewed metal.

"Cut it out!" Todd screams, unable to control his fear and revulsion. "Stop!"

The roar fills the world.

The planes return, flying low to the ground, and strafe the valley floor with Gatling cannons spraying dozens of rounds per second. Todd can feel the electric buzz of the cannons in his forehead, deep in his chest, in his teeth.

Something crashes into the branches over his head. A human head, shattered to a pulp, flops smoking at his feet followed by a rain of leaves.

"Sons of bitches," Todd says, feeling rage unlike anything he has ever felt, so strong he wonders if he is infected. His cannot hear himself scream. "Motherfuckers!"

The boy runs into the grisly downpour, howling at the sky, and stumbles over a naked, mangled torso. Falling to his knees, he grips a handful of earth and flings it at the departing planes, already just dwindling dots in the sky.

"You didn't have to do this!"

His rage spent, he looks at the smoke and dust drifting across the wasteland of the valley floor, his ears ringing. He presses his forehead into the grass and moans.

"You didn't have to do this," he whispers into the dirt.

All I wanted to do was say goodbye to her.

Alarm bells ring in his brain, warning him to get out of here. The noise will attract every monster within miles. The sun is falling, and he will be caught out in the open in the dark. But he does not move.

I need a little time with this, okay?

It's not fair, it's not fair, it's not fair.

IT'S NOT FAIR.

He raises his head and gazes down at the scene of Biblical devastation. A massive wall of smoke rises above the valley, reminding him of Pittsburgh. Piles of the dead lay half buried in dirt. Nothing moves. The land has been scrubbed of life.

He stares at it for over an hour, watching the shadows claim the land.

The air fills with a rhythmic shrieking sound, growing louder. Snapping out of his reverie, Todd jumps to his feet and runs to the tree where he left his rucksack and carbine. Shouldering the weapon, he flicks the selector lever from SAFE to BURST, and waits.

The high-pitched rhythm is too regular to be a monster. It's a machine, close enough for him to hear the roar of the engine. The shriek sounds like tank treads.

The beat-up armored vehicle crashes through the foliage fifty yards away on the hill, chugging puffs of exhaust, and grinds to a halt at the top of the slope, where it stands idling. Whoever is inside it is apparently stunned by the scenes of devastation in the valley below.

The sun is bleeding into the horizon. Todd could get away from these people easily if he wanted. He doubts they have spotted him. All he has to do is back into the trees.

He needs people, however. Shouldering his rifle, he steps away from the tree, hands raised in the air, and approaches the vehicle.

I hope these guys are friendly.

As he closes the distance, he spies the legend on the turret through the humid, smoky air: BOOM STICK.

Despite the horrors he has seen, Todd laughs. It is the laugh of the Infected, a sound one cannot easily distinguish from crying.

A dismembered leg falls from the sky and thuds onto the turret with a final arterial spray of blood, bouncing into the grass. Two bearded men and two women, dressed in motley uniforms, scurry from the back of the tank, glaring at him over the barrels of their rifles.

Todd keeps his hands in the air, his heart racing.

"I don't know you," he says, starting to worry.

The Bradley's hatches open and Sarge and Steve emerge.

"Oh my God," Todd says, swallowing hard.

"Hey Kid," Sarge says, using his old nickname. "Where you been?"

Todd barely notices them, his attention focused on the beautiful woman striding toward him in a black T-shirt and baggy camo pants, a police-issue pistol slung low on her hip.

"Wendy," Todd says, bursting into tears.

She breaks into a run and launches herself into his embrace.

"Hi, Todd," she says, grinning.

DR. PRICE

Travis tells Fielding to take off his watch and any jewelry and badges. To remove anything sharp in his pockets, such as pens or keys.

"Step into the coveralls," Travis instructs him, finding a certain satisfaction in giving the man orders. "Now get the boots on. After that, we'll put on the facepiece."

Fielding pulls on the suit, flexing his hands inside the attached black gloves, while Travis closes the zipper running diagonally from his hip to his throat. Using the coupler, he connects the air hose to an appendage jutting from the mouth of the faceplate.

"Now we'll put the air tank on your back using the harness," Travis murmurs, concentrating on his work. Fielding's breath hisses rhythmically through the respirator. "How does it feel?"

"Hot as hell, but it works," Fielding says.

"Now you even sound like Darth Vader."

"Very funny, Doc."

"We put the suits on using the buddy system. I check your suit for rips and you check mine. The idea here is to achieve an isolated atmosphere within the suit. If one germ gets in, you're toast. Especially check for holes along the seams."

"Got it," says Fielding.

The soldiers are returning on their motorcycles. Travis watches as Sergeant Rodriguez walks away from the Stryker to greet them. He likes the sergeant, wishes Fielding were a little more like him. It's too bad they are enemies.

"Hope they brought the spray paint back so we can cover up this yellow," Travis says.

"I would keep it," Fielding tells him. "The yellow makes us look friendly. We want the guy not to see us as a threat, so he doesn't get spooked or decide to attack us."

Travis unzips the man's coverall and then removes the facepiece and harness. "Do you really think he might attack us?"

"We won't know what he's going to do, Doc. Hell, we don't even know what he is. He may walk like a duck and quack like a duck, but he's not a duck. For all we know, Wildfire is guiding his every thought and action. He might not even be able to tell the difference."

"What are we going to do if he does attack us?"

Fielding sneers. "Doc, leave that to me. Just pray real hard he shows up."

"I'll bet you wish he doesn't," Travis says, sneering back at him. "You're the kind of guy who'd be perfectly happy to see the world end, as long as you get to shoot me with a big told-you-so smile on your face."

Fielding laughs. "You know me too well, Doc."

"Why do you hate me so much?"

The man steps out of the coveralls, stretches and punches him in the solar plexus, knocking the air out of him. Travis doubles over, hugging his ribs and gasping.

"Her name was Sandra Forbes, you piece of shit. The woman you got kicked off the helicopter so you could save the world. She was a travel planner. She worked for the chief of staff."

Travis comes at him, fueled by sudden rage. He throws an awkward punch that connects with Fielding's chin. The response is quick, vicious. Travis wakes up on the ground lying on his back.

"Breathe, Doc. Breathe."

He rolls onto his side, coughing and gasping. "I never would have guessed she was a friend of yours," he hisses. "I didn't see you rushing to give up your seat."

"So it's my job to rescue everyone?" Fielding says, standing over him, his hands clenched as if itching to hit him again. "And if I don't, their death is my fault, is that it?"

"What's wrong with wanting to stay alive?"

"You're a freak, Doc. You don't know shit about honor or principle. If it were me, I would give up my life without a second thought if it meant ending the epidemic. You? You want to save the world, but only if others take the risks and do the dying. You're a coward."

"Hey!" Sergeant Rodriguez shouts, jogging toward them. "What's going on here?"

"Just some personal business, Sergeant."

"Captain, you are fucking up my op. Take a hike."

"Fine, you can babysit him. He's all yours." He leans and whispers to Travis, "I really do hope I get to kill you, Doc. It almost makes me wish your guy never shows."

Fielding walks away as Rod approaches and kneels next to Travis. "You all right, Dr. Price?"

"Yes, I think so," Travis says, rolling onto his back and looking up at the blue sky, enjoying the simple act of breathing. "Thanks for that."

"You mind telling me what that was all about?"

"It's complicated."

"Your body is your worst enemy," the soldier tells him. "Your breathing, your vision."

"Tell me about it."

Rodriguez laughs harshly. "You don't know the half of it. When the Infected come screaming at you, it's not them you got to worry about the most, it's your body's response to stress. That's their greatest advantage over us; the Infected, well, they don't know fear. Even now, when I see one of them running at me, I get a jolt to my system, like an electric shock. But then the training takes over and I do what needs doing."

"What are you trying to tell me?"

"The point I'm making is a fistfight is not so different. The body reacts the same to fear. Maybe you'll remember that the next time you decide to take a swing at the Captain. You could never beat him fair and square. The guy has military training from somewhere, and you'd never get past it. He knows how to take punishment, and he knows how to dish it out. He let you off easy with what you got. So don't antagonize the guy, okay? We happen to need you."

"Thank you, Sergeant. I'll remember that."

Travis watches Fielding walk toward the Stryker, and spits into the dust.

You're making a big mistake underestimating me. When I took that seat on the plane, that wasn't me being a coward. That was me fighting to survive. You have no idea what I will do.

I just fight differently, that's all.

RAY

As the sun melts into the horizon, Ray veers off the main road, taking a short detour north to a town called Milford. The idea was to drive into the night to gain more distance from the shooter on his tail, but he is exhausted. And he once had a friend who lived in Milford; he knows the ground, how to get in and out. Lola does not seem to mind.

"Tonight, you're going to sleep in a real bed, honey."

She says nothing.

"I know I'll appreciate it. I'm dog tired."

After everything he has been through, he feels like he could sleep for a week.

The truck passes an overgrown cemetery on the left, a white delivery van with its back doors wide open, driveways, mailboxes and a sign reading, SCHOOL BUS STOP AHEAD.

"Man, I haven't been here in years."

Dozens of corpses lay clumped around a roadblock of two trucks blocking both lanes; traffic cones direct him toward an abandoned checkpoint on the side of the road. Ray drives over the bodies, breathing through his mouth.

It is not hard for him to figure out what happened. The townsfolk set up the roadblock to keep people out. Like many roadblocks set up in the first days of the epidemic, however, it was overrun from within. On the right, a sign is riddled with bullet holes: KOCH FUNERAL HOME.

Moments later, Ray is in downtown Milford, consisting of an IGA, hardware store, tavern he knows well from back in the day, convenience store and post office. He spots a house where an old chemist ran a meth lab; someone spray painted VAYA CON DIOS across the front door. Further on, an American flag hangs limply from the top of a white pole set in front of the town firehouse.

The Infected creep from their hiding places, grimacing and reaching out to him as the truck rolls past. He is too tired to play around with them this time. He is too tired, and they are too goddamn pitiful.

We'll make this right, he broadcasts.

The Infected wail in response, an eerie cry that sounds like laughter.

♦

Ray makes a right turn at a stop sign and drives ahead to a small, shabby motel where he remembers two prostitutes who worked 2A. The sign out front says NO VACANCY, which makes him chuckle. He stops the truck in front of the manager's office and kills the engine.

The Unit 12 cops jump down, holding the weapons they were given by the mob back in Sugar Creek.

Clear the motel, he orders. The last thing he needs is another vigilante or some gun toting survivalist taking a shot at him. Then he tells the other Infected in the area to bring food and water. First aid kit. And candles and a razor. Oh, and some booze.

Then arm yourselves. All of you. Guns, knives, whatever you got.

"Come on, honey. Let's find us a room."

Ray enters the office and emerges with a handful of keys.

"Second floor has a nice view of the woods out back."

He finds a blackened corpse in the first room, its leaking, congealed body fluids fusing it to the bed next to the night table, which is covered in empty pill bottles and a jug of wine. He backpedals and slams the door.

After skipping the next two doors, he tries the third.

"Now, this is more like it."

The air is stale and smells like dust, but it was cleaned before the epidemic, and the bed is made. The bedroom window in the back offers a view of the swimming pool, bone dry and half filled with a tangle of dead bodies.

Beyond the pool, Infected stagger out of the darkening woods, moaning.

And above the tops of the trees, he sees flashes of light along the horizon. The battle for Washington, DC, still playing itself out.

Ray sighs and closes the curtains.

In the living room, he inspects the drab couch, wood paneling, dead TV and painting on the wall of an empty rowboat grounded on an ocean beach. Two of his cops set boxes on the floor, brought to the motel as tribute by the Infected still living in the town. He can see them down in the parking lot, staring up at his room and moaning.

The sound of bottles clinking against each other brings a grin to his face.

"Jim Beam!" he says, inspecting one. He unscrews the cap, takes a sip, and sighs. "Here, honey, have a snort. You deserve it."

Lola takes the bottle and drinks it like water, wincing.

"Whoa there, Nelly," he says, taking it back and screwing the cap back on.

She's like a child. I have to take care of her.

Working by candlelight, he undresses her and inspects her body for wounds. She has multiple bite marks on her arm, one of which broke the skin and appears red and inflamed, and her feet are cut and bloodied. Otherwise, her long legs are bruised but she appears to be healthy.

"Let's get you fixed up, honey."

Dipping a washcloth in the basin of water the Infected provided, he rubs her face and arms, clearing away the dirt. He dips her head into a second basin, washes her hair and brushes it out, taking his time. Then he washes the rest of her body.

"I'm sorry, you know," he says, glancing at her face for a reaction.

Her face twitches, her eyes open and staring at the blank face of the TV. He wraps a blanket around her shoulders, covering her nudity.

"I'm sorry I hurt your boyfriend. Remember that? Long time ago, right? Well, I'm sorry about it, Lola. It was just me hating everything. This might sting a little, honey."

Ray dabs her feet with hydrogen peroxide, making the tiny wounds fizz. Lola stiffens but says nothing. He reaches for the tube of antibiotic cream.

"I hated everything because if I liked something, I hurt it until it was gone. Stupid, huh?"

He takes another swig from the bottle of Jim Beam and inspects his work. The wounds on her feet and arm are now clean and bandaged.

"You know, you were the closest I ever came to loving someone. Even more than Tyler, and he was my best friend."

Rummaging through other people's luggage, he finds a simple sundress and pair of comfortable sneakers that appear to fit her. She puts them on obediently.

"The weird thing is I hated my dad, but I act just like him. I know right from wrong and all that. I just can't help myself after a few beers."

He stops, wondering how to continue. It is hard to explain.

"Screw it. You don't even know what I'm saying anyway. Open wide, honey."

He winces; Lola's mouth smells like an open grave. He takes a needle from the first aid kit and flosses pieces of meat wedged between her teeth. Putting a large dollop of Crest on a motel toothbrush, he brushes her teeth and tells her to spit into the basin.

"You look real beautiful, honey." His heart aches looking at her. "Why don't you climb under that blanket and go to sleep? You need a rest."

I'm going to save this girl, and then marry her, if she'll have me.

Outside, the Infected pace and grunt. Ray looks out the window and sees their eyes gleaming in the dark. They seem to want something from him, but he cannot guess what it is. He takes another swig from the bottle and belches. He is well on his way to becoming blissfully drunk.

"Rest in peace, Tyler."

The Infected rustle in the dark, filling the empty parking lot. They do not scare him anymore. He feels oddly at home with the damned.

"The only hope the rest of you have is if I turn myself in."

Ray places his hand against the window.

"You're all my second chance."

WENDY

They set up the Coleman stove in the abandoned warehouse and heat some of the MREs, or meals ready to eat, the Army provided as part of its supplies for the NLA. Sitting in a circle on the cement floor, they eat in a thoughtful silence, the Bradley crew watching Todd, Todd studying the blue ring of fire on the Coleman. This is fine with Wendy; she just wants to look at him. They all know it is a miracle they found each other again.

He has grown up a lot in the past two months, but at this moment he looks like an exhausted boy on the verge of tears. She is not even sure why she missed him so much. They fought and scavenged in the same group for just two weeks. Once they reached Camp Defiance, they split up with hardly a goodbye.

But they went to hell and back. For those two weeks, they were a tribe, relying on each other with their very lives. Wendy remembers standing in a dark hospital corridor with him, guns readied, waiting for the Infected to attack. She held her Glock against his head after the monster bit him, praying he would not become infected and she would not have to put him down. They escaped while Pittsburgh burned, pursued by the Demon. They made it to Defiance and later fought a horde to save the camp.

The simple fact is she feels safe with him there.

And yet he makes her a little sad, too. He makes her remember Paul and Ethan and how they died on the bridge. Deaths that now seem utterly pointless, seeing as the camp fell anyway.

Wendy tells Todd about their journey to Camp Immunity near Harrisburg, where they told Ethan's wife about his death on the bridge, and how they joined up with the New Liberty Army, taking the fight to the Infected all over southeastern Ohio.

Todd nods and accepts a cup of coffee from Toby.

"You're going to be okay, Kid," Toby tells him. "You got your whole life ahead of you."

"We're leaving soon," Wendy says.

The boy glances at her.

"We're leaving the war," she continues. "We're done."

Wendy studies him for a while. He watches her intently, waiting.

"Where are you going?" he finally says.

"South. We're going to find an island. A state park or something, where it's warm all year around. Make a stand. Live as long as we can."

She and Toby heard the bombing, saw the smoke, and decided to check it out, which led them straight to Todd. There can be no other reason they found each other like this.

It's meant to be.

"You should come with us," she says.

TODD

Wendy's idea is the same as their original plan back in Pittsburgh, before they learned people were resisting, before the Army came home to wage its impossible war against Infection. They would leave humanity to fend for itself, and find a place for themselves. Find sanctuary with people you could trust to watch your back, and survive as long as possible. Not just survive, but *live*, on their own terms, not in some miserable, overcrowded refugee camp. It is either the wish of a dreamer or the most rational thing he ever heard.

Sarge said he has his whole life ahead of him. At seventeen, it is hard for Todd to understand what that means. It is the kind of thing someone who has been alive a long time would say. He remembers Anne saying she does not get to come back. *What about me? Can I leave the road and build a new life somewhere?* Anne and Paul taught him your demons can never touch you if you keep moving. It's dangerous on the road, but some of the worst monsters are in your head.

And yet finding a remote place that is defendable and self-sustaining is possibly the one rational course left. People like Sarge and Wendy are best equipped to survive not just today, but what is coming. In just a year, civilization could finally collapse, Todd believes, at least in the North. Everywhere he has traveled, people were using up what they had while producing nothing, and nobody seems to be planning ahead for the lean times coming in the winter. Salvage is not enough to keep the nation going. Winter, hunger and disease may finish it.

The nightmare, sadly, is about to get worse, with no end in sight. The apocalypse is taking its sweet time, but this is still the end of the world. The final collapse will come suddenly, and then the human race will no longer be able to stage large-scale organized resistance to Infection. Out in the open, humans will become part of the food chain, somewhere near the bottom.

We will all go down together, and we will go down fighting.

In the first days of the epidemic, he saw a small band of exhausted police fight until a mob of Infected overran them. They shot at the Infected, and when they ran out of bullets, they clubbed at them with the butts of their guns. They knew the entire time their fight was futile, and yet they did not submit to the inevitable. They fought back, tooth and nail, to the final second.

FUTILE BUT BRAVE; that will be our epitaph.

The one logical alternative to going down with the ship is to find a good place, dig in and hold onto it for as long as possible. Fortify it, make it self-sufficient, and defend it with people you can trust with your life. If there is one thing Paul's death taught Todd, it is people don't matter, only certain people do. If there is one thing Erin's death taught him, it is to take whatever happiness you can get for as long as you can get it.

Wendy is right. They should go. Todd wants to join them.

One hope still exists, however. One major hope for the human race.

We could find a cure.

And for this reason, it is not time to leave just yet. He has one more thing to do.

He still wants his revenge on Infection.

"Ray Young is alive," he tells them.

COOL ROD

Dear Rod,

We're all okay.

A man dropped by the dorm today to tell us that the Marines have retaken the White House. It won't be long now, he said. Soon, our nation's capital will be free again.

He called the infected people demons. I'm not sure I'm willing to go that far. They may be crazy and evil now, but they still look like us. They used to be us. They are so sad.

The monsters we hear about are another story altogether. They sound like something out of Hell. Have you seen any during the fighting? The kids try to scare each other during the day by pretending to be monsters, and it makes them laugh, but at night they're terrified. Sometimes, late at night, you can hear the real monsters howling outside the wall.

Victor was starting to make such a racket at night that he now sleeps with me and Lilia, and then Kristina didn't like that so now we all sleep on the floor on an old mattress. Okay, I admit, a part of me likes it. I make them feel safe, and they make me feel needed. The more they need me, the more it takes my mind off other things, like the end of the world.

I'm sorry I sound so down in the dumps in this letter, Rod. Most times I write, I put a big smile on my face because I want you to not worry about us. Things aren't great, but we're doing okay. We're alive and we have enough to eat, and that's plenty to be thankful for these days. You have enough going on in the war without wondering if your family is all right, because we really are.

It's just that every day things get a little harder. The other night one of those things got inside the camp and the MPs were chasing it around with flamethrowers. They had it surrounded—this horrible, hoofed, screaming thing—and they were shooting it with jets of fire. We were hustled into the rec center, where we stood shoulder to shoulder in the dark until the coast was clear, and came out to find our dorm tent had burned clean to the ground and all our possessions were floating away in the dark as ash and sparks on the wind. Our photo albums are gone, Rod. All those years of memories. Our entire past. I now have only one photo of you to keep me company at night and remind our kids that they have a daddy, and it's falling apart from all of us holding it so tight.

Today, a salvage crew brought in a truckload of clothes to replace what we lost in the fire. I try not to think that the clothes our kids are wearing once belonged to other kids who are now probably dead. Dead and eaten, from what I hear the crazies do to children.

If the Marines have taken the White House, I hope that means you'll win this important victory, and get to rotate out for a few weeks of rest. You could come home and live with us for a while. I really need you, Rod. There was a fire and the photo album is gone and now I can't stop crying. I feel like it wasn't just pictures but our past that got burned up and forever lost. Right now, our past is all I have of you.

As time goes on, I feel your absence ever so much. You should be with your family right now. Your place is here. I freely give up this demand, my right as your wife, in the hopes that you will win and be able to save not just us, but the entire country. Do your duty, Rod. The wolves are at the door and your family is counting on you to put this to an end. Fight hard, without mercy. Kill them all. Do whatever it takes to win, no matter how hard, no matter how horrible. Put this to an end. And then come home to us so that we can build new memories.

I love you more than myself. Your children miss their father. We are all praying for you.

Your loving wife,
Gabriela

ANNE

Sitting cross-legged on the road, Anne cleans and oils her weapons by starlight while her team sleeps fitfully on the bus, dreaming their bad dreams. With swift, deft movements, working by feel, she reassembles her rifle and dry fires it. The forest crowding the road is alive with the song of insects and nocturnal critters scampering through the undergrowth. The air feels warm and wet against her skin. Most people are terrified of the night these days, but not Anne. She welcomes it. The Infected can hide in it, but so can she. In the dark, Anne becomes a hunter.

The asphalt feels warm against her ass and legs. She finishes her granola bar and washes it down with a few chugs of Red Bull. This is what passes for breakfast, but Anne does not mind. Food is for fuel, not pleasure, these days. And speed is paramount; it is time to get back on the road and narrow Ray's head start. She reloads the rifle and stands, dusting her pants and stretching like a cat. In the dark, she feels calm, thoughtful and safe, as long as she does not think too much about the past.

About two months ago, she started her day serving breakfast to her husband and three small children in their kitchen. After dumping the dishes into the sink to soak in steaming water, she started rolling out pie dough. Her friend called to tell her there was trouble downtown—mobs of people running amok, doing horrible things to each other. By the end of the day, her husband disappeared and her children lay slaughtered in a neighbor's living room. Three days later, she surfaced from a state of shock in a deteriorating government shelter. By the end of the week, Sarge taught her the basics of sniper craft, and she began the killing. She learned from the pros who worked the camp watchtowers. She often volunteered for a shift in the towers herself, practicing range finding, estimating elevation and wind. With endless practice, she turned murder into an art. Mostly, she has a knack for it. Some people have a natural talent for certain things. It is a strange thought, considering how she came to be a killer, but sometimes she feels she was born to do this.

Which is good in one way, because it is all Anne has left. Hurting Infection, in fact, is one of the few things that make her feel something besides guilt and loss.

The guilt of allowing her children to be slaughtered, the loss of everything she loved. The guilt of letting Ray Young live, only to see him return and slaughter tens of thousands.

Ray Young has become Infection. All that matters now is catching and killing him before he does even worse because Anne, in a moment of weakness, showed mercy.

Stepping onto the bus, she slaps Marcus's boot and steps back as the man lunges awake, growling in the dark with a knife in his hand.

"Time to go," Anne tells him.

"Anne? Christ, it's still pitch black out there."

"It'll be light in less than an hour. We already spent too much time here."

"Wait a minute." Marcus sits up and rubs the sleep from his eyes. "Listen, Anne. I need to know you're okay."

"Since when I have ever been truly okay since you've known me?"

"You know what I mean."

"I'm upset, Marcus. There's a guy who can control the Infected, and spreads Infection, as far as I know, just by looking at you, and he's on his way to Washington, DC, where our military is in a fight to the death to take the city back."

"Look, you think we don't get it about what kind of threat Young poses to all of us, but we do. We get it. It's just hard to put your life on the line for something, you know? And that's what you're asking us all to do here. You're asking us to die for this. Most of us would rather go somewhere safe and let someone else figure it out."

Anne blinks at him. She forgot most people still place a high value on their lives.

"The stakes," she says finally, unsure how to finish the statement.

"We'll get him," Marcus assures her. "We will, or the Army will."

They remember the planes roaring overhead, the distant thunder, the rising wall of smoke on the western horizon, veiling the setting sun.

"We both know he got away before they dropped those bombs."

"Anne, let me get to the point. I'm worried about you."

"I'm worried about Todd." For Anne, even this is a big admission.

"He can take care of himself."

"He ran off to snoop around a horde of a hundred thousand Infected, and then was close to ground zero when the bombs fell. Marcus, I'm worried."

"Let's talk about you. Anne, you shot and killed a woman today."

"So what? I've shot lots of people."

"Jean was a crazy, but she wasn't Infected. You shot her in cold blood and didn't even blink. As far as I know, that's a first even for you."

"You know what she did in the art gallery."

"Jean and Gary did what they had to do to survive. You've never judged anyone before for what they've done to stay alive. Christ, we all have blood on our hands. If we didn't, we wouldn't be here."

The truth is I lost control.

"I don't want to talk about it," Anne says.

"All right. Forget why. What I don't get is what's going on inside your head. Me, I honestly can't picture doing what you did. Shit, what do you feel about it? Do you feel anything at all?"

Anne's mind flashes to pointing her pistol at Jean's face and squeezing the trigger.

"I don't feel anything," she says, a little surprised at the realization.

Marcus nods, taking this in. Another major admission.

"We're wasting time here," she says. "Can we go now? Please?"

He says nothing, and they regard each other in the dark, their eyes gleaming.

"I need you, Marcus," she tells him, her voice strained.

"I'll come," he says. "We'll finish this."

"Good. Let's wake up the others."

"But I want more."

"More?"

"I want you."

As much as Anne loves Todd as a son, she has come to love Marcus as a man. The thought of giving herself to him fills her with panic, however. For one thing, it is too soon. Just two months ago, she was mother to three children given to her by a man whom she loved with her whole heart for nearly ten years of her life. She never properly mourned them. She cannot just let go.

On the other hand, no more perfect time exists. She could die within the next five minutes.

"If you want sex, I can give you that."

"It's not about that, Anne. I want *you*."

He is asking her to feel, but she doubts she has anything to give him. She remembers Sarge in the government shelter, what seems like a lifetime ago, calling the Infected the living dead.

Us? he added. *We're the dead living.*

The words shocked her at the time. Now she understands.

How can you ask me to love you, Marcus, when you might die before sunrise?

"I want you," he repeats. "Don't we deserve to be happy, even if for a little while?"

"I don't know what that means anymore. I want to but I don't know if I can."

Marcus nods. "All right. Then I'll settle for that."

He smiles at her in the dark and Anne smiles back, a rare sight at any time of day.

RAY

While Ray twitches and sweats in a deep snoring sleep with his arms wrapped around Lola, he dreams the Infected are normal again. In the dream they stand outside where he left them, but it is bright and sunny instead of dark, and all of them are well dressed and clean and looking up at the sun, tears flowing down their cheeks as they smile. The men and women look at each other with wide, sparkling eyes. There is no hate here, no rage, just the thrill of freedom.

Lola, accustomed to dreaming of billions of monsters writhing like maggots across the scoured face of a red planet, finds herself at her house in Cashtown, weeding her garden while her children shriek and run barefoot through the sprinkler spray on the lawn. Her husband winks at her as he enters the garage to take out the lawnmower. She vows to hold onto the feeling she has looking at her family—a sense of her soul being filled to the brim with contentment—knowing nothing perfect lasts forever in this world. That night, as they drink wine and barbecue steaks and eat them outside in the cool dusk, she tells herself if she had to pick a day to relive, she would pick this one, this beautiful summer day spent doing almost nothing.

Outside, the other Infected moan in the darkness, free of the dreams of the red planet and the long exodus through space. They dream of the time before, reliving the past. They are free of the bonds of slavery at last, while Infection waits patiently until morning to reclaim its hosts.

ANNE

Dawn is coming fast and the bus flies down the road, chasing a paling sky. The V-shaped snowplow retrofitted onto the front, peppered top to bottom with blood, sends the occasional Infected flying into the ditch with a thud. The engine growls as Marcus changes gears with the stick, slowing down and speeding up to navigate occasional wrecks blocking the road. The Rangers peer through the metal firing ports welded over the windows, Anne looking for any sign of Ray Young, the others watching for threats that specialize in the night. The air feels humid but cool against her skin. This has always been her favorite time of the day; it's a new day, and anything can happen. For as long as she can remember, Anne has been a morning person.

Holding the edges of the seats to stay balanced as the bus bangs over potholes, she navigates the center aisle until she finds Gary, huddled against the window with his arms crossed.

"I'm sorry about Jean," she says.

"How did you know what we did in the art gallery?"

"I found the evidence. It wasn't hard to piece together."

"You shouldn't have judged her," Gary tells her. "Her one sin was she refused to accept that things have changed. She honestly thought the whole thing would blow over and her life would pick up again almost where she'd left it. I think she thought once we got to Nightingale, she would find a Starbucks with Wi-Fi."

Anne frowns. "Jean had bigger sins than that."

"What we did, we did to survive. We were trapped. It was either that or die. But it wasn't her. It was me. I was the one who did it. I made a choice. You should judge me, not Jean. Jean just ate."

Anne nods. Her suspicion has been confirmed. "She just ate."

"That's right."

"And that's why I judge her, Gary. You, I don't judge."

Gary stares back at her stricken, on the verge of tears.

"I killed my friend and then we ate him," he says. "You need to understand this."

"You survived."

"If you call living with that surviving."

"Can you handle a weapon?"

"I've never fired a gun in my life," he says. "I killed my friend with a knife."

"We don't talk about the past," she says.

"I killed my friend with a knife," Gary repeats with a shrill laugh. "It actually feels good to say it out loud. I was selling his paintings in my gallery and then a week later I cut his throat so Jean and I could eat him and live. It was hard work. Once I had him down, I had to lean and put all my weight into it. He hardly struggled. He just looked at me in surprise while I did it. I was pretty surprised too. I mean, I was outside my body, watching myself do it. I should be in jail, but here I am, alive, and he's dead. Do you see what kind of person I am?"

"Are you willing to kill again to survive? If you had to?"

"I want to live," Gary says after a pause.

"All right. We'll give you a nine millimeter. If the Infected get close, you point it, you shoot it. You watch our backs, we watch yours. Think you can do that?"

"I can do it."

"Good," says Anne. "If you killed a man to survive, I can't absolve you. None of us are shining examples of virtue; we've all done terrible things or we wouldn't be here. But it tells me you have what it takes. That's the only qualification that matters these days."

"Anne!" Marcus calls from the driver's seat at the front.

She feels the tug of gravity test her balance. The bus is slowing.

"Thank you," Gary says, crying.

Anne stands and hurries toward the front.

"We've got people waving us down, about a hundred yards up the road," Marcus says. "Cops having some car trouble, from the looks of it."

Anne braces her feet with a wide stance and takes a look through her rifle scope. Standing next to a state police car, two large men wearing black T-shirts and load-bearing vests and jeans wave at the bus, flagging it down. The badges on their belts glint in the morning sun.

Something is wrong with their faces.

Anne blinks, thinking: *Impossible.*

The cops raise their guns, grinning at her across the remaining distance.

"Go, Marcus!" she screams, taking aim. "Keep going!"

Marcus obeys instantly, throwing the bus back into its highest gear and stepping on the gas. The machinery roars in response, lurching as it accelerates. Anne loses her footing and falls hard onto the floor, the rifle clattering away from her.

BANG BANG BANG BANG

Bullet holes pop through the windshield, spraying the interior with bits of glass. The Rangers drop to the floor, wrapping their arms around their heads. Marcus bellows with rage and pain, half out of his seat and driving blind.

BANG BANG BANG BANG

The bullets shatter the windshield and rip through the air, thudding into metal and bursting through the seats, sending bits of stuffing swirling around them. Wind rushes through the open windshield, carrying the faint tang of rotting milk.

Anne feels the hard, dusty floor under her scarred cheek and wonders how many kids stepped on this spot on their daily commute to school. She pictures their little sneakered feet. She closes her eyes and remembers visiting one of the many orphanages at Camp Defiance. She wanted to see children again. Pastor Strickland gave her a tour and showed her the rows of boys and girls drawing on construction paper with crayons—art therapy, he called it, endless scenes of fire and slaughter, Infected mommies attacking crying daddies, children running through the woods, red eyes identifying the Infected, slashes of blue representing the tears of the victims.

Strickland asked about her spiritual health and she told him she was spiritually dead. He said she should return to her faith, which could serve as a source of strength for her as it has for so many others, reminding her there are no atheists in foxholes. Anne answered there are no believers either. There is just you, dying. And that is the true sadness of life.

You're here, and then you're not.

BANG BANG BANG BANG BANG BANG

The cops step aside as the bus roars past, emptying their guns at point blank range, the bullets punching holes through the thin metal skin of the vehicle.

The firing stops. Marcus straightens in the driver's seat, his face flushed with rage. Anne climbs to her feet and looks through the back window to see the two cops standing in the middle of the road, staring at the bus as it zooms away from them.

"Who's hit?" Anne says. She has to shout to be heard over the rush of wind whistling across the seats.

"Just glass," says Ramona. "Nothing major."

"I'm all scratched up," Marcus says. "I'm all right, but I'm bleeding."

Evan and Gary tell her they are okay.

"Ramona, get the first aid kit," Anne says. "Gary, take a look at Marcus and let Ramona know where he's hurt and how bad. Ramona, patch him up first if you can."

"Shouldn't we stop?" Gary says.

"Not after that. Those people who were shooting at us were Infected."

"How can that be?" Evan says.

"Ray Young," Anne answers. "Evan, I need you to fetch the machine gun."

Despite everything that has happened, Evan grins. The M240 is his baby. He hurries into the back, dodging Ramona, and returns with the gun.

"Where do you want it?" he says.

"We're going to mount it right up there next to Marcus where the windshield used to be."

"Hot dog," Evan says. "Here, take the gun. I'll go get the ammo."

Their boots crunch broken glass as they lug the twenty-six-pound machine gun to the front of the bus and mount it on the hood, the barrel resting on the integrated bipod.

Marcus glances at them as they set it up for firing. Evan pulls the charging handle, locking the bolt to the rear.

"Give me the ammo," he says.

Anne opens one of the ammunition boxes and pulls out a long belt of shiny rounds, which he connects to the machine gun, sliding the first round into the firing chamber. Locked and loaded.

"We're in business," he grins, the wind ripping through his hair. "It's set for a cycle of eight hundred fifty rounds per minute. Just keep feeding me the belt."

"Gary!" Anne calls out. "Sit right there. When I say so, get behind Evan, brace your back against the pole here, and put your hands against his back right about here. Keep him stable, okay?"

"I can do that," Gary says.

"Good idea," Evan says, hunched over the machine gun, one hand wrapped around the firing handle and the other hugging the gunstock.

"You're a long way from designing electrical circuits now," Anne tells him.

Evan laughs into the wind. "Seems like a dream." Past or present, however, he does not elaborate.

"People in the road!" Marcus says.

Anne raises her rifle and peers through the scope. A crowd of some fifty grim-faced people, holding knives and baseball bats and hockey sticks, stands in a line across the road next to a massive billboard proclaiming, WELCOME TO SUGAR CREEK.

"Fire, Evan."

"They don't look Infected!"

"Fire!"

"Anne!"

"FIRE YOUR GODDAMN WEAPON."

The machine gun fills the air with its loud chatter as fifteen rounds per second rip downrange into the crowd, every fourth a streaming tracer. Dozens of people crumple under the withering fusillade, body parts and guts torn and hurled across the asphalt, while the rest charge howling, throwing bricks and waving their weapons.

A rock sails past Anne's ear and falls into one of the seats behind her. The town's welcome sign collapses into pieces. The snowplow strikes a rushing knot of people with a jarring bang and sends them cartwheeling into the fields bordering the road. Next to her, Evan fires, his body shaking, Gary holding onto his back and trying to keep the man steady. Anne feeds the belt into the machine gun, which spits the rounds at a murderous rate. She catches Marcus's profile while he drives, ramrod straight in his seat, gripping the wheel with white knuckles, bleeding from a cut in his forehead, tears flowing down his stubbled cheeks and drying in the wind. She knows how much he hates this. The endless slaughter. He hates all of it.

The bus zooms down the town's main street, scattering garbage and scraps of paper. Hundreds of people emerge from houses and buildings, throwing rocks and waving homemade weapons. Stones and shards of brick clatter against the sides of the vehicle.

Evan continues firing, cutting them down and chewing up the fronts of houses. Anne eyes the ammo belt's shrinking length with alarm. The sides of the bus thud and vibrate as the Infected throw themselves at it. The street behind them fills with clouds of dust. Signs flash past proclaiming zero down financing, world famous tacos, propane for sale.

"Reload!" Evan screams. "Reload me!"

Anne pulls out the second belt of ammunition as the bus approaches another mob of Infected at the other end of town, arrayed in ranks like a medieval army.

RAY

Ray awakens on musty sheets with a pounding headache and a mouth that feels coated with moss. Lola smiles in her sleep, and as Ray gets out of bed, yawning and rubbing his belly, she frowns, stirs, wakes up Infected. Feeling a little nauseous, he plods into the bathroom and pisses loudly. Then Lola pulls up her dress and sits on the toilet, and he thinks: *At least I have her potty trained.*

"I had the weirdest dream. Did you sleep well, honey?"

Lola barks, making him laugh. His body is paying for last night's bender, but it did the trick. Overall, he feels better than he can remember.

"Today, we're going to find ourselves some Feds and make a deal."

He gives her some fruit juice in a plastic jug, which she gulps. While he brushes his teeth, he wonders what it is like to wake up every day driven by hunger and rage. *Maybe a lot like my twenties*, he thinks with a snort. The whole thing seems so pointless but then he remembers the Infected are just a means to an end. The bug's real goal is to plant new life on the planet.

Ray lights a Winston and pats the lump on his ribs, which vibrates like a tiny hummingbird.

"This is not going to turn out the way you wanted, Mini Me," he tells it.

We like this world just the way it is, and we don't appreciate you messing with it.

He pulls on his T-shirt and steps into his jeans.

"Let's go, honey. We'll get something to eat on the road. The world's our oyster."

She takes his hand and he leads her outside into the bright day.

His guards step aside to let him pass: French, Anderson, Cook and Salazar. Ray walks to the edge of the balcony and waves at the Infected gaping up at him with hopeful expressions. The sun is already high in the sky. He overslept, and yet he is still exhausted.

Thank you for watching over me, he tells the Infected.

The sun's glare makes his eyes tear up. He takes a last drag on his smoke and steps on it.

"There's just four of us now," he tells the survivors of Unit 12. "You've always been good guys, normal or Infected, don't matter which. I'm taking you all the way with me. If they want me, they're going to have to cure you too."

He leads his entourage down the cement steps and into the parking lot, where he left his truck. The Infected stare at him, sweating and grunting, their skin burned red by the sun, their hair greasy and matted. They touch his shoulders lightly as he passes, growling deep in their throats. Some of them show him weapons they scavenged, baseball bats and shovels, while others try to give him gifts of food. The air is thick with their stench.

"Come on, now," he says. "I ain't the Second Coming."

A massive vehicle rumbles past the motel. Ray freezes, watching it roll past. It is shaped like a school bus, painted in a camouflage pattern, with a large snowplow fitted onto its front, stained the color of rust, and metal slats welded over its windows and doors.

"Wow, what a great rig," Ray says.

The bus stops with a squeak, idling before it reverses, stops again, and executes a slow turn into the parking lot.

Ray watches it turn with mounting terror until it faces him, giving him a clear view of the giant blond-haired driver, a skinny man with glasses hunched over a machine gun, and a woman standing next to him, pointing at Ray and shouting.

"You," he gasps.

Even from this distance, he can see Anne Leary's face shining with fierce excitement at catching her prey.

Of course it would be her.

He flashes back to sitting on the bridge, trying to hold onto a happy thought while she stood over him with a very large gun pointed at the back of his head.

Protect, Ray tells his cops.

The Unit 12 officers raise their weapons and fire as the machine gun opens up, it rounds hacking through the crowd and plowing into the Infected around Ray.

The firing stops. The dying Infected thrash and howl in their own blood. Someone screams on the bus. The air smells like smoke.

Ray emerges from his daze gasping for breath. He pats his body, amazed he got through the exchange without a scratch.

Lola.

She lies on the ground, her brains splashed across the pavement among old cigarette butts. Behind her, Cook crawls on his hands and knees, vomiting blood, his tattered shirt smoking.

Lola!

"Oh, honey."

Oddly, she seems to be smiling.

There goes your second chance, bro.

As his rage mounts, the Infected around him tremble, shaking their fists and weapons, jaws snapping like animals.

Ray turns to the bus, where Anne is struggling to right the machine gun.

"Kill them!" he commands.

KILL KILL KILL KILL

The Infected howl as one and charge, surging toward the bus in a human flood. The driver puts the vehicle into reverse, inching away slowly, too slowly, making Ray laugh harshly.

Oh no, you don't. You're not going anywhere, Anne Leary. You're going to stay right here and get what's coming to you.

"Kill them all!"

The air fills with the pop of weapons as the Infected clamber onto the snowplow and force their way into the bus.

"Whatever you think is best, Ray!" he screams. "Whatever you think is best!"

ANNE

The bus slowly reverses while Anne tries to pull the machine gun from under Evan's legs. The Infected shot him. The man shakes violently, bleeding out, his eyes glassy and unseeing. Behind him, Gary sits with his back against the pole, wincing and licking blood from his lips.

"I can feel it in my lung," he says. He sounds like he is being strangled. "The bullet. It went through Evan and popped into my chest."

"I'm sorry," she tells him.

Thrashing in his final death throes, Evan knees Anne in the face and pain flares through the lines of her scars. Above her, Ramona screams and fires her automatic rifle on full auto at the Infected clambering onto the hood of the vehicle.

Anne frees the gun with a final jerk.

"This is your fault," Gary says. "It's all your fault."

She looks up in time to see Ramona fire her last round and slam the butt of her rifle into a man's face before the hands reach in and pull her out into the mob, which tears her apart. Blood splashes onto Marcus but he ignores it, gritting his teeth, firing a massive handgun into the snarling faces with one hand while steering with the other.

"I'm scared," Gary says.

This is what you wanted, Anne's mind whispers.

Your murdered your own children through your stupidity and arrogance and you can never be happy so you kill and kill and kill the Infected in the hopes one day your luck will run out and they will tear you to shreds and eat you like you deserve.

That day has finally come.

"It's going to be okay," she says.

Gary does not hear her. He stares into oblivion, his eyes blank, his face pale, his final expression one of pure terror.

Anne glances down at the machine gun in her hands and realizes she could just drop it. Dying would be that simple. She has already gotten enough people killed. Let Ray kill the world. What does she care?

Not yet. Soon, but not just yet.

They can have me, but only after a fight. They have to prove they are stronger. They have to earn it.

The will to survive floods her body with energy. She stands and levels the heavy weapon, putting her back against the pole for support and firing from the waist, holding the ammo belt with her other hand. The barrel lights up with muzzle flashes that fill the air with hot metal.

Anne screams with something like joy. This is how she wants to die.

The hot metal slugs punch through skulls and torsos, spraying brains and guts back into the crowd. Soon she can no longer see individuals, just torn and charred flesh and muscle and clothing, shattered bone, ripped organs and blood.

Then she no longer sees even this, struck by a vision of a single face, watching her without expression, as if lobotomized, a human face with an alien mind.

A human face constructed entirely of seething maggots.

No, not maggots. Monsters.

The face snarls with recognition and hatred before it explodes into millions of howling things hurtling into the void.

"I am Life," it tells her. "I am Life and you are the enemy of life. You are Death."

Empty shell casings clatter across the floor. She grunts, sweat pouring down her face. Her arm trembles with exhaustion from the constant recoil.

The bus continues to gain speed. The Infected fall behind, howling and waving their weapons and shooting their guns. Anne lunges and slams the M240 down onto hood, hugging the stock and resuming fire.

The Infected collapse in waves under the withering fire of the machine gun.

"Come on," she screams, her body jerking from the recoil. "Come and get it!"

The bus steadily puts more distance between them and the Infected. The tracers arc and drop among the crowd, punching more bodies to the ground. The ammo belt runs out.

Marcus stops the bus, turns and finds another way out of town.

Ray fled during the attack. The pursuit is back on. And Anne has survived again.

As with every other time, she is almost disappointed.

COOL ROD

Sitting in the shade of the Stryker, Rod watches his squad tear the plastic wrapping off their MREs and sink their hands into the yellow pouches, producing brown packets containing entrees and seasonings and HOOAH! energy bars. They compare meals and barter like Wall Street traders. Sosa trades a cigarette for Lynch's hot sauce. Tanner puts his chicken fajitas on the market, but gets no takers. He takes a long pull on a stray bottle of water they liberated from the Walmart's shelves and passes it on. Lynch suggests lighting some C4 to cook their meals properly, but the air is so hot the others do not seem interested. Sosa, constipated from the steady diet of MREs, calls his a *meal ready for enema*, making them laugh.

Rod joins in the laughter, enjoying the banter during this rare calm while Davis stands twenty meters away with his rifle providing security and Arnold monitors the recon equipment on the Walmart roof. He tears open his own MRE and inspects his beef brisket with mild disdain. It is not his favorite, but he needs the twelve hundred calories.

Hellraisers 3, this is Hellraisers Eyes, over.

That's Arnold calling in from the observation post. Rod places his meal on the ground between his feet and keys the push-to-talk button on his headset, chewing. "Hellraisers 3 here. Go ahead, Eyes, over."

Contact to the west. A uniform victor, moving fast, over.

An *unidentified vehicle*, Rod understands. "You got eyes on it, over?"

Not yet, over.

"Let me know when you get eyes on it. Hellraisers 3, out."

Roger, Three. Out.

The others wolf down their meals, knowing what is coming, but waiting until he gives the order.

"We've got a vehicle inbound," he says. "You know what to do. Let's get to it."

The soldiers take final bites of food and slugs of juice and scramble to their feet, pocketing their energy bars and candy for later. They snatch up their weapons and run off. Lynch stays behind to help Sosa pull on his flamethrower harness.

"Corporal, when you're done there, go tell spooky and the doc we're expecting company," Rod says.

"Aieeyah, Sergeant."

"Hart, I need you on the fifty," he shouts, banging his fist against the Stryker's armor. The gunner appears in the cupola, gives him a thumbs up, and grabs hold of the mounted heavy machine gun, locking and loading it.

Checking his shotgun, Rod walks to the checkpoint they built using sawhorses and STOP signs, placed in layers running every twenty meters along the road up to the gas station. The theory is Typhoid Jody will either stop, or try to bypass or drive through the roadblock.

If he tries to bypass or drive through, he will slow down, and the Stryker's fifty will make quick work of him. If he fails to cooperate, he is a dead man.

Rod's body rebels, his heart racing and his breath becoming fast and shallow, but not from fear. No, he is simply excited. *Can this really be it? Can this guy really offer a cure? If not a cure, maybe a vaccine, or even a weapon?*

Is this the operation that ends the war and allows us to retake the country?

He whistles to get Davis's attention. "Corporal, change of plans for you. I want you to find a safe spot fifty meters behind us, watching our rear. Same plan if something happens to me, though. You're to take command."

"Got it, Sergeant," Davis says, jogging away.

Rod blows air out his cheeks, raises the hood on his MOPP suit, and pulls on his gas mask.

"It's time to earn our money," he says.

Hellraisers 3, this is Hellraisers Eyes, over.

"Go ahead, Eyes, over."

I have eyes on the uniform victor. Range, about three kilometers. Break. It's a military vehicle, Sergeant. An APC. Over.

"Shift to overwatch, Eyes. Hellraisers 3, out."

Rod frowns at the waves of heat rising off the warmed road and wonders about the odds of this being a coincidence. *What's an armored personnel carrier doing in this exact place at this exact point in time? Could this be our guy?*

He had the impression Typhoid Jody is a civilian, but he might be military, and he might know how to drive an APC. Alarms flash through Rod's mind.

How are we going to stop him if he's driving an amored vehicle?

Fielding and Price approach in their bright yellow spacesuits, carrying what appear to be suitcases made of yellow plastic emblazoned with ominous biohazard symbols.

"Stay behind me," he tells them.

The vehicle appears in the distance, approaching with a metallic scream, and crushes the first line of sawhorses before rolling to a sudden stop in front of the second.

Rod waves, his heart pounding against his ribs.

The turret turns rapidly, aligning the cannon barrel with the Stryker. Five shooters in a motley collection of military uniforms fan out from behind, taking cover and aiming their weapons at his men.

"Hold fire, Hellraisers," Rod says into his headset.

"Any idea who they are?" Dr. Price says.

"I believe we're about to find that out."

The hatch opens and a large man appears. "Who's in charge here?" his deep voice booms across the roadblocks.

Rod takes off his mask and pulls his hood down.

"I'm Sergeant Hector Rodriguez, Fifth Stryker Cavalry Regiment. And you would be?"

"Sergeant Toby Wilson, Eighth Infantry Division, Fifth Brigade—the Iron Horse."

Rod grunts with respect. From what he heard, elements of Fifth Brigade fought hard all over Pennsylvania in the first days of the Wildfire epidemic, and were destroyed piecemeal. If Wilson is from that unit, he and his crew are among its few survivors.

This guy must have one hell of a story to tell.

"Where's your original dismounts?" he asks, referring to Wilson's infantry squad.

"Dead just like all the rest. We're militia now."

"Well, Sergeant Wilson, it's an honor, but I'm going to have to ask that you exit my area of operations. If you want to pass through, you've got my blessing."

"No can do, Sergeant. This is important. I need you to tell me about your operation."

"What the hell?" Rod mutters, then calls back, "Go fuck yourself, Sergeant! Is that enough information for you?"

He hears his boys laughing at their positions. Wilson's shooters continue to scurry to new cover, fanning out further on his flanks. Preparing for a fight. Soon, they will have him flanked on the left, where he's weak. He doubts they know about Arnold looking down on them with his machine gun.

The situation is deteriorating fast.

"I ain't playing with you, Sergeant," Wilson says. "This is important. I'm going to ask one more time. What are you doing here?"

"I'm telling you for the last time: It's none of your goddamn business, Sergeant."

The next few seconds appear to stretch as nobody speaks or moves. Rod has a sense of everyone lining up iron sights on a human target, settling in for the order to fire.

"Sergeant," Dr. Price says.

"If I were you, I'd get down, Doc," Fielding says, kneeling behind cover.

"He's right," Rod says. "Get your ass down."

"We're looking for a man!" the scientist cries, rushing forward.

"Jesus," Rod groans. "Get down before you get shot!"

Price ignores him, running toward the distant Bradley and shouting: "We're looking for the man who brought the Wildfire Agent into Camp Defiance! We believe he is coming this way! We want to bring him to a special facility because we believe his blood may hold a cure to Wildfire! Come on, we're all on the same side!"

Wilson whistles and Rod tenses, raising his shotgun and aiming it center mass at the figure sitting in the open hatch of the armored personnel carrier.

Go ahead, Wilson. I'm taking you with me.

Wilson has some connection to the camp, and has been tracking Typhoid Jody in the hopes of killing him. Simple justice.

To his surprise, Wilson's shooters pop up from their concealed positions, weapons lowered.

"Good call, Doc," Rod says absently, blowing air out his cheeks and lowering his shotgun. He watches Wilson jump down from the Bradley and march toward him unarmed. A woman exits the back of the Bradley and joins him. Rod gives the order to stand down.

"I want you back to observing the road, Eyes. Out."

Roger that, Three. Out.

Rod steps out from behind the row of sawhorses, and jogs to meet Wilson and the woman.

"Looks like we're on the same side, Sergeant Wilson," he says, extending his hand.

"Sorry to step on your op," the large man says, taking it.

"Hate to see what would have happened if we weren't on the same side."

"That's a topic best avoided, don't you think?"

"Agreed," Rod grins. "And you can call me Rod."

"Rod it is. I'm Toby. The guys call me Sarge. This is Wendy, my gunner."

"Pleasure to meet you, Ma'am."

"Likewise," she says.

Rod blinks as he shakes her hand, feeling his cheeks burn. Wendy smiles wryly in response. *God, this woman is gorgeous.* He introduces them to Price and Fielding.

"Anything we can do to help, Rod?" Wilson asks him. "We appear to have the same mission."

"Let me be clear about something, Toby. Our orders are to bring the man in if we can. We are going to do everything we can to make this happen. If we can't, well, then I'm afraid we'll have to put him down. Those orders are not open to discussion or compromise."

"Understood," Wilson says with a nod.

"In that case I will take you up on your offer of help," Rod says. "I could use your vehicle a hundred meters behind us and to the left, in front of the strip mall there, with your shooters deployed around it, out of sight, but accessible, and everyone in gas masks if you've got them. Provide rear security, and act as reserve."

"Happy to do it."

"What do you know about the man?" the scientist asks them.

"His name is Ray Young," Wendy says. "We came across his trail yesterday, and we've been tracking him. Lost him somewhere after Mechanicsburg."

"Why were you tracking him?" Fielding wants to know.

"He infected Camp Defiance," Wilson answers. "We figured he uses spores. And if he's using spores, it's something we haven't seen before, something unique. We thought we might be able to get him to where some scientists could take a look at him. Maybe come up with a cure."

"That's why we're here too," Dr. Price says.

"Smart thinking," says Rod.

"Not me," Wilson says with a grin. "We got a smart aleck kid named Todd on our team."

"So what are we dealing with here, Sergeant?" Rod says. "Do you know the extent of his influence over the Infected?"

Wilson and Wendy exchange a glance.

"We had to shoot our way through two towns," Wilson tells him. "The Infected attacked us, with weapons. Some of them had *guns.*"

"Fascinating," Dr. Price says.

"I was thinking, *horrible,*" Rod says. "If Mr. Young has that kind of command and control over the crazies, he could be a hell of a lot harder to deal with."

"After Mechanicsburg, we stopped being attacked, so our guess he went to ground between there and Spring Lake, probably up in Milford, which is around a ten-minute drive off the road."

"The man is close, then," Rod says, nodding. "Assuming he's still coming east."

As if to confirm his assumption, Arnold's voice buzzes in his ear.

Hellraisers 3, this is Hellraisers Eyes. Contact, west. Repeat. We have contact.

DR. PRICE

Travis catalogs his symptoms: shaking, loss of peripheral vision, lips tingling, heart racing and eyes and mouth feeling dry, which he knows is a result of stress inhibiting the lacrimal gland. Sergeant Rodriguez was right; when it comes to fight or flight, you may end up fighting your own body.

As they wait for the vehicle to approach the roadblocks, Travis remembers what he felt his first day at the White House, and the last, when he fled the building in a helicopter. That sense of history in the air. He glances at the men next to him. Their eyes are gleaming. They can feel it too. The Berlin Wall coming down. Fireballs erupting from the World Trade Center. The Screaming, the first days of the Wildfire epidemic. Fulcra around which history bends. The sense that after today, nothing will ever be the same. After today, everything, everywhere, will be different.

And now this. Bringing Ray Young to a special facility, where they will capture a pure sample of Wildfire and save the world.

He remembers Sandra Forbes swooning in the grip of the Secret Serviceman just before the man flung her into the crowd like so much garbage. *I'm sorry, Sandra. But I did it for this. I have a responsibility to the human race far greater than to any single individual.*

He turns and studies Fielding's profile. The man is grinning. He feels it too. For this one moment, these enemies are like brothers, united in common cause.

I owe you an apology as well.

I'm sorry, Fielding, but you won't be able to come with me for what I must do.

ANNE

Anne stands hunched and gasping over the hot machine gun, her dead comrades crumpled at her feet. She and Marcus say nothing for several minutes, just watching the road. They are approaching another town. Anne tenses, but it appears to have been burned off the map. A charred ruin that smells like ash, utterly dead.

The bus jolts over a pothole and Marcus moans in pain.

Anne stares at him with growing horror. The large man hugs the steering wheel, gritting his teeth, his face pale and waxy. Marcus looks like a corpse.

Blood drips from his seat into a dark puddle on the floor.

"You stupid—" She drops the machine gun and hunts for the first aid kit. "How bad is it?"

"Bad," he manages. The simple act of speaking appears to give him pain. "Shot."

"Stop the bus."

"No."

"Marcus."

"Can't. If I stop, don't know if I could drive again."

"Then don't," she says simply, surprising herself. "I'll get you patched up, and then take you to Nightingale."

"The mission. . ."

Anne shakes her head. "I don't care. I can't let you die."

"Not up to you," he says, his eyes a fiery blue in his pale face. "Saw what this guy can do. Understand now. Have to stop him."

She chokes back a tear, conquering the urge to weep by sheer force of will. Crying is like death, a threshold. Once she starts, she knows, she may never stop.

"I don't want you to do anything for me anymore."

"It's not about you, Anne. Always my choice."

She probes him with her eyes, looking for the gunshot wound, and finds it in his hip—a small hole with charred edges, the surrounded area blackened with blood. Probably a ricochet, or one of the Infected shot him point blank from the hood. She checks for an exit wound but finds nothing. The bullet is lodged in his pelvic bone.

While Marcus focuses on the road, Anne uses her knife to widen the hole in his jeans, and studies the ragged, broken flesh around the wound. It is still bleeding, but the bullet missed the arteries. She opens a bottle of alcohol.

"This is going to hurt. Get ready."

She pours the alcohol onto the wound, making Marcus gasp with agony. Anne marvels at his endurance. He has strength of a bull. She wipes away the fluids and pushes a bandage against it.

"I can put a dressing on it but the bullet is still in there. You need a doctor."

"After," he says.

"We could go to Nightingale, get you fixed, and then we could live there together, you and me," she offers. "I could be your wife."

Marcus does not speak for several moments. Anne studies his face hopefully. Finally, he shakes his head with a tight smile. "Now you ask. Too late for that." He gestures to the bodies on the floor, the smile turning into a grimace. "Otherwise, they died for nothing. Besides, unless Ray dies, nowhere safe. Must give him mercy."

"I don't know if we can get him," Anne says. "He's too well protected."

"Find a way. Always do. Ranger way."

"We're not real Rangers, Marcus. I'm just a—"

Anne pauses, surprised she cannot recall what she was before. Instead, she remembers the cries of children washing over her like waves from the distant burning ruin of Camp Defiance. In her mind's eye, a military helicopter lunges into the sky, wobbling unsteadily, people tumbling out of the back and falling screaming to the ground.

"All right," she says. "This time, I need you to get me close. We'll wear gas masks. We'll drive straight into him. I get out, I shoot him in the head. All or nothing. Then I get you to Nightingale."

"Can get you close," Marcus tells her. "Can do that."

Anne runs her hand along his heavily muscled arm and wonders at the life they might have created together. She kisses it, tasting blood. Presses her scarred cheek against his bicep.

This is her way of saying goodbye.

"Look," Marcus says. "The road."

She stands, facing the wind rushing through the open windshield, and sees the billboard looming in a grassy field. The board is plastered with a wilting ad for a gun store and shooting range in the next town, five miles ahead. Morgantown.

The content of the ad barely registers with her. Someone has spray painted over it in bold black capitals:

DEFIANCE? FIND SOLDIERS IN MORGANTOWN

"I think things have just gotten more complicated," she says.

RAY

The old truck lurches down the road, careening around abandoned wrecks, its driver feeling terrified and elated, still riding high on the adrenaline rush. The ferocity of Anne Leary's pursuit makes Ray shiver even now.

She was one tough broad. But I took care of that, yes sir. I got her, I'm sure of it. Her and her entire crew, all dead or infected now, and good goddamn f'ing riddance.

"No more Mr. Nice Guy, honey."

He glances right for a reaction but the seat next to him is empty. French, Anderson and Salazar are in the back, clinging to the sides of the truck, and Lola is dead, her brains splashed across a motel parking lot like so much litter.

Nothing ever works out the way you want it to, he tells himself, filled with bitter anger.

Lola is dead, but the plan is the same: go to Washington and help to make things right again. The lump in his side purrs in response to this thought. *Yes, yes,* it says. *Find more people.*

After driving through the burned-out husk of Horseneck, he saw the first billboard. He knew it was meant for him. Whatever doubts he had about trying to work out a deal were silenced by the apocalyptic horrors of Horseneck, which reminded him of the dead world of his fevered dream. Infection showed him that world as if it were an offering that would please him. To the bug, a dead world is beautiful. Lots of space for new life.

An epiphany makes him blink. The bug, he realizes, has no master plan other than to diversify and compete. Ray is not particularly special; he is just another mutation, an experiment, part of the Brood. Just like all the monsters. They are not things from another planet, recreated on Earth. They were specially created, like him, from genetic material the

Brood found here. The Brood is not an alien race. It is life itself. A runaway program for building life.

You are my seed, the bug hums happily against his ribs, as if they are on the same side.

"I'm your cure, asshole."

He passes another billboard, this one reading: DEFIANCE GO TO MORGANTOWN.

A feeling of calm washes over him. Every time he drives past a message the military left for him, he feels a little more control slipping away. Soon, it will all be out of his hands. He knows in his gut they are here for him. They know who he is, and they have come for him.

As he drives along happily, he keeps checking his rear view, wondering if Anne Leary really did die. The woman is indestructible. He can feel her back there somewhere, hunting him with that look of fierce glee on her scarred face.

It was just blind luck that prevented her from killing me. Twice.

As terror seeps back into his consciousness, he wonders if the government is going to make an honest deal with him. Maybe the idea is to treat him real good until they don't need him anymore, and then put him down like a dog. Dissect him and throw him out like garbage. Hell, maybe no lab is out there waiting for him, no salvation, no redemption. Maybe the soldiers are waiting for him up there in Morgantown with flamethrowers.

What an idiot I sure am. I was about to give myself up without making sure I get what I want. I can't trust anyone. Force is the one thing people respect. The only thing you know for sure is the sucker punch is coming. The only thing you can control is whether you are going to get it or give it.

He scans the forest on his left and sees nothing but trees in the gloom. Then he scans the grassy fields on his right, empty except for giant steel pylons carrying dead transmission lines.

Returning his attention to the road, Ray broadcasts: *I can sense you. I know you're out there. Meet me in Morgantown, but do not show yourselves to the people there. Hide and wait. Hide and wait for me. I will be with you soon.*

He hears them murmur across the ether. Not the garbled, agonized voices of the Infected, but the obscene babble of monsters, clicking and chewing and grinding teeth.

He grunts in surprise. He did not know he could control the monsters.

This is a whole new ballgame, folks.

NEXT TOWN STOP WALMART

He barks a harsh laugh. *What am I afraid of? I command MONSTERS.*

The roadblocks appear at the outskirts of town. Ray taps the brake pad, downshifting, breathing fast and trying to ignore the sensation of falling in his gut. He becomes aware of a large military vehicle on his left and, in the distance, a Bradley like the one Sarge commanded. A big gas mask-wearing soldier with a flamethrower stands next to the Stryker. Ray waves at the man, who hesitates before waving back. Despite all of the anticipation, he is kind of surprised to see them here, just for him.

Straight ahead, another soldier in a gas mask stands with two men in biohazard suits holding plastic suitcases. This, he assumes, is the welcoming committee, rolling out the red carpet.

COOL ROD

Rod watches the truck stop and waits for the man to cut the engine, but he doesn't; he lets it idle and even revs it once, as if having second thoughts. He studies the distant figure and decides this must be Ray Young. He raises his hands, showing he is unarmed, and waves his arms over his head. *Stop, stop. Kill the engine.*

The beat-up pickup slowly turns and pulls into the parking lot of the office building across the street from the Walmart. The engine dies and Young steps down from the truck, slamming the creaky door. Rod gets his first good look at the man and feels like he already knows him. Dressed in a wrinkled black T-shirt, dirty jeans and, oddly, a brand new STEELERS ball cap pulled down low over a scowling unshaven face, Ray Young looks like any number of rednecks living around Dallas, where Rod grew up.

Young whistles and three men jump down from the truck bed dressed in bulletproof vests, T-shirts, jeans, cowboy boots. Empty holsters on their hips, guns in their hands. Rod watches them take up positions in a defensive formation around Young, acting like bodyguards.

Friends of his?

No, it looks like Sergeant Wilson was right. The man can control the Infected. Incredible.

Rod checks out the Bradley on his left. Sergeant Wilson watches the scene from the commander's hatch, wearing a gas mask. His shooters are gone, dispersed into concealed positions. Wilson catches him watching and gestures as if to say: *It's all yours, Sergeant.*

"What's your name, sir?" Rod calls out.

"I'm Ray Young?" the man answers tentatively, as if he's not sure.

"Bingo," Rod says to the scientist, who grins behind his faceplate. "You guys ready?"

Dr. Price gives him a thumbs up.

"We're going to send our scientists over to talk with you," Rod calls out again. "Is that okay, Mr. Young?"

The man shrugs. "I guess that'd be fine."

"Do you need anything? Food, water, medical attention?"

Young snorts and spits onto the asphalt. "No, I'm good."

"You're on, *vatos*," Rod tells Price and Fielding.

The two men approach the distant figures carefully, their spacesuits gleaming yellow in the bright sun. It's hot as hell in the MOPP suit, but Rod is used to it. *So far, so good.* All they have to do is get Ray to put on the orange Racal suit and ditch his entourage, and they can pack him up and get him to the USAMRIID facilities at Fort Detrick in Maryland.

USAMRIID: the United States Army Medical Research Institute of Infectious Diseases, part of the Medical Research and Materiel Command, where the Army's top disease experts are working around the clock on ways to fight the bug.

Rod watches the men talk and realizes he should have equipped them with radios and given one to Young. *It's too late now.*

Something is wrong. Young is shaking his head, chopping at the air with one of his hands for emphasis. Price waves his arms at Rod, and jogs back. Rod decides to take the risk of meeting him halfway. As they close the distance, he eyes the scientist's bright yellow suit and wonders how hot it is with live spores.

"What's the story, Doctor?" Rod asks him.

"He says he won't come with us unless we can give him a guarantee about his safety."

"Is he crazy? Does he understand why we're actually here?"

"He's concerned about later," Price explains. "What if he turns out to be unhelpful in the fight against the Wildfire Agent? Or what if he *is* helpful, and we win the war, and now here's this one guy who can bring Hell back? Either way, what happens to him?"

"Well shit, Doc, that is far above my pay grade," Rod says. "I can't give that type of guarantee. Not one that would mean anything to him, anyway. Didn't anyone think of this kind of thing when the op was being planned?"

Price clears his throat, sounding like, *ahem*. "I was rushed into the field, Sergeant. I barely had enough time to collect the right equipment. I couldn't think of everything."

"All right, all right. Then I guess we're going to have to negotiate something." He makes a call on the radio to Tanner to meet him at the last checkpoint with the spare JTRS radio from the Stryker, and then hands his own radio to Price. "Give this headset to Mr. Young."

"Will do."

"But then take it right back the second we're done with the conversation. We don't want him hearing squad chatter. It's bad enough I'm sharing our communications."

"I understand."

Shit, this is complicated, Rod realizes, jogging back.

Soon he and Young are communicating on the radio while Price swabs down his and Fielding's bio suits, hoping to capture spore samples.

"Mr. Young, I'm Sergeant Rodriguez, U.S. Army."

Nice to meet you, Young says. *Now listen. I want you to get on the phone to your people and tell them I ain't going nowhere until I get some simple assurances.*

"We can talk about that."

Ain't nothing to talk about. You must think I'm flat out batshit nuts to go anywhere with you without some type of guarantee about my safety. In fact, I'm plenty goddamn insulted you took all this effort to come on out here without it. Get on the phone with your people.

"Fine, Mr. Young," Rod says. "But what type of guarantee would satisfy you?"

Young considers this. Rod watches him light a cigarette.

I want a letter from the President, he says after a long pause.

Rod growls. He knows the man is scared and he can empathize with that, but this is ridiculous. "Do you want him to deliver it personally?"

No need to get smart. But now that you mention it, it should be on White House letterhead and I want a high-ranking officer to give it to me. I want to trust you people, but this is my life we're talking about. You want it, you got to earn it. Get on the phone. I'll wait.

"I cannot do what you are asking. The President doesn't even know we're here. By the time the message works its way up the chain of command. . . We're talking a long time, Ray. My orders are to bring you in, or shoot you in the head. I suggest you come in."

To his surprise, Young laughs. His guards raise their guns, covering Price and Fielding, who respond by raising their hands.

I wouldn't threaten me, man. You have no idea what you're dealing with.

"We basically have you surrounded with automatic weapons. If I give the order, it will take all of three seconds to turn you into Swiss cheese. Whether you have hostages doesn't matter."

Ray drops his smoke and grinds it into the road with his boot.

Even if you're the hostage?

Rod frowns, but says nothing.

Look behind you, but don't panic. Make no sudden moves, and you won't get hurt.

Sergeant, Davis cuts in. Christ, *Sergeant, they're right behind you.*

Rod wheels and stares in shock at the two monsters approaching with arms outstretched, tottering on spindly legs oddly articulated like a grasshopper's. They're like deformed albino children, mewing and flashing sharp little teeth.

He doesn't care about the teeth. Instead, he stares in horror at the massive erect stingers swaying between their legs.

Cascading voices blast the radio channel.

Contact, several men shout at once, calling in hoppers and requesting orders.

Ay, wey, Sosa says quietly.

Oh shit is right, Rod thinks. The hoppers are everywhere. Dozens of them. One has ventured close enough to sniff at his boots, its stinger buzzing. So far, nobody is shooting. He is amazed at his boys' fire discipline.

"Easy, Hellraisers," he says, aware Young can hear everything he is saying. "Nobody shoots unless I give the order. Understand?"

Sorry, Sergeant, Arnold says from the roof of the Walmart. *I can't cover the target and run the surveillance equipment, over.*

"Get on the recon gear and tell me what you see," Rod tells him. "We need to know what we're up against."

Can I torch them, Sargeant? Sosa asks him.

"If you shoot, then people are going to die," Rod says, hoping his voice is not as shaky as the rest of him is right now. "Mr. Young is just showing us he has big guns too."

That's right. Do I have your attention now?

"Roger that, Ray."

Then get me my damn letter, says Ray.

I see dozens of them, Three, Arnold says. *At least a hundred. And more on the way, over.*

"Roger that, Eyes. Out."

He's giving me no choice, Rod realizes. *He knows I can't deliver his letter. Even if I could, it would still be symbolic. The President wouldn't have to honor it. This is all about Ray Young's stupid redneck pride. So I'll have to give the order to shoot, and then whoever can't make it to the Stryker will die. We're all going to die because this son of a bitch feels insulted.*

Arnold: *Contact west, over.*

Rod presses the push to talk button. "What you got?"

Large vehicle approaching fast, over.

Rod can hear it already.

"Friend of yours, Mr. Young?"

I can't believe it, Young answers, sounding panicked.

"Mr. Young, if you want any of us to survive this fucked up situation, you'd better tell me right now what's going on."

It's Anne Leary. She's been hunting me since Defiance. She's trying to kill me. If you want to make a deal, then I'm going to have to ask you and your guys to kill her, Sergeant.

Rod opens his mouth, closes it. He does not want to kill any American who is not infected.

He also has no choice.

"Hellraisers, I want you to smoke that vehicle and anyone in it. Weapons free."

RAY

Ray has a sense of events spiraling out of control. A moment ago, he was enjoying flexing his power in front of the soldiers, but now he needs their help. His jumpers are deadly and terrifying, but he does not trust them to kill Anne Leary before she kills him. In his mind, she has become the angel of death. He flinches as the whir of the bus engine grows louder.

Fade, he tells his monsters. *Get out of the way. Hide until I need you.*

Ray sees the bus approaching, the driver crouched low over the wheel and ignoring the squad's warning shots. Then the Stryker's heavy machine gun opens up, the pounding fire loud and urgent, like a hammer striking an anvil next to his ear. The gun chews up the thin metal, punching gaping holes in its walls and blowing out the seats, which fly away in clouds of cheap stuffing.

Another machine gun opens fire from the roof of the Walmart. Hundreds of rounds stream into the vehicle and rip it to shreds. What's left of the roof flops away like aluminum foil and slams into the road, dragged along with a grating, ear-splitting screech. The bus appears to disintegrate into pieces as it roars across the final distance, trailing smoke and rolling debris.

"Come on," Ray shouts into the roar. "It's just a freaking bus! Kill the goddamn thing!"

He watches the vehicle continue its approach and feels rooted to the spot.

I never had a chance. The woman is indestructible. It's not fair.

BUMP BUMP BUMP BUMP

He flinches again and spins around as the Bradley fires its main gun, flinging cannon rounds downrange into what's left of the vehicle. Empty shell casings topple down the Bradley's metal chest, knocking off a withered wreath of wildflowers someone had placed there. Ray watches the wreath fall away and suddenly he is on the bridge again, watching the Infected come howling at him like an army boiling up straight from Hell, standing his ground and firing because there is nowhere safe to go, and to run is to die.

"Sarge?" he says. *Can it really be you?*

The cannon rounds slam into the front of the bus, which flies apart in a series of fireballs. Ray glimpses the crumpled hood flying end over end through the air. Then, miraculously, the rig emerges from the cloud of smoke trailing fire and pieces of metal, heading toward him as if in a final death lunge, the driver's seat blown away. Then it flips.

The soldiers stop firing, watching the flimsy wreck roll several times and collapse, the culmination of a long streak of smoking debris stretched back along the asphalt like metal road kill. A horde of metal parts continues to clang and tumble along, and then the wreck is finally still.

"Ha!" Ray whoops, clapping his hands. "Ha, ha, ha! You're dead now, Anne Leary! You're fucking dead! I win!"

Price and Fielding, lying on the ground with their hands over their heads, return to their feet.

Mr. Young, Sergeant Rodriguez says over the radio. *Are you all right? Anyone injured over there?*

"We're just great," Ray tells him, lighting another Winston with shaking hands.

"What now, Mr. Young?" Price says, his eyes wide behind his faceplate. "Are we still your hostages?"

"I don't know," Ray says, blowing a stream of smoke and chewing on his lip.

"Give it up," Fielding tells him. "What you're asking for can't be gotten. You're going to just have to take a chance. Either way, isn't it worth the result?"

"You really think what I've got inside of me could save the world?"

Fielding glances at Price, who nods.

"I believe it," the scientist says. "I know it."

We need to talk this out, Ray, Rodriguez says. *Let's keep the hoppers out of it for now.*

Ray realizes they're right. It's time to give up. He'll never get a guarantee that would mean anything, and he has a real chance to end Infection.

I want to save the world, he decides.

"That's weird," he says, staring at Fielding.

"What? Why are you looking at me like that?"

"You're one of mine."

Ray's chest explodes and his blood sprays across Dr. Price's suit and faceplate, followed by the sound of a gunshot. Then he's spinning, spinning, falling to the ground.

Over the ringing in his ears, he hears a woman screaming an inhuman cry of joy.

Protect, protect, protect—

DR. PRICE

Travis watches in shock as the hoppers flood from their hiding places, bounding across the empty parking lots like a swarm of locusts. The crackle of small arms fire fills the air. Standing over Ray Young, two of the Infected cops level their guns and open fire at one of the windows of the low-rise office building. The third sits on the ground, holding his throat and gurgling as blood flows between his fingers.

Young sits with his back against one of the truck's tires, legs spread wide, breathing in rapid, shallow gasps. One of the cops topples to the asphalt next to him, a neat hole drilled through his forehead, the back of his skull a smoking, shattered ruin. Young clutches his chest with a bloody fist and stares at Travis, his eyes communicating his desperate need to live.

"Help," he croaks.

Travis falls to his knees and opens his plastic suitcase, which contains first aid supplies, and stares at it, his face tingling. He feels like he is about to pass out. The last Infected cop appears to do a jig in the air, blood spraying, and then collapses to the ground grinning.

"Fielding, do you know how to treat a gunshot wound?"

Fielding stands over them, fists clenched at his sides, oblivious to the bullets and the monsters flying past. "What do you mean, I'm one of yours?"

"This man is going to die if we don't treat him!"

Young grimaces in pain. "Thought you were a doctor."

"I'm not a medical doctor, Mr. Young."

"Figure it out quick," Young tells him, "or you're a dead man."

Travis takes a pair of scissors and cuts away Young's T-shirt, exposing the small hole that bleeds down his front. Moving the man as gently as possible, he finds another hole in his back, a little below the first one.

"The bullet passed through."

Fielding screams, "What do you mean, I'm one of yours?"

Young's eyes shift to him. "Infected."

Wadding up a thick bandage, Travis jams it behind Young's back, and then pushes another against his chest, running tape over it. The man's face is pale and waxy, but his breathing is steady and his eyes seem alert. Travis has no idea what kind of damage the bullet did inside of him, however. Young needs a medical doctor.

"Doc, what did you do?" Fielding says.

Travis ignores him, watching the hoppers swarm over the Stryker. They rip apart the gunner, tossing shreds of his body high in the air like tissues from a Kleenex box, and then eat their way inside the cupola to get at the rest of the crew.

The big soldier with the flamethrower throws a long jet of fire onto the vehicle, torching the hoppers, which flop to the ground shrieking.

"What did you do to me?" Fielding demands.

The air fills with tracers, flashes of light bursting in all directions, cutting down the leaping creatures. Behind the Bradley, one of Wilson's people runs with a hopper on her back, another swinging from her outstretched arm, until collapsing a short distance later. The earth around her erupts as bullets kill her and the hoppers both.

Sergeant Rodriguez mows down a pair of hoppers with his shotgun and joins the big soldier with the flamethrower, waving his arm and shouting.

Fielding picks up one of the guns dropped by the dead cops and points it at Travis's head. "Doc, I'm going to ask just one more time. What did you do?"

Travis turns so that Fielding can see his face through the plate.

"I cut a hole in your air hose. You've been exposed the whole time. Young infected you. It was a one in three chance. You're just unlucky, I guess."

"Jesus, Doc." The man's eyes are wild. "How much time do I have?"

Young shakes his head, staring up at him, breathing hard.

"A few minutes, maybe," Travis tells him.

"What the hell are you saying? Why, Doc? Why'd you do it?"

"I wasn't about to let you carry out your orders to kill me if things didn't work out here. Let's just say I needed my own guarantee."

"I'm going to kill you anyway, you idiot. You just killed us both for nothing."

"You said you would give your life to save the world. See? Ray Young is here. We still have a chance to gain viable samples. If you kill me, you will prevent me from saving the world. So give your life. Go somewhere and die."

Fielding lowers the gun, considering this.

Travis turns to Young and says, "You're bleeding through your dressing. I'm going to put another dressing on top of it, okay? We've got to stop the bleeding."

Fielding raises the gun again. Travis stares up at him, feeling real terror for the first time. His gamble failed. The man is going to kill him.

"I gave it some thought, Doc," Fielding tells him, his face a mask of rage. "I realized I don't give a shit about the world if I'm not in it—"

The man disappears in a blur, the gun cracking once, burying a bullet in the asphalt. Travis blinks in shock several times before realizing Fielding is at the bottom of a pile of hoppers. The man screams as they rip into him with their teeth and tiny hands, stingers pounding.

"Doc," Young says. "Hey, *Price.*"

He stammers several times before answering, "Yes?"

"Heal me, or you're next."

ANNE

Anne crouches next to the window, tears streaming down her cheeks. She shot the bastard, she shot him good, and he's dying now, but Marcus is dead, dead like everyone else she ever loved, and now that the tears have come, they won't stop, flowing down the channels created by her scars.

A hopper launches itself against one of the room's windows, cracking the glass and bouncing off with a scream. The next crashes through in a burst of glass shards and falls to the carpet writhing and spraying blood. A third peers into the window on her other side, hissing at her with its jagged mouth as she shoves the barrel of her rifle against its forehead and squeezes the trigger, splashing the contents of its little skull across a photocopier.

More scratch at the walls, trying to figure out a safe way in. Anne can hear their glottal clicks and grunts. In the distance, she catches a glimpse of an arc of fire streaming from a flamethrower. The air is still filled with gunfire. Ray must have summoned every monster from miles around. The hoppers, being fast, got here first. Others will follow. Already she can hear the booming foghorn calls of the juggernauts. When they get here, anyone still out in the open is going to be slaughtered.

It's time to make a quick exit if she wants to live. Sadly for her, Anne appears destined to survive this fight as well. She backs away from the front of the building, her rifle banging in her hands as the hoppers appear in the windows. It is hard work without someone watching her back, but it is work that is second nature to her, work that she's good at.

Even now, with the hoppers pouring through the windows into the withering fire of her rifle, she sobs, mourning Marcus, the man she believes died to save the world from the plague spreader. At the end, when he saw the soldiers and realized their desperate plan was certain to fail, he told her to jump off the back of the bus and save herself, and then stepped on the gas for his suicide run while she rolled away and disappeared into the office building.

The rest was surprisingly easy.

Anne swore she would kill Ray Young for what he did to Camp Defiance, and she has fulfilled her oath. She wonders if it was worth the cost. All of her Rangers are dead. Todd is missing. What if Marcus had taken her up on her offer to go to Nightingale? He was strong; he could have made it. They might have had a life together. Is it possible she could ever be happy?

I don't get to go back, she knows, shooting a hopper in the face.

She hears another window shatter somewhere to her left. The hoppers have found another way in and are hunting her among the cubicles. Anne continues to retreat into the gloom, backing toward a door under an EXIT sign, which she knows accesses the stairs and offers a route to the rear of the building.

The creature flies hissing at her. She catches a glimpse of mottled gray flesh and large black eyes before putting a round through it, sending it spinning among the cubicles. She turns and shoots another two creeping up on her other side, arms outstretched like children wanting a hug.

As her back connects with the door, she feels a tremor jolt through the building, bumping her body an inch off the ground. Then another.

Something's wrong.

A violent, agonized roar rakes her ears, sending massive vibrations through her body that leave her feeling shaken.

"Demon," she whispers, paling.

The building shakes, filling the air with dust. Something is crashing through walls and pounding the floor with giant feet. Behind Anne, a workstation shelf collapses, spilling staplers and tape dispensers and photos of smiling children.

Anne backs away from the door, eyes wide with terror.

The monster roars again. The building continues to shake violently, spilling light fixtures and pieces of acoustical ceiling tile into the workstations. She can hear drywall crumbling into dust on the other side of the door.

Anne has stopped crying. A wave of calm washes over her. She is going to need everything she's got if she's going to escape.

And if I can't escape, if this is my time, I'm ready for that too. Tom, Peter, Alice and Little Tom, I'll be with you soon.

She turns and runs back toward the front of the building.

Behind her, the wall explodes, flooding the room with a thick, rolling cloud of dust.

WENDY

Wendy plants a final long, deep kiss on Toby's mouth and breaks away with a gasp.

"Wish me luck," Wendy says, pulling on the gas mask.

"Be careful, babe," Toby tells her. "We'll have you covered."

"I love you," she tells him, winking. "It's show time."

She touches the Bradley's instruments lightly, as if saying goodbye to an old friend, and climbs into the passenger compartment. Toby is already dropping the hydraulic ramp and she keeps moving, exiting at a crouch with her police-issue Glock in her hand.

A rifle pops to her right and a hopper flies skidding and tumbling across the asphalt. Wendy turns and sees Todd running toward her, pausing to shoot at distant targets. She points at herself and then Ray. Todd gives her a thumbs up and pats his rifle. He will cover her.

They parked the Bradley in front of a strip mall housing a Thai restaurant, dry cleaners, flower store and 7-Eleven. Across the parking lot, side street and another parking lot, Ray lies with his back against his truck, thirty yards from the office building from whose windows someone shot him, triggering this whole mess.

Her plan is simple—at least, once she reaches Ray Young. First, she just has to run a hundred yards through Hell.

Wendy starts running.

Bullets rip past, taking her breath with them, tracers flashing red in her eyes. Someone shrieks in pain. A fireball blooms in the distance, a single figure making his stand with a flamethrower at the center of a circle of scorched, blackened ground. Over the constant thunder, she hears the *ping ping ping* of Toby's AK47.

She dodges a hopper thrashing howling on the ground, pausing to glance over her shoulder. Toby and Steve lean out of their hatches firing their rifles, while Todd paces her on the left. A hopper comes flying at her and the pistol bangs in her hand, the bullet hitting it midair and sending it tumbling lifeless against the side of a mailbox.

She does not have far to go now. Wendy puts her head down and launches into a final sprint.

As she approaches Ray, a pair of hoppers land in front of her, hissing and waving her away.

"Screw you," she says, shooting one in the head, then the other.

She hops over the bodies and holsters her gun, looking down at him.

"Officer Saslove," Ray greets her.

The man kneeling next to Ray turns and glances at her through his faceplate flecked with blood. "You're taking a chance being near him with just that gas mask," he says, his face pale.

"I know," she tells him, crouching so her eyes are level with Ray's.

"Good to see you, honey," Ray tells her.

"You need to stop this right now, Ray."

"I won't let them hurt you."

"You shouldn't let them hurt anyone."

"Too late for that." He chuckles. "Whatever you think is best, Ray."

"I thought you came here to save us," she says. "You can still do that."

"What do I care?" Ray answers, his eyes blazing. "Nobody ever gave a shit about me. My old man was right. Hit them before they hit you."

"Does that include me?"

Ray smiles. "No, not you, Wendy. I would never let anything happen to you. See all these people? None of them are innocent. But you are. You remind me of how things were."

Wendy turns and gazes with longing at the Bradley, where Toby and Steve and Todd are still shooting. She wishes they could all drive away together. Find their island. Try to be happy and forget this long nightmare ever happened.

He pats the ground next to him, and adds, "Sit with me for a minute. Tell me what you've been doing with yourself. Don't worry about all this other stuff."

Foghorns boom in the distance, getting closer. The juggernauts are coming.

"Please stop this, Ray."

"It'll be over soon. It really is good to see you again."

She remembers her promise. Hates herself for making it. Hates the world for making her do it. *It's not fair.*

But it's meant to be.

"I need you to do just one thing for me, Ray."

"What's that, honey?"

She raises her hands and takes off her mask. Lets it slip between her fingers.

"I want you to save me," she tells him.

Ray howls like a dying animal.

"*NO!*"

"Save me, Ray."

Then she turns, surprised, as a woman staggers out of the office building at the edge of the parking lot in a cloud of dust, firing a rifle back at the open doors through which she exited moments earlier.

Anne? Anne, is that you?

Wendy shields her face as the front of the building erupts and the Demon comes spilling out snorting with crashing wings, clawing up the asphalt.

TODD

Todd shoulders his carbine and fires. The little corpse skids to a stop against his boots and he leaps over it, shuddering in disgust. Its erect stinger continues to stab at the ground. Even dying, Todd knows, these things are a threat.

A massive roar rends the air, vibrating deep in his chest. He turns and sees Wendy crouched next to Ray, while Sarge and Steve run toward her from the Bradley. Beyond Ray's truck, a woman retreats from the office building, shooting into the massive dust cloud billowing from its collapsing face.

Anne.

It was his idea to pursue Ray and try to bring him to the authorities based on the theory his body might contain a new strain of the bug. His theory was simple: If Ray infected others using spores, weren't those spores evidence of Infection? Evidence that could be used to isolate a pure sample of the organism? A pure sample that could be used to produce a cure?

Sarge and Wendy agreed. When they found Dr. Price and the soldiers, Todd felt overjoyed. Excited. Vindicated. *This is it*, he believed. *The moment we win the war. We will look back on this day and say, "This was when the tide turned."*

Then Anne shot Ray and destroyed what could be mankind's last hope.

Cruz is dead; he can see her body from here. He heard Noel scream just moments ago. Someone fires from Yang's position, but Guthrie has disappeared. Ray is shot and possibly dying. The soldiers are fighting for their lives.

They died for an idea. Todd grew up with the proverb that the road of good intentions is paved with the dead, but had never truly understood it. Now he does.

The dust cloud rolls outward from the building like a massive wave. Todd catches a glimpse of a hideous thing inside the cloud, a massive horn jutting from where its eyes should be, bellowing in pain and rage. He knows what it is. *Demon.*

Todd raises his rifle and fires into the dust. On his left, Sarge and Steve start shooting.

Run, Anne, he wants to scream. *Run as fast as you can.*

Anne stops running, throws down her rifle, and pulls out her Springfields, making a stand against the monster.

She is firing both guns as the dust cloud rolls over her. Then the shooting stops.

She can't be dead, he reasons. *She can't be killed. It's impossible.*

Nearby, juggernauts stampede through the auto dealership, crashing through the vehicles with tentacles waving, flinging cars and glittering clouds of safety glass into the air.

It's over. We're dead.

He watches them come. As much as he hates them, they really are quite beautiful.

RAY

As the dust cloud flows over him, turning the world brown, Ray asks Wendy if she believes in second chances.

"I'm living proof," she says, glaring into the dust with wide-eyed fear. "What about you, Doc? Do you believe in second chances?"

"I believe in redemption," the man answers.

The scientist has stopped treating him. Ray knows he is dying.

"Me too," he says, blood spurting from his mouth.

He believes in second chances. He believes in redemption. He just wishes it mattered.

When you know you're going to die, not a whole hell of a lot matters, even saving the world.

He thinks about what Fielding, the government agent, said when he realized he was doomed: *I don't give a shit about the world if I'm not in it.*

"Ray, please," Wendy says, tears streaming down her cheeks. "It's not too late."

He smiles, remembering the vision of Anne Leary firing her guns as a massive shadow swept over her, just as the brown cloud covered them both.

I won. I beat her.

"There's nothing more that I can do," Price tells him.

"Too bad it's not enough."

"Are you going to kill me now too?"

"No, I'm not going to kill you. At least you tried."

"I want redemption," Travis says. "I want that just like you. I also want to live."

Ray closes his eyes. "Bingo."

Wendy squeezes his hand. "Ray, you can still make things right."

His eyes flutter open and he takes in her beautiful face, wet with tears. He can hear Sarge and Steve calling her name in the swirling, blinding dust.

The Demon roars, drowning out their voices.

The rage is gone now, spent. Ray feels calm. He knows what is coming, and accepts it. And he finds he does care what kind of world he leaves behind.

"I remember," he says. "You want me to save you. All right. I can do that." He closes his eyes and whispers, "Go."

"Where?" Wendy asks him with alarm. Then she understands.

The children of Infection are leaving. The gunfire slackens off as the hoppers retreat into the forests surrounding the town. A group of them hiss at her as they lope past, bounding over the truck and disappearing.

The soldiers are cheering.

"You did good, Ray," Wendy says. "You did real good."

Ray's eyes shift to the scientist. "You'd better get my blood or whatever it is you need, Doc. I don't think I'm going to be around for much longer."

Price scrambles for a syringe. Ray watches the man tie a tourniquet around his bicep, wipe the inside of his arm with an alcohol pad, and plunge the needle in.

"Ow," he says. "Wendy, I hope you'll stick around for the cure. You got your whole life ahead of you with that jerk boyfriend of yours."

Wendy smiles, fighting tears.

"I got a sample," Price tells him, holding up several vials containing Ray's thick, dark blood.

"Hell, you can have more if you need it. Take it all. In fact, I can do even better, Doc. Do you want to see Infection? Would you like to meet the little bastard?"

He pulls the cut remains of his T-shirt aside, exposing his ribcage, and touches the pink bump on his side. The mound of flesh vibrates happily in response.

"Meet the enemy," he tells them.

"My God," Price says, clearly fascinated.

Wendy says nothing, eyeing it with revulsion.

"This is where I was stung. See? Instead of a hopper, a new me grew out of it. This is Infection, Doc. Take it. Cut the little sumbitch out. Do it now before it's too late. Before it changes my mind."

"I'll kill you if I do that," Price says.

"Dead already," Ray says. " I want to see you do it. I want to see us win."

"All right," Price says.

"I already know you got what it takes, Doc."

"I'll do it."

"Wendy, reach into my pocket and give me a cig, will you?"

She finds his crushed pack of Winstons, puts a wilted cigarette between his lips, and lights it. Ray inhales and spits it out, coughing and spitting blood.

"Lousy day to have to give up smoking," he says.

"I'm ready when you are," Price tells him.

"Tell everyone about today," he asks. "Tell them I did good."

The dust is settling; he can see the sky, and it has never looked so blue. *The earth abides. Yes, it does. And death is the biggest sucker punch of all.*

He tightens his grip on Wendy's hand and fixes his stare on her face.

You are my reason, Wendy. My second chance. My redemption.

You remind me of the way things were.

"Don't cry, honey."

"I'm sorry, Ray," she says, wiping her eyes. "I can't help it."

"Do it, Doc."

As the scalpel approaches his flesh, the lump flutters with terror, as if trying to escape.

Ray screams during the cutting.

By the time the operation is done, he is dead.

WENDY

Wendy cries into her hands until her face and fingers are wet. She wipes at her eyes and nose until she can see and breathe again, wondering how much time she has before the lights go out and she attacks the people she loves. She can bear the thought of becoming something else, something monstrous. But if the bug makes you hate your loved ones while otherwise you are still you, Wendy thinks she would rather put her gun in her mouth and end it now.

The dust has settled and the sun is shining. She sees the scores of corpses carpeting the parking lots and shattered vehicles, wonders how much of all that dead flesh is human. The soldiers stopped cheering long ago. Toby, Steve and Todd watch her from a respectful distance, waiting in silence, their expressions unreadable behind their black gas masks.

Steeling her nerves, she glances at her watch, anxious she wasted so much of her remaining time on regret. Next to her, Price kneels next to Ray's body, continuing his gruesome dissection while Ray stares into oblivion, his face a cross between a smile and a scream.

"Why are you still cutting him?" she asks.

Price pauses, his scalpel gleaming in his blood-washed hand. "I need everything I can get," he snaps. "And I don't have much time."

"But he showed us the tumor. That was Infection."

"Maybe. We don't know what we saw. Welcome to the scientific method."

She hesitates, stung by his words. "How much time do I have?"

Price says nothing, his trembling hand poised over Ray's open chest.

"Dr. Price?"

"I'm sorry I was rude, Wendy. I'm very tired. I think I might be in a state of shock."

"How much time do I have?"

"I don't know," he says. "You were exposed five, ten minutes ago? I'd say you have another five or ten minutes before you show symptoms."

"Is it sudden? I mean, what's it like?"

Price turns his torso so she can see the man behind the faceplate.

"You fall down," he tells her. "And then you get up, and you're changed. But you might not have it. The odds are something like two in three you don't. So there's hope."

The math is simple. She has a one in three chance of becoming infected within the next few minutes. She remembers standing in the ruins of a hospital a long time ago, holding a gun against Todd's head after he was cut by the teeth of a monster, while Ethan counted down on his watch and then pronounced him clear.

Now it's my turn.

He adds, "If anything happens, I will cure you. I swear I will."

"Thank you," she says.

"Thank you, Wendy. We'd all be dead if it weren't for you."

She stands and dusts her knees slowly, carefully, aware of a tingling in every inch of her body. Turning, she sprints toward Toby, needing his arms around her, the one place in the world she feels safe outside the Bradley's gunner station.

Instead of extending his arms to embrace her, he pulls his mask off and falls to his knees, his shoulders shaking. Steve and Todd look away, too stricken to speak.

"Why?" Toby asks her. "Why, Wendy?"

She falls to her knees and puts her arms around her man, providing what comfort she can. "You know why. You would have done the same."

"It's not worth it," he sobs. "They can all die except you. Me included. But not you."

"There's a good chance I don't have it."

He takes a long shuddering breath, gathering his strength, and puts his large arms around her. She nestles against him, feeling safe again.

"Tell me it's nothing," she says.

"How long until we know?" he asks her.

"Five minutes, maybe. I don't know for sure. Where are the others?"

"Yang and Guthrie are helping the soldiers. They don't know you might have the bug. Cruz and Noel didn't make it."

"Bury them deep, Toby."

On the road, it is common practice to burn the dead so the monsters don't dig them up and eat them. The alternative is to bury them extra deep. It's considered a high honor.

She says nothing, her ear pressed against his barrel chest, listening to the rhythmic beat of his heart. Then she becomes aware of ghostly wailing in the distance. The sound appears to have no source. It seems to come from everywhere. Then the foghorns join in with their sad lowing that ripples through the air.

"What is that?" Toby says.

"They're mourning him. The Infected. They're mourning Ray Young."

"I love you, Wendy."

"I love you, Toby."

She says it repeatedly, hoping she will take the thought with her when she crosses over.

Then she stiffens in his arms.

COOL ROD

Rod finds Davis's body, scattered across the sidewalk as if a pack of wild dogs had fought over it for an hour. After Arnold, Davis was supposed to be in the safest place in the operation. Shaking his head in anger and sadness at the waste of a good man and a reliable soldier, Rod pockets the man's tags and brings the field radio back to the Stryker, setting it on the ground.

"Davis is dead," he tells Arnold. "Back that way."

"I'll get him, Sergeant," the soldier says, sounding strangely subdued. They are all humbled by what they have endured and accomplished this day.

"Bury him deep," Rod tells him. "Find Sergeant Wilson and ask him if he minds our boys sharing the hole he's digging for his people."

"Will do, Sergeant."

He wonders how the dead will ever find peace. He grew up in a small town near Dallas with his parents and grandmother. Sitting in her rocker, his granny often told ghost stories from Mexico, Rod's favorite being the little boy who haunted one of the oldest restaurants in Mexico City. The little boy was often spotted running through the kitchen walls, and would call the restaurant on the phone repeatedly, asking the staff to play with him. The boy choked to death at one of the tables in the forties, she explained, and that is why he cannot leave this world for the next. He died in violence, and is confused; he thinks he is still alive.

The world will be filled with ghosts by the time Wildfire is done. Angry ghosts of both the normal and the Infected, wondering why they died, demanding justice.

The bodies of the dead hoppers, which in life exuded a smell best described as sour milk cologne, are already starting to stink like rot. He wonders if they will leave ghosts as well.

Christ, I'm tired. The sooner we can be rid of this cursed place, the better. I want to go home.

Sosa ignites the flamethrower, sending an arc of fire across Ray Young's remains, the bodies of his guards and Fielding, and the truck. Anything his spores might have come into contact with. The scientist tosses a garbage bag filled with clothes into the flames, and steps away.

Ray Young is gone now. All that is left is a few vials of blood and chunks of flesh in a cooler, one of them still eerily pulsing and alive, looking for its host.

These tissue samples, packed in ice, might hold the key to beating Wildfire. *The organism*, Dr. Price explained, *hides in plain sight, disguised as something else, something common.* Using the tissue samples he collected, he hopes to unmask it once and for all. And once unmasked, it can be defeated. He can make no guarantees, however. It might be another dead end, another trick.

It's out of Rod's hands in any case. The mission is almost over; another will begin upon his return. *The war goes on.* His next step is to report the action up the chain of command, and receive orders. Either he will be told to drive the samples to Fort Detrick, or more likely, given the possibility the specimens might decay, they will send a helicopter.

Then Rod can go back to the fighting. The idea of getting up tomorrow morning and doing this all over again, day in and day out, makes him want to lie down and quit. His boys deserve better. Unfortunately, there is nothing else.

He watches Dr. Price sitting on the ground, holding his head in his hands, and thinks: *It's your war now too, Doc. You against the thing in the cooler. Have courage, man. We are all counting on you.*

It's time to bring this mission to an end.

◆

Rod finds the designated channel and initiates contact. The radio/telephone operators recognize his call sign but pass him around, unsure what to do with him. Finally, he finds himself talking to Corporal Carlson, who hands him over to Major Duncan.

"Message follows, over," Rod reports.

Send message, over, the Major answers.

"I send 'Typhoid Mary,' over."

Code for *mission accomplished.*

Next he will say, "Immunity failed," which means the *subject is dead.*

Then he will say, "Frankenstein found," which means they obtained *viable tissue samples.*

Finally, he will provide map coordinates and say, "Antidote rising," a request for *air units to come and extract Dr. Price and the samples*, and take them to Fort Detrick.

Rod glances at the twilight sky, hoping the day has enough light left for an air extraction. The birds will have to leave soon, or Rod and his people will be driving to Fort Detrick.

The radio dips into white noise, over which Rod can hear shouting in the background.

I don't have the codebook for that mission, over.

Rod blinks, stunned by this information. "Say again, over."

That mission was scrapped. Your unit was recalled, over.

"Negative on that," Rod says. "We are in the field executing the original operation order, over."

Did you not receive new OPORD, over?

"Negative. " He cannot think of what else to say at this point. "Over."

Target was ordered terminated by Higher, and was killed in an air strike, over.

Rod feels the old rage returning, bit by bit. It is as if the dead are here, with him, lending him their anger in the hopes he will give that anger a voice.

Report your location, over.

Rod no longer cares that it's an open channel. "We accomplished the mission. Subject was killed during recovery, but we were able to obtain biological samples for Fort Detrick. Will provide map coordinates for extraction. Repeat request for air extraction, how copy?"

Another long pause. Duncan starts to say something, but the words become garbled. Rod can hear more shouting in the background.

"Negative contact," he says in frustration. "Say again, over."

Negative on that air extraction. Subject was terminated by air strike—wait one. Rod hears someone scream. *Wait one, out.*

"What's your status, over?" he asks.

He waits for nearly a minute, wondering if headquarters is under attack. If the Infected penetrated the Green Zone, the war is over, at least in this part of the world. America would be lost. And there would be nothing for Rod and his men to come back to. Nowhere to go.

Hard to hear you, Hellraisers 3. There's a bit of a celebration going on here, over.

"What?" Rod shakes his head in disbelief. "Say again, over."

The power's on, Hellraisers 3. The whole town is lighting up like a Christmas tree. Wish you were here to see it, over.

"Holy sh—" Rod says before catching himself. "We won, sir?"

We sure did, Hellraisers 3. Washington is ours. We took it back. Over.

A grin flashes across Rod's face. "Outstanding."

The credit is yours, Hellraisers 3. It belongs to you and every other service member we have in combat. Now let's finish up our business so you can get back here. Your mission was scrapped, and a new OPORD issued. We need to get your unit back to the operating base for rest and refit. Comanche has been given two weeks' leave. You can go home, Hellraisers 3. Over.

A memory flashes of Gabriela and his children running toward him at the airport after one of his tours in the Sandbox. Their happy faces.

He pushes the memory from his mind with an almost physical effort.

How copy?

"Major, please listen to me. We have identified Typhoid Jody and secured viable biological samples from his remains. They must be delivered to Fort Detrick immediately—"

Negative, over.

Rod's rage boils over. "No, not fucking 'negative,' sir—"

Sergeant, Higher scrapped the mission and ordered the subject terminated, which you apparently accomplished. If you obtained samples, I don't know what to do about that. I don't know who to tell, or who to call. The higher-ups will want to know what the hell you're doing out there going against orders. I cannot get the assets to do anything—

"Are you ordering us to return to base, Major?"

Affirmative. I am ordering you to return to base. I expect you to use maximum individual initiative in accomplishing this order. Understood? Over.

"Roger that, sir. Hellraisers, out."

He slams the receiver down and growls. He can't believe it. He can't believe Higher Command won't accept Ray Young's remains.

And yet he can. It's typical Army bullshit, amplified by the ongoing stress of fighting Wildfire with steadily dwindling forces.

The Major gave him an out, however. When he said he expected Rod to show individual initiative in getting back to base, he was saying if Rod thought it necessary to stop at Fort Detrick first in order to accomplish his mission, then go ahead and do it. On his own.

He does some quick calculations. If he goes north to Detrick, he will officially be off the reservation, cut off from reinforcement, casualty evacuation, supply. They have enough fuel, but they don't have much in the way of provisions, and they burned through at least half their ammo in the fight today. He lost three men during the fighting, giving him just two shooters besides himself.

They could just go home and forget the whole thing. Duncan said they have rest and refit waiting for them. Two weeks with their families. Hearing this made him feel like he'd won the lottery. Like the soldiers under his command, he desperately wants to see his wife and children again. Two weeks is a long time these days. It may be the last time he ever sees his family.

He remembers the words in Gabriela's final letter: *I freely give up this demand, my right as your wife, in the hopes that you will win and be able to save not just us, but the entire country.*

Do your duty, she said.

The survivors of the squad gather around, watching him. They buried Davis and Tanner and Lynch, along with the Stryker's gunner and Sergeant Wilson's dead, and expect him to say something over the mass grave.

Rod tells them what Duncan told him. The boys hiss obscenities under their breath.

"Was it all for nothing, then, Sergeant?" Arnold asks him.

"Well, that's the thing," Rod says. "I'm going to do something I've never done before as a sergeant in the United States Army. I'm going to call a vote."

TODD

Night is falling. The soldiers load their remaining gear into the Stryker for transport while the big soldier named Sosa, manning the vehicle's heavy machine gun, provides overwatch. Yang and Guthrie are still at the mass grave, holding each other for comfort. Sarge and Steve are in the Bradley, watching over Wendy, who sleeps fitfully in the back, pumped full of sedatives. Todd finds Ray Young's remains scattered around the burned husk of the truck, just ashes and bits of blackened bone. But he came here to pay his last respects to Anne.

The face of the office building is shattered, a ghastly black maw choked with debris. Rubble and standard office junk litter the parking lot in front of it, carpeted in a thick layer of dust. Todd sifts through it looking for signs of her. He finds a warped length of pipe. Crushed ventilation duct. Smashed pieces of office cubicles. Staplers and pens. Upright office chair. Hastily scrawled notes on Post-Its. Photos of loved ones. Of the Demon itself, he sees no sign. Presumably it returned inside the building and, from there, who knows?

Todd kicks at the dust, unveiling a Springfield pistol. He picks it up, checks the magazine, and tucks it into his belt. A little further on, he finds a shred of clothing. Past that, a piece of bone. Anne pursued death, he knows. In her mind, she died the day she discovered her dead children at her neighbor's house, murdered and half eaten by an infected man named Hugo. She woke up every day with the knowledge she was already dead. By conquering her fear of death, she conquered fear itself, and that made her a good survivor—that and the fact she was far better at dealing death than she was at pursuing it. But in the Demon, she met her match.

Was this really what you wanted, Anne? He has a feeling she would have called it a good death. He knows he will miss her. She was the best person you could have watching your back, a real monster slayer. But her hate consumed her until there was nothing else. People like that become another kind of monster.

Goodbye, Anne.

He thinks about the people he has known since the epidemic began. Most of them are dead and gone forever. Anne. Paul and Ethan. Ducky. Cruz and Noel, Marcus and Evan and Ramona and Gary. Ray Young.

Erin.

They did not die for nothing, he believes. *They died for something. All of them died to ensure Ray Young would end up here, today, and give his body and blood for a chance to save the world. They all played their part.*

That makes them all heroes, in a way. A sappy thought, but accurate.

The Bradley starts its engine and sits idling in the dead town. The Stryker is already rolling across the parking lot, executing a U-turn until it points east.

East, and then north. To Fort Detrick.

We're going to do this, Todd understands. *Perhaps there we can end this nightmare.*

Goodbye, heroes.

There is still a chance we can win this war, and we will fight for that chance. We will never give up. We will win, or we will all go down together.

THE INFECTION

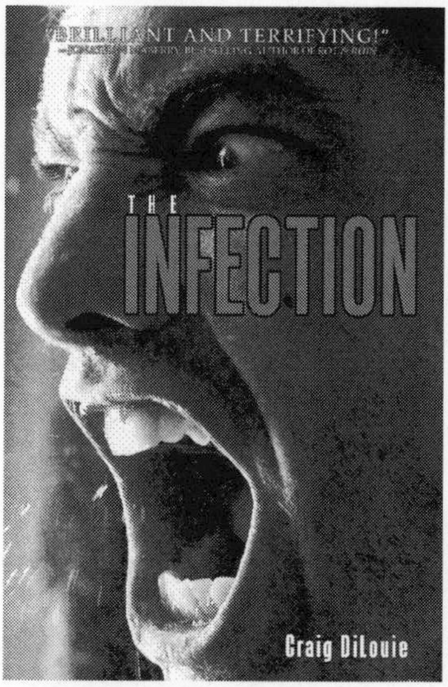

The world is rocked as one in five people collapse screaming before falling into a coma. Three days later, the Infected awake with a single purpose: spread the Infection. A small group—a cop, teacher, student, reverend—team up with a military crew to survive. But at a refugee camp what's left of the government will ask them to accept a dangerous mission back into the very heart of Infection.

ISBN: 978-1934861653

BY CRAIG DILOUIE

PETER CLINES

EX HEROES

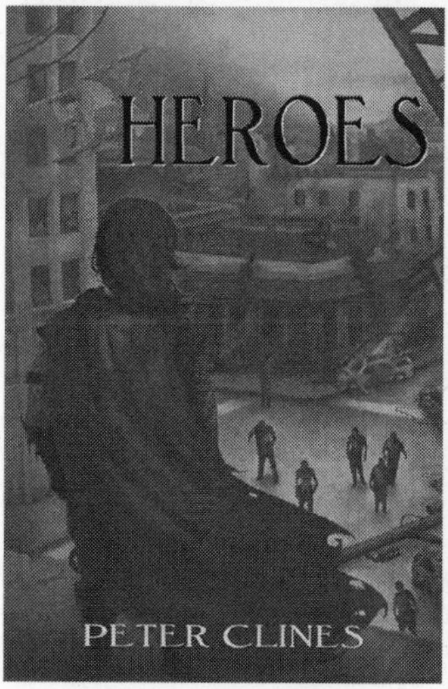

The plague of living death spread around the globe. Despite the best efforts of the superheroes, the population was decimated, heroes fell, and the city of angels was left a desolate zombie wasteland like so many others.

Now, a year later, the heroes lead teams out to scavenge supplies, keep the peace within the walls of their home, and try to be the symbols the survivors so desperately need. But the exhumans are not the only threat left in the world, another group has grown and gained power.

And they are not heroes.

ISBN: 978-1934861288

MORE DETAILS, EXCERPTS, AND PURCHASE INFORMATION AT

www.permutedpress.com

PLAGUE OF THE DEAD

BY Z A RECHT

A worldwide viral outbreak brings the dead to life. On one side of the globe, a battle-hardened General surveys the remnants of his command: a young medic, a veteran photographer, a brash Private, and dozens of refugees, all are his responsibility. Back in the United States, an Army Colonel discovers the darker side of the virus and begins to collaborate with a well-known journalist to leak the information to the public...

ISBN:978-1439176733

DYING TO LIVE

a novel of life among the undead

BY KIM PAFFENROTH

After wandering for months in a zombie-infested world, Jonah Caine discovers a group of survivors. Living in a museum-turned-compound, they are led by an ever-practical and efficient military man, and a mysterious, quizzical prophet who holds a strange power over the living dead. But Jonah's newfound peace is shattered when a clash with another group of survivors reminds them that the undead are not the only—nor the most grotesque—horrors they must face.

ISBN: 978-0-9789707-3-4

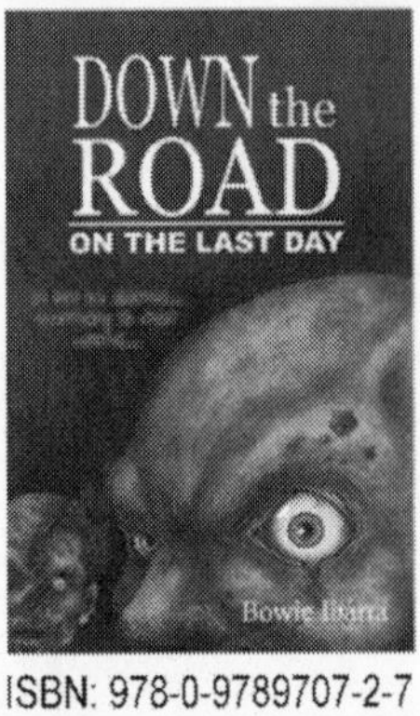

ISBN: 978-0-9789707-2-7

DOWN the ROAD

on THE LAST DAY

by Bowie Ibarra

In a small south Texas town, the mayor has rallied his citizens against the living dead and secured their borders. When two strangers from San Antonio stumble into town, they bring news of a global peacekeeping force sweeping toward the city. Led by a ruthless commander, the force is determined to secure the republic of Texas on its own terms, and establish a new, harsh government for the plague-ravaged nation.

www.permutedpress.com

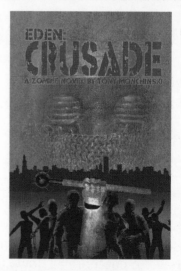

EMPIRE

A Zombie Novel by David Dunwoody

The outbreak began in 2007. It's now 2112.

The crippled U.S. government is giving up its fight against an undead plague. Military forces and aid have been withdrawn from the last coastal cities, leaving those who choose to stay in the "badlands" defenseless against hordes of zombified humans and animals.

It's been a hopeless battle from the beginning. The undead, born of an otherworldly energy fused with a deadly virus, have no natural enemies.

But they do have one *supernatural* enemy... Death himself.

Descending upon the ghost town of Jefferson Harbor, Louisiana, the Grim Reaper embarks on a bloody campaign to put down the legions that have defied his touch for so long. He will find allies in the city's last survivors, and a nemesis in a man who wants to harness the force driving the zombies—a man who seeks to rebuild America into an empire of the dead.

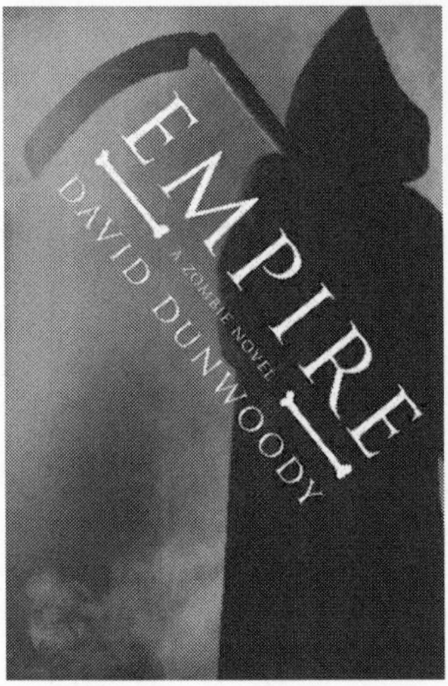

ISBN: 978-1439180723

EMPIRE'S END

By David Dunwoody

The dead refuse to stay dead. The Reaper is here to put them down.

As winter sets in and America's survivors struggle to rebuild a semblance of civilization terrifying new enemies are gathering. Death's questions about his origin haunt him, but the worst of both the living and the dead are rising in his path, and he'll have to cut them all down to reach the cosmic endgame.

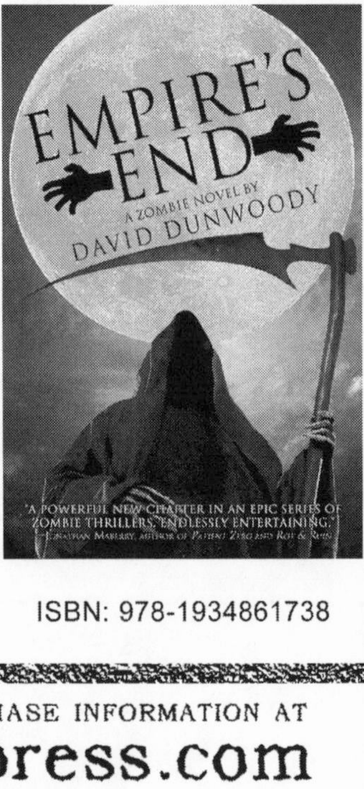

ISBN: 978-1934861738

More details, excerpts, and purchase information at

www.permutedpress.com

15504886R00173

Made in the USA
Lexington, KY
01 June 2012